A TYLER ZAHN NOVEL

I0575010

STABLE

SOMEONE IS TAKING THEM...

CAM TORRENS

Black Rose Writing | Texas

The author grants the final approval for this literary material.

First printing

This is a work of fiction. Names, characters, businesses, places, events, and incidents are either the products of the author's imagination or used in a fictitious manner. Any resemblance to actual persons, living or dead, or actual events is purely coincidental.

ISBN: 978-1-68513-234-7
PUBLISHED BY BLACK ROSE WRITING
www.blackrosewriting.com

Printed in the United States of America
Suggested Retail Price (SRP) $22.95

Stable is printed in Minion Pro

*As a planet-friendly publisher, Black Rose Writing does its best to eliminate unnecessary waste to reduce paper usage and energy costs, while never compromising the reading experience. As a result, the final word count vs. page count may not meet common expectations.

ACKNOWLEDGMENTS

STABLE is not my first book—but it *is* my first published book. My writing journey continues to be one of the most challenging endeavors in my life. Fortunately, I've had a team of support practically carrying me the entire way. The following people helped make this book possible. I'd like to thank:

My wife, Linda, for hours of listening to plot twists and turns and politely keeping the glaze off her eyes. My mother, Susan, and sisters, Amy Torrens-Harry and MaxieJane Frazier, for beta reading and cheerleading. My daughter, Natasha, for battling on the front lines to help me overcome Boomer-speak. My father, Fred, for mastering the one-word opinion, and my sisters-in-law, Donna and Sandra, for their comprehensive beta reads.

The Chaffee County Writers Exchange and our critique group of fellow authors: Linda Ditchkus, Laurel McHargue, Dan Bishop, Susan Bavaria, Wendy Oliver, Robin Hall, Tom Dury, Danielle Frost, and Monica Young, for their sharp critiques and loving hearts.

My beta reader team for showering me with firm patience as I continue to grow as a writer: Liz Brown, Stephanie & Bill Summers, Mary Riley, Terry Williams, Sue & Ben Paganelli, Nathan Small, Terry Kelly, Alta Beren, Diane Haven, Shane Bumgarner, Jane Venohr, Scotty Cain, Kathy Keidel, Chris Pike, Penny Martin, Gina Williams, Joy Knight, Lori Johnson, Chris Kaufman, Kate O'Connor, and Jim Hight.

Brad Grant for sharing his experiences as a Jefferson County Reserve Sheriff and his daughter, Beth Grant Helmke, for serving as an inspiration for the Search & Rescue portions of the book. CCSAR-N members: Josh Schwenzfeier, Erik Rasmussen, Rebecca Hinds, Kevin Powers, Bobby Lewis, and Brandon Ove for supporting my efforts.

Authors Martin J. Smith, CJ Box, Craig Johnson, Mary Kubica, Mark August, and Nikolas Butler for the mentorship they don't even know they provided. Ed Roberson of *Mountain & Prairie* podcast for his author interviews and reading lists, and literary agent Amy Collins for investing her personal time to help a non-client. Finally, Black Rose Writing for believing in my work, and Brooke Dillon for showing up in my life as the perfect editor at the perfect time.

PRAISE FOR *STABLE*

"Tyler Zahn is a hero to love — deeply wounded, undeniably flawed, but determined to do the right thing in Cam Torrens' intensely dramatic debut thriller. The stakes of Zahn's search-and-rescue work in Colorado's Rocky Mountains have never been higher, or more personal. Trim your fingernails before you start this one."

–Martin J. Smith, author of the Edgar, Anthony, and Barry Award-nominated *Memory Series* novels of psychological suspense, and the stand-alone thriller *Combustion*

"*Stable* pulls you in and won't let go. Search and rescue expert, Tyler Zahn, is a hero as likable as he is fiercely capable. And, when a kidnapper abducts his daughter, Zahn will stop at nothing to find her. *Stable* will have you holding your breath all the way to a harrowing, edge-of-your-seat ending."

–Brooke L. French, author of *Inhuman Acts* and *The Carolina Variant*

"*Stable* crackles with suspense! Nestled in the wild beauty of Colorado's Rocky Mountains, the small town of Buena Vista is a peaceful retreat from the troubles of the modern world. Until the girls begin to disappear–first one, then another. The time to find them–and whoever is taking them–is running out. In *Stable*, Cam Torrens has created an edge-of-your-seat, cheer-on-the-heroes, just-one-more-chapter great read!"

–Joan M. Griffin, author of *Force of Nature, Three Women Tackle the John Muir Trail*

"Cam Torrens's 30-year Air Force career and his experience as a search and rescue volunteer shine through in this impressively realistic debut novel that's packed full of Colorado-style adventure and enthralling suspense. The characters are vivid, the dialogue is spot-on, and the tension never lets up. But *Stable* isn't just a thriller–it's a layered, compelling story that delves into the complexities of trauma, grief, family ties, and most of all, forgiveness. Looking forward to more from this author!"
–Regina Buttner, author of *Down a Bad Road*

"A fine thriller with loads of action and suspense, and a great read for anyone wanting a novel filled with plenty of twists and turns."
–Parman Reynolds, Author of *All For Summer* and *The Boys*

"Cam Torrens has pulled out all the stops and created a spell-binding mystery that will keep the reader on the edge of their seat. *Stable* is a definite must read for anyone who loves suspense."

–LeeAnne James, author of *Justice for Loretta*

STABLE

CHAPTER 1

"I'm not ready yet. He's out there taunting me. Give me another ten minutes."

Tyler Zahn's gaze moved from his daughter's CU Boulder T-shirt and brown-skinned arms to the clear bobber on the end of her fishing line, jerking underwater. Again. "We need to leave in five if we're going to make it on time. I told Kristee we'd be there by noon."

Daria jerked her pole, but didn't hook the trout teasing the bait under the lake's mirrored surface. Zahn already had three fish on a stringer and was hoping his twenty-year-old daughter would catch her first of the day.

His technique, crude by local fly-fishing standards, rarely failed. He'd rig up a regular fishing pole with a float bobber and fly, an amateur's fly-fishing rig that eliminated the entire process of whipping the line back and forth to fling it out in the water. Then the *coup de grâce*. He'd stuff a piece of worm on the fly. Every time he pulled out the worms, he glanced around the shores of Aspen Lake, checking for purists. Not the way locals caught fish around here. But it worked for Zahn. Why wasn't it working for his daughter?

Zahn opened his appointment book for the number to the front desk of River Ragers, where his friend Kristee guided rafts. He frowned. No way would they make it on time. It was at least a twenty-minute drive down Cottonwood Pass and across the Arkansas River Valley to the raft company.

Zahn looked up and saw his daughter staring at him and shaking her head.

"Are you marking off fishing with an 'X' or planning out tomorrow?"

"Neither. I need to call the rafting company and let them know we're running behind."

"The only reason we're running behind is because you're over scheduling everything, Dad." Daria held her pole with one hand and gestured with the other. "Look around. We're literally at ten thousand feet, on a mountain lake tucked into the Colorado Rockies. This isn't something you just 'log off' on a to-do list. Do I look like I'm not having fun?"

Zahn gave a half-smile. "You haven't caught a fish yet."

"Because you're tracking the wrong things. It should be 'go fishing' instead of 'catch a fish.' I bet your afternoon goal says 'raft The Numbers' instead of 'enjoy the river.' Am I right?"

Zahn didn't dare look at his appointment book. She was right. "I want you to experience everything out here, Dar. You've only got a couple of weeks, right?"

Daria sighed. "I finished my Psych finals. I'm with my dad who I haven't spent time with in six years," she said, smiling at Zahn. "Do you think you could relax a little and let me enjoy it on my own terms? You spending every day trying to schedule my vacation is making me nervous." She paused. "I thought you were going to work again. You know, after that thing you did last year?"

Zahn stayed silent, staring at Daria's bobber. No movement. He thought about the *thing* from last year. He and his deputy sheriff friend had stopped those guys from blowing up the dam on Dillon Reservoir. Kind of funny, actually. Everyone had been congratulatory and had lauded Zahn for saving lives, but the truth of the matter was that the experience had literally—stealing one of Daria's oft-used words—saved his life.

Stepping up and taking action had reversed a ten-year spiral of depression that started when he lost his son, Jacob, Daria's brother, to the flu while Zahn was deployed in Iraq. Then he lost an aircrew under his command to a missile. His marriage to Sheila had fallen apart, not because of the challenges of a mixed-race relationship, but because he couldn't handle the grief and shame accompanying the tragedies. He had wallowed away at a desk job in the Pentagon, followed by a contractor job on the outside, gaining weight and perfecting the ancient medicinal art of numbing pain with beer.

Yep, the *thing* his daughter referred to was an understatement.

"I've got a slot for training," Zahn said. "But the Law Enforcement Academy is backed up after the pandemic shut things down. They canceled two cycles of training before they finally determined it was safe enough to start up again. So I'm going in July."

"Well, maybe you ought to study or something. Give me a break." Zahn saw Daria's bobber plunge below the surface again. This time it didn't resurface. He shifted his gaze back to his daughter and saw her pole bent toward the water.

"Got him!" Daria smiled at him over her shoulder.

Zahn may have caught the most fish, but Daria won the prize for the biggest. Fourteen inches long. Enough for a night's meal for him, since Daria didn't eat meat.

"Nope," she said, crouching next to the fish in the shallow water and working her hand up the line to the trout's gills. She'd hooked the fish through the mouth and didn't need an extractor to remove the worm-wrapped fly. "This guy gets to live for another day. You already caught enough fish for dinner." Daria twisted her wrist underwater and pointed the nose of the fish toward the mountains overlooking the far side of the lake. "Swim free, buddy." The fish sped away.

Zahn smiled. His daughter loved animals unconditionally. He suspected she held humans to a higher standard.

• • •

Zahn took the gravel road to the main highway at about forty, pushing up a cloud of dust behind his truck. Rounding a sharp corner, his back tires swung wide as he corrected to avoid a maroon pickup truck. He snapped his head toward the oncoming driver, but couldn't see a face through the dust. Zahn slowed and regained his side of the road, shaking his head.

"Dad, stop."

Zahn pulled over and looked at his daughter. "Did you forget something?"

"Look at me."

Zahn kept his eyes on Daria and thought how much she looked like her mother. Deep brown eyes that flashed warning signals when she was upset. Like now.

The dust caught up with the parked truck, and he coughed as he felt his nose tickle.

"I had a blast. I caught a fish. I loved the lake. Rafting's next. Let's go." She tilted her head. "But you need to slow down. Relax." She checked the rearview mirror. "You just blanketed that truck in dust."

"We're late…"

"Live with it. Because if you don't slow down and lighten up a bit, I will kindly ask you to take me home. How's that sound?"

Zahn sighed. Sounded like his ex-wife. A force of nature combined with a voice of common sense. And rarely wrong. He put the truck into gear and pulled onto the road.

"You're right, Dar," Zahn said, smiling. "I got it."

CHAPTER 2

The dog in Janae Longmont's arms stiffened like a board, and the girl woke at his low growl. She opened her eyes to Dobby, a Chihuahua-Corgi mix—a Chigi—staring at the door. A floorboard creaked. Janae rolled over toward the door. She stuck her fingernail between her teeth and nibbled. The shadow beneath the door shifted from right to left, gliding by just like last night and the night before. A little less scary in the dim light of dawn, especially since Janae knew who it was.

Dobby settled back in her arms when the shadow disappeared, and Janae heard muffled footsteps descending the stairs. She exhaled and reached for the book next to the bed.

Crack. This noise came from the window side of the room. From outside.

Dobby froze again, now staring at the window.

"Stay."

The nine-year-old girl climbed out of bed and padded to the far window facing a hill marking the edge of the Arkansas River Valley and the start of the Collegiate Peaks.

Visiting her aunt and uncle's house in the Colorado Rockies always reminded Janae of the *Wizard of Oz*. She glanced back at her dog. "We're not in Oklahoma anymore, Dobby."

The window framed tall Ponderosa pines thrusting from jagged rocks only a stone's throw from the house. "There's no place like home," Janae said, then raised on her toes to click her heels together.

A movement below the window caught her eye. She dropped her heels back to the floor and pressed her face to the window. A mother deer and her fawn nibbled at the dry, brown grass next to the house, the larger deer popping her head up, alert, after each bite, while the fawn nibbled away, oblivious to the fact that their breakfast was in someone's backyard.

Janae checked Dobby again and smiled. Already back asleep.

Tiptoeing to her bed, she grabbed her tablet computer off the nightstand. Back at the window, she took pictures of the tawny mother standing guard over her hungry, white-spotted offspring. The angle was off; all Janae captured were the tops of the two deer.

She could grab a better shot from the dining-room window downstairs. Or even the ultimate shot if she ventured outside and took the picture. She normally avoided the dining room because sometimes Uncle Mike was the only one awake this early. Janae hated talking to him by herself. Ever since her cousin Meghan—Uncle Mike's daughter from his first marriage—had left, her uncle was just awkward around kids.

Outside would give Janae the better photo. But alone? The woods scared her. And her mom didn't want her going far.

Scaredy-cat. That's what they'd called her last year at the elementary school in Oklahoma because she wouldn't climb through the tire tunnel on the playground. She didn't enjoy the nickname. But it was true. Put her somewhere dark or alone, and she was the complete opposite of her best friends. Well, her imaginary best friends, that is.

She knew Harry Potter's bold housemate, Hermione Granger, wasn't real. Just as Percy Jackson's friend, Annabeth Chase, was only part of a story. But Janae spent more time with those two girls than with any real girls, and they wouldn't blink at going outside. Especially to snap a shot of a doe and a fawn.

Janae took a deep breath and tiptoed to the door while watching Dobby. No invisibility cloak needed here—Dobby seemed to have dropped back into a deep slumber. She crept out the door and down the carpeted steps. A kitchen light shone, but the house was quiet.

Janae sat in the entryway and slid her bare feet into her pink cowboy boots. Last fall, her dad had asked her if pink cowboy boots were the right choice for the first day of school.

"I like them," she had said. It's not like the kids at school would not make fun of her, anyway.

Janae donned her pink windbreaker and opened the front door. No need for alarms at Uncle Mike's place. Who would drive eight miles into the woods to break into a house? She closed the door behind her and walked toward the backyard, trying to avoid awakening the sleepers inside.

Poking her head around the wooden siding, she could see the mother deer staring at her. The fawn munched grass between Janae and the doe, clueless about the impending photo shoot or any potential threat. Janae's eyes rose toward the cliff overlooking the house, and she shuddered. Perfect spot for a mountain lion, according to the movies she'd seen. Didn't the deer know that? Like, from instinct or something?

Janae breathed in, then pointed the tablet at the two deer. She tapped the button, and the picture froze. Perfect. The doe's eyes seemed to look straight into Janae's. *Isn't my little fawn beautiful?*

Oops. The tablet's camera made a noise just like a real camera. The smaller deer's head whipped toward Janae. It glanced at its mother, then swung its head back to Janae and took a step toward her. The girl raised her tablet again. "Hey there, little guy. Want to be my friend?"

Janae pressed the button on the tablet, startling both deer into full attention. She snapped another shot before the doe leaped toward the rocks jutting from the steep slope, with her fawn close behind. Where mountain lions liked to hang…probably.

She should have stayed inside.

The mother deer stopped, her little one tucked at her side, and looked back at Janae. And then Janae felt a hand drop on her shoulder.

CHAPTER 3

Breakfast at Zahn's house had evolved since Daria's arrival. She'd let him know she wasn't a picky eater, but she didn't eat meat. So this morning was his first effort at a veggie omelet, and judging from the way Daria dug into her plate, he'd produced a winner.

Yesterday he had made avocado toast. Daria said it was a *thing* at school, but it still looked like green peanut butter smeared on toast to him. Not too bad, though. Especially when he draped two ribbons of bacon across the top of his serving while smiling at Daria.

Zahn's smile dropped as an Active 911 alert lit up his phone. Search & Rescue, or SAR, call.

Damn. Had to get a call today. His open day planner read *Take Daria hiking.*

He grabbed the phone and tapped to open the alert.

Need hikers. Missing woman on La Plata. Report to the bay.

La Plata was a 14-er, one of the fifty–four Colorado peaks stretching past the 14,000-foot elevation mark. Climbing these peaks, or *bagging* them, as the veterans called it, was a popular pastime for hundreds of Coloradoans. And hundreds more if you counted the folks road-tripping from out of state.

Scaling these peaks was a challenge. It wasn't just the jagged cliffs above the tree line, or the unpredictable weather—including July snowstorms—making the climbs difficult. The altitude also impacted the hikers' minds and bodies. The elevation sucked like a vacuum, drawing energy from even the most physically prepared and siphoning mental acuity from all who ran into trouble. Every year brought a spring-summer uptick of search and rescue missions for Chaffee County SAR North.

Last year, Zahn had been just as physically unprepared for a 14-er as the crowds of Texans who made the weekend treks to Colorado. His SAR teammates Kristee Li and Deputy Sheriff Rick Perez didn't care and had finally dragged his butt up his first 14-er, Mt. Harvard, as a victory climb following the *stop-the-terrorists-from-blowing-the-dam* incident. US Marshal Randall Williams had gone along for the ride.

Zahn would remember it as his first 14-er. Rick Perez most likely remembered the climb as the day where Williams had body-blocked Perez's attempts to win over Kristee, stealing her away for himself. The Marshal and Kristee had been dating for the last year, and Perez remained terminally single.

Zahn smiled. Not that there was anything wrong with that.

Since Mt. Harvard, he'd summitted five more of the local peaks, including La Plata, just three weeks ago.

"SAR call?"

"Yep. Lost hiker on La Plata. Just this side of Independence Pass to Aspen. I climbed it with Rick Perez last month."

"So…?"

"So, you and I are hiking up Horned Fork Basin. As planned. SAR has enough hikers. They don't need me."

"You should go, Dad."

"I told you—" His phone rang. He glanced down and saw Mary Morgan on the caller readout.

"Tyler, I need a favor," she said.

"What's up?"

"I'm on the desk for this La Plata thing, but I can't get there for another thirty minutes. My car's on the rack at BV Automotive. I sent out the 911 alert, and teams are responding, but can you get them organized and out the door until I get there?"

Zahn looked across the table at Daria, who was emphatically nodding her head. Guess he wasn't the only one who thought Mary had a loud phone voice.

"Go," Daria mouthed.

"Yeah, I got the 911 call you sent. I can cover until you get there. I have some plans later in the day, though, so that's why I didn't respond to go search."

"Thirty minutes. Forty-five tops, Tyler, and I'll be there," Mary said. "I appreciate it."

"Got it."

Zahn punched off his phone and looked at Daria. "All right, since you're pushing me to go, how about you take care of the dishes and get packed for our hike? I'll be back in an hour."

"Got it," Daria mimicked Zahn's business voice. "Take your time. Sounds more important than our afternoon day hike."

Zahn pushed through the SAR bay door twelve minutes after the phone call with Mary. Three members were already in the bay, grabbing gear and loading packs. A dark-haired Asian woman turned to him as he entered the bay.

"What's up, Z-man? You going hiking with us today?"

Zahn walked to the whiteboard at the front of the room, glancing Kristee Li's way. "I'm filling in for Mary just long enough to kick this thing off. How'd you get released to do this? I thought raft guides didn't get any time off this time of year."

"It's a training day, and my boss says I'm already the most trained guide he's got!"

Zahn started writing the details Mary had given him onto the whiteboard, the smell of dry-erase marker taking him back to the Air Force briefs he used to lead before big missions. His flying days might be over, but he liked the mission-driven purpose of Search & Rescue.

Subject: Abby Lamont

Reporting Party: Jackson Twain (boyfriend)

Last Known Coords: 39°02'05.8"N 106°28'45.1"W

He turned toward Kristee. "How about Randall? You still seeing him?"

Kristee emerged from the storage closet with three granola bars and a digital radio. "Yeah, we're still a thing. He's only been out visiting twice since the new year, but I've been in to see—"

Zahn turned around to see why she'd stopped talking. Rick Perez, in full deputy sheriff uniform, strode through the door.

"Nice hiking clothes, Rick," Kristee said with a smile.

Perez smiled back. "I know you're worried about getting lost without me, Kristee, but I actually just stopped by to pass some mission info on to the Incident Commander. Guess that's you, Tyler?"

Zahn grinned. "For another hour." He liked how Perez and Kristee had remained friends even after the awkward Williams incident.

Perez moved to the front of the room, reading Zahn's notes on the board. The other team members moved closer to hear whether Perez had any updates or additional information to help them find Abby.

"So they started hiking yesterday at 10:00 a.m. and took the Ellingwood Ridge route," Perez said.

Zahn looked at Kristee. She had pointed the route out to him when he was preparing his own La Plata summit. There were three ways up La Plata: the standard route on the north side, the longer route on the south side, and Ellingwood Ridge, which required Class III+ rock scrambling for six hours to reach the summit. You needed to know what you were doing to take the Ellingwood route.

"Late start for Ellingwood," Kristee pointed out. "Guess they were pretty confident in their pace?"

"That's the thing," Perez said. "The boyfriend is pretty experienced. Abby isn't. So instead of six hours up Ellingwood, it took them eight. They summitted about six o'clock yesterday evening and started down the standard route. Abby was dead tired. So, halfway down, the boyfriend—his name is Jackson, by the way—gets the idea that he'll run ahead to the car at the bottom. Move it up the dirt road from the trailhead to where the trail heads off in the woods, so Abby doesn't have to hike as far. Then he figures he'll cook her dinner and have it ready when she comes off the mountain."

A voice piped up from the back. "That sounds like a long way of saying the dude left his girlfriend on her own on a fourteen thousand foot mountain."

Zahn stifled a smile and looked around the room. Seven SAR members, including Kristee Li, looked back at him.

"You all packed and ready?" They nodded in return.

He grabbed a binder from the incident command desk, flipping to the briefing guide. Ten minutes later, the search teams were on their way.

Zahn spent the next thirty minutes checking the communications with the teams en route to the trailhead and gathering more information on Abby and Jackson. He tried to give the boyfriend a call, but Lake County Dispatch reported the young man had returned to the trailhead to wait for the SAR teams.

By the time Mary walked in, shaking her head, Zahn had projected the search area from the computer onto the mounted flat screen and was talking to the SAR teams arriving at the trailhead.

"Sorry, Tyler, they were backed up at the shop," she said. "I owe you one."

"No biggie." He glanced at his watch. Still plenty of time to get Daria out hiking.

He briefed Mary on the status of the mission, and when he was sure she knew everything he knew, he headed toward his truck, tapping Daria's name on his phone while he walked.

"What's up, Dad?"

"You ready to go in fifteen?"

"Ready. Did you guys find the hiker?"

"Not yet. But they're off to a good start. They'll find her."

CHAPTER 4

Janae screamed and broke free from the firm hand gripping her shoulder. She stumbled forward and turned her head. She froze.

Uncle Mike wore a big smile.

"Morning, Nae Nae. Fancy meeting you out here."

Janae hated Uncle Mike's pet name for her.

She glanced from Uncle Mike's grinning face to the house and saw her mother smiling and waving at her from the guest bedroom window. Janae waved back, then dropped her hands and looked back at Uncle Mike.

"You scared me," she mumbled.

Uncle Mike laughed. "Not as much as I scared that doe and her fawn. I must be losing my stealth skills." He stepped toward Janae. "What are you doing out here all by your lonesome, anyway? I thought you hated the outside?"

"I wanted a picture of the deer."

"And you didn't even bring that little yapper of yours?"

"Dobby would have scared them away."

"You should keep that thing outside. Ain't normal for a dog to sleep in your bedroom."

Janae glanced up at her uncle, then back to the ground. "He keeps me safe."

The day got better. Perfect, in fact. Her dad and Uncle Mike headed out to fix the little treehouse they used for hunting deer, and her mother and Aunt Marcie wanted to run down to Buena Vista to wander through the shops. They gave Janae the choice of tagging along or staying home.

Janae didn't give it a second thought. Uncle Mike wasn't around. She had two books to finish. And she could stay inside.

"I'll stay," she said. "I want to read."

Her mom left her with the cellphone and Aunt Marcie's number. "Two hours, max," her mom called from the front door. "You are NOT allowed to leave the house, okay?"

As if. Janae had no plans to venture into the unexplored and potentially dangerous forest outside.

"Okay," she called back. "Take your time!"

Decision time. Should she read the last third of *Maze Runner*, a book she hadn't read before, or burrow back into *Harry Potter and the Deathly Hallows*, a book she'd read at least three times? After the shadow under the door and Uncle Mike sneaking up on her, she picked Hogwarts. She needed a dose of courage. The book might have Harry's name in the title, but Hermione, Harry's fearless sidekick, remained Janae's kindred spirit.

When disaster loomed in JK Rowling's books, you could be sure Harry would prevail in the end. But it was actually Hermione's poise under pressure and quick wits that allowed Harry to be the hero. Hermione was exactly who Janae wanted to be.

The only problem was that Hermione existed between pages. Not in real life. Janae recognized that, even if she sometimes forgot. The memory of the playground tire tunnel never failed to remind her. All the kids egging her on... *it's easy... do it, scaredy-cat.* Without a thought, Janae had pointed toward the tunnel and blurted, *Wingardium Leviosa*, as if she could levitate it out of the way. Mike Phillips had stood close enough to hear and turned to the small crowd. "She tried to put a spell on the tunnel!"

Janae had run from the playground, mortified, with the raucous laughter and calls of *petrificus totalus* pursuing her. Most. Embarrassing. Moment. Ever.

She opened the Harry Potter book and kept *Maze Runner* at the ready on the end table.

Aunt Marcie and Janae's mom ended up shopping for close to three hours, allowing Janae enough time to finish the first book and half of the other. After spaghetti and meatballs for dinner, Janae talked the four adults into playing Catan with her, which lasted until almost nine o'clock. She had more fun than she expected, especially because Uncle Mike didn't act as weird with others around.

Yep, she mused, as she shrugged under the thick covers of the guest bed with Dobby at her side. Vacation wasn't so bad when you stayed inside. She grabbed *Maze Runner*. Time to find out what happens in the end.

A low growl woke Janae two hours later. Her lamp reflected off the cover of the book on her chest, and the small clock on her nightstand read 11:00. She looked at Dobby, staring at the door.

"Shhh," she admonished the dog.

Janae turned toward the light under the door. Light on the left. Light on the right. Shadow in the middle.

How come her parents didn't think it was weird someone was walking the hallways this late? Or Aunt Marcie?

She shifted the dog lower on her legs and reached for the lamp, clicking it off. Not that she welcomed the dark, but she wanted the shadow to believe she was asleep. She turned back toward the door. The shadow remained.

Janae's first instinct? Point her finger at the door and use one of Hermione's special spells. Unfortunately, she was a fourth grader now and understood spells weren't real. She thought about that. It wasn't always magic that made Hermione brave. Often, her willingness to face her fears and to stand up to whatever scared her the most were the traits that made her courageous.

Janae slipped out from under the comforter and approached the door. The shadow shifted in the light at her feet. She reached out with her hand and grasped the doorknob. It turned between her fingers and she jumped backward. Dobby let out a sharp bark that filled the room.

Janae stared as the shadow shifted back from the door. Feet padded down the hall and the shadow disappeared.

• • •

Janae woke, her heart pounding. She stared at the crack of light beneath the door.

No shadow.

She sat up and looked around the bedroom.

Nothing. *What woke her?*

Dobby lay fast asleep at the foot of her bed. The clock next to her read 7:04. Earlier than she normally rose.

Pulling back her covers, she climbed from the bed and walked to the window, ready to face the wilds of Colorado…through the paned glass. Below her second-story room, a fawn munched new cheatgrass thrusting through drifts of pine needles. The same one as yesterday. She knew it. She scanned the yard for the doe. No movement. She stared into the woods surrounding the house. *Where was mama deer?*

Her eyes returned to the fawn, and she nibbled on her pajama-wrapped thumb. Maybe that's what woke her. The lost fawn.

Decision time. She could sit in her bed and worry about a baby deer with no mother, or she could put on her big girl pants—she wasn't sure that was what Hermione or Annabeth called them, but her uncle certainly did—and go resolve the situation.

She dressed quickly, in jeans, socks, and a t-shirt, and headed downstairs. The light from the dining room spilled into the entranceway, and the smell of coffee hovered in the air. Uncle Mike and Aunt Marcie talked in low voices. Maybe Aunt Marcie would keep Uncle Mike busy, and he wouldn't sneak up on her again.

Janae glanced at her cowboy boots, then slipped on her tennis shoes instead, grabbing her windbreaker from the coat rack by the door.

"I'm going to play outside," she called to her aunt and uncle. Her parents were still asleep. They had been sleeping late since they had arrived four days ago. A much-needed vacation, her dad kept explaining to Uncle Mike.

"It's just past seven, Janae. What are you doing awake?" Aunt Marcie called.

"Let her go," Uncle Mike said. "She's been so scared to go outside since she got here. If she wants to go, let her."

Aunt Marcie mumbled something. Uncle Mike called out, "Stay close to the house, Nae Nae."

Ugh. Uncle Mike was telling everyone how scared she was. And she hated the name *Nae Nae* almost as much as *Scaredy Cat*.

"Okay!" Janae pulled the door shut behind her and scanned the trees, looking for her fawn. Rounding the corner, she glimpsed movement at the base of the cliffs. The terrain looked dangerous...and Janae didn't like danger.

Slowly walking toward the rocks, her arms wrapped around her body, Janae spotted the fawn standing frozen, looking back at her.

"Hey there, sweetheart," Janae called. "I won't hurt you." She sat down, about fifty feet from the baby deer, and stared at it. The fawn stared back for a minute, then lowered its head and nibbled some more.

"Where's your mama?" The animal jerked its head and stared again at her as if reminded it was indeed missing a mother. Dropping its head for another bite of cheatgrass, the fawn turned around and started picking its way up the slope between the rocks. Janae watched the fawn, then turned and looked at the house. She bit her lip, hesitant to walk away from the property. *I'll just make sure it finds its mama.* She stood and followed her new friend.

The girl and the deer made slow progress up the hill, with the fawn stopping every twenty feet to check on Janae. Or so it seemed. When the baby deer paused, Janae scanned the rocks for lions...or tigers, or bears. "Oh my!" she said, shaking her head.

Get a grip, Janae!

She looked back down the hill where the corner of her uncle's house poked from the trees. Definitely farther than she'd ever gone.

Janae stayed quiet. Suddenly, the fawn bolted, dashing up the hill.

I wonder if it hears its mama? Janae thought. She took a last glance at the house, then followed. *I'll turn back as soon as I see the mama deer.*

After a few minutes of running—shuffling was more like it, as it was harder to breathe here in Colorado than in Oklahoma—Janae stopped. The deer was nowhere to be seen. Neither was the house.

She listened.

Nothing.

Janae's lips trembled. *Maybe it found its mama.* Retreating toward the house, she flinched as she heard branches crashing to her right. Did the fawn circle around? Or the mama deer? Janae hesitated, then climbed over a log and moved toward the sound. Exiting a stand of tall pine trees, a flash of color caught her eye. A tawny-haired girl in a pink windbreaker crossed the clearing. Janae froze, her legs rooted.

She would remember later how strange her first thought was. *That girl's wearing my jacket!* Janae raised her arm. Not to wave, but to double check she had worn her own pink jacket. Definitely pink.

Wait. Jacket or not—*why is a girl my age running through the woods?*

"Hey," Janae called. "What are you doing?"

The pink flash stopped, and a wide-eyed girl, maybe a year or two older than Janae, gaped back at her. Janae walked closer. The girl's lips and chin quivered above her dirt-smeared shirt. She gasped for air, and a cottonwood leaf dropped from her hair onto a blood-stained sleeve. Her eyes blinked rapidly before shifting toward a noise to Janae's right.

"They're coming," the girl said. "Run."

Janae sucked in her breath and turned toward the noise. She saw nothing, but heard loud crashing and branch-breaking through the wood. She turned back toward the disappearing pink jacket, her throat closing, cutting off her breath. *Who was 'they?' Coming to do what?* She spun again toward the sound. A dark shape materialized from behind a tree, heading toward her.

Her head swiveled back to the girl.

Gone.

Janae clutched her jacket above the zipper with both hands, her feet frozen in place. The dark shape moved closer. Not completely dark. Two eyes above a camouflaged bandanna stared at her as the man continued climbing the hill.

Janae screamed and began running.

Janae was a fast reader, not a fast runner, and the man quickly closed the gap between them. He kept calling out in a soft but firm voice, as if he didn't want anyone else to hear him.

"Kendall, hold up there. Let's get you back home."

And again.

"Kendall, stop. I'm your ride back."

Janae tripped over a log and sprawled on her face. Her legs were lead—as if all her blood was racing to her heart instead of her muscles. Attempting to regain her feet, she felt the man grab her shoulder, shoving her harshly back toward the earth. She screamed as another arm circled around her, pressing its hand against her mouth.

"Shhh! Relax, sweetheart. Everything's okay now."

The hand relaxed and Janae tried to scream again, her eyes widening in terror, as she stared at tufts of reddish hair thrusting from under the man's hat. His hand pressed harder against her lips and moved up against her nose. She tried to breathe, but couldn't. Her vision tunneled gray, and she stopped struggling. He adjusted his hand, and Janae desperately inhaled fresh air through her runny nose.

"Listen now, sweetheart. If you make any noise, I'm going to cover your mouth and nose until you can't breathe. Do you understand?"

Janae nodded between his hands, snorting for air through her nose again.

"You want to test me?"

Janae shook her head, squeezing her eyes shut.

"Anything you want to say before I get you back?"

Janae nodded, and the man loosened his hand.

"My name is Janae, not Kendall," she whimpered.

Janae's head whipped to the side as the man slapped her face. "Nice try, little lady." He pulled her to her feet. "Let's get you back where you belong. Remember, any noise and you get to stop breathing. Got that?"

Janae nodded again between rasping breaths and stared with horror at the man's sterile eyes above his mask, before returning her gaze to the ground.

The man barked a laugh. "We're going to stick together like white on rice, the whole way back. Got that?" He grabbed Janae's hand and tugged her behind him, keeping to the ridge above the lot where her uncle's house lay hidden.

Janae scanned down the hill, hoping to glimpse the house or one of the adults. Nothing.

• • •

Janae and her captor stood in front of a red ATV.

"Time to go home, Kendall girl," the man said, lowering his mask and exposing red sideburns. "Guess I don't need to blindfold you."

Janae clapped her hands over her ears. "I'm not—"

"Shut up," the man snapped. "Get on." He pointed at the rear seat on the ATV.

Janae scrambled aboard and grabbed the passenger handles. When the man mounted the machine's front seat and started the engine, she slid off the back end and began running downhill as fast as her legs would go, praying she was moving in the house's direction.

The motor went quiet. Janae heard the man call out. "Kendall, this shit just got real!"

And then she fell again.

• • •

After twenty minutes of bumping on the back of the ATV, Janae stopped sobbing. She didn't know if her tears arose from fear, from the slap in the face, or from the bruises after the man tackled her and dragged her back to the ATV. She tried to control her breathing and make sense of her predicament. The man thought she was the other girl, Kendall. No wonder Kendall had run away. This guy was mean, meaner than any adult she had ever met. As the ATV sped across the trail along the ridgeline, she thought about Kendall's escape. *She made it a long way. Wonder if I could do that? Where did Kendall come from?*

The man slowed gradually and then veered the ATV off the path, descending a tree-covered slope. He brought the ATV to a stop in front of a wire fence.

"Don't go anywhere," he said. "I'll get you if you do."

Janae nodded her head in agreement. She wasn't going anywhere.

He walked over to the fence and lifted a wire hoop off a fence post, swinging a makeshift gate open.

"Passenger's job is to get the gates," he said. "Should've made you do it." He drove the ATV through the gate, stopped, and repeated the gate process in reverse.

"Home, sweet home," he said, mounting the ATV.

The trees thinned, and Janae recognized structures in the distance. First a shed. Then a barn. And behind the barn, a house with two trucks parked in front of it. Like a small ranch. They pulled in between the buildings, and Janae watched a man rise from a chair and walk toward them. He didn't look happy.

"Got her, Jefe," her captor said, switching off the ATV and twisting toward Janae.

"The hell you did," said Jefe. "Who is this?"

Her captor looked at Jefe, then at Janae, then back.

"What are you talking about?" Her kidnapper's voice sounded nervous. "You said a young girl, scared, in the forest alone… how many of those can there be?" He paused, then gestured toward Janae. "Here you go."

Jefe looked at Janae. He looked disgusted.

"That's not Kendall." He scowled at Janae's captor. "And why is she looking at me? Where's her hood?"

"Why would I hood her? I thought she'd already seen everything here."

Jefe shook his head.

"We got ourselves a problem now, don't we?" He paused and looked at Janae again. "What's your name, sweetheart?"

Janae opened her mouth, but no words emerged.

Jefe stared at her. "You want to try again?"

"Janae," the girl managed.

Jefe sighed and turned to her captor. "Get back on your rig and keep looking. Dirty blond hair, not pure blond like her," he pointed at Janae. "We need to find Kendall, or we have a huge problem."

The ATV man scuffed the dirt at his feet and looked at Jefe. "Got it," he said.

Jefe reached out to help Janae from the ATV. She recoiled, shaking away his hand and stepping off the opposite side of the ATV without help.

As the ATV disappeared, Jefe glared at her.

"Janae, Janae, Janae," he mused. "What are we going to do about you?"

CHAPTER 5

Zahn rolled through the stop sign at the Elk Trace exit. Daria exhaled from the passenger seat.

"What? There's no one coming for a mile each direction." Zahn pointed left, then right to the road tracing the Collegiate Peaks foothills.

"It's not that. I told you after yesterday's hike we didn't need to schedule anything today, and you still scheduled something. A ropes course? I was doing those when I was like thirteen."

"Useful skills," Zahn said under his breath.

"And now you're worried we're late to the course I don't even want to go to?"

The silence between the two was broken by Zahn's phone trilling with a SAR alarm. *Trilling* wasn't part of Zahn's daily lexicon, but he couldn't come up with a better word to describe the special tone these 911 calls broadcast. Not a ring. Not a buzz. A distinctive trill. He glanced at his daughter.

"I need to read this, Dar, okay?"

Daria nodded her head, and Zahn pulled over to the side of the road, unhooking his cellphone from the holder mounted on the truck's unused CD player.

Active 911: Hikers needed at 4 Elk Road. Meet at bay.

Zahn peered left out the driver's window. The address was only two miles north of his house and crammed right up against the steep Collegiate Peaks. Driving south to the SAR bay first would add forty-five minutes to his response time. He scanned for the incident commander's name. Josh Rasmussen. He smiled and dialed with his phone on speaker.

"Josh, it's Tyler. Still need hikers, right?"

"Right—you responding?"

"Maybe. I was taking my daughter out to do—" Daria's head whipped toward Zahn. "Uh… to go fishing. What's going on in 4 Elk? Lost hiker?"

"It's not a hiker. There's a nine-year-old girl visiting relatives over at the northwest corner of the loop in 4 Elk—one of the offshoot roads. She was outside playing this morning and now she's disappeared. Hang on…" Josh came back. "31665 Wagon Trail…you in?"

Daria shifted toward Zahn when Josh mentioned the girl. "You need to go," she mouthed.

He nodded. "Yep, I'll go. It's right by my house. I'm going to respond directly. Can you send whatever radio I need with someone else?"

"Yeah, sounds good. We'll use VHFs up there. I'll send one up for you with Deb. She'll be in the tech rig running trailhead command duty."

"All right, Josh. Thanks for running incident command. I'll be up at 4 Elk in five."

"Thanks, Z-man. See ya."

Z-man. Kristee's nickname for him was spreading through SAR like the flu in an elementary school. Zahn pulled up Google Maps and entered the address. Not within town limits—but close to where he sat in his truck. Daria stared at him with concern in her eyes. He glanced at his day planner—this was going to throw off his schedule for Daria's visit—and accepted the fact that he could get her to the ropes later. She'd appreciate it once she hung thirty feet above the Arkansas River.

"Thanks for understanding, Daria. We'll hit the ropes tomorrow."

"You're the one excited about ropes, not me," Daria said. "I just said 'yes' to keep you happy. I'll go for a run and check the mail." She looked directly at her father. "Go find the girl, Dad. Can you imagine how worried her folks must be?"

"I've got a key for the mailbox in the glove compartment. Go ahead and grab it," Zahn said.

Daria opened the glove box and extended her hand, then froze.

"There's a gun in here," she said, wincing as she spoke.

"That's mine. I've got a permit."

"They have permits allowing you to carry a gun in your truck's glove compartment?"

"Actually, I can carry it anywhere I want. A concealed carry permit." Zahn sighed. "The sheriff's department recommended I get a weapon and get current before I started the Academy. I just use it over at the range." He tilted his head. "Not a big deal."

"Whoa. Seems like a big deal to me," Daria said, sticking the mailbox key in her pocket and closing the glove compartment.

The drive over to 4 Elk only took seven minutes once he had returned Daria to the house. Zahn pulled in behind the sheriff's Tahoe and started prepping his 24-hour bag. Each SAR member carried the key essentials, not just for treating the injured, but for their own survival as well. Sleeping bag, food, lighter. Enough supplies for an overnight. As he packed, he felt a pang of guilt in his gut for leaving Daria alone at home on her vacation to visit him. Or was it guilt for his excitement about the mission?

His ex-wife, Sheila, had been the one to encourage Daria to visit Zahn for a week during her March college break. Two days after Daria arrived, the college had called and extended the scheduled break to six weeks because of water issues back at the school, something about contaminated pipes. Zahn was surprised they didn't make the students take class online, but Daria said they weren't happy with how that went during the pandemic and were hesitant to try it again. The good news? Zahn and Daria's together time this March would surpass the previous six years added together. Of course, the not-so-good-news was that Daria's spring classes would now extend well into the summer.

Sheila and he had agreed that Daria might as well spend the extended vacation up here in Buena Vista, since Daria spent time at Sheila's during the school year on weekends. Zahn had made a pact with himself. He'd give Daria a spring break she'd never forget. The Buena Vista locals boast the mountain town has 25-30 activities to choose from: skiing, rafting, mountain biking, trail running, all part of an almost endless list. The challenge is always picking the four or five where you most want to spend your time. Zahn was trying to have Daria experience all 25 activities. 30 if it worked out.

Zahn shouldered his pack and walked past the law enforcement vehicles to a uniformed officer talking to two couples in the driveway.

Rick Perez.

Zahn smiled. His partner in crime. Zahn had met Perez the year before during SAR training and had joined him on a couple of ride-alongs in the deputy sheriff rig. One thing led to another and both men found themselves knee-deep in a case involving an escaped prisoner, a kidnapping, and a terrorist plot. Zahn gained a little notoriety around town for his successful role in cracking the case and at Perez's urging had signed up for the Reserve Deputy Sheriff's program.

After the pandemic scare, however, everything was delayed with the Reserve program, and Zahn had fallen back on SAR to keep busy.

Perez turned and nodded at Zahn.

"Zahn," Perez said. "This is Jack and Kate Longmont from Oklahoma. They're out here staying with Mike and Marcie for a week. Jack and Mike are brothers."

"Hey," Jack Longmont said, then leaped back into an earlier conversation. "Janae told Mike and Marcie she was going outside. Both of them heard her leave, right Mike?"

Mike Longmont nodded. "Even told her to stay close," he said.

"You shouldn't have let her go alone," Janae's mother wailed.

Marcie jumped in. "We know it was early, but she's been so scared about everything. We thought it would build her confidence."

"She went out yesterday to take pictures of deer. I thought she was probably doing the same this morning," Mike said, shaking his head. "I never thought she'd go any farther—"

"It's okay," Perez said. "Anybody see her after she left?"

The four adults looked at each other and shook their heads.

"No," Kate said.

Perez continued. "And what time was that? When she left?"

"Just past seven," Mike said.

"Any idea what she was wearing?"

"Probably blue jeans and a t-shirt," Kate said. "That's what she usually wears, right, Jack?"

Her husband nodded. "Her windbreaker's gone, you know, that pink one. But her cowboy boots are still there, so she must've worn those red tennis shoes."

"So red shoes, jeans, and a pink jacket, right? Any hat? Does she have a phone?"

"Janae's only nine," Jack said. "No phone."

"And she doesn't wear hats," his wife said in a quiet voice, staring at the ground.

Perez finished recording the information and glanced at Zahn before addressing the group.

"Okay. Here's what we got planned. It's coming up on two hours since you last saw her, so there's a good chance she's lost, right?"

Most of the group nodded. Except Jack Longmont.

"We've got Search and Rescue from both ends of the county responding. We've got the Buena Vista police coming, and I got a helicopter en route who's going to help." He pointed east toward the valley. "Our primary focus will be downhill through the forest and out into the valley. In most of our missing child cases, they don't wander off uphill—" Perez pointed back to the mountains sloping up to the west. "—Especially something as steep as that. We'll run a line of folks up the hill, just in case, but our main effort will run east." He turned and pointed toward the parked cars.

"We'll help," Jack said. His brother nodded.

"I want you and Janae's mother to stay at the house," Perez said. "You and Marcie, too," he said, turning to Mike. "Couple of reasons. First, if Janae comes back, I want you guys to be here. Second, I'm going to use the BV police to sit and talk with you some more. See if we can figure out what she's thinking. If she was upset, or—"

"She didn't run away," Jack barked. "We're a tight church-going family and she's only nine years old. Something's happened and we need to find her."

Perez nodded slowly. "That's the plan, Mr. Longmont. We're going to find her."

CHAPTER 6

Daria paused in the driveway after Zahn dropped her off and surveyed the mountains to the west. Her dad might live in the middle of nowhere, but you couldn't beat the view. Over the tops of the Ponderosa pines surrounding the house, the sun reflected off the snow-capped peaks of Mt. Princeton, Mt. Yale, and Mt. Columbia. While nursing a beer last night, her dad had told her more than she'd asked for about his 14-er adventures over the past year.

Daria was willing to try a climb, but was finding it hard to adjust to the altitude. Not enough air. She kept in good shape at college, but the first time she went out for her daily run here, she'd had to stop at a half mile, hands on her knees, chest heaving. Maybe she'd try to get closer to her three-mile standard today. She could see the faint outline of a trail disappearing into the woods across from the house. Great day for a jog.

Ten minutes later, clad in Lycra and trail running shoes, she locked the house and followed the path into the forest. Cutting across a vacant lot, she halted abruptly to keep from falling into a barbed wire fence. *So much for staying within the housing development.* The trail continued on the other side. She was positive her dad was familiar with this path. According to her mom, the man had never met a fence he wouldn't climb.

Daria crouched under the bottom strand of barbed wire, then dusted herself off as she stood. The trail forked north toward the mountains into a twin-track dirt path showing signs of regular use. She considered putting in her earbuds, a regular habit on her college runs, but changed her mind. Who needs distraction with sunshine and a view? She picked up her pace, ignoring the *Private Property* sign next to the trail.

After a mile, she still felt okay. Maybe she was getting used to the lack of air? The path ran into a chained gate—no lock, though. Another *Private Property* sign hung on the rails, and Daria decided the gate was too obvious and forbidding a barrier to ignore. She angled right on an adjacent path, following the fence line. A flash of movement in the distance brought her from a run to a walk.

Daria peered ahead. *Crap. People.* She looked closer. People on horses. Coming her way. She glanced left at the fence. Crawling under the wire with people in sight didn't seem like the best idea. She veered off the path toward the trees.

A sharp whistle pierced the silence of the woods from the direction of the riders and Daria watched as they reined to a stop.

"Hello there," a male voice called.

Daria waved at the voice. The figures drew near, and she counted two horses, each with a man in the saddle. The first rider was younger, maybe Daria's age, wearing a baseball cap, blue jeans, and cowboy boots. Thick brown hair poked from his cap, and his eyes squinted from a smile. The second rider was much older and had *cowboy* written all over him. A grayish-white handlebar mustache on a lined face topped with a cattleman's hat. No smile. His piercing gray eyes looked at her, then behind and around, as if checking for others.

"Hi?" Daria called, one finger twisting her hair. Not a confident salutation. But not meek either.

"What're you doing out this direction?" The young man cocked his head at Daria.

"Jogging," Daria said, crossing her arms. "It's beautiful out here."

The older man snorted, and his chiseled face broke into a smile. "Sure is, young lady. And you picked the right day for a run. Welcome to Beyond Adventure."

Daria gave the two men a blank stare.

The younger man jumped in. "What Mr. Elliot is saying in his gentlemanly fashion…" The young man grinned and glanced at the older man.

"I'm saying that this here is private property, and you, young lady—" Elliot interrupted, looking again at the younger man, as if he was teaching him the correct term to use when addressing a woman, "—are trespassing on church land."

Daria's eyes widened. The private property part didn't surprise her, but she didn't know it belonged to a church. The closest town was Buena Vista, six miles away. She hadn't seen a church out here.

"Church?"

"Yup." Elliot waved his arm toward the forest. "The Christian Scientists run a camp out here—Beyond Adventure—and this property belongs to them."

"I didn't know that." She raised her eyebrows. "And you all are with the church?"

Elliot leaned forward in his saddle, cocking his head toward the younger man. "Kevin here is with the church. I'm not a member, but I work for them. I run the stables back that direction." He turned his head over his shoulder.

Kevin's grin faded. "What's your story? Didn't you see the signs?"

Daria considered adopting the *innocent young girl feigning ignorance* approach, then nixed it. She looked at Kevin, then lowered her eyes.

"Yeah, I saw them. Sorry." Her chin dropped. "I'm visiting my dad over in Elk Trace, and all they have over there for running is gravel roads. They suck. I saw the trail through the fence and couldn't resist. Sorry," she repeated.

Kevin laughed and glanced at Elliot, who wore a big smile.

"Understandable," Elliot said. "Don't blame you. But you're currently heading right toward the center of camp, and the staff there might not be as accommodating as we are. Probably be wise to turn around."

Daria's shoulders slumped in relief. They would not make a big deal about it.

"What's your name, Miss?"

"Daria. Daria Zahn."

"Nice to meet you, Daria Zahn. I'm Gabe. Gabe Elliot." Elliot pointed to the young man. "And this here young buck is Kevin Kilgore."

Kevin touched the brim of his ball cap.

Elliot looked at Kevin, then turned back to Daria. "You like horses?"

"I love horses," she said. "My dad used to take me riding when we lived in Abilene…that's in Texas. He was in the Air Force."

Elliot nodded. "I know Abilene." He turned to the younger man. "Kevin, why don't you offer Daria here a ride back to Elk Trace?"

Both Daria and Kevin tilted their heads at Elliot. Kevin glanced back at Daria.

"Come on up," he said, after a brief hesitation, patting the space behind his saddle.

Daria had mentally rejected the offer as soon as it left Elliot's mouth. Middle of the woods, two strange men. 'Need a ride, sweet thang?' She was already hearing banjos.

But her resolve softened as she admired the tall horse. Kevin's smile wasn't too bad either. It was a beautiful day for a ride in the forest. And it was a church camp, for crying out loud.

"I don't have riding clothes."

Kevin grinned. "Oh, did they use fancy stuff back in—what'd you call it, Abalone?"

"Abilene." Daria looked down at her running tights. "I just wore jeans back then."

"Then hop on up," he said. "That running getup ought to work just fine."

Daria laughed. "Sounds great," she said, striding toward Kevin and his horse. He moved his foot out of the stirrup, extended his arm, and Daria swung up behind him. Tight fit.

"What's a Christian Scientist doing way out here? Aren't you guys the ones who don't believe in medicine?"

"That's what everyone always thinks," Kevin said. "Misconception. We just believe in the power of prayer for healing. Doesn't mean we don't believe in common sense. We get shots, use band-aids, wash our hands. All that stuff."

"Huh."

"More common sense than Elliot there," Kevin said. "He doesn't believe in that vaccine stuff."

Elliot snorted. "Take more than a little flu to bring me down."

The two men pointed their horses back toward Daria's fence crossing. The ten-minute ride seemed like two, with Elliot acting as a social facilitator.

"Where'd you grow up, honey?"

"I was a military brat. We lived all over. Florida, Texas, Germany, Virginia."

"What part of Virginia? Kevin, here, he grew up in southwest Virginia. Tell her, son."

"Yep, I grew up in Blacksburg, Virginia. You know, where Virginia Tech is?"

"We were up in northern Virginia. My dad worked at the Pentagon." She lowered her voice. "So you're a Hokie, Kevin?"

"Yep, my dorm room at VT was just ten minutes from my house. But I only watch the football games on TV now. Once I saw these Colorado mountains, I was hooked."

By the time the three pulled up in front of Daria's corner of the fence, Elliot had set up an invitation for Daria to come over to the stables and join the two on a real ride—one where she could ride a horse on her own.

"We'll see you Thursday, Daria," Elliot called. "Now that you have an invitation, you can crawl under the fence and come on over without worrying about getting caught."

Daria waved from the fence.

"See ya, Mr. Elliot, Kevin. Thanks."

"You can call me Gabe, young lady. Nice to meet you," Elliot said.

The men waved, and Kevin called out, "You forgive your dad yet?"

Daria froze. *What the heck was he talking about?* He didn't even know her father.

She cocked her head. "For what?"

Kevin grinned. "For moving you away from Abalone and those horses. I can tell you miss riding."

Daria laughed and gave another wave.

"Abilene… not Abalone."

Kevin glanced back over his shoulder in her direction as he rode away.

She turned toward the house, breaking into a jog. Busted while trespassing. Could have been worse. Met some new friends. Going to get to ride horses. And maybe see that Kevin again.

CHAPTER 7

Perez and Zahn left the Longmonts huddled in the driveway and walked toward the growing fleet of volunteer vehicles parked on the side of the road. They stopped at the SAR command vehicle as a tall, solid woman stepped out of the driver's seat. Debbie Coffman.

"Hey, Deb," Perez said. "Thanks for getting out here so quick."

"That's what we do." Coffman stood with her feet apart. "You've been listening to the radio?"

"Not in the last five minutes. Zahn and I were talking to the subject's family."

Coffman nodded. "Two choppers are on their way. There are three ponds over there." She pointed to the east. "Sheriff is coordinating to drain them if needed."

Perez nodded and said nothing.

Zahn smiled. When Deb started, it was best to let her keep going until she got it all out. Type-A to the bone. She rubbed some of the SAR and law enforcement members the wrong way, but Zahn had watched her run incident command from the bay and from the trailhead, and thought she might be SAR's most valuable member, given her sharp mind for detail and the ability to juggle multiple inputs while giving direction.

Coffman continued. "I'll run two ATV teams on a grid covering the approaches to the ponds. I think the drone team should focus on the valley since the choppers have the ponds, don't you?"

Perez nodded again.

"So that brings us to the ground teams. Rick, why don't you tell me how you want to run those?"

"I like what you've got planned, Deb. You said Chaffee County SAR South is responding, right?"

Coffman nodded and pointed at a line of cars waiting to park. "Some of them are already here. They're bringing their drone as well, so we'll have two."

"Great. So let's use the Longmonts' house as the east-west dividing line. Use one team on a north-south line, and walk them east into the valley. Use the other team and walk them west up into the mountains. You decide who goes where."

Coffman nodded again. "Already have."

"And why don't you have the south team run their drone on the opposite sector as your own?"

"That's the plan."

Perez turned to Zahn. "Got to check in with the Sheriff. See you out there."

Zahn nodded, turning to Coffman. "Where do you need me?"

"I'm going to go coordinate with South's team leader. I'll have them search downhill to the east. You rally our folks and set up the uphill search line to the west."

"Got it."

He walked toward a group of three SAR members clad in red shirts. SAR North. His team.

"Morning, folks," Zahn greeted the team. "Hey, Kristee." He nodded and smiled at his friend. "We're going to form a search line and do the mountains. Can I get you all to move to the driveway and start spreading out our folks as they arrive? Hold them there, and we'll start when Deb gives us the go-ahead."

"Got it, Z-man." Kristee smiled. "Missed you on La Plata the other day searching for the abandoned girlfriend. Climbed anything worth bragging about lately?"

Zahn smiled. "How did that mission turn out? I got the message you found her."

"Yeah, the girl, Abby, was working her way down the mountain. Completely lost. The team that found her had the boyfriend with them, and he was crying a river when he saw her. I thought she was going to slap him upside the head for leaving her, but, noooo…she just gave him a big old hug." Kristee rolled her eyes. "So what have you and Daria been up to?"

"Lots of hiking and fishing."

"Good for you. What did she think of the raft trip? Better than fishing, I bet."

"She had a blast. Thanks for setting it up." Zahn's smile faded. "And sorry about being late."

Kristee laughed. "Customers are always late. That's why we tell you to show 30 minutes before we really need you." She grabbed Zahn's arm. "I'm glad Daria liked it. Better than your fishing and hiking plan. You need to let me take her out and show her what the gals do in town."

Zahn nodded and gave Kristee a wry grin. "I will. Got a busy schedule lined up for her, though."

Kristee shook her head. "I know you, Z-man. You're trying too hard. Let me guess…you're trying to give her the vacation of a lifetime to make up for the last six years. Am I right?"

Zahn scuffed his boot in the dirt. "We were heading off to the ropes course when I got the call."

"Ropes course? Seriously?" Kristee laughed, shaking her head. "Have her call me."

The group moved toward the driveway, spacing themselves a few yards from the Longmont family. Zahn continued directing SAR North members. He nodded at a SAR South member in an orange shirt doing the same thing with his team.

Ten minutes later, Coffman briefed the two teams on the situation.

"Okay. Here's what we got. Nine-year-old Janae Longmont left this house at seven this morning to go play."

Coffman checked her watch.

"It's now nine-fifteen. She was wearing a pink windbreaker, blue jeans, and red shoes. The aunt and uncle talked to her as she left, but no one saw her after that. We have no reason to think she had a destination. She is not a local. She and her parents are visiting her aunt and uncle, Marcie and Mike Longmont."

Coffman paused and looked over the heads of the teams. Zahn followed her gaze. Jack Longmont was striding toward the group, his face twisted in a scowl. Zahn started edging around the group toward Janae's father.

"Listen to me, guys. You don't know my daughter." Longmont's voice rose. "She's not the kind to wander off. She's scared of the woods. Someone took her. You all need to be looking at this as an abduction. I need—"

Zahn saw a small arm reach out and grab Mr. Longmont's arm.

"You're Janae's father?" Zahn heard Kristee Li's calm voice.

"Huh? Right. I need to—"

"You've probably got just what we need. You're closest to her. Can I talk to you for a second?"

Longmont's head turned to the group, then to Kristee. "Of course." He followed the young woman away from the searchers.

Coffman nodded in Kristee's direction, and Zahn smiled. The diminutive Kristee Li had saved the day again.

Coffman continued.

"Here's how it's going to go. I want SAR North lined up north-south searching west into the mountains. Keep the member in line next to you in sight. The SAR North drone will be overhead—up high because of the trees. I have SAR South doing the same thing in the opposite direction, heading east into the valley. Each sector will have helicopter coverage. They'll be on Simplex-1 on the digitals, but you can keep your radios on the mutual aid freq, Chaffee MAC. If you need to talk directly to a helicopter, call me on Chaffee MAC or on MRA-1 on VHF and I'll set you up with them. The ATVs will focus on the east sector in the valley."

Coffman glanced briefly at Kristee and Jack Longmont and then at the rest of the Longmont family huddled closer to the house before turning back to the SAR members.

"The Sheriff has coordinated teams to work the ponds. So stay out of their way. Questions?"

"Hat? Phone?" someone called from the back of the crowd.

"Neither," Coffman said.

"What's she go by? Jan? Janae?"

"Jan-nay," Coffman emphasized. "Anything else?"

Silence.

"Okay. Move out."

CHAPTER 8

Jefe strode across the driveway with Janae in tow. *No damn way to run an operation.*

He slid open the barn door and tugged Janae inside.

"Stay here."

Jefe closed the door and paused, breathing through his nose. The smell of horse manure and hay hung pungent in the stillness of the stable air. A good smell. *She would have called it 'nostalgic.'*

He grimaced. No time for a walk down memory lane.

"I'm going to introduce you to some friends, Janae. No sense you getting lonely out here, right?"

The girl stared back at him and sniffled. Still scared. Probably would be for a while. The new ones always were.

He reached up into a coil of rope hanging on the wall and yanked on a metal handle. The lever notched in the forward position and released a locking mechanism on the floor beneath the feeding trough facing Janae and the man. He wedged his fingers under a wooden plank and lifted, raising a trapdoor underneath the stationary trough. Drawing a headlamp from his pocket, he stretched it over his head and flicked on the beam.

"All right, Janae. It's a ladder. Drops about ten feet. Turn around and face me, and lower yourself using the rungs, okay?"

The girl shook. "I'm scared."

"I won't hurt you. We're going to a place where you can rest, while I straighten this all out. I'll be right behind you."

Janae stepped back and glanced toward the barn door.

Jefe's voice hardened. "Let's go." He grabbed Janae by the shoulders and positioned her above the ladder.

The girl crouched, tentatively poking a foot into the black hole. When her foot rested on the first rung, she lowered the second foot, gripping onto the metal side rails.

Jefe nodded. "That's it. Not too hard, is it?" He pointed his headlamp beyond Janae, illuminating the concrete floor at the bottom. Janae continued descending, one careful step at a time, and Jefe followed her.

Stepping off the last rung, he scanned his headlamp over Janae before reaching for a metal door, then turned a horizontal latch in the opposite direction. The door swung open, and he pulled Janae into a small, walled room with another door. He flipped on a light in the entranceway and dug for a key in his pocket. Silence permeated the small room.

Swinging open the other door, Jefe called out. "Girls, we've got company." He guided Janae in front of him.

The underground room was a bunkhouse. A front alcove for shoes and jackets funneled into a wide corridor set up as a library or playroom. Shelves in the hallway held books and board games. A young girl sat against the wall, a book in her hands.

Jefe stopped at the girl's feet. "How you doing, Rachel?"

"Fine." She glanced from Jefe to Janae before returning to her book.

"Say hi to our new guest, why don't you? This is Janae."

Rachel glanced at the unfamiliar girl and said nothing.

"I said say 'hi', Rachel," Jefe said, louder.

"Yes, Jefe," the girl looked directly at Janae. "Hi."

She looked at Jefe's feet. "Where's Kendall?"

"She's coming," Jefe said. "But you won't see her for a while. Going to spend some time in the hole, she is." He raised his voice and projected to the back bunks. "Just like anyone else who tries to run away. Time in the hole."

Jefe looked at Janae. "Go down the hall."

Janae didn't move.

Jefe reached forward, gripping Janae's neck between his thumb and forefinger, and guiding her forward.

The two stepped into the bunkroom. Another girl sat on the bottom bunk, staring at them with her chin thrust forward.

"Nicole, say hi to Janae," Jefe ordered.

"Hi, Janae," the girl said. "Welcome to paradise."

"Hi," Janae whispered.

Jefe shook his head at Nicole, pointing to the bunk above her head. "Nicole, you and Rachel move all that shit up there somewhere else. Janae, this is your bunk. At least until we figure out what to do with you."

No one moved.

Jefe turned back toward the corridor and yelled. "Rachel, move it. Get in here and help Nicole."

Rachel shuffled into the room, and Nicole climbed out from the bottom bunk. The two girls transferred clothes and books from one bunk to another while Janae watched.

"That's Kendall's bunk," Nicole said.

"Maybe," Jefe said. "If she gets out of the hole." He turned to Janae. "You're going to stay with us for a while, Janae. New family. How's that sound?"

Janae shook her head. "I already have a family."

"It's okay, sweetheart, you'll get used to things real quick. The girls will help you settle in, right, girls?"

The two girls stiffened at Jefe's question, then continued moving items off Janae's bunk.

"So here are the rules in the House of Jefe…you ready?" He looked at Janae and cocked his head. "Do you even know what a Jefe is?"

Janae looked at her feet and shook her head.

"Jefe. Spelled with a 'J.' J-E-F-E, pronounced with an 'H,' H-E-F-E. Originally derived from the French word for 'Chief' or 'Chef.' The word has a long history in this part of the country. It means I'm the boss. What I say is what you do—understand? That's rule number one."

Janae nodded, tears welling in her eyes.

"Rule number two. You will not leave your new home—these two rooms—unless I'm with you. If you leave, I will find you, and you'll spend time in the hole. Got it?"

Janae nodded again, panting as she sobbed. The two other girls stopped cleaning the bunk and looked from Jefe to Janae.

"Rule number three—keep this place clean." He pointed toward the corridor. "There's a cupboard with cleaning supplies next to the door. Rachel and Nicole will show you what to do."

Jefe put his hands on his hips. "And that brings us to the most important rule, rule number four." He looked at the other two girls. "You girls want to let her know about rule number four? About field trips?"

Both the girls looked at their laps. Janae stopped sobbing and turned toward the girls.

"Tell her, girls."

Nicole shot a glance at Rachel. "Don't let the marketers touch you."

"And?" Jefe pushed.

"And if they do anything inappropriate, tell Jefe."

Jefe smiled and nodded. "There you go, Janae. Welcome to the stable."

CHAPTER 9

Daria punched the code on the front door and walked through the mudroom of the house, kicking off her shoes before entering the living room. She smiled, recalling her encounter with Kevin and Elliot. Not a bad outcome for trespassing. The invite to ride horses at the church stables was practically a date. Maybe this father-daughter visit would go more quickly than she expected.

She filled a glass with tap water and sat at the dining room table. Her dad had left his day-planner open at her seat. *The horror... how would he know what to do next?* She smiled as she grabbed the book and read the current date's entry:

Morning: Ropes course with Daria
Noon: Lunch with Daria at Minimalist Eats
Afternoon: Hike with Daria to Harvard Lakes
Evening: Make Daria veggie lasagna.

Tiny boxes aligned with each event where he could check off progress.

Daria's smile disappeared. How many times did she have to tell him to stop scheduling every minute of their time together? She flipped back a few pages to the week before her arrival. Fewer entries. *Morning: Library shift; Afternoon: Jog 4 miles.* But still the little boxes. With the *X* in them. Daria wondered if this was like a pilot thing, a leftover from her dad's Air Force time, or a new habit. Tracking everything. She'd have to ask her mom.

She gazed around the room. This was a big step—this trip out to visit her father. When her parents had divorced eight years before, she visited her dad twice a year. A week at Christmas and two weeks in the summer.

She had stayed with her mother after the divorce, and they moved to Colorado Springs. Zahn—everyone called him *Zahn*—remained in northern Virginia, finishing out his Air Force career before moving to Florida to take a contracting job. It was a long flight from the Springs to Florida. After two years, they stopped the summer visits. Too hot in July, and one year Zahn couldn't get the vacation time.

Her mom took her to Hawaii for Christmas one year, and so she skipped the winter visit. Before she knew it, she was entering college and hadn't seen her father in six years.

Daria checked her cell phone for a message. Nothing. Not good news. If SAR had found the girl, then where was Zahn? Even if he had to help wind things down—he would have called.

Not visiting him for six years—Daria couldn't decide if that was a good thing or a bad thing. He seemed so sad, yet obviously eager to see her. Sometimes when he stared at Daria, she couldn't tell whether he saw her, or Jacob. And she couldn't really ask. Because no one talked about Jacob.

She barely remembered her brother. She was eleven, when he died, and old enough to remember. But, oddly, she remembered little. Her dad was gone—off flying his airplanes in the war. Jacob got sick with the flu. Two days later, he was dead, and her dad was home. A week later, something happened back in the war, and Lt Col Zahn went back to Iraq, or Afghanistan, or wherever he was.

Just a blur after that. She couldn't remember her parents ever being in the same house again. When her dad left, she wasn't even sure if it was because of the war or because her mom and dad decided they couldn't stay together anymore.

Daria finished her water, glancing back at Zahn's list as she set the glass on the table.

Lunch with Daria.

Screw that. She was going to the J-Stroke Brewery for a veggie burger instead. Alone.

On the drive into Buena Vista, Daria thought about how the loss of Jacob had ripped her family apart.

His death had devastated her mom, but at least she had been there to support Daria. When she could finally talk about it, Sheila had relied on her faith to explain to Daria about how God must have a plan. Looking back, Daria thought she was probably right.

It's not like their family was ultra-religious, but they went to church every Sunday. Or at least Daria and her mom did. Zahn's attendance was haphazard before Jacob's death. Non-existent since then, she suspected.

When she and her mom moved to Colorado Springs after the divorce, the church was their welcoming committee. They embraced her newly single Black mother and her only child, wrapping them in a whirlwind of activities that continued to dominate her mother's days even now, and providing Daria with an instant network of friends in the youth group.

And God was a comfort. It was easy to forget her dad had ever been even a small part of her life. Memory of the men in their family faded, and Daria grew up.

When Zahn had moved out to Colorado, only three hours away from her mom, Daria hesitated to visit him again. Not scared of him. Just scared about it being awkward.

She was pretty sure he didn't believe in God's plan. And he hadn't handled the time since Jacob's death very well. But so far, besides his annoying tendency to micromanage the entire visit, it hadn't been awkward. The events of the previous year seemed to have snapped him out of his funk, and he had found a network of friends.

She had already met Rick Perez, and Zahn was lining her up to spend time with his other friend, Kristee Li. Maybe Kristee would line up something more exciting than the ropes course. She smiled, then sucked in her breath at a flash of blue lights in the rearview mirror.

Crap. She glanced down at the speedometer rapidly decreasing toward forty-five and flipped the turn signal to ease onto the shoulder.

Daria watched the police officer striding toward her car, then squeezed her eyes shut. What was she thinking? That you could fly through a town of two thousand people at 55 mph? She fished her registration from the glove box and her license from her pocketbook, then lowered the window.

The officer stood a foot from her door and stared at her before lowering his sunglasses and breaking into a smile.

"Well, hello there, little lady. What brings you out from the big city?"

What the heck? Daria thought, but responded in an apologetic tone. "I know, I know. I didn't slow down coming into town," Daria said, her eyes on the officer's nametag. LINZMEIER. "Why do you think I'm from the city?"

"Yeah, I clocked you ten over back there by the hardware store," Officer Linzmeier said. He stepped closer, and Daria felt his eyes wander over her legs. Either that, or he was looking for something.

Linzmeier continued. "I just assumed you were from Denver, or one of our college towns. I know most of the local ladies. Not many with your complexion." He paused. "Nor as pretty. You remind me of my ex-fiancée."

Daria was officially creeped out. An officer of the law was trying to convince her how open-minded he was while commenting on her skin color and trying to flirt with her. She didn't return Linzmeier's smile.

Linzmeier pressed his lips together. "License and registration, please."

Ten minutes later, Linzmeier returned to Daria's window. "Knew you were from the city." He smiled. "Listen, Ms. Daria, I'm going to let you off with a warning. Are you staying in the area or just passing through back to the Front Range?"

None of your business, she thought—then reconsidered. "Actually, I'm staying with my dad for a while. Tyler Zahn? I'll make sure and watch my speed in town. It won't happen again."

She watched Officer Linzmeier snap his eyes to her face when she mentioned her dad. He knew the name.

"Okay, then. I'll see you around town. You have a good day now."

Daria shook her head in disgust, as she pulled onto the road. First time anyone had mentioned her skin color since she'd been to Buena Vista, which was kind of surprising since she'd only seen two other Black people since she arrived. Maybe one who was biracial, like herself. And it was definitely the first time a cop had tried to pick up on her. He had to have been mid-thirties. Ugh.

She was definitely going to tell her dad about this. He wouldn't be happy about the speeding, but she was more curious about his reaction to her traffic stop. Bet he'd be less pleased about that.

Her dad seemed okay. Not perfect. Kind of weird to have him living all by himself out here, but he came across as pretty normal—for a dad.

She wasn't nervous about talking to him anymore. The visit was working out, and she had a date to ride horses. And no speeding ticket.

Not the worst spring break.

CHAPTER 10

Zahn and the remainder of the North team spread out. Twenty searchers with twenty yards between them meant Zahn couldn't see the ends of the lines. Not a problem. That's what radios were for.

SAR North search line, this is Trailhead on Chaffee MAC. Call if you're not ready.

Trailhead, this is Stu. I'm ready.

Zahn rolled his eyes. Stu was a new guy, participating in his first mission and nervous he'd screw up—and he just did. You only answered if you weren't ready.

Copy that, Stu. Thank you. SAR North search line, start the line.

Zahn looked over at Kristee and nodded as the line advanced toward the mountains.

Here we go.

His heart pounded. They didn't search for kids very often, and he could see why Jack Longmont was up in arms. *Imagine if you lost Daria.*

Scanning the line, Zahn watched the search unfold as he expected. The quick move across the typical Rocky Mountain backyard—Ponderosa pines and a carpet of pine needles—before hitting the gradual slopes of the Collegiate Peaks foothills. Then the slow unraveling of the line. Everyone felt the burn of the nine thousand foot elevation differently, with the young, athletic SAR members maintaining their starting pace and calling out Janae's name every ten seconds, while the older, less active members slowed, their legs burning and their breath coming in gasps. They didn't call Janae's name as often.

Zahn fell somewhere in between. When he first joined SAR, his conditioning had left something to be desired. His fitness had also failed him the year before in the frigid waters of Lake Dillon—the botched attempt to stop a bomb from destroying the Dillon Dam spillway. Although it all worked out in the end, Zahn hadn't forgotten the paralyzing combination of icy water, atrophied muscles, and lazy lungs.

He spent the next year changing his walks to runs, snowshoeing these same peaks they searched today, and lifting some weights. Sure, Zahn still had the body of a man in his late forties, with a persistent tire around his gut and a hairline receding faster than spring snow in the Rockies, but everything worked better. He was at home at this altitude, in these mountains.

"Janae...Janae," he called. He heard other searchers using whistles in between their calls. If Janae was below tree line, she'd be able to hear them, that's for sure.

Trailhead, SAR South search line.

SAR South, Trailhead, go ahead.

Trailhead, we've got something for Deputy Perez to see. We've got a member on Wagon Trail that will flag him down and walk him in, copy?

SAR South, Trailhead copies. Perez is right next to me and copied as well. He's on his way.

Zahn looked over at Kristee and raised his eyebrows. She shrugged. Not the lost girl, or they would have said something. Must have found a potential clue and didn't want to put it out on radio. It was like the mission the month before, where someone had called in a pair of running shorts and a sports bra. You hear that on the radio and the first thing you think of is foul play. In that case, the dog handler search team had pulled articles of the subject's clothing from the residence to give the dogs a scent...and then had inadvertently left the clothes on the trail. Took two days of rumor control to quash the *we found the subject's clothes, but not the subject* storyline generated from the radio traffic. The good news? SAR radio procedures had tightened up, and searchers were thinking more carefully before they used their radio.

Zahn and Kristee's search line continued. SAR used unspoken rules—you kept searching until you found the subject, you still drove to a trailhead even if another SAR team already responded, you kept hiking toward an injured hiker even if a helicopter was on its way. The Colorado Rockies, especially in and among the cluster of 14,000-foot peaks here in the Arkansas River Valley, were no joke. Weather, terrain, and fatigue could impact a search team or helicopter in minutes. So, no one ever stopped and waited when a radio call hinted the search might be over. You kept going until you got the call to '*Stand down.*'

"Janae?" Zahn heard Kristee's call behind a stand of trees to his right, and another searcher calling the same name out of sight to his left. The search line strung out now as the team hit the steep slopes leading up the side of Mt. Columbia. Another mile until treeline. Hopefully they would find something before then; at this rate, the mile search would take close to two hours.

Zahn joined the chorus calling Janae's name, blowing the whistle dangling from his pack every minute. Between calls, he pictured Daria back at the house. Nice that she urged him to take the SAR call. He could have skipped this one. Family in town was a valid excuse for not reporting for a mission, especially if a lot of other volunteers were responding. Zahn wasn't sure if Daria was more concerned for the missing girl or just not that interested in the ropes course. He smiled. No contest. No way she'd let her dad take her climbing while there was a missing girl in the mountains.

Zahn couldn't believe it when she'd agreed to come visit during her spring break. It surprised most parents when their college kid picked a visit home over a beach trip to Florida. Nice of his ex-wife, Sheila, to agree to that as well.

An hour later, the search line remained a line in name only. Zahn could no longer see Kristee on his right, although he heard her check in on the radio. He stopped and looked to his left, where he'd last seen Justin Mitchell. Nobody. Unless Justin was wearing pink. Zahn squinted his eyes and took off his sunglasses, staring at a flash of pink in the middle of a deadfall. Trash? Logging flag? Janae?

"Janae!" he called, keeping his eyes on the fallen tree. No movement. He shook his head before turning back up the mountainside.

Then he stopped and looked back. Still something pink. Maybe. *Got to check it out.* It wasn't as if he were falling ahead or behind the other searchers. They were nowhere in sight. He turned and walked back toward the fallen tree where he'd spotted the glimpse of color. Approaching the dead branches, he peered ahead, looking for the pink. Nothing. *What the hell?*

He stepped back and approached the tree from a different angle. Still nothing. He stepped back again and looked around. He had seen something inside this tangle of dead branches. Or had he? He turned uphill to rejoin the line, staring at the deadfall as he walked. *There it was again.*

Zahn stepped over the branches closest to him. He bent, looking toward the trunk, and stepped further into the pile. The tree had fallen, and the broken branch stubs from the impact kept the trunk from touching the ground. A hollow opened between the tree trunk and the ground. Big enough for a critter.

He pulled his headlamp from the pocket of his cargo pants and stretched it over his head, flicking on the power switch. Lowering himself to his hands and knees, he peered into the darkness.

A white face poking above a pink windbreaker stared back at him.

CHAPTER 11

Jefe sat on his porch steps, Janae safely locked away in her new home, when the ATV returned. The driver idled the machine in the driveway loop. Alone.

"Where is Kendall?"

"Couldn't really search where I found that first girl," the man said. "They're all out looking for her. They got cops, helicopters, their own ATVs, and there are search lines in the woods."

Jefe shook his head, pondering the wooden planks of the porch. "Clusterfuck. That's what it is."

"How'd Kendall get away in the first place?"

"Not your business."

"Just thought if you needed help to fix the place where you keep them…"

"The stable's fine. It's my marketers that are the problem. It's aways my marketers."

The ATV man remained silent and Jefe continued.

"My video guy was bringing her back to the rendezvous point. Kendall told him she was sick and needed to stop. When the guy pulled over and released his door locks, she bolted. Straight into the woods. My guy—who's no longer part of my team—chased her for a while, then gave up. Came and told me, and I called you." Jefe paused. "Thought you were supposed to be an expert tracker, all that hunting you do.

"I think I was close. No way I could've known there were two girls."

Jefe shook his head again. "And now we have two problems. A missing girl problem and a new girl problem." He stood up from the porch and walked to the ATV. "You're done for the day. I'll put the ATV away."

The man climbed off and stood aside as Jefe mounted the ATV. Tilting his head, he asked Jefe, "So what're you going to do with Janae? She's kind of pretty."

Jefe exhaled. "You want to keep her? You ready to take that on? Missing girl three miles from this house—you go ahead. My daddy always told me, never get your meat from where you get your bread."

The man gave Jefe a blank stare.

"The whole idea is to use out-of-state girls," Jefe said. "That way no one looks for them around here. This local girl, they're going to be searching for her forever. I can't very well rent her out in our own backyard, can I?"

The ATV man nodded. "So you're going to…"

"I'm going to take care of it. And you're done for the day. Go home."

"Can I…" he looked at his feet and scuffed the dirt in front of where he stood. "Can I take one of the others?"

Jefe started up the ATV and raised his voice. "You got no clue, do you? You not finding Kendall? And now this new girl? It could bring this whole little setup to a stop. And all you can think about is a live performance instead of video?" Jefe revved the throttle. "Get the hell out of here."

CHAPTER 12

"Shit!" Zahn's heart raced as he jerked back from the hole. He took a breath and bent forward again.

"Sorry," he said to the figure cowering beneath the tree trunk. A girl. Scared. Pink jacket. Definitely Janae.

"Are you Janae?"

The girl shook her head slightly and remained scrunched under the tree with her knees to her chest.

Zahn crawled forward a few inches. The girl's eyes widened, and she shrank farther back in the hollow.

"Sorry, just wanted to see if you're okay."

The girl stared at Zahn's face.

"Janae, we're all out looking for you. Don't be scared. We're here to help."

The girl said nothing.

"Do you want to come out of there now?"

The girl remained frozen.

"Are you hurt?"

Nothing.

Zahn paused, staring at the frightened child. *This isn't a lost girl. This is a girl hiding from someone. Maybe there was more to this story than what they briefed. Maybe Janae had run away.*

"Janae, listen to me. I'm going to step out of these branches and make a radio call, okay? I'll be right back."

The girl's wide eyes followed him as he backed away. Zahn climbed over the branches and stood up next to the deadfall, reaching for his radio.

Trailhead, 741.

741 was Zahn's SAR number. When it was just SAR North, they sometimes used first names, but this was a big search. Best to keep it formal.

741, Trailhead, go ahead.

Trailhead, 741 is part of the SAR North search line. I'm about a mile west of the reporting party's house at the center of the line, and I've found the subject. Uninjured.

741, come again? You've found the girl?

Trailhead, 741, that's affirmative. Found the girl. She's uninjured. I'll text you the coordinates when we're done talking.

Trailhead copies. Can you just walk her out?

Zahn paused. The girl sure didn't seem too eager to get home.

741, Trailhead, did you copy? Can you walk her down to us?

Trailhead, I copied. Uh, did Rita respond today?

Rita was SAR North's certified counselor. Most of the time she was available to talk with SAR members after a traumatic mission, often involving the recovery of a corpse. She might be just the ticket for talking with Janae.

741, that's affirmative. She's over talking to the parents right now. You want her to come up?

Zahn pulled out his GPS and started a text to Trailhead with the coordinates.

Trailhead, yeah, send her up, please. She'd be a good person to help me walk the subject out. Code words for *hey, we've got some unexpected issues here.*

Roger that. Pause. What about the parents?

Yeah, yeah. Tell the parents she's okay, but I think you should keep them there and tell them we'll bring her down.

741, Roger that.

Zahn sent the coordinates, then crawled back to check on the girl.

"Janae, I just sent for a lady who's going to come up and talk to you, okay? After you guys talk, we'll walk you on down to your parents."

The girl lifted her head when Zahn said the word *parents*, a blank look on her face. Zahn stared back.

"I guess, we'll just wait until Ms. Rita shows up." Zahn crouched among the branches across from where the girl remained huddled beneath the tree trunk.

It seemed like the longest thirty minutes ever, even though Rita and two other SAR members cut Zahn's hour-long trek to find the girl in half. They knew exactly where the two were and just followed the GPS. Zahn crawled out and greeted the team.

"She's in there." Zahn pointed to the opening in the branches. "Scared as shit, not saying a word. When I asked her if she was Janae, she shook her head 'no.'"

"Doesn't sound like someone who just got lost," Rita said. "More like someone trying to run away."

"That's what I figured." Zahn nodded. "That's why I thought it might be better for you to talk to her before we took her back to her parents."

Rita nodded and stepped past Zahn through the branches covering the girl's hiding place. Zahn heard Rita calling softly to the girl.

"Hey, there, sweetheart. How are you? I'm Rita."

Silence.

"Are you scared? Hey, look…look at my face now. See? I'm a girl too." Zahn guessed Rita had crawled close enough to show the frightened girl her face.

A choked wail came from the deadfall, and Zahn heard rustling. A soft grunt from Rita, then muffled sobbing.

"Hey…there you go. Let it out. You're safe now. We're going to take care of you."

"He wouldn't let us go home, he made us live down below, he's…he's…bad," the girl wailed.

"Janae, Janae…it's okay now—"

"My name is not Janae," the girl paused her sobbing, and Zahn heard her voice gathering strength. "My name is Kendall."

Silence.

Then, "Okay, Kendall. Shall we climb on out of here and see about getting you home?"

"Yes, please."

Rita called out to Zahn. "We're coming out now. Can you guys give us some room?"

One of Rita's teammates pointed across the downed tree. "Looks like we got company."

Zahn turned from watching Rita and the girl climb out of the deadfall and saw Jack Longmont, Janae's father, charging up the hill, like a moose running from a forest fire.

"Janae! Janae!" he called, approaching the group huddled around the deadfall.

As Rita pulled back a branch to allow the girl to step out from under the dead tree, Longmont pulled up short.

"Where's Janae?" he bellowed. "You guys said you had my daughter. That she wasn't hurt. You said you found her."

Zahn looked from the girl to Longmont and back to the girl again.

"That's not my daughter," Longmont screamed behind him.

Zahn heard the girl whisper to Rita. "I told you my name was Kendall."

CHAPTER 13

Daria stepped onto the front porch and waited as Zahn locked the door. Part of their daily routine since she had arrived was to walk a mile to pick up the mail at the community mailboxes. She quickly learned to don her hiking boots because Zahn always had a different way to get home. The jaunt usually ended up being a three- or four-mile round trip. Cutting between houses and crawling under fences wasn't out of the question either. Maybe that's what had inspired her trespassing adventure the other day…her genes.

Daria's decision to spend her spring break with her father had exposed forgotten memories. Their first brief hug had offered a scent from her childhood, when Daria curled up in her father's lap, spellbound as he read aloud *The Adventures of Robin Hood*. Right Guard deodorant, he had told her. A distinctive man smell.

"Good enough for basic training, good enough for the rest of my life."

Then there was his smile. Not as often as she remembered. But now more spontaneous. All she had to do was talk about some part of her life after he left—the powderpuff football game in which she had scored a touchdown while the varsity boys donned cheerleader outfits, Rush Week at her school in Boulder—she'd tell the story, and the familiar grin would burst out on his face.

Daria glanced back at Zahn as they approached the road's shoulder. "Any word on the girl?"

"Which one?" Zahn lightly pulled her arm, steering her to his right, away from traffic. "Janae, or Kendall?"

Daria cocked her head at her father's move. So old-fashioned, putting the woman on the inside.

"Well, I was asking about Janae, the one you didn't find," Daria said. "But, yeah, I'd like to know Kendall's story too. Did they find out where she's from?"

"I got an update from Rick last night. You remember Deputy Sheriff Perez?"

"The guy I met the first day? From the bomb thing last year? He was like your Batman, and you were like his Robin for the investigation, right?"

"Right. Not sure I agree with the analogy. I don't wear my underwear outside my pants."

"Gross. Dads don't talk about underwear. It's weird."

They turned the corner and picked up Zahn's mail path.

"They haven't found Janae. But it's no longer a SAR mission. It's a criminal investigation now."

"Why? Did they find something?"

"Because of the other girl. Kendall. And her story. Turns out Kendall is from Texas, and she's been missing for close to a year." Zahn glanced at Daria. "Her parents are flying up today to take her home."

"Texas? A YEAR???? How did she end up in Colorado?"

"That's what everyone is trying to figure out. Kendall was slow to talk, and she won't talk to men at all. No memory of what happened between Texas and her escape. She didn't even know she was in Colorado. She saw a chance to get away while they were moving her in a car and she took it. Kendall had been moving through those woods for hours when we found her. Said she was followed."

"Wow. Brave girl to make a run for it."

"Right—but get this. She said she saw another girl just before she found the place to hide. The place where we found her."

"She saw Janae?"

"That's what we're thinking. Who else could it be?"

Daria's brow furrowed. "So the assumption is that whoever was following her took Janae instead?"

"That's the theory. Would be hard to believe she just got lost in the exact same area where another girl escaped her kidnapper or kidnappers, or whoever's behind this. I mean, we combed that area for two days—and the second day we had the Colorado Bureau of Investigation, the CBI, with us. Lake and Park County SAR teams, as well. Looking for clues."

"Kendall can't remember anything? No memories of where she was being held?"

"She doesn't have a clue. She doesn't know where they kept her. She didn't know where she was when we found her. Hell, they could've just been transiting Colorado when she got away. Just because we found her here doesn't mean she was being held nearby." He paused, then went on. "But everyone is guessing it's local. And that's pretty big. I mean, she couldn't have gone much over ten miles after she escaped, right? So if you assume the car she got out of was near where they kept her, well, there's only so many people living in that area. And...get this, Daria. Rita—our SAR counselor—was the first one to talk to Kendall. And those first sentences were critical because it seemed like the more Kendall believed she was safe, the more she completely blocked what had happened to her. They tried to do a child forensic interview on her, but she wouldn't talk."

"What did she say to Rita?"

"I was standing right outside the downed tree where we found her. One of the first things she said was, 'He wouldn't let us leave,' something along those lines."

"Us?"

"Right. There might be more missing girls out there."

"Oh, no. So, are you going to be involved in the investigation?"

Zahn pulled the mailbox key from his pocket and opened the small door. Daria smiled as he bent and peered into the empty slot. This was the third time they'd walked together for mail, and she'd only seen him get two letters. Both offered the opportunity to refinance the house, which was funny, since he was renting and didn't recognize the name on the envelopes.

"Nope. Search & Rescue might get called back to help if they keep searching up there for clues, but as far as actual investigating, I'm not involved. Got to go to that Reserve Sheriff's course before they can use me. Who knows when that will be back on schedule?"

"What about that stuff you did last year? With the dam. You weren't a Reserve Sheriff then, and they let you help."

"Right. But I didn't have my favorite daughter visiting last year." Zahn smiled.

Daria stopped. "Don't you dare use that as an excuse. If you can help, you should help. And I already told you, I could use some *me* time on this vacation."

Zahn held up both hands. "Whoa! I already told them, if I could help, I would. I'm just not planning on 12-hour shifts down at the office."

"Good." Daria nudged Zahn's shoulder. "You should have opened with that."

Zahn walked past the mailboxes and started heading west toward the mountains.

"The house is back that way." Daria pointed back at the path.

"Come on, girl." Zahn grinned. "Let's get some exercise."

The two circled the neighborhood, adding an extra mile to the walk. Zahn led Daria between two three-acre plots until they hit the fence separating Elk Trace from Beyond Adventure, the church camp.

Zahn pointed toward the fence. "The best trails in the neighborhood are over there on the church camp side. I've ducked under a few times to do some snowshoeing."

"I know."

"How do you know where I go snowshoeing?"

"No. I know the best trails are over there. I went jogging there the other day when you were on your SAR call."

"Hey, that's private property."

"Really? You just got done bragging about crawling under the fence, and now you're going to give me a bad time about doing the same thing? Is it because I'm a girl? Or because I'm your daughter?"

Zahn stopped and stared at Daria before breaking into a smile. "Okay. You got me." He went on. "I'm an overprotective sexist, I guess. But what if you would've got caught?"

Daria stared back. "I *did* get caught."

"What?"

"Yeah, I turned the corner by the gate about a mile up." Daria pointed to the left. "Ran into two guys on horseback from the church camp."

"What did you tell them?"

"Well, I thought about playing dumb and giving them the 'Oh, I'm lost' story, but that seemed like it would be kind of sexist on my part. I mean, how stupid do you have to be to climb a fence and then claim you're lost? So I just told them what you told me—that these are the best trails around."

The two continued walking along the fence before picking up the faint trail leading back to Zahn's house.

"And…?"

Daria smiled. "Well, I ended up getting an invitation to go ride horses. I'm going over there Thursday afternoon."

Zahn said nothing.

"Is that okay?"

"I don't know. I don't know much about the camp. They're Christian Scientists, you know?" He glanced at Daria. "Not that there's anything wrong with that…"

"I know. Gabe told me. He's not one, though. He's just in charge of the horses. You'd like him. Probably the only guy around here older than you."

"Hey!" Zahn laughed and nudged her shoulder.

"Kevin was the younger guy I met. He's with the church."

"What was he like? I know nothing about Christian Scientists except they don't believe in medicine. Which seems weird to me."

"That's all I knew about them too. But I asked Kevin about it, and he said it's not just a fanatical 'no medicine' thing. I mean, he gets shots and goes to the dentist and stuff. He says they just believe prayer is a powerful healer and ought to be the primary medicine."

"Huh," Zahn said.

"Huh," Daria mimicked.

Zahn stayed silent.

"I believe in prayer," Daria said.

"Hmm."

The two kept walking in silence.

"Do you?"

Zahn glanced at Daria, then back at the trail. Then he spoke.

"So I guess it's a protective Dad thing, but would you mind if I went with you when you go horseback riding? Not on the actual ride, but to meet the guys? I'm a neighbor. Introducing myself would be a neighborly thing to do."

Daria decided not to push it. "Sure. I don't care if you come along. Just don't embarrass me."

"What do you mean? I told you I wasn't planning on asking them if I could ride."

"No, it's not that. It's Kevin."

"What?"

"He's kind of cute."

CHAPTER 14

This was nothing like Janae's books. No Harry Potter or Percy Jackson to save the day. A masked man in the woods captured her and took her to this Jefe guy. And now…this place? Beyond creepy. The underground home terrified her. Beds, board games, roommates. Like it was summer camp or something. Her dad used to tease her in his scary voice, "Welcome to the House of Longmont…you can check in but you can't check out. Mwa ha ha ha." *That* was funny. This wasn't.

Janae cowered in the corner, resting her forehead between her folded arms.

"How did they get you?"

Janae raised her head. The girl, Nicole, stood at the foot of Janae's new bunk. Rachel sat crosswise in the doorway to the outer room, picking at her fingernails.

"Did you have to ride in the back of a truck? That's how I got here." She glanced over at Rachel. Rachel's eyes never left her hands.

Janae shook her head and focused her red, swollen eyes on Nicole. "No. A man just brought me here from my uncle's house. On the back of one of those ATV things."

"Really? You live by here? Where are we?"

"Not supposed to talk about 'before.'" Rachel said in a dull voice, not moving her head.

"I don't live here," Janae said. "My aunt and uncle do. I'm from Oklahoma. This is Colorado."

"Told you," Nicole said to Rachel. "Remember, I told you I saw that license plate that one time under the blindfold."

"Don't care. Not listening," Rachel said.

Nicole turned back to Janae. "Are you going to be on the team?"

"What team?"

"Jefe calls us his team. Me, Rachel, and Kendall. Before I got here, there was another girl. But she didn't follow the rules. Rachel won't tell me her name." Nicole glanced over at Rachel. "If Kendall is in the hole, then she didn't keep the rules either. Maybe you'll take her place."

"What's the hole?"

"It's the pla—"

"Shhh," Rachel said, looking up from her fingers. "He'll hear."

Janae looked at the girls. Her voice was soft. "I don't think Kendall is in the hole."

Nicole ignored Rachel's warning not to talk.

"Why?"

"Because the man who caught me thought *I* was Kendall. He brought me back here, and that man—the one who said his name was Jefe—got mad at the guy for bringing him back the wrong girl." Janae shook her head. "Before I got caught, I saw another girl running through the woods. In a pink jacket."

Rachel looked up from her fingernails again and stared at Janae. "Kendall has a pink jacket."

Nicole looked at Janae. "Did they catch her?"

"I don't think so. Jefe sent the man back out to look for her."

"You hear that, Rachel? Kendall got away."

"They'll catch her," Rachel said, looking back at her fingers. "They always do. And we won't see her again. That's what happens when you try to run away." The girl stood up in the doorway and moved into the playroom.

Janae watched her leave, then looked back at Nicole. "What are we doing here? What's the 'team?'"

Nicole put her foot on the frame of the lower bunk and pushed her face up closer to Janae. Janae moved forward.

"It's not like soccer or softball...those kinds of teams," Nicole said. "Jefe says we're a team of artists. And he's our agent."

"Artists? What do you mean?"

"Like actors." Nicole's smile looked uncertain. "We just play, and the men take movies of us. Jefe says it's called marketing."

Janae glanced sideways at the girl. "What kind of movies? Like, you know...bad ones?"

"No. That's against Jefe's rules. Just movies of us talking and playing with toys and stuff. Weird. But not like bad stuff."

Janae heard a loud exhale, and she and Nicole both turned toward Rachel.

"What?" Nicole sounded defensive.

"If you're going to tell her stuff, then tell her everything," Rachel said.

Janae's voice quivered. "But he said...he said, rule four was no touching.

Nicole nodded. "Right, no touching. But we have to take our clothes off."

CHAPTER 15

"Namaste," Zahn murmured to Ruth with the rest of his Monday morning mat mates at the community center yoga class.

A year and a half after signing up, he still found the class to be his anchor when things got tense. Besides mending his frozen shoulder and eliminating his knee pain, Ruth's exercises and calming voice always set an upbeat tone for the rest of Zahn's week.

Not that he believed in any of the new-age mumbo jumbo that came with the class. Not that he'd ever try to explain to Perez how the session slowed his resting heart rate. It just worked. So he kept doing it.

Zahn grabbed his gear and walked west on Main Street to meet Perez for coffee at The Elkhead. The rising sun cast an aura on the Collegiate Peaks in front of him. Ice-capped ridges still reflected the sunlight off the remaining snow. He smiled. Buena Vista had brought him peace. God's country? Namaste? No idea. Zahn just knew he had arrived two years before, a broken man, afraid to assume responsibility for his own shadow.

He wasn't yet completely healed. Probably never would be. There was a hole in his heart that Jacob had once filled. There were also wounds in his pride, his dignity, and his confidence—fractures that didn't exist before the war, before his squadron mates limped their missile-ravaged C-130 out of Iraq and died as the plane smashed into the ground just miles short of the runway in Kuwait.

But the beauty of this mountain town, the compassion of its people, and the unexpected involvement in foiling last year's terrorist attack had changed Zahn. He'd always been good at faking confidence—looking folks in the eye, keeping his shoulders thrust back. But now it radiated from the inside. Not invincibility. But a new inner confidence that no longer feared getting involved would make things worse.

On an existential level, he had no idea what he believed. But at ground level, he believed in himself.

Perez raised his eyes from his conversation with another uniformed man and nodded at Zahn, kicking the third chair at the table out a bit. Zahn nodded back and turned toward the smell of fresh grounds behind the counter. Black. No sugar. No fancy name.

"Morning, Tyler," the young woman called over her shoulder as she filled his cup. "How was yoga?"

Zahn glanced around to see if the yoga question had drawn any stares. It was one thing for this young lady to respect his workout choices…but the rest of these guys? He turned back and cocked his head at the young woman.

"My grandma told me about you. Maddie Bodin? From eight o'clock pickleball? She says you guys always chat in the parking lot before your yoga class."

Grandma? Zahn knew the barista was young, but found himself surprised he was on a first name basis with her *grandmother*.

Perez greeted Zahn as he approached the table. "What's up, old man? How's that community yoga stuff working for you?"

"Better for my body than running fifty miles at a pop. I didn't ask you the other day—did you run while you were in Utah last month?"

"I did. Snow was already gone out there."

Zahn met Perez's tablemate's eyes and nodded. The man nodded back.

"And how'd you do?"

"Finished. That's the goal." Perez shifted his eyes. "Tyler, you know Adam Linzmeier? Buena Vista Police?"

The guy who pulled over Daria. Zahn reached across the table and shook the other man's hand, forcing a politeness he didn't feel.

Linzmeier smiled underneath a thick black mustache. He nodded at Zahn. "Good to meet you. Heard about your work with Perez over at Dillon last year. Nicely done." He turned back to Perez. "Both of you."

"Thanks. How long have you been with the BV Police?"

"Going on five years. Moved out here from Jefferson County."

Perez spoke. "We were just talking about the SAR mission. About Janae?"

"Any more info on her? Get anything more from the girl we found, Kendall?"

Perez stirred his coffee. "No. She's still not talking. Drawing, though. She gave us a picture of some kind of bunkroom and other girls."

"You think it's a picture of where she was held? Could you tell if it was close by?"

"Don't know. Rita talked to the counselors the CBI brought out. They said they can't determine whether it's an actual memory, or if she's just drawing stuff." Perez looked at Linzmeier and then back at Zahn. "Adam, here, he's got some thoughts about where we ought to look next."

Zahn turned to Linzmeier. "What do you got?"

"No evidence. No proof. But maybe a theory," Linzmeier said. "I was looking at the map where you all found her, drawing out some distance lines to see where she might have come from. Figured much over ten miles was unlikely. You guys agree?"

Zahn and Perez nodded.

Linzmeier continued. "That area's outside our city jurisdiction. It's county, so that stuff falls to Perez and his sheriff guys." He nodded at Perez. Perez nodded back. "But we've responded to two calls in the past year here in town involving people from that area. Those Christian Scientists? You heard of them?"

"The ones out at Beyond Adventure? I live next door to them in Elk Trace."

Linzmeier nodded. "Yep. Nothing in the calls is that weird. We had a lady call in that she saw the kids changing out of wet clothes from rafting. She thought it was odd because they were changing and the camp counselors were there too. That was last June when the river was running high. Then, at the end of last summer, they lost a kid in town, and we ended up finding her over at the skateboard park."

Zahn squinted at Linzmeier, then looked at Perez.

"I know. I know. None of this is anything substantial," Perez said.

Linzmeier nodded. "Right. But there're the rumors."

Zahn stared at Linzmeier, then bit. "What rumors?"

"Well, not really rumors," Linzmeier backtracked. "It's just that people don't know what kind of religious stuff goes on out there, so they guess at it. And then you got rumors."

Zahn and Perez said nothing.

Linzmeier continued. "Okay, so some people say it's a cult thing. You got to be one of those Christian Scientists to be in the camp, and once they got you up there, you can't leave unless you're with the staff or going home."

Zahn shook his head. "Show me a camp that doesn't operate that way. They're responsible for parents' kids. Of course they can't leave on their own."

Perez looked at Zahn. "I told you up front, Adam had nothing concrete. We have to cover everything in that ten-mile swath, anyway; he's just helping us find a place to start."

Zahn thought about that. "How are you going to 'cover' it? Searching?"

Perez took a sip of his coffee. "Not without evidence and a warrant. But we can do 'knock and talks.'"

Zahn nodded, tilting his coffee back. "I got kind of an invitation out there to Beyond Adventure. On Thursday." He paused. "Well, Daria does. To ride horses. I'm walking her over there."

Perez smiled. "I haven't seen her since the first day she arrived. How's the visit going?"

Linzmeier got up from the table to refill his coffee.

Zahn smiled. Perez was a friend—the only guy in town who knew his past and his family situation.

"Going great. Getting some hiking in. Almost had her out to the ropes course before the last SAR call canceled that," Zahn said.

Linzmeier returned to the table and sat, blowing air out from his cheeks.

Perez glanced at the officer. "What?"

"The pastries look pretty good." Linzmeier smiled, looking back at the young lady serving coffee. "But the buns behind the counter are just outstanding."

Zahn glanced at Perez, who returned a blank stare. *Huh.* Linzmeier was what? Mid-thirties? Zahn remembered talking like this with the guys when he was younger. He'd grown out of it—either because he'd matured, or because societal norms had changed. Or both, he hoped. But it sounded weird coming from Linzmeier, a grown man wearing a uniform.

"Anyway, about Beyond Adventure," Zahn said. "I can talk with the folks at the stables, see if they'll show me around. Get a sense of the place. If you're interested?"

"That would be awesome," Perez said. "We can follow up—hell, we have to follow up—with our standard drive-by, but I like the idea of you going in first and kind of feeling them out. Lot more subtle."

"Subtle." Zahn laughed. "Listen to you. Getting all 'nuanced' on your investigative techniques. The knock-down-the-door technique not working for you lately?"

Perez and Linzmeier shared a glance across the table, smiling.

"Knocking down doors is like bread and butter for law enforcement," Linzmeier said. "But you gotta mix it up, right?"

Zahn finished his coffee and turned to Perez. "Going to try again for the ropes course with Daria. Got to go." He looked at the two men. "Don't you guys do any work around here?"

Perez stood, taking his coffee with him. "Yep, I'm up Highway 24 today, starting at the north end of the ten-mile area of interest. Asking questions."

Linzmeier stayed in his chair. "I'm in no hurry. Got a 'Don't Do Drugs' talk at the school in fifteen minutes." He looked at his empty plate, then back up at the girl behind the counter. "Hell, got time for another bagel."

Perez glanced at Zahn then back to Linzmeier.

"What? You're expecting me to order a donut, right? Because I'm a cop, is that it?" Linzmeier laughed as Zahn and Perez walked out.

CHAPTER 16

Jefe decided to hang on to Janae. He'd kept his ear to the ground. Heard the talk around town. Janae was from Oklahoma, not from Buena Vista. Not a well-known face.

HAVE YOU SEEN THIS GIRL? posters were already popping up on the doors of local businesses, printed in bold, with a photo of Janae and a small white dog on the bottom. The search wasn't going away any time soon.

Jefe figured it was like this: he stood on thin ice. The fractures already radiated out from his little enterprise like a chip on a windshield. Losing Kendall was just the latest failure. He could either hold still, waiting for the ice to give away, or he could run like hell and try to make it off the pond. And Jefe wasn't a *hold still* guy.

He thought about the woman who had left him. The name he couldn't even say out loud. Her journal was his inspiration. The only thing of hers they had returned to him he kept. It was his window into what her life was like after she had gone.

The secret is in the fundamentals. Build a solid team. Develop their talents. Market your product. Expand on your successes.

We're in the 'develop their talents' phase right now. It feels like we are on the cusp of greatness. All I have to do is believe in my team. And make sure they believe in me. It's going to happen!

It had taken Jefe a while to build his own team. Like hers—but different. And he was definitely a novice when it came to developing their talents. When he started with the first girl, he had kept her to himself. Not for himself. Not that way. He wasn't a pervert. He just reveled in the rush of power he felt in owning her. He didn't even consider marketing her.

But that wasn't enough. After he got the second girl, impatience crept in. He wanted to get the team out there. He needed someone to know there was a new agent in town. Someone besides the faceless contacts he'd made on the anonymous part of the Internet. That place they called the Dark Web. He started by posting a couple of pictures of his girls playing in the barn. Let folks know he had a stable. A stable for hire.

Cellphone photos didn't cut it, though. If he was going to represent these girls, he needed to market them. Professionally.

He had used the Dark Web to find a videographer only twenty miles away. Walter from Leadville would shoot video and send it to Jefe. Jefe would use his local contact to integrate the video onto his website.

When Jefe brought up payment, he was surprised to hear Walter offering *him* money to do the shoot.

"It's good advertising for my business," Walter had claimed. That should have set off alarm bells.

He briefed Walter in person. No physical contact. He could watch them. He could talk to them. And he should shoot the required shots—subject to Jefe's approval, of course. He couldn't risk some idiot filming his girls next to a *Welcome to Leadville* sign or something like that.

But Walter broke the no physical contact rule on the first visit. What a shame. For his girl. Didn't work out so well for Walter either. But it sure helped pave Jefe's reputation.

After the incident, his first urge was to take Walter—the pervert—out. Eliminate him. Instead, barely keeping his rage intact, he'd taken the girl back to the stable and gone online for a little revenge. By week's end, Walter was in prison. The anonymous tip about the child porn on Walter's computer not only put the son of a bitch behind bars, but it also served as a deterrent for all his future marketers. The Arkansas River Valley was a small community—hell, Chaffee and Lake County together only had around 25,000 people. When he briefed the rules, one mention of poor Walter ensured total compliance.

Of course, they all claimed ignorance. Perverts don't admit to knowing other perverts.

But they all knew what had happened to Walter. Perverts pay attention to what happens to other perverts.

It's how they keep their guard up.

Yes. Janae would join Team Jefe. He might hold off marketing her, but after this hullabaloo died down, he could rent her out. He could make up for losing Kendall.

Maybe *more* than make up for Kendall. Kendall's videos had stopped attracting attention when she started refusing to talk. His online customers judged the merchandise from these short videos his marketers produced. They expected to see happy, outgoing girls, doing the things you expect girls to do. Dolls. Toys. Stuff like that. Watching a mute Kendall staring at a tea set turned them off, and lately the videos of Rachel and Nicole were the only ones drawing views.

The challenge kept him up at night, trying to figure out how to deal with it. The girls had to know who was in charge—so Jefe knew discipline was important. But they had to relax too. His marketers liked to film them at play. Jefe understood he would never convince his girls their situation was normal, that this was now home, that he was in charge, and that they should accept this as their new life. Wouldn't work. The girls were too old to hoodwink. They knew they were prisoners. He was the Jefe. They had a job to do.

And then? Well, the *and then* part was the most important. There had to be a light at the end of this tunnel. That if they did their job well, they got to go home.

He thought maybe Nicole believed it. The first girl, Mandy, was gone when Nicole arrived. He'd told the girls she'd been allowed to return home to her family. But he questioned whether Rachel or Kendall ever believed it. They both knew Mandy and what had happened with Walter up in Leadville. They had watched her downhill slide as she gradually stopped talking, stopped eating, and stopped engaging. Jefe had tried everything to bring Mandy out of her funk, but nothing had worked.

Jefe knew one bad apple could spoil the lot. So he had to remove Mandy from the team.

It certainly was not something he enjoyed and not a decision he took lightly. He did it for the others on the team.

He told Rachel and Kendall he'd sent Mandy home to heal and grow stronger. When Nicole joined the team, he told her the same story. Whenever Mandy's name came up with the girls, Jefe could see glimmers of hope in Nicole's eyes—an avenue out. But Rachel's eyes never brightened. Jefe didn't think she believed.

He worried about Rachel. Can't have more bad apples.

Janae was a tough one to figure. Still crying all the time and had a hard time meeting his eye. But every once in a while, Jefe thought he saw a glimmer of spunk in her. He had a nose for that kind of thing. It would be interesting to see how she adapted to the stable. Maybe she'd be a team player. Inspire Rachel. Help the team.

CHAPTER 17

Daria followed her dad out the driveway and northwest toward Beyond Adventure, on a different route than what she'd used for her run. He held up the bottom strand of barbed-wire for her at the fence.

"Like to mix up my entries," Zahn said.

They walked the perimeter path a half mile to the north, aiming for the stables. A flash of movement caught Daria's eye, and she turned her head toward the mountains. Through the trees, a large cow elk sheltered a calf.

"You see that?" she pointed. "Elk. Two of them."

Zahn paused next to her, studying the forest.

"More than two. Look past them."

Daria squinted her eyes and nodded. The mother and her baby had caught her eye because they were moving, but there was an entire herd—maybe thirty—staring motionless at them.

"You live in God's country." Daria smiled, looking at Zahn.

He smiled back. "Namaste."

Another half mile later, she could smell the stables and glimpsed Gabe and Kevin saddling two horses. Daria raised her arm.

"Hey, Gabe. Kevin," Daria called.

"Daria, hi!" Kevin waved, looking from Daria to Zahn. Gabe Elliot cinched the saddle he was fastening and gave them a nod.

"Only two horses? You guys forget I was coming?"

Kevin reddened a bit before Elliot stepped forward. "I got a little work to do here. Thought you and Kevin could find your way around

78

the place without me. That okay?" He shifted his gaze from Daria to Zahn.

Daria looked straight at Elliot. She didn't need her dad's permission. "Sounds good—sorry you can't go." She looked at Kevin. "Think you can keep up?"

Kevin laughed. "We'll see." He turned to Zahn. "Gabe was joking about finding my way around this place. I work here."

"I figured as much." Zahn smiled.

"Guys," Daria said, "This is my dad…Tyler Zahn. He's the one I'm visiting over in Elk Trace. He wanted to meet you."

"Gentlemen," Zahn said.

Kevin nodded awkwardly, thrusting out his hand. "Kevin Kilgore."

Elliot walked over to Zahn and shook hands. "Gabe Elliot."

Daria stared at the group of men, wondering if this was how knights of the middle ages introduced themselves before doing battle.

"Nice to meet you guys. Thanks for taking Daria out on the horses. We used to ride…but it's been a few years," her dad said.

"Well, heck, Tyler, we can get you out today too. Want to go along?"

Daria smiled at Elliot breaking the ice, but then widened her eyes as she heard the invite. *Please say no.*

Zahn glanced at her and smiled before answering. "No, no—just wanted a chance to see your operation and introduce myself. Feel like we're neighbors who never see each other, even though my house is right across the fence and all."

Elliot nodded. "Let's get these two on the trail, and I'll show you around a bit."

Elliot and Kevin finished prepping the horses. Zahn held the bridle of Daria's horse while she mounted and then waved goodbye as she and Kevin departed.

"I'll meet you back at the house," Daria called. She hoped her dad didn't stay at the stable the entire time waiting for her. She didn't want Kevin cutting the ride short out of concern for an overbearing father.

• • •

Zahn watched Daria ride off toward the Collegiate Peaks with Kevin trailing. He turned to Elliot and saw a smile on the man's face.

"He's a good kid," Elliot said. "Daria will be just fine."

Zahn nodded. "I know. Hell, she's all grown up."

"They do that, you know." Elliot laughed. "But if you want a safe place to leave a kid, it doesn't get much safer than Beyond Adventure." He turned to Zahn. "You want me to give you the overview? I can't really give you the full-fledged tour—supposed to shoe one of the horses here," he said, pointing toward the corral where a group of four horses tossed their heads. "But I'll walk you out toward the center of the property and show you what's what." He swung his hand away from the horses toward the mountains.

"Sounds great," Zahn said. "What's so safe about Beyond Adventure?"

Elliot walked them around the two trucks facing the stable and motioned toward the gate. Zahn stepped through.

"It's a church camp. Nothing safer than that."

Zahn watched as Elliot fastened the latch behind them. "Right. But this church is a little different, right?"

"Follow me. We're going to walk up there to the hay barn, right in the center of the property." Elliot said, as Zahn joined him. "So you're nervous about the 'crazy Christian Scientists?'"

Zahn glanced over at Elliot. "No. Well, I'm not sure, actually. Maybe you can help me out. All I know is that Christian Scientists differ from the Baptists and the Methodists and all those mainstream churches. And that they don't believe in doctors." He cocked his head at Elliot. "Am I right so far? What else should I know?"

"Well, I'm not a Christian Scientist myself, but I've been working out here for sixteen years and got a pretty good sense of what they're about. They're good folk. And you got some of that right about them. They're different from other mainstream churches. They keep to themselves. And it's not just a *no doctors* thing—they believe God can heal the body through the power of prayer."

"Huh," Zahn said. "So what do they do when it's flu season? Or what about the coronavirus thing last fall when we were all wearing masks? They just pray they don't get it?"

"Nah, they're way more pragmatic than that," Elliot said, bending and stepping between the strands of a barbed-wire fence. "When the sun's out, they put on sunscreen. When the bugs are out, they use bug spray. So when the germs are out, they'll put on masks…if it's serious. Hell, most of the folks I've met up here even go to the dentist. That's like maintenance stuff." Elliot held the upper strand of wire, widening the gap for Zahn. "But if they take ill up here, they don't call the doctor. They pray. More importantly, others pray for them."

They walked toward the foothills forming the base of Mt. Columbia and stopped next to a brown-stained two-story barn.

Elliot pointed toward the mountains. "From here, the property line looks like the shape of Nevada. You go about a third of the way up toward Columbia there—" he pointed straight ahead, "—and the boundary runs north-south. We got a trail on the property that joins up with the Colorado Trail." He turned to Zahn. "But if you're anything like your daughter, you might have already explored that…I saw a lot of snowshoe tracks up that way last winter."

Zahn grinned at Elliot, then dipped his head. "Might have run across that trail."

"Right. The property goes all the way north past the long building up there," Elliot said, pointing toward a structure resembling a mountain resort. "That's the school. It belongs to the Christian Scientists as well, but it's separate from Beyond Adventure. They got their own staff. Sometimes they bring the kids down here for activities and stuff."

Elliot swept his hand across the valley until he pointed east. "Then it runs straight down to 361, the same road that runs by the entrance to Elk Trace. South to the Elk Trace boundary and then back up to where you and Daria walked from." He looked at Zahn. "That's it. Except for people in your neighborhood climbing the fence, this place is pretty private. Fenced all around. What goes on in Beyond Adventure stays in Beyond Adventure." Elliot smiled.

"Man, you guys got the perfect piece of property for a camp," Zahn said. "Where are the kids?"

"They're up closer to the mountains doing this conservation camp thing we got going. No horses for that, so the stables are pretty quiet. That's why I could let Kevin go riding with Daria."

Zahn tried to think of a subtle way to bring up Janae, the missing girl. He drew a blank. "I work with Search & Rescue. You hear about the girl we found? And the missing one?"

Elliot turned toward Zahn. "Oh, yeah. Heard about that. I think everyone in the valley heard about that situation." He paused. "Why are you asking? You think the church camp here has something to do with it?"

Zahn looked at Elliot, then at the ground, shaking his head. "I know the sheriff's folks are canvassing all the residents from here north on this side of the valley, and I thought I'd just ask, since this place has— or at least normally has—a bunch of kids. And since I'm here."

"Let's walk back to the stables," Elliot said, nodding his head the way they had come.

The two men ducked through the fence and walked without talking.

Elliot broke the silence. "Do you believe in a higher power, Tyler?"

Zahn stepped around a pile of horse manure and glanced at Elliot. "Are you asking whether I've accepted Jesus as my personal savior?" Zahn snorted. "You're either proselytizing for your employer, or you think you know me better than you do."

"I said nothing about Jesus. I asked whether you believed in a higher power. A force out there spurring our heart, driving our actions, and giving us meaning?"

This was why Zahn avoided men's groups and Bible study. His parents didn't raise him in the church, but he had explored the Christian religion during his 14-year marriage to Sheila. He had visited the Baptist churches like what Sheila had grown up with when they were stationed stateside, as well as the non-denominational churches during their overseas assignments. Sheila never missed church, and Zahn was convinced she had raised their children right—even after Zahn left. Zahn's tentative attempt to know God had come to an abrupt halt the night their son, Jacob, died from the flu. The night that started the breakup of Zahn's family. The night that told him loud and clear that no loving God would stoop so low as to steal the lives of innocent children.

But Zahn had no wish to share any of this with the stranger next to him.

"No, Gabe. I don't guess I do," Zahn said. "I believe man is in control of his or her destiny, not a higher power. I believe you should love your neighbor—but not because a God says so, but because that's how a successful society works. The alternative is chaos, and we see it every day."

Elliot nodded his head and said nothing.

"What about you?" Zahn wondered where Elliot's interest in his religious beliefs was coming from.

The older man laughed. "Oh, yes. I believe a higher power guides our actions. It's how we've survived so long." He paused. "I asked because if you understand the faith driving the folks running this place—" he swept his arm around the forest to their left and toward the stables "—then you understand how incongruous it would be for them to harm a child. Oh, sure, they might lose a member because they didn't go to a doctor for a burst appendix—not that I've heard of that happening here—but they would never abuse a child. It's counter to their foundation of faith."

Incongruous? Zahn was getting big words from the cowboy here.

"So, my two cents?" Elliot said. "You got to put yourself in the heart of whoever is behind these two little gals' situations and ask yourself. What's driving that person? Do they believe they control their own destiny—like you? Or do they believe in a higher power driving their actions—like the folks running this camp?"

"That would be one crazy-ass Christian to believe God drove him, or her, or whoever, to harm little girls," Zahn said.

"Damn straight," Elliot said, and kept walking.

CHAPTER 18

Janae's eyes sprang open, as she waited, motionless, for Jefe's wake-up call. It was as if her internal clock knew it was coming.

Back home in Oklahoma, Janae had loved routine. Get up at 6:35. Check and see what Dad packed in her lunchbox. Make herself a gold mine.

No one knew what a gold mine was in Colorado. Well, they knew a different kind of gold mine. The Rockies had actual gold mines—a hole in the ground where you searched for gold.

It meant something far better at an Oklahoma breakfast table. You butter up a slice of bread. Put a hole in the middle. Start frying it. Add a dab of butter in the hole, then crack an egg in it. Two minutes, then flip it. Two minutes and, *ta-da*, a gold mine. Called a gold mine because when you started working around the edges with your fork, the scent of buttered toast filling your nose, you eventually struck gold—the bright yellow yolk running out like a rivulet of lava, soaking into the remaining bread. Nothing tasted better.

After devouring her favorite breakfast, then she would change her clothes, brush her teeth, and pack her backpack before her dad drove her to the bus stop on his way to work. Same thing the next day. And the next. Until Saturday. Janae clung to the house routine because the rest of the school day was terror. Who would pick on her today?

Recess was the worst. She'd try to disappear in a corner of the playground with her book, but inevitably the mean kids found her. *Scaredy-cat, it's playtime. Want to come play with us?* She would attempt to ignore them, but eventually, one of the girls or boys would yank her upright and start pulling her toward the tire tunnel. The hallways were just as bad. They surrounded her and then jostled her through the hall like those pinball machines her dad played when he was a kid. And in two years it would be even harder. No recess in middle school. That was good. But eight classes? That was a lot of hallway time. Too much exposure for Janae's peace of mind.

Jefe's voice barked over the intercom, and Janae knew it was 6:00.

"Wakey, wakey, ladies. Up and at 'em. See you in fifteen." Jefe's voice, always cheerful, but never cheering, broke the silence of their bunkroom.

Fifteen minutes to get out of their nightclothes. Brush their hair. Brush their teeth. Put on their shoes and coats. Line up in the playroom.

Routine in the stable sucked.

Jefe claimed morning air and brisk walks were the keys to well-being. So every morning, he herded them from the bunker, up the ladder, and into the bay for harnessing. Not like horses. More like a chain gang. Jefe used zip-ties to hook them to a rope rigged with loops every five or six feet. Then he'd lead them on horseback, a mile-long circuit on a trail. Jefe said he was economizing his time. He was giving his girls a workout, his horse exercise, and he got to enjoy his coffee.

"Don't want you gals getting lazy. You never know when we might have to leave in a hurry. Got to keep you and my horses in shape." Jefe patted his ride.

Sometimes he stopped and pointed out things. Deer munching on low-hanging branches of the cottonwoods bordering the small stream. Chipmunks chasing each other as the forest awoke. Once they saw an owl.

Janae's eyes remained frozen on Nicole shuffling in front of her the first few mornings. Fear kept her from noticing anything. But after a few days of the same morning walk, she began to appreciate anything that was different. Like the owl.

Afterward, they returned to the bunkroom. First, breakfast. That didn't change either. A refrigerator in the bunkroom's corner harbored the milk for the cereal. The toasted oats were some store brand she didn't recognize. She remembered her dad telling her the store brand saved you money.

Then, dishes, taking turns at the shower, and reading the same stack of old books. Maybe a board game, but Janae didn't like playing those with Nicole and Rachel. Like zombies, they would just roll the dice, mechanically count, then stare at the board.

Six days after Janae had arrived at the stable, the routine changed. The intercom still broke the pre-dawn silence at 6:00, but everything was different after that.

"Ladies, good morning. No morning walk today. We got ourselves a video shoot." Janae heard Jefe pause, then his voice cut in again.

"Drumroll...and the lucky winner is...Rachel. Nicole, Janae, you two help Rachel clean up. Then eat your breakfast. I want her looking sparkling clean and ready to go at 7:00."

Janae swung her feet out of bed while Jefe was talking and looked at Rachel's bunk. Two bumps under her comforter. One was where Janae expected Rachel's knees would be. The other at her head. No movement.

The intercom fell silent. Janae saw the top of Nicole's head on the bottom bed below her. She was looking over at Rachel's bunk as well.

"Rachel?" Nicole called. "Did you hear that?"

Silence.

"Rachel?"

The sheets in Rachel's bunk shot downward and Rachel stared at the two girls. Nicole first, then up at Janae. Back to Nicole. Her eyes registered no emotion. Dead and calm, like lake water on a cloudy day.

"I hate video shoots," Rachel said. "Why can't Janae go? She's never done one."

Nicole tilted her head and looked at Janae. Janae tried to mirror Rachel's lack of emotion. She didn't know why Jefe hadn't picked her yet. But she wasn't volunteering. Not for a video shoot. She remembered what Nicole told her the first day. *We have to take off our clothes.*

Janae didn't want to do that.

Nicole turned toward Rachel. "He didn't pick Janae, Rachel. He picked you. You have to do it. Mandy did it right, and she got to go home. Kendall tried to get away, and you said we'd never see her again. Which do you want, Rachel?"

Rachel sighed and swung her legs out of bed, dangling her toes above the linoleum floor. "Home. But we don't know for sure that's where Mandy went." She rose and stuffed her feet into the slippers tucked underneath her bunk. She shuffled toward the door, then turned.

"Nicole? I'm going to shower. Will you please brush my hair and make it pretty after I get out? Like you did last time? I like it when you brush it."

Nicole nodded her head. "Of course I will. We'll both help you, won't we Janae?" She met Janae's eyes. Janae nodded.

Nicole called out to Rachel. "Don't forget to put your suit on after the shower."

"Suit?" Janae eyes widened. "I thought you said she had to take her clothes off. Why would she need a suit?"

"Her swimsuit," Nicole said. "You wear a swimsuit underneath when you go to the video shoots. That's what's left after you take your clothes off." She squinted at Janae. "If you forgot your suit, then you would be naked underneath. Ew."

CHAPTER 19

Daria exhaled and relaxed into the saddle. Her horse knew the narrow path, and Daria's muscle memory transported her back to her riding days. The scent of pine hung in the air like an invisible mist, and the sun broke through trees, reflecting off the white outcroppings of rock. Daria smiled, grateful she wasn't hiking and gasping for air as the elevation increased. It was so much easier to deal with the nine thousand foot altitude on horseback. She glanced back at Kevin. It was also easier to enjoy spring break with a cowboy following you.

"You doing okay? How's Gus doing for you?"

Daria slowed Gus at a wide spot in the trail, making room for Kevin to pull beside her.

"Doing great!" She patted her horse on the neck. "I was just thinking how lucky I am to be riding a horse in the Rockies. Thanks, Kevin, for the invite. This is the best thing I've done all break."

Kevin grinned, nodding. "Yeah, I knew you were a horse gal the moment you swung up behind me the day we met. Not afraid. Riding like you'd been doing it your whole life."

"Well, it's nice of Gabe letting you and Goober—" she nodded at Kevin's mount, "—have the time off to take me for a ride."

"Oh, I'll have to make up for it when we get back. Plus, I think he kind of likes the matchmaker role."

Daria looked at Kevin and tried to hide her smile from him. She kind of liked Gabe's matchmaker role, as well. But Kevin didn't need to know that…yet.

"Huh." Her eyebrows raised. "First date for the horses?"

Kevin laughed. "Right, how'd you guess?" Daria felt him size up both her and the horse. "So you're looking pretty comfortable there. You want to pick up the pace?"

"I don't know. You think you can keep up?"

"I'll try," Kevin said with a smile. "The trail runs straight for a while, then skirts right, around the slope. When it forks right and opens up, that's when we hit the field. We can push it up a bit."

"Okay. Got it."

The horses continued picking their way up the hill until the rocky trail intercepted a well-worn dirt path.

"That's the Colorado Trail," Kevin called. "Or at least part of it. It splits up north at Twin Lakes. More trees on this route."

Daria turned her horse onto the trail and called back to Kevin. "This is nice—a lot easier on the horses."

"Technically, we're not supposed to ride on it," Kevin said. "We'll just go a half mile, then turn off to Beyond Adventure property."

Daria squeezed her legs and clicked her tongue, moving Gus from a walk to a lope. "Keep up?"

"Are you kidding?" She heard Kevin urging his horse faster, and then he was next to her.

This.

The smell of forest. Rippled muscles beneath her propelling her forward. A new friend…one she wanted to get to know better. All the trepidation about visiting her father during one of her only breaks from school washed away. This beat bikinis in Mazatlán and stupid beer games any day. Not her scene.

No, this was perfect.

She prodded the horse and edged past Kevin. She heard him call out "—Right?"

All right? She was great.

She snapped a glance over her left shoulder for Kevin. He was no longer there. She whipped her head right and saw him slowing his horse, veering right on a path she'd missed.

Crap.

She tugged the reins and eyed a game trail cutting straight down the mountain and intercepting Kevin's trail. She veered off the Colorado Trail and leaned back as Gus dug his rear legs into the loose pine needles, adjusting for the downslope. This horse thing was like riding a bike. She felt confident as she looked ahead at Kevin waiting beyond the trees.

Later, she only recalled raising her hand to Kevin and letting out a whoop. Kevin had to describe the rest. A branch the size of her thigh flashed in her face. She twisted her shoulders and ducked her head, trying to avoid it, but she couldn't get low enough and the branch was too large to push away. Bases loaded, and nature was up to bat. The branch connected squarely on Daria's shoulder and swept her off Gus's back. A home run. She landed directly on her opposite shoulder among the stand of trees responsible for her fall.

Her next memory was Kevin's urgent voice.

"Daria? Daria? Are you okay?" A shadow loomed over her, blocking the sunshine from the side of her face. White-hot pain shot down her neck and shoulder as she tried to turn her head.

"Kevin?"

"I'm right here. Are you hurt? That was a heck of a fall." She felt him kneel beside her and lay his hand on her injured shoulder.

Daria shifted her eyes toward him without moving her head. "I'd love to tell you I'm okay," she said, pressing her lips together. It wasn't just the pain. Something felt wrong with her shoulder and neck—like pieces might be in the wrong place. "But I'm not. I think I broke something. On the side I'm lying on."

Kevin leaned closer.

"Hang in there, Daria. I'm going to go get help."

CHAPTER 20

Zahn raised his head at the sound of a familiar horn. He stepped out of the garage where he was replacing the spark plug on his snowblower and waved at Perez. The deputy sheriff lowered his window and peered around Zahn.

"What's going on in there? Spring cleaning?"

Zahn grinned. "Nah, just changing plugs. Should have done it before last winter."

"Where's Daria? What happened to the minute-by-minute schedule?"

"Believe it or not, she's doing her own thing today. Over riding horses at Beyond Adventure."

"That's right. You were going to check it out. Find anything?"

"Nothing weird. I mean, I just talked to one gentleman, an employee over there, but he's been there for years—it all sounded on the up and up to me." Zahn looked at the Tahoe. "What're you doing up here? Harassing the good citizens of Elk Trace again?"

"Nope. There's a guy out on parole working up here. Had some questions for him." Perez tapped his steering wheel. "Got an update on the Longmont case. Thought I'd share."

"You all found Janae?"

"No, but they're putting together a task force." Perez paused. "Guess who's back?"

"Who?"

"Randall Williams, our favorite US Marshal."

"No shit?"

"No shit."

Zahn smiled. Williams had been part of the Fugitive Task Force the year prior when he and Perez were working the terrorist case. With the inevitable bureaucratic friction between the Colorado Bureau of Investigation, the Federal Bureau of Investigation, and the US Marshals, Williams had found himself the odd man out. Rather than sit back and watch the other two organizations muddle through the investigation, he had followed a couple of leads Perez and Zahn had uncovered. While the two local men worked the case, Williams stayed with them step-by-step, but gave them all the credit when the case was solved. They liked him—even though Perez was still pissed about Williams and Kristee getting together.

"Yeah, so Randall is definitely in charge of this case. Marshals have a national task force looking for missing kids, and this one was right up their alley with Janae being from out of state and all."

"He find anything yet?"

"Yep. You remember Mike Longmont? The uncle? It was his house where we started the search for Janae." Zahn nodded. "So during a search of the house, they found a bunch of pornography on his computer."

"Let me guess," Zahn said. "Child pornography?"

Perez gave a half smile. "That would be too easy." He paused. "So they found these pics and videos hidden away on his computer. And it's kind of weird, but not like illegal weird."

"What do you mean?"

"I mean, it's not children. It's like women dressed up like girls. You know, in school uniforms and stuff."

"That's still weird. What did he say about it?"

"Randall said Longmont was in denial at first, but when it became clear what they had found and whose it was, he flipped and went on the offensive. You know, like 'so what, it's a free country ain't it?' and 'I got more where that came from and it's not illegal, either…want to see it?' That kind of shit."

Zahn's phone rang in his pocket. While he dug for it, he tilted his head, looking at Perez. "Nothing you can do with that?"

"Nothing immediately. But it gives us a sharper focus on possible suspects. Know what I mean?"

Zahn nodded and glanced down at the phone. *Unknown caller.* Another one of those automated calls? *We're calling because the warranty on your Toyota Tundra has expired...*

He punched the phone's green button. "Zahn."

"Tyler, it's Gabe Elliot," a voice on the other end said. "From Beyond Adventure?"

Odd. Zahn didn't remember trading numbers.

"What's up, Gabe? How'd Daria's ride go?" He felt a twinge of unease. Why the call?

"Daria took a fall. We're getting her down to the main lodge on a stretcher. Shoulder or collarbone or something. Got the EMTs on the way."

Zahn raised his eyebrows at Perez, then turned away, pressing the phone to his ear. His heart hammered. "Did she hit her head? Is she conscious?"

"I just heard the calls on the radio and figured you'd want to get up here. I don't have the details. Come on over, and I'll meet you at the gate and take you up to the lodge."

"Five minutes," Zahn snapped, and hung up the phone. He turned back to Perez, who was listening to the radio in his Tahoe. "It's Daria. Horse accident over at the church camp."

Perez nodded. "Hop in. I heard them dispatching the EMTs. Didn't know it was Daria."

The deputy hit the flashers and bolted down the Elk Trace entrance to the main county road heading north. Five hundred yards later, he turned west on a gravel road framed by a large wooden arch with *Beyond Adventure* burned into the wood.

"We'll beat the EMTs," Perez said. "It's over six miles from town."

Gabe Elliot stood next to the gate which blocked public access to the lodge. He waved his cattleman's hat and swung the gate open.

Perez abruptly stopped and lowered his window. Zahn leaned across and called out to Elliot. "Where's she at?"

"I'll show you if that's okay with you?" Elliot looked from Zahn to Perez.

"Jump in," Perez said, nodding toward the back seat. Elliot threw open the rear door and climbed into the Tahoe. He reached forward and tapped Zahn's shoulder.

"Got another update. They're not sure if she hit her head, but she's fully conscious. Fully coherent. Just in a lot of pain." He pointed through the front windscreen. "Quarter mile farther up, then turn left toward the lodge. You'll be able to see it from this road."

Perez nodded and sped up.

Zahn turned to Elliot. "What are they doing to treat her?"

Elliot sat back in the bench seat. "Well, I don't know for sure about that, but considering where we're at, I suspect they're giving her a lot of prayers."

"Shit," Zahn said.

As Perez's Tahoe pulled up to the lodge, an ATV approached slowly from the other direction. The tail end of a stretcher thrust out the back of the vehicle with a person walking on each side to stabilize Daria.

Zahn bolted out the passenger door and jogged to the ATV. The driver nodded at him and pointed toward the lodge. Zahn slowed to a walk and tucked in alongside the stretcher. He stared at Daria, still wearing her helmet, looking at him with a weak smile.

"Hey, Dad," she said.

Zahn could barely hear her voice over the motor.

"Are you okay?" he shouted. "Can you move your arms and legs?"

Daria nodded her head as the ATV pulled to a stop where the parking lot met the entrance to the main lodge. Her hand reached to one of the helpers, and Zahn recognized Kevin Kilgore.

"It's my shoulder, Dad," she said, dipping her chin toward her right side. "Well, maybe my head too. They're not sure, yet."

"What the hell happened?" Zahn raised his eyes and stared at Kevin.

Kevin looked at Zahn, his eyes wide. His mouth opened, and Daria winced before interrupting.

"Dad, it was an accident. I missed a turn and went down a side trail fast, without checking it first. Tree branch took me out." She turned her head an inch toward Kevin. "It wasn't Kevin's fault."

The ATV driver hopped out from the front seat and wheeled around to where Zahn stood. "Sir, I'm Patrick Donnelly, and I work emergency response here. I take it you're the father?"

Zahn nodded. "Yep, what's your plan here?"

"We're going to leave her on the ATV stretcher until the EMTs get here," said Donnelly. "No sense moving her twice." He turned to Zahn. "I've been through Wilderness First Aid—that's the extent of my training, so take what I say as an opinion."

Zahn nodded.

"She fell on her right side, shoulder and head striking first. I'm pretty sure she has a broken collarbone. Doesn't appear to be any neck injury. It's the head I'm concerned about. No bleeding. Could be a concussion, though."

"Got it, Patrick," Zahn nodded again. "Thank you. Have you given her anything for the swelling?"

Donnelly shook his head. "No. As you might have guessed, we don't have a lot of medicine up here." He paused and went on. "Not that I would have given her anything, anyway. Not until the medical folks look at her head."

"Right. I meant a cold pack. Or ice. What about that?"

"We can do ice." Donnelly nodded at Kevin.

When Kevin returned, he handed several ice packs to Donnelly and stepped out of the way.

Donnelly turned to Zahn. "I'll need some room here."

"I'm not leaving. I'm going to ride in the ambulance with her."

"I just need you to step back for five minutes, sir, and let us get a set of vitals and do the ice."

Zahn looked at Daria and said, "I'll be right back, sweetheart."

He walked over to Perez and Elliot next to the Tahoe. Approaching the men, he heard sirens coming from the main entrance to the camp.

Perez tilted his head toward the front of his Tahoe and Zahn followed him.

"She all right?"

"Not sure. I think so, but everyone's pretty unsure about her head."

"You going to ride with the ambulance?"

"Yeah, why?"

Perez nodded. "I'm not trying to make light of Daria's situation, but it looks like I'm just in the way. Since I'm here, I'm going to ask some questions about her accident and see if I can get a feel for this place. See if Linzmeier's theory on weird stuff up here holds any water."

Zahn gave Perez a grim smile. "Makes sense to me."

"Call me from the hospital when you find out more. I'll take you guys home when you're ready."

Zahn nodded and walked back to where Elliot stood near the rear of the Tahoe. The man was watching the group surrounding Daria. Donnelly was packing ice between Daria's jacket and her shirt. Kevin Kilgore had his hands tightly clasped together over Daria's body with his head leaning over the side rails.

Zahn pointed to Kevin "What's he doing?"

"He's praying," Elliot said, staring at the young man. "Praying she'll heal."

CHAPTER 21

This was not the way Daria had planned to spend spring break. Propped in her dad's easy chair, arm in a sling, and shoulder strapped to her side, she stared at the bottle of pain meds, trying to decide whether she could get by without taking any more. The good news from the Rocky Mountain Regional Health Center was no concussion. The bad news, and not unexpected, was the broken collarbone diagnosis. The tree branch that had swept her off the horse had twisted her body and guaranteed her first contact with the rocky trail would be the crook between her head and her shoulder. Then the rest of her body. Good thing she was wearing a helmet.

She continued staring at the bottle of pills. No concussion, but even taking the minimum dosage to dull the aches fogged her brain.

The memory of intense pain still lingered. And she'd never forget the jolting ATV ride. But the strongest memory was a surprising moment of bliss amidst the pain. When Kevin had laid his hands upon her, she had felt the burning in her shoulder lift. Like steam rising from a lake, dissolving into the sunshine, Daria could almost see her pain wisp away. She had turned her head toward Kevin and watched him pray. When he finished, they both knew the pain was better. He had smiled, given her hand a squeeze, and promised to see her after she saw the doctors.

Maybe she didn't need medicine. Maybe she had been underestimating the power of prayer. She hadn't underestimated the power of her attraction to Kevin. He was coming by after he finished work later today.

She stared out the living room window and watched her father climb the porch stairs. "Hey, Dad," she called, as she heard the front door close.

"You were sleeping when I left. How're you feeling?"

"Well, the shoulder's a little sore, but I bet this thing's going to be more of an awkward heal than a painful heal." She heaved a sigh. "No running for six weeks? It's going to kill me. I'm going to be so out of shape."

"How about the meds? They working?"

"Yeah, I was going to talk to you about that." Daria smiled. "I'm thinking about not using them. Or, if I do, just once in a while. I took one, and it helped with the pain. But it makes me so funky. Like I can't hang onto a thought."

Zahn nodded his head. "I don't have a problem with that. Never been a huge fan of pills, anyway. But I do think you need to figure out how you're going to handle the pain."

Daria glanced at the clock, smiling. "One of my methods is stopping by in about ten minutes."

"Not happy with that young man. I don't understand how he could have you in the lead, at a gallop, on a strange trail."

"Maybe you should lighten up on Kevin a bit? I was the one who went ahead, who missed the turn, and who made a bad decision to go down a steep trail. He did nothing wrong. When I fell, he was there. When they transported me to the lodge, he was there. I'm practically an invalid now, and he's coming to visit."

Her father stared at her but didn't speak.

"My point is that if someone is there for you, even if it *was* their fault, which it wasn't, then you forgive them." Daria tilted her head. "Right? I mean, if Kevin went silent on me now and stopped visiting, that would be different. But he's on his way."

Her father remained silent. That's when Daria realized what she had said. She might have been talking about Kevin, but her dad was taking it as a judgment on him.

He hadn't been there for Daria when his only son, and her only brother, Jacob, had died. Not really. He was at the funeral, then disappeared back to the desert. Then her parents got divorced, and that started the infrequent visits.

Daria was willing to be over that. Water under the bridge. A fresh start with this visit.

She just wasn't ready to talk about it yet.

"Just think about it from Kevin's perspective. Give him a chance." Daria said. She spotted movement behind her father through the living room window. Zahn followed her gaze.

"See? He's five minutes early. I know you're a fan of that," she said.

"Nice." Zahn walked toward the tapping on the door.

"Do you think maybe you could give us some alone time after you let him in?"

Zahn looked back at Daria. His grin looked forced. "You mean no long conversation in the living room, just the three of us?"

Daria rolled her eyes. She heard her dad open the door.

"Kevin."

"Tyler. I was wondering if Daria—"

"She's right around the corner. Make yourself at home. I'm off to run some errands."

"Okay. Thanks. I—"

"Got to run, Kevin. Catch you later."

Daria watched through the living room window as her father walked to his truck, head bowed.

That didn't go well.

CHAPTER 22

"Gotta walk." Zahn gasped for air, halting a slow jog up Mountaintop Road in Elk Trace.

Perez paused until Zahn caught up, then settled into a brisk walk. "Walking's good. You can't expect to maintain a run uphill at 9,000 feet."

"You do," Zahn said.

Perez laughed. "It's not a matter of 'if you walk,' it's a matter of 'when you walk.' Guarantee you, I'd have been walking, too, in the next five minutes."

Zahn wasn't sure that was true. Perez was just trying to make him feel good. The deputy was an amateur ultrarunner. One of those ubiquitous Colorado crazies, looking for trail runs longer than the standard marathon distance. When Zahn met Perez two years earlier, the lawman had just finished the Red Hot 55k, almost 35 miles of running across slick rock in Moab, Utah.

After the two men had worked together on the case the previous spring, Zahn had gotten serious about getting his late-forties body in shape. And he'd made progress, moving from one-mile gasping efforts to five-mile runs a couple times a week. After he'd boasted to Perez about a ten-mile stretch on the treadmill in his garage, the deputy had thrown down the challenge. Join him at Moab for this year's run.

Zahn had balked at the distance, whined a while, and then refused before Perez told him about the shorter version. The 35K fell just shy of 22 miles…not even a marathon. When February rolled around, Zahn had found himself in the Utah desert at 8:30 in the morning, shivering in the below-freezing weather and waiting for the sun to crawl above the sandstone mountains. He had made it farther than ten miles, running the flats and the limited downhills. But by mile fourteen, running was no longer an option. He had reluctantly hiked to the finish line. His fitness journey remained a work in progress.

He liked it, though. Perez had helped him to get stronger. That's why he was out here with him countering the burning in his lungs and legs with the dazzling view of the snow-capped Collegiate Peaks and the smell of sun-warmed pines.

Zahn caught up with Perez. "Any developments with the Longmont girl's case?"

Perez grunted, shaking his head. "We've been kind of sidetracked the last 24 hours. Internal affairs at BV Police."

"Internal Affairs is investigating you guys?"

"Ha!" Perez laughed. "They ain't big enough for an Internal Affairs section." He turned to Zahn. "They've asked the Sheriff's Department for someone to take an independent look at a situation. And that someone is me."

"What's the situation? Or can you tell me?"

"Can't talk about it officially, but I think after last year, we're past the formalities. I value your thoughts." Perez snorted, "Hell, I'm surprised you haven't heard about it already. You remember meeting Linzmeier at coffee the other day, right?"

"Right."

"He left us after that. Headed over to the elementary school for the 'don't do drugs' brief. Things went downhill from there."

"Let me guess. Inappropriate words to the kids, and now the teachers are in an uproar?"

"How about *did*, not *said*, the wrong thing, and we only wish it would have been in front of a teacher?"

"What?"

"He gave his brief. Teachers said it was typical Linzmeier—strutting around, telling them right from wrong, and making lots of references to his weapon. Kids loved it. They always do. Teachers roll their eyes. But they're used to it." Perez stopped for a minute and Zahn pulled up as well. "So, afterward, the kids come up and ask questions, touch the badge, that kind of thing. There's always a line. A young girl—fifth grader, they said—came up and told him her dad was a criminal, and asked if Linzmeier was going to catch him?"

"How did Linzmeier react?"

"Linzmeier said he laughed it off. Told her to tell her dad not to be a criminal because they always get caught." Perez opened his hands at his side. "So, the girl says, 'But my dad is inappropriate with me.'"

"Oh, shit."

"Right. So Linzmeier tells her they need to talk about it privately, and they should get a teacher to sit in on the conversation."

Zahn nodded.

"The girl says 'no.' She says she can't say it in front of a male teacher because she's too embarrassed. And a female teacher wouldn't understand. She says she tried telling her mom, and she just ignored her."

Zahn tilted his head. "Where are you reciting this conversation from? Linzmeier or the girl?"

"Linzmeier. He told me he walked around the corner with her. An alcove with two chairs next to the counselor's office. No one else in sight. He sat there and talked to her, and she told him her dad was reading her books with bad words in them like 'hell' and 'damn.' Words she knew were inappropriate."

"That's it? Dad's reading a PG-13 book to a 10-year-old?"

"That's it—as far as Linzmeier is concerned. But it doesn't match the other story."

"Which is?"

"The principal walked around the corner and saw Linzmeier's hand on the girl's back. She jacked him up for being alone with a student and escorted him from the school. The girl then told the principal that Linzmeier told her it was okay for men to be inappropriate with girls."

"Oh, shit. And then she told the teacher the topic? Reading books with bad words?"

"Nope—that's Linzmeier's story. The girl stopped talking, and the school is spinning through the roof—as you can imagine."

After twenty-plus years of military service, Zahn knew what it was like to be the one in uniform, charged with protecting those out of uniform. Special trust is awarded to institutions paid for by the taxpayers. The people who served took that value seriously, and when you heard these kinds of accusations? Well, you wanted to believe the one who chose to serve. But sometimes that one percent violated the trust. Zahn had seen it happen, read about it happening, heard of it happening. He hated all of it.

He thought about his one interaction with Linzmeier. At the coffee shop. A half-baked rumor about child-stealing church groups? Linzmeier bragging about staring at a 16-year-old's backside? And Daria telling him about Linzmeier's comments when he pulled her over?

Zahn said nothing. Just because he didn't like Linzmeier didn't make him a pedophile. But, still...

"I'm ready to jog again." Zahn started shuffling up the gentle slope, pushing his thoughts away. He didn't have enough facts yet to pass judgment on Linzmeier.

Perez pulled even with Zahn. "Thoughts? What's it sound like to you?"

"Sounds like you've been sidetracked—just like you said." Zahn's breath picked up, a freight train leaving the station. One-syllable words easier than anything more. "Met him once. Wasn't impressed."

Perez's head bobbed. "Yeah, he's kind of off. We all know that. But whether he's just weird, or whether he's a pervert? Guess I'll have to figure that one out."

"Yup."

"This case is leaving a bad taste in my mouth." Perez turned toward Zahn. "You mind if I keep you in the loop on this one? Might need some of those insights you're famous for."

"Which case? Janae Longmont or Linzmeier?"

Perez stopped and stared at Zahn. "Exactly."

Zahn met Perez's gaze. "Nope, I don't mind. Something weird is going on in this valley. We need to stop it."

CHAPTER 23

Zahn walked to the stables—cutting through the neighbor's property and ducking under the fence. The tapping of metal on metal rang through the woods as he neared the corral. From the building's corner, he watched Gabe Elliot hard at work shoeing a gray mare.

He wasn't sure why he had come. Daria was still asleep at the house, sleep she sorely needed. Between the fall from the horse, her indecision on taking the pain meds, and her blossoming interest in Kevin, she had a lot going on. Zahn wasn't so sure about her stopping the pain meds. It was obvious she was hurting. Sleeping late was a good thing.

He had sat at the dining room table that morning pondering life. Not in an existential sense. He'd given up on that some time ago—but rather considering how one's beliefs factored into one's worldview.

Zahn was self-aware enough to recognize his progress. Last year a six-pack over an evening numbed his thoughts, put him to sleep, and guaranteed he would regret it in the morning. Not much pondering.

But that was before. Before the ride-alongs with Deputy Perez. Before they stopped the dam from washing away and put the bad guys (and gal) behind bars. Now he was a one-beer-a-night man with a purpose in life…and he was happier with this new version of himself.

Except what good was purpose without family?

His conversation with Daria had left him unsettled. He had family. He had Daria. But the awkwardness in their father-daughter relationship hadn't improved since she arrived. It was something beyond Zahn's neurotic—and he recognized it as such—drive to schedule every moment of Daria's time with him. She had immediately picked up on that, and he was attempting to throttle back. No, it was something else.

As he had sat next to Daria yesterday afternoon, and she had explained why she forgave Kevin for his role in her accident, Zahn's heart had sunk. Her words stung. *If someone is there for you, then you forgive them.* Was she talking about Kevin, or was she admonishing Zahn?

Because he wasn't there. After Jacob died.

He left.

He left Sheila the job of raising Daria. His ex-wife nailed that, both in the home and in the church. He was grateful Daria had something he lacked—a bedrock of faith to carry her through trials and turmoil. Something she believed in.

But did that belief include forgiveness for her father? That was the awkwardness, he realized. That was the big unknown. Until yesterday. *If someone is there…*

She hadn't forgiven him.

Zahn didn't know how to fix that. It was clear that scheduling more father-daughter time on this vacation was not the answer. But he was also nervous about those trying to influence, change, or convert Daria. People like Kevin Kilgore.

And what was the deal with the church next door? Zahn stopped his personal pity party and thought about Beyond Adventure. Should he allow Daria to be with Kevin from the church, or had both he and Daria already outgrown the *allowing* stage of parenting? But what if Linzmeier had something legitimate when he pointed the Janae Longmont investigation toward the Christian Scientists? And, if there was something going on there, did Zahn have any power to keep Daria away?

Elliot said the church was harmless. And he didn't seem to have a reason to defend them. He wasn't even a member. Zahn liked Elliot. He made sense when he talked, and Zahn needed some of that right now.

Zahn rapped his knuckles on the half-open sliding barn door, and Elliot raised his head from the horse's hoof.

"Morning," Elliot said.

"Gabe. Good to see you. How're things?"

"Fine. Just fine. You know anything about shoeing horses?"

"Nope. Ridden a few, but never owned one. Someone else always did the horseshoeing."

Elliot nodded toward the opposite corner of the room. "Bring that stool over here and pull up next to me." He patted his hip. "On this side, not opposite."

Zahn retrieved the stool and set himself up next to Elliot.

"Finished the first three, already. This is the last one," Elliot paused and raised a horseshoe. "I used a nipper to get the old shoe off, then a hoof pick to scrape all the stuff that either grew or got stuck in there. Basically, making a clean, stable place to mount the next shoe. Once that's clear, I take the new shoe, like this one, and tack it on. We use a farrier knife and rasp for the final manicure just to smooth it all out."

"And it doesn't hurt the horse at all? I've seen the process from a distance, and it never seems to upset the horse."

"Well, I wouldn't say never," Elliot said. "Horses aren't always predictable. Like Daria's ride the other day. Most horses would have pulled up short from that branch rather than duck below it, but it sounds like Gus ran through it. Not normal. But it happens." Elliot started tapping the nails into the shoe again. "But you're right. It's all dead skin and nail here—so no pain. It's like putting pieces of armor on their feet."

Zahn thought about that. It felt that way when he was with Daria. Like she wore armor around the things that hurt. The things not discussed.

"You got something bothering you? Daria doing all right?"

"Yeah, she's doing great. Starting the healing process. I guess I'm just interested in hearing some more of an outsider's perspective on this place." Zahn scooted his stool back a couple of feet from Elliot to give him room to finish the shoe. "She's quite taken with Kevin. And I guess I'm okay with that. He seems like he's squared away."

"I can vouch for that," Gabe said. "Solid young man, and he'll treat your daughter right."

"I'm kind of worried about where he's coming from. This church. All the praying."

"Prayer stuff?" Elliot smiled.

"You know, when you pointed out Kevin and the others praying for her after the fall? She felt something when they did it. I suspect she's still doing it with Kevin. She said she wanted to try going without the meds and using prayer to help with the pain."

Elliot nodded. "Is it working?"

"I don't know," Zahn said, shaking his head. "She thinks it helps, and I guess that's what matters. What kind of place is this?"

Elliot finished mounting the shoe. He stood and untied the horse, then led it into the adjoining corral, patting the animal on the flanks as he released it to join the others. Zahn followed. After Elliot closed the corral gate, he propped his foot up on the bottom rung of the fence and leaned on his elbows across the top rung, looking up at the foothills of Mt. Columbia. He nodded toward his right, and Zahn joined him at the fence.

Elliot returned his gaze to the mountains. "You want the party line, or my opinion?"

"Your view. I already looked them up on the Internet and got the public affairs version."

"Uh-huh." Elliot nodded and stayed silent for a moment.

Zahn waited.

"I lost someone I loved. About ten years back." Elliot kept his gaze focused on the mountain in front of him. "My daughter." He stopped and took a breath. "My entire world."

Zahn turned to look at the man. No wonder he felt drawn to this stranger. Elliot recognized Zahn's pain. He'd likely suffered with it even longer.

"I'm sorry."

"I'm sure you are, and I appreciate that. Not looking for sympathy, though—trying to explain something about this place." Elliot turned his head toward Zahn. "When I lost my girl, this church wrapped itself around me. The men kept me company. The women fed me. They all embraced me in prayer. I got explanation after explanation about why bad things happen to good people. If ever I was to step into their fold, that was the time."

"But you didn't?"

"I didn't." Elliot shook his head. "I thought their explanations were a bunch of shit. What kind of God takes the innocent?"

Exactly. Zahn felt a sense of *déjà vu*. What kind of God would take Jacob?

"I worked—hell, I still work—through the pain myself. By honoring my girl's memory. Her dreams of what might have been. Her aspirations." Elliot stepped back from the fence and looked into Zahn's eyes. "But here's the deal. It was the church's *intent* that earned my respect. Not their religion. They were wrapping me into their fold because they cared about my pain. They weren't recruiting. Weren't trying to prove how their religion was better than others. Just trying to help me because they cared." Elliot looked at the ground, then back to Zahn. "That meant the world to me, and it's why I still work here. I don't believe in their worldview. I don't believe in their God. I believe in what they gave me—grace, with nothing expected in return. Screw outcomes. Their intent is what mattered."

"Screw outcomes?"

"Right. Take Daria, for example. If the prayer doesn't work, then have her take the damn medicine. But no need to blame the church. They mean well." Elliot nodded. "I guess that's what I feel about this place. You don't need to worry about Daria here. Their intent is good."

Zahn nodded. He had asked for a straight answer and got it. From a man he'd just met. But a man he had quickly grown to respect.

Elliot spoke again. "Another thing."

"What's that?"

"I know your friends are still poking around out here trying to figure out where that little girl is, right?"

"Of course they are. They'll poke until they find her."

"Uh-huh. Well, they can keep poking, but my gut tells me they won't find anything strange going on here." Elliot swept his arm toward the main lodge. "This place means well."

CHAPTER 24

Rachel was gone all day.

That changed things for Janae and Nicole. Not externally. They still made half-hearted attempts at the Battleship game before giving up and retreating to the pile of books and magazines. But inside, Janae's stomach churned. She couldn't stop thinking about Rachel. Where was she? What was she doing? With whom?

"How long do you think she will be—"

"Don't talk about it. She'll be back when she's back." Nicole shifted with her book, turning away from Janae.

She's worried too.

Janae had inventoried the book selection the first day. Jefe seemed to think they either wanted to read Clifford books or murder mysteries. Nothing much in between. A Ramona book by Beverly Cleary and, thank goodness, one Percy Jackson book, *The Last Olympian*. She'd moved it under her pillow and read it twice in the first two days. Not like she hadn't read it three times already back in Oklahoma.

The book's adventures took on new significance now. Suddenly she was trapped in a situation as bad, or worse, than those Percy and Annabeth faced. She found a pen in the book room and underlined a quote from Annabeth. *I am never, ever, going to make things easy for you, Seaweed Brain. Get used to it.* Of course, Annabeth was flirting with Percy when she said it. But she liked the idea of calling Jefe *Seaweed Brain.* And not making things easy for him.

Maybe it was time for Janae to channel her inner Annabeth.

A muffled sound came from the entrance. Both girls turned their heads. The door swung open and there stood Rachel with Jefe behind, herding her into the hallway.

Rachel's eyes were glassy again. Like a zombie.

Jefe followed Rachel into the room, a scowl on his face.

"A dead fish?" Jefe was continuing what appeared to be a one-way conversation. "He said filming you playing today was like watching a dead fish floating in an aquarium."

Rachel walked through the hallway, past the other girls, and into the bunkroom, where she sat, eyes straight ahead.

Jefe watched the girl walk away and then turned to Janae and Nicole.

"Why don't you two follow her in there?" he said. "What I got to say, you all can hear."

Neither Janae nor Nicole moved. Janae caught Nicole's frightened expression.

"Move it," Jefe bellowed. "It wasn't a question."

The two girls scurried after Rachel. Nicole sat on her bunk. Janae sat on the far side of Rachel and looked back toward Jefe.

Jefe moved forward and filled the frame of the door. He glanced at Rachel and then looked at the other girls, shaking his head.

"Let's review our team strategy," Jefe said. "Some of us seem to have forgotten."

He froze his eyes on Rachel. "Look at me."

Janae already had her eyes fixed on Jefe. She shot a quick side glance at the other two girls. Nicole was staring wide-eyed at Jefe. Rachel turned toward Jefe, but kept her eyes pointed at his feet. Janae swung her eyes back to Jefe.

"You are mine. This is your home," Jefe said in a monotone. "You work for me. Do your work well, and you can go back to your old home. Screw up your work, and you go in the hole." He glared at Rachel. "It doesn't seem that complicated. Is it complicated, Rachel?"

The girl kept her eyes on Jefe's feet.

"What about you, Janae? Do you think you could do your job right?"

Janae's lip quivered, and she felt something sour in her throat.

"I don't know." So much for standing up to Jefe.

"You don't know what?"

"What to do."

Jefe sighed. "What the hell, don't you guys talk in here?" He paused. "It's like a zoo. Your job is to act like a little girl—which shouldn't be hard since you are one—in front of someone who's making a movie. Does that sound so difficult?"

Janae shook her head.

"Nicole, can you tell Janae the other reason it's like a zoo?"

Nicole turned to Janae. "If we do a good job, people will pay money to watch us."

CHAPTER 25

Zahn was running behind for yoga class. Lately, he'd been arriving first or second, a marked improvement from the year before when a hangover often kept him from class. He dropped his gear in his coveted corner spot.

The community center only charged $5 a session. A year-and-a-half into it, and Zahn still hadn't met a patron younger than himself. Not a matchmaking opportunity. But the perfect place to keep the aging body limber. When he'd started, he could barely touch his ankles with his fingertips. Now? He was grabbing his toes. And making friends. He liked the old-timers that made up Ruth's class.

But this morning he'd stopped and grabbed Greek yogurt for Daria and filled up with gas. The community center parking was already full. Zahn parked at the tennis courts—although he noticed the pickleballers seemed to be taking over—and walked toward the playground to shorten the distance to the front door. He threaded between two cars, nodding at the driver parked in a Blazer on his right. No nod in return. The young, clean-shaven man with hair to his shoulders and a big grin was focused on the three kids chasing each other around the monkey bars. Probably watching one of his own. Zahn pegged the two women sitting on the park bench as more likely candidates for the role of caregivers.

He glanced back as he stepped over the curb and into the playground. The man hadn't even noticed him, fixated on the kids, and still smiling. Weird.

The Janae Longmont case was lodged in Zahn's head. He was seeing potential perverts everywhere. No law against sitting in your car in a public parking spot.

But that smile…

He stopped and turned toward the Blazer. The man's jaw hung loose, a wide smile still on his face, and his eyes focused on the kids.

Aw, hell.

Zahn turned around like he'd forgotten something in his truck and started walking back. The young man kept his head pointed toward the playground. Zahn approached the Blazer from the rear. He caught his reflection in the Blazer's rearview mirror about the same time the man behind the wheel noticed him. Zahn watched a flurry of motion as the man reached across the center console.

He motioned for the man to lower his window. Through the glass, he could see a newspaper, *The Chaffee County Times*, covering the man's lap.

The man fumbled with the window latches. *Electric windows don't work when your car ain't running, buddy,* Zahn thought. The man stared over Zahn's shoulder and turned the key in the ignition. The Blazer roared to life, and he lowered the window halfway. Zahn flinched at the pungent scent of aftershave.

"What?" the man said, still not meeting his eyes.

Zahn had nothing on this guy but a gut feeling.

"Saw you sitting here and thought maybe you were looking for the yoga class?"

The man snorted and shifted his eyes to Zahn's other shoulder. "Me? No way, man. I just dropped my aunt off for pickleball." He raised his eyebrows. "Waiting for her to finish." He lifted the newspaper, and Zahn noted with relief the man's pants were zipped.

"Reading the paper," he said.

Zahn smiled. "You ought to give the yoga a try if you're coming, anyway. They got extra mats."

"Not for me, man."

"All right. I'm headed in." Zahn turned, then pivoted back. "So who's your aunt? I know a lot of those pickleballers."

Something about this guy still felt off. Time to check the story.

"Maddie Bodin," the man said, returning his eyes to Zahn's shoulder. "You know her?"

Zahn knew her. The coffee server from the Elkhead had mentioned a grandmother. The woman who always parked next to Zahn's usual spot and chatted with him in the mornings. Huh.

He smiled and tapped on the Blazer's door. "I do. I know Maddie." He tried to look into the man's eyes. "I'll tell her I met you. I'm Tyler Zahn. What's your name?"

"Roger Fulhart."

"Good to meet you." He turned away from the Blazer. Handshake didn't feel like the right move. Zahn heard the window powering up behind him.

He ducked into the yoga room and aimed for his normal spot. Still empty. Everyone had *their* spot. He wasn't sure if it was a yoga thing or an old people thing. Creatures of habit.

He took off his shoes and socks, unrolled his mat, and did a couple of quick stretches before joining the group routine. Zahn hated showing up late. Ruth's first five minutes were his favorite part. Relaxing the mind. Pushing out thoughts of the past or the future and focusing on the present.

It was the only thing he'd found that approximated his experiences flying a plane. Like he had in the Air Force.

They called it *compartmentalization* in the flying world. Ruth called it *being in the now*.

Regardless, Zahn liked it. But it was hard to get into *the now* when you were late…and thinking about a strange man watching children in a playground outside.

Yoga closed with five minutes of cross-legged breathing exercises where Zahn hoped to achieve that *presence*.

Which didn't happen today.

Zahn passed Roger and his Chevy Blazer on the way back to his truck. He gave the young man a nod, and this time Roger noticed him and waved. Unlocking his truck, Zahn heard a female voice calling from the pickleball court gate.

"Tyler."

Zahn turned and saw Maddie Bodin latching the gate behind her. She walked to his truck with a smile on her face.

"What've you been up to?"

"Not a lot. Got my daughter in town, so staying busy." Zahn paused. "Got a chance to meet Roger this morning."

Maddie's expression froze. "Did he do something? How did you meet Roger?"

"No, no." Zahn tilted his head toward the playground. "He's just sitting out in his car. I thought maybe he was trying to find the yoga class, so I introduced myself."

A wave of relief crossed Maddie's face. "Oh, thank God." She wrinkled her nose at Zahn. "Roger gave me a ride this morning. My car's in for a tune-up and oil change."

She paused. "Family can be a challenge, you know."

Zahn smiled. "I know. But you're lucky if you've got a nephew who can take care of you when you have appointments."

"Oh, you have no idea. I'm paying Roger to run me around today. Not that he wouldn't do it for me anyway, but he needs the money, and I don't want to just hand cash to him, you know?" She went on. "Roger can't hold a job. He's got, how would you say it, special challenges. I mean, the boy couldn't finish high school, but wrote the code for the school counselor's computerized scheduling program and filmed the school play. He can talk to a seven-year-old all day long, but can't look an adult in the eyes."

"That's not uncommon these days. The whole 'socially challenged' thing."

"Well, my sister is an enabler that way. She still pays for his phone and pays the internet bills, if you can believe it? And Roger's like mid-thirties, you know? I mean, on the one hand, I can understand, because he can't afford to pay it himself. And she wants him to be able to call her if he has an emergency. She pays for his mobile home over at Riverside, as well. You know how it is when it's your kid. You can't ever completely give up on them. You keep hoping they will come around."

Zahn nodded, as if he understood. He didn't. His daughter was a mature young adult. His son was dead.

But Maddie didn't need to hear about that.

"Maybe he will." He nodded his head, then repeated. "Maybe he will."

"That's what Molly, his mom, says. I have my doubts, though. There's just something off about Roger. The only people he relates to are children. And that's just strange." She paused. "I mean it's one thing if you have your own kids, and you're like Super Dad, and you're great with other kids, right? But it's a worry if a parent sees their kid just talking or hanging out with a thirty-something-year-old man who doesn't have a job. You know what I mean?"

Zahn nodded his head. He knew exactly what Maddie meant. Same gut feeling he'd felt when he first saw Roger.

"If only my niece hadn't left," Maddie said. "She was like the one person who he connected with. After she left, Roger kind of went downhill."

Zahn remained silent, unsure what to say.

"Oh, it's not her fault. She went to college. Got married. She's got a life to live too." Maddie sighed. "I don't know why I felt like I had to saddle you with my family drama. Sorry. You're a great listener."

"Feel free to unload any time. You're not alone with the family stuff. What did that Russian author say? '*Every family is dysfunctional in its own way?*' Or something like that?"

"You're a reader? I'm impressed," Maddie said. "It was Tolstoy, from *Anna Karenina: 'each unhappy family is unhappy in its own way'*"

"I knew it was something like that. Anyway, you're not alone."

"No," Maddie said. "But I don't think it's going to get better."

Zahn said nothing, turning toward the Blazer parked across the street. He couldn't disagree with the woman. Something *was* off about Roger.

CHAPTER 26

Jefe turned to the back seat. "You excited?"

Janae said nothing.

"First time out of the stable? First time contributing to the team? Come on, Janae…how about a little enthusiasm?"

Jefe had hoped for some spunk from the girl. Hell, they'd found her alone on the side of a mountain. What nine-year-old ventures out by herself without some get up and go? Some initiative. But now, nothing. Maybe Nicole and Rachel were bringing her down. Or, maybe he didn't know shit about motivating young girls.

No more Mr. Nice Guy. Business was business.

"Hey," Jefe barked. "I'm talking to you."

Janae sat up in the rear seat and turned her blindfolded eyes toward him.

"Enthusiasm. You got it? My guys are paying money to film young girls who want to be there. It's cutthroat out there in the big leagues. Ladies are fighting tooth and nail to get on film. Here I am, putting opportunity right in your lap and you're treating it like it's a chore." Jefe checked the road and glanced back at Janae. "I don't care if you want to be here or not. Fake it until you make it. You understand?"

He flashed to the journal back at the house, and what the one who left had written:

I'm a tiny fish in a big ocean out here. The only way to survive is to fake it until you make it.

Janae nodded her head.

"I'm not sure you do," Jefe said, glancing at the girl in the rearview mirror. "I can tell you this: Rachel pulled the 'dead fish' routine on her last shoot. The guy showed me part of the footage. She sat there and moped for the entire time. I ended up giving him his money back." He coughed and glanced back at Janae. "Should've put her in the hole." He paused. "Are you interested in the hole, Janae? You going to be Happy Girl or Dead Fish Girl?"

Janae dipped her chin. "Happy Girl."

"That's right," Jefe said. "What name are you going to use?"

"Janae?" Jefe heard the uncertainty in her voice

"No. I thought Nicole and Rachel gave you the brief. You need to pick a name. We call it a stage name."

Jefe checked the mirror and watched the girl think.

"Annabeth," she said. Jefe stared at the mirror, nodding at the timbre of confidence in her voice.

"Fine. And what do we call the cameraman?"

"Boss."

"You got it."

Jefe pulled his truck into a mobile home park and worked his way to the rear of the property. The road wound between several trailers before dead-ending in a cul-de-sac with a long green trailer on the far side. A man with shoulder-length hair sat on the steps. Jefe parked next to a Chevy Blazer in the driveway. The man gave a weak smile, stood up, and shuffled toward the truck.

"You stay here for a moment...Annabeth," Jefe said, reaching behind him and patting Janae on the knee. "Don't be forgetting the names. Annabeth. Boss. You remember?"

Janae nodded.

Jefe exited the truck and met the man halfway across a gravel-strewn yard.

"Morning, Roger," he said with a head tilt, trying to catch the man's eyes.

Roger thrust out his hand, then dropped it.

"Is she in there?" He raised on his toes and looked over Jefe at the truck.

"Hold your horses there. Let's review the rules." He looked closely at Roger. "You remember the rules?"

"I remember."

"Well, let's hear them," Jefe said. He wrinkled his nose. Roger sported some kind of aftershave or something. He smelled like a high school sophomore on his first prom.

"Rule number one: I can watch her, and I can film her, but I can't touch her." Roger looked at Jefe for approval.

Jefe nodded.

"Rule number two: Don't ask her questions about where she lives or—" Roger scrunched up his nose.

"Anything about her past," Jefe prompted.

"Right, no questions about where she's from." Roger's face fell. "I think I forgot the last one."

"Don't use my name," Jefe said.

"I—I don't know your name," Roger stuttered.

"Right. Keep it that way," Jefe said. "The girl's name is Annabeth. I verified the money dropped into the account. You've got two hours." Jefe turned, scanning the two neighboring trailers. "Anybody going to see her go inside?"

"No," Roger said. "They work. No one's there but the dogs." Roger gave a staccato laugh. "And they don't talk."

Jefe nodded. "Let's do this."

He walked over and opened the truck door, reaching for Janae's blindfold. "Let's go, Annabeth."

Janae slid from the truck and squinted at Roger. Jefe looked from Janae to Roger and saw the man sporting an eager grin.

"Hello, Annabeth." Roger edged sideways, allowing Janae a path up the stairs without touching him.

Janae looked at her feet.

"Answer him," Jefe said.

"Hello, Boss," Janae said, glancing at Roger, then back at her feet.

Roger grinned wider, looking from Janae to Jefe, and back at Janae. Jefe nodded and gave him a thin smile.

Going to work out just fine.

Roger followed Janae up the steps, closing the trailer door behind them.

Jefe glanced at his watch. Two hours starts now.

CHAPTER 27

Janae moved across the linoleum-covered entryway as Boss closed the trailer door. The room smelled just like the man behind her. Like some kind of men's perfume. The living room was a mess. Funny, her hands shook and her heart pounded, but all she could think of was that the girls kept the stable neater than this.

A low brown couch butted up against a picture window dimmed with threadbare curtains. The glass coffee table carried a layer of dust; Janae could see remains of a cleaning effort, but circles of dried liquid crusted the surface. Probably from beer cans. She'd seen Uncle Mike leave the same stains with his Budweiser cans back at his house.

A small pink travel case sat atop the table, and Boss saw her looking at it.

"Want to see the toys?" Boss strode to the case. He looked straight at her and spoke with a confidence that had been missing when Janae watched him with Jefe. Boss held it up so she could read the front.

Safari Barbie.

Really?

Janae's last Barbie session lay three years in the past, roughly the same time she'd discovered Hermione, Annabeth, and the worlds of magic and adventure. Even before that, she hadn't quite fit in with her friends during Barbie play dates, always turning Beautician Barbie into Ninja Barbie or making the pink Cadillac into a demolition derby entry.

She inhaled and noticed her fingers had stopped shaking. Playing with Boss's Barbies was better than the scenarios she had imagined. What did Jefe say? *Fake it until you make it.*

Boss handed her the case. "Here. You set it up on the table, and I'll get you something to drink? Does that sound okay?"

Janae could hear Boss's breathing getting louder as he stood next to her. Was he nervous? Like she was?

"What would you like to drink?"

"Water," Janae said, walking over to the couch and sitting with the Barbie case in her lap.

While Boss bumped around the small kitchen for a glass, she opened the travel case and examined the contents.

A tan Barbie in khakis.

Two more sets of clothes.

A small plastic pair of binoculars.

Barbie was ready for the safari. At least *she* knew what was next.

Boss nodded across the Formica counter toward the couch.

"The Jeep is over there. You know, what she rides in." He brought Janae a glass of water.

She reached over and placed the plastic car on the table. Bending Barbie at the waist, Janae sat her inside the Jeep, draping the small binoculars over the doll's head.

Boss sat on the opposite end of the sofa. He watched her and said nothing.

Janae sipped the water, swirling the cool liquid in her parched mouth before swallowing. She stood, holding the Jeep and the Barbie, and walked to the center of the cramped living room. Lowering herself to her knees, she ran the car over the carpet. Forward two feet. Reverse two feet.

"Like this?" Maybe he liked watching her play.

Boss leaned forward, tense. "That's good, Annabeth. Just like that." His voice trembled. "Why don't you go back to the bathroom and get ready, while I set up the gear?"

Janae's heart sunk. No. No. No.

"What do you mean 'get ready?'" Her hands began trembling again as she realized this was the part Nicole had been talking about.

Boss stared at Janae. "You know what to do."

CHAPTER 28

US Marshal Randall Williams had been in town almost a week before he gave Zahn a call.

"Tyler, it's Randall."

Zahn laughed.

Randall. Not *Randy.*

Zahn knew Williams didn't like *Randy.* Unless, of course, it was Kristee he was talking to, and then he'd answer to Randy, Rander-boy, the Rand-meister, or whatever.

"Randall," Zahn said. "Thought you'd be too busy with the case to remember your old friends. What's up?"

"Coffee. You, Perez, and me, down at the Elkhead. Can you make it tomorrow at seven?"

"Hmm. Let me check my schedule."

"Yeah, right," Williams said. "You're old, retired, and bored. See you tomorrow."

The three men gathered the next morning in the back corner of the coffee shop, Perez with his quiche, Zahn with the house black coffee, and Williams sampling a cranberry-orange scone with a double latte.

"You think you might need a little sugar with that?" Perez needled Williams.

"No, both the scone and coffee already have sugar—" Williams eyed the two men. "Oh. That's sarcasm, right?" He smiled, white teeth gleaming from his ebony face. "Got it." He set the scone on his plate. "You're probably wondering why I asked you two here today."

Perez cocked his head. "Not really. You don't have any other friends."

"Kristee's busy?" Zahn laughed and reached for his coffee.

"You know, after a year I had almost forgotten the joy of conversation with you two. It's coming back, though. Like I hardly left." Williams took a pull from his latte. "I wanted to talk a bit about the missing girl case—the one I'm out here for."

"Janae Longmont? You guys making any progress?" Zahn returned his cup to the table.

Perez winced and Zahn looked from him to Williams.

"Rick's right," Williams said. "Not much. I got a couple of CBI guys giving me a hand in this thing, but we've sort of hit a dead end."

"No leads at all?"

Williams sighed. "You start with family, you know. Statistically, it's going to be someone the girl knows, and since she was out visiting from another state, that narrows down the choices. Either one of her parents, or her aunt or uncle."

"The parents are still here," Perez said to Zahn. "Randall talked to neighbors back in Oklahoma. Marriage appears to be sound. No problems that anyone knows about between Janae and her folks." He shoved a forkful of quiche into his mouth.

"No ransom note. No financial issues. Parents are in plain sight and the girl's gone—so it doesn't look like it's the folks," Williams said.

Zahn turned to Perez. "What about the porn you guys found on the uncle's computer? Anything with that?"

Perez continued chewing for a moment, then swallowed. "Nothing. I mean at first glance you have a missing girl, and then you find that stuff—kind of related to girls, you know—and you think, well, hell, there's got to be a connection. But we can't find one." He looked from Williams to Zahn. "We looked around on his internet usage to see if maybe he had a ring of guys or some sort of Dark Web group, but came up empty. Just a standard porn site, and he's paying for it off a pre-paid card from Wal-Mart—probably so his wife wouldn't find out."

Zahn's gaze wandered past Perez to the window where he watched Adam Linzmeier—off duty in civilian clothes—exit the outdoor gear shop across the street.

He turned his eyes back to Perez. "What about Linzmeier's theory, the church folks up at Beyond Adventure?" He glanced to the window as Linzmeier stopped on the sidewalk between the restaurant and the row of diagonally parked cars on the street. Linzmeier stood talking to a man Zahn didn't recognize, the stranger's hands moving up and down as Linzmeier's eyes widened.

"Rick talked to me about that," Williams said. "I went up there and interviewed a few folks, but got nothing." He looked closely at Zahn. "Rick told me you've been spending some time up there. What's your sense of the place?"

Zahn glanced back at Williams. "Yeah, the whole 'no medicine, prayer is the cure' mantra, that's pretty out there for me," he said. "But that's a personal thing. Same as you, I got nothing from my time there making me think they're involved."

Movement across the street caught Zahn's attention again, and he rose slightly in his chair as he saw the man talking to Linzmeier throw a roundhouse right at him.

"What—?" Perez looked puzzled.

"Looks like they need you across the street." Zahn pointed. Perez and Williams turned as the man swung again at Linzmeier. The police officer crossed his arms in front of his face and backed into the corner between the door and the display windows.

"Holy shit," Perez said, striding across the floor toward the exit. Zahn and Williams stood and followed Perez out the door.

Zahn wondered how this would go down. Perez wore his sheriff's uniform, but this was Buena Vista Police jurisdiction. And Linzmeier was obviously off duty. *How does that work? An off-duty assault in your own jurisdiction?*

As Perez checked the street for traffic, Zahn watched the man crowd Linzmeier into the corner, flailing punches against his ribs and yelling.

"Pervert." He drove a fist into Linzmeier's right side.

Thunk.

Linzmeier made no sound.

"Probably a molester too." The man used his opposite fist and drove it under Linzmeier's left arm.

Thunk.

Linzmeier grunted.

Perez approached the man from behind, Zahn and Williams following. "Sir, that's enough. Step back."

The man didn't turn his head.

Perez stepped forward and slapped his hand on the man's shoulder, pulling him from one side to face the street. The man turned, swinging a right at Perez. Zahn saw recognition light up in the man's eyes mid-swing. Not that he recognized Perez, just a glimmer of knowledge in his eyes as he saw the deputy sheriff's uniform, hat, and weapon. Amazing what the brain can process in less than a second.

The man's arm dropped to his side, and he stood, shaking, trying to catch his breath. Linzmeier looked at the man and Perez through crossed arms.

"I didn't fight back," Linzmeier said, dropping his arms. "You saw it. I just let him hit me."

"What the hell are you doing, man?" Perez turned to Linzmeier's attacker.

"This is the son of a bitch who tried to molest my daughter." The man sucked in a breath. "Law and order, my ass. I'm showing him how we deal with perverts in this town."

Perez eyed the man, then shifted his gaze to Linzmeier. The officer's head shook from side to side.

He returned his attention to the man. "You're Alyssa Peterson's father, sir?"

"See? The whole damn town has heard about my little girl, thanks to this asshole."

Zahn wondered how Perez would handle this one. Hadn't the girl gone to Linzmeier with an allegation against her father? Who was in the wrong here?

"What's your name?"

"Chuck. Chuck Peterson."

"Listen up here, Mr. Peterson," Perez said. "I'm familiar with the situation with your daughter. And I know it's being investigated through the proper channels. Now you and your actions—? That's not part of the proper channels. That's called assault, and that's why I'm arresting you." He reached for the cuffs hooked to his belt.

"Rick, no," Linzmeier said from behind Peterson.

"What?"

"I'm not pressing charges," Linzmeier said. Zahn noticed he looked shaky, as well. "I mean you're spot on about Chuck here being out of line, but I understand how he could have the misperception—"

Peterson whirled around and raised his arm toward Linzmeier. "Misperception, hell, you son of a bitch. You sat alone in a room with my daughter trying to get her to say bad things about me."

"Mr. Peterson," Perez barked. "You drop that arm now, or I'm taking you in. How do you want it?"

Peterson twisted his head toward Perez and dropped his arm to his side. Then he turned and fixed a glare at Linzmeier, shaking his head.

"Ain't over," Peterson said, and spit on the sidewalk near Linzmeier's feet. He turned to Perez and the small crowd of people gawking from the sidewalk.

"Screw this," he muttered and walked away.

Perez drilled Linzmeier. "You sure?"

Linzmeier nodded. "I'm innocent. That's why I didn't fight back. I'm not going to lose my job."

Zahn watched Alyssa's father walk away, then looked at Linzmeier's heaving shoulders. He caught Williams's questioning stare.

Something's off here.

CHAPTER 29

Daria assumed the whole point of a relationship was having a partner with whom you could talk. Sharing the special things that happened to each of you. Someone to lean on when life got rough.

Sitting in the living room recliner, waiting for Kevin's morning visit, gave her plenty of time to ponder. To be honest, she hadn't had a lot of relationships. She was always moving as a military brat. High school had been a blur after her parents divorced; she seemed to remember far more concern about her mother's mental health than in chasing boys. Jacob's death lingered over everything, like when a motel room converted from smoking to non-smoking. You still knew.

They'd talked about relationships in the church youth group she attended while in high school—the man and the woman, their respect for one another, and their love of God, serving as pillars supporting the relationship. Each pillar strong enough to carry the relationship on its own if the others showed signs of stress. But mostly bearing the loads together.

Kevin came and saw her twice a day, right after her fall. By the third day, it was routine. They had just begun to get to know one another before the accident. Now, after hours of conversation in the living room, she felt like she had known Kevin for years. They discussed favorite foods—dried bananas for her, brisket for Kevin, first loves—Daria's high school boyfriend, Nick, whom she lost contact with after he joined the Navy, and Kevin's Angie Diaz who practically left him at the altar to pursue a career in publishing in New York City. No topic seemed to remain off limits.

So, when Kevin didn't show up on the fourth day after the accident, it was odd. She'd never asked for daily visits. It was just something he'd started doing. And she liked it.

He didn't come the next day either. And he didn't call. When she texted a *hey you,* she never got a response. Now that was strange, strange enough to put a pang in her gut. But she wasn't going to call him.

Today was day three with no visit, and when noon came and went, Daria made a decision. She climbed from the recliner, figured out how to wrap a jacket around her sling, and headed outdoors. She wasn't on a search for Kevin. No. She would cut through the woods to Beyond Adventure and check on the horses. She'd wanted to go see Gus, anyway. It wasn't his fault she'd made the horse take that trail, and she needed to let Gus know they were still friends.

At the stables, Daria poked around, trying to appear as if she were looking for Gus. Elliot walked in on her as she scanned the stalls.

"Kevin's not working today, Daria," he said. "How's the shoulder doing?"

"Hi." Daria turned and smiled. "The shoulder's good. I'm good, thanks." She paused. "How do you know I'm not looking for you?"

Elliot chuckled.

"Actually, I'm looking for Gus. Is he around?"

Elliot dipped his head toward the door behind her. "Out in the pasture. You're welcome to head out there."

"Thanks," Daria turned for the door, then spun back to Elliot. "Will Kevin be here later?"

Elliot looked directly at Daria, then lowered his eyes to her feet. "Kevin's not working at Beyond Adventure for a little while." He looked back up at Daria and raised his eyebrows. "He'll be back, though, I figure."

Daria stared at Elliot. Something was going on. Something wasn't right.

And Gabe didn't want to talk about it.

Daria crossed her good arm over her sling. Elliot stared back at Daria.

"Okay, it's not like the word isn't getting out, anyway," Elliot said with a sigh. "They suspended Kevin from Beyond Adventure pending an investigation."

"Investigation of what?"

"An investigation of inappropriate behavior," Elliot said in a softer voice.

Daria stepped closer to Elliot. "You mean for taking me out on the horse ride? And me getting hurt? I thought that ended up being a non-issue? It was Kevin's day off."

"Not that," Elliot said, shaking his head. "Something else. Two of our campers—two young ladies—have accused Kevin of inappropriate behavior while he was alone with them."

Daria's mouth dropped open. "Like what kind of behavior?"

"Daria, the details aren't important, what's important is to figure out why they would say such a thing. You know—"

"Just tell me what they said."

Elliot stared at Daria. "They said he exposed himself to them while they were on a horseback ride. During a break, they said."

"How old are the girls?"

"Like eleven or twelve," Elliot said. "And of course Kevin denies it, but—"

"But you can't ignore a sexual harassment or sexual assault claim. I'm a college female, Gabe Elliot, which makes me a Title IX expert. We all know this stuff." She paused. "Here's my question, though."

"What's that?"

"You know Kevin's been visiting me every day. Checking up on me and stuff?"

Elliot nodded.

"I don't know if he's mentioned it, but we've gotten kind of close."

Elliot smiled and said, "Oh, he's quite smitten. I'm guessing you feel the same way?"

Daria nodded. "I do. Or I did—"

"Daria, you don't believe for a second—"

"It's not that. It's the fact that this is going on, and he hasn't told me about it. Daily visits. Texting back and forth for almost a week. And now he runs into a bit of trouble, and I'm the last one to find out? That's a great way to kick off a relationship." Daria felt heat rising in her cheeks. "If he's hiding his troubles from me, what else is he hiding? And I shouldn't have to find it all out from you."

"I'm sure he's embarrassed—"

"I'm sure he is…but hiding it from me is the way to end our relationship before it even starts." Tears filled Daria's eyes and she brushed them away with her hand. "It makes me question his judgment." She sniffed. "And character."

Daria strode for the door, without looking back at Elliot. "It makes me think I don't know what to believe about what happened with those girls."

CHAPTER 30

"Where've you been?" Zahn tried to hide the edge of concern in his voice.

He had walked in the door, ten minutes earlier, expecting to see Daria propped in her chair, reluctantly working through a series she'd started about the British royal family. He knew she felt trapped in the house. And he knew she was fighting the pain without pills. But she hadn't ventured outside since returning from the hospital, so, the silent house surprised him.

Zahn had checked her room, and sighed in relief at the still empty suitcase leaning against the dresser. She hadn't gone back to her mother's house or to school. He wasn't sure why that possibility had run through his head. The whole daily schedule that had driven her crazy had lightened up after the accident. She wasn't still mad about that, was she?

He knew he shouldn't worry about his 20-year-old daughter leaving the house. She was a big girl. But things were strange around here lately. His idyllic small town was putting off a strange vibe, and it made him nervous.

A missing girl. Janae, not Daria.

The lurker—he knew Roger was off somehow—at the park.

Linzmeier and the situation with the student at school.

Not like these things all related to each other. They couldn't. But it was still an odd time around the home front.

So he was a little unnerved at Daria's absence. Probably not missing. But not home. He noticed her jacket and boots were no longer stationed by the front door, which gave him a bit of relief. She must have felt good enough for a walk. He put on his jacket and left the house. A hundred yards later, he spied Daria ducking through the fence, heading his way.

"Hey, Dad," she said. "I was over at the stables talking to Gabe Elliot."

Zahn smiled and fell in next to Daria, walking between the pines back toward the house. Questions ran through his head: *Are you sure you feel well enough to do that? Do you think it's smart to take your first walk outside after your injury all by yourself? Do you know how worried I was?*

Zahn said nothing.

Daria looked sideways. "How was your day?"

"Good," Zahn said. "Well, more like interesting." He told Daria about the dad attacking Linzmeier downtown.

"So do you think Linzmeier did it?"

"Did what?"

"You know, something inappropriate with the girl?"

Zahn glanced at Daria. "That's a loaded word…'inappropriate.' Do I think he was incredibly stupid for letting himself ever be alone in a room with a minor? Yes, I do."

"But the other stuff?"

"It doesn't feel right," Zahn said. "I don't even like Linzmeier that well. And I know you don't after that stunt when he pulled you over. Kind of a crude guy. But do I think he's stupid enough to do something like that at a school, in uniform, with a young girl? Nope."

"Well, then why would a girl make something like that up?"

Zahn thought about that. Why would she?

"It's hard for me to believe a girl that age would lie out of cruelty. Trying to get an adult in trouble," he finally said. "I mean, either something happened, or it didn't. If you go with the assumption that it didn't, then you have to ask why a young person would say it did." Zahn turned to Daria. "Why do you think someone would say something happened if it didn't?"

"Maybe a cry for help?" Daria suggested. "Something going on at school or at home the kid can't talk about, so they do something else to draw attention to them. Maybe hoping the attention will make the other thing stop?"

"Well, now, it's interesting you say that."

"Why?"

"Because that was why Linzmeier said he met the girl. She said her dad was doing something inappropriate."

"Are you guys looking at that?"

"I'm not looking at anything," Zahn said. "But Rick Perez is keeping me in the loop."

Daria glanced at Zahn. "Has he said anything about stuff going on up at Beyond Adventure?"

"Like what? We've had some conversations about the missing girl and the church up there, but there has been nothing to point that way. Why? Have you heard something?"

Daria sniffed and stopped in her tracks. Zahn pulled up short, keeping his eyes on her.

"It's Kevin. They're investigating him for inappropriate behavior around minors. Like what you're talking about with the police officer."

"What? Like being alone with them, or did they say he did something?"

Zahn watched a tear squeeze from his daughter's eye.

"I can't...I don't know—"

He wrapped his arms around Daria and pulled her close.

"Honey, I'm sorry. So sorry."

Daria pushed back and looked into Zahn's eyes. "But what are you sorry for?"

"What—"

"Are you sorry for me because you think Kevin is some kind of pervert? Or are you sorry for the girls because of what happened? Or are you sorry for Kevin because they accused him of something he didn't do? Which is it, Dad? What are you sorry for?"

Zahn kept his hands on Daria's shoulders and looked into her eyes. It was none of those reasons. "I guess I'm sorry about not knowing how to fix the way you feel right now," he said. "Do you know the details of what allegedly happened?"

"No. Gabe said the girls accused Kevin of…of…showing himself." She looked up at Zahn. "There's no way, Dad. Do you believe that?"

"I believe you're usually an excellent judge of character." Zahn paused. "How long have you known Kevin?"

Daria stepped back, and Zahn's arms dropped to his side. "Less than two weeks. But wouldn't I know? I mean, if he was weird that way? Wouldn't I be able to tell?"

"I don't know." Zahn sighed. "What does Kevin say about the whole thing?"

Daria started walking toward the house again. "That's the thing. He's gone totally silent on me. I wouldn't have even known if I hadn't talked to Gabe today." She turned to Zahn. "Doesn't exactly inspire confidence in his innocence, does it? When he doesn't even tell me and just hides away. I mean, did he think I wouldn't find out?"

"Do you want me to check it out, Daria? See if I can get the details?"

Daria looked at her father and slowly shook her head. "No. Please don't." She stared at Zahn. "I'm going to look him in the eyes and ask him why he's keeping these allegations to himself. Not telling me about it."

Zahn tilted his head. Daria might be an adult, but letting her confront this issue alone, with Kevin, felt wrong. "Daria, I'm not sure—"

"I am," Daria said. "You can track me on your cellphone, or have Gabe Elliot there—whatever makes you comfortable, but I'm talking to him." She sniffed. "And after I get his explanation, I'm going home. To Mom."

"Home?"

"It's not you, Dad. Well, maybe a little with your scheduling issues and such. It's this." She raised the sling on her injured arm. "And him." She tossed her head toward the fence surrounding Beyond Adventure. "I've had it."

CHAPTER 31

Daria stared at her cellphone screen. She wouldn't see Kevin alone. As bold as she sounded—*I'm going to look him in the eyes and ask him*— she wasn't actually comfortable with that plan. And she knew her dad wouldn't be either. She had finally agreed to let her father call ahead and work it out with Elliot. Daria and Kevin would meet to talk at the stable. Elliot didn't need to listen, but at least he'd be close. She still trusted Kevin—but this plan would keep her dad happy. And Elliot, as well. Elliot was…avuncular.

Daria smiled at the word and knew her English 101 instructor from freshman year would too. *Friendly, kind, or helpful—like an uncle.* No one in her life fit those qualities. These brief interactions with Gabe Elliot—on the horse, in the stable—had changed that. He said little. But when he said something, it usually was worth a listen.

And her dad liked him too. As Daria rebuilt her relationship with her father, one thing she noticed was that he chose his friends carefully, and he chose them well.

They needed Elliot to contact Kevin, anyway. Daria still had gotten no text replies from the young man, and her phone calls went unanswered. Her father had given her Elliot's number, and she called him to find out how to reach Kevin.

"Tell him to 'man up,'" she had said. "Tell him I know he didn't do it, but the longer he goes without talking to me, the less and less conviction I have."

Elliot had chuckled. "Well, that ought to light a fire under him." He paused. "Let's meet about five, okay? Kevin's not supposed to interact with any of the campers, and I got a passel of them out here riding until 4:45. Does that work for you?"

"I'll be there." She punched off her phone.

Five hours later, as the sun neared the tips of the Collegiates, Daria adjusted her sling and walked from the house to the stable. The pain had almost disappeared, but the joint remained stiff. No horseback riding any time soon, but at least she could get off the recliner and away from the TV. She quickened her step, curious to find out if she had misjudged this young man who had occupied her thoughts for the last week.

Daria walked into the stable and ran into Elliot, currying the horses they had ridden that afternoon. The scent of sweat, straw, and manure still took her back to her Abilene horse days—and, more recently, to her first days with Kevin.

"Daria." Elliot nodded his head toward the aisle of stalls. "He's down there."

Daria walked down the aisle to the open stall door. Rounding the corner, she saw Kevin leaning against the stall wall. His boot pushed at a clump of straw, his eyes tracking its progress. He had definitely heard her coming.

She paused at the stall door, watching him, and waiting for him to look at her. Kevin kept his eyes on the ground. Daria waited. Finally, he lifted his head. Tears squeezed from his eyes.

Daria said nothing. If Kevin had reached out, made any sort of effort…had acknowledged their relationship. Anything, and she would have initiated this conversation. But falsely accused or not, Kevin's refusal to include Daria put the ball in his court.

Kevin spread his arms out to his side. "Well? Aren't you going to say anything?"

Daria didn't.

Kevin stared at her, then sighed. "I didn't do it. I think you know me well enough to know I didn't do it."

Daria exhaled. Her head had always known he didn't do it. Their time together had been short, but intense. Deep and personal conversations, as opposed to long kisses and teen-age groping. Kevin's words validated what she already knew, and a weight lifted from her heart. This wall dividing them would never have existed if he would have just called her and told her what he was telling her now.

"Do you believe me?"

Daria stared back at Kevin, expressionless, and nodded. "I do. And I think it's terrible you're being accused. It's not right." She stopped nodding. "But how dare you run into trouble and just shut me out? What kind of friend does that?"

"But—"

"I don't want to hear it. There's no excuse. They accused you of something bad that you didn't do...and then you followed it by ignoring me. Leaving me out. Shutting me down."

"Because I can't bear the thought that people see me as some kind of monster." Kevin clenched his fingers into fists. "You. My parents. My church. Do you know how hard it is to have people lose all trust and respect for you overnight?"

Daria's eyes softened. "I don't. And I'm sorry you're dealing with that. But bottling it up inside? I just don't see how that helps you." She moved her good hand to her hip. "And it certainly doesn't help me."

Kevin nodded. "I know. When Gabe called me, and when he told me you were insisting on seeing me? I realized that what I'd done—or hadn't done—with you was wrong. I mean, here you are, hearing me out, asking for my side of the story." Kevin shook his head. "I'm so sorry, Daria. I should have come to you from the beginning." He looked back at the clump of hay at the toe of his boot.

"Why would the girls say you did it if you didn't do it? I've told you I believe you, so that means the girls either misinterpreted something or are lying."

Kevin raised his eyes. "I don't know. Absolutely nothing happened out of the ordinary on the ride. I mean, we don't take campers out of sight of the stable unless we have two or more adults. So, I wasn't even alone with them, really." Kevin looked toward the barn door. "Maybe a couple hundred yards out there in the field. I found out what they said about an hour after I got back."

"What were you talking about? Are either of them having problems in camp? Why would they lie?"

Kevin dropped his eyes to his boots, then raised them back to Daria. "We were talking about horses." He spread his hands at his side. "I have no idea why they said this."

"So what happens now?"

"They can't let me work. They can't let me interact with the campers. Not until the investigation finishes," Kevin said. "Which makes sense, right?"

"Guilty until proven innocent?"

"Right. But if you look at it from a parent's point of view, let's say it took two weeks to complete the investigation, and at the end you found out the adult was guilty. Can you imagine the fallout if that adult could have interacted with kids during those two weeks?" Kevin shook his head. "They'd sue this place and shut it down within days. So, I guess I can understand where they are coming from."

"But two weeks?" Daria said. "I mean, it's basically your word against their word, right? How long can it take?"

"Right. And there are two of them and one of me. And let's say they recant. I still have this stigma hanging over me. I'm not sure I can work here anymore."

"You can't just walk away. That'll look like you're guilty."

"That's not the only reason I can't walk away," Kevin said. "I'm required to stay here until the investigation is complete."

Daria stared at Kevin. "What about worst case? What if they find you guilty? The girls don't change their story? Will you go to jail?"

Kevin stared back. "I don't think so. They'd investigate my past. Find nothing. Charge me with a misdemeanor, and fire me. But that's not the worst part."

"What is the worst part?"

"It would be on my records, Daria. Sex offender with a history of exposing himself to kids. How do you live with that?"

"What about a lawyer?"

"Right. My boss mentioned that, as did the cop who came up and talked to me." He looked at his feet, then returned his eyes to Daria. "I could. It would wipe out my savings and, in the end, it would still be my word against the girls." He cocked his head. "If it ends up sticking, I might hire one to get the misdemeanor off my record." He paused. "What would you do?"

Daria didn't answer right away. He'd already resigned himself to losing this battle. *He's giving up.*

She pictured her own reaction if she read a story in the newspaper about a counselor exposing himself to young girls at church camp. She'd read, shake her head, and say *lock him up.* She'd assume he was guilty.

That was what was facing Kevin. Unless the girls changed their story, everyone would judge Kevin guilty, and convict him through the court of public opinion.

Daria was still furious. She hadn't forgiven him either. But this? It wasn't fair.

He had to do something. He couldn't just sit back and hope to be absolved. It wouldn't happen.

She looked up at Kevin.

"You need a lawyer."

CHAPTER 32

"You ever questioned how well you know someone?" Elliot kicked at a weed beneath the fence.

Zahn cocked his head. "You said Kevin was a good kid. You stood here and told me my daughter would be safe with him."

Elliot nodded. "And I'd do it again. You know why?"

Zahn shook his head.

"Because from the outside looking in, they don't come any better than our young Kevin here," Elliot stared at Zahn. "A heart for the Lord. Compassion toward others. And a damn good work ethic."

"What do you mean from the outside…?"

The two men leaned against the fence in the dusk, watching the horses eat. Zahn remained shaken from his conversation with Daria that afternoon and was searching for answers. She'd stormed in, told him Kevin didn't do it, then disappeared to the guest room before he could question her further. He'd tapped on her door and gotten only a brief reply.

"Later, Dad. I'm going to need your advice on this, but I need a moment."

Had the real danger in Daria's visits to Beyond Adventure been much more serious than a broken collarbone? Was she going back to her mother's place because of Kevin? Or because of Zahn?

Before coming to see Elliot, Zahn had spent the afternoon at the house, using a trowel and a ladder to clean out his gutters after the winter. Anything to distract himself from everything going on. And it gave him time to think.

The allegations against Kevin most likely hadn't risen to law enforcement level...yet. Private matter on private property with no claims of actual contact. If Zahn took it to the authorities, the pressure and intensity would spin up, with the police looking at associations between Kevin, Beyond Adventure, and the Janae Longmont case.

But Daria thought Kevin was innocent. He trusted her judgment. Plus, how could Kevin kidnap a little girl when he spent his days working at the stables and his nights in a dorm room?

Nope. Zahn wasn't ready to talk to Perez. Maybe one of his other close friends? *Yeah, right. Who?*

He'd almost finished the gutters when he thought of Elliot over at the stable.

He'd hoped for straight answers about Kevin. Instead, Elliot was skirting the subject. Talking about external perceptions?

"The reason I said from the outside looking in?" Elliot said. "Is because you can never truly judge a man's, or a woman's, inner soul. You'd have to see it, and that's impossible."

"I'm not sure I under—"

"What's Daria doing right now?"

Zahn started. Did Elliot know something he didn't? Was Daria okay?

"She's at the house, probably packing up to leave. Why?"

"Let's do a hypothetical here," Elliot suggested. "Let's say you walked back to the house and stood outside the front window."

Zahn nodded, still unsure where Elliot was taking the conversation.

"Say you looked through the window and saw Daria crying. What would you assume made her cry?"

Zahn considered the scenario. "Well, based on this afternoon's conversation, I'd say she was crying about Kevin."

"But you couldn't be sure, right?"

"Well, I know she was pretty upset when I talked to her earlier."

Elliot moved his hand from the fence and slapped his thigh. "That's what I'm talking about. You're probably right. I mean, you know Daria, and you know she cares for Kevin, so you're judging her reaction based on her character." Elliot turned toward Zahn. "The thing is, you can't be certain. She might cry because she's afraid it's true. That Kevin did it. She might cry because now she's leaving you." Elliot lowered his voice. "You said you lost a boy—her brother, right?"

Zahn nodded.

"She could cry because she's about to lose another man from her life. One she thinks she might be falling in love with. But you can't know from watching. Either you ask her and believe what she tells you, or you continue to trust your judgment of her character," Elliot said. "Why did you allow Kevin to meet Daria over here today?"

"Because you were here. I trusted you to keep her safe."

"But you just met me last week, Tyler."

"I'm an excellent judge of character."

"Exactly. I've known Kevin for two years and feel the same way." Elliot smiled. "That's all we got to go on. Sometimes evil lurks behind the facade of character. But we'll never know unless we see it."

Zahn slowly nodded. He would not get a confirmation of Kevin's innocence from Elliot. Nor a confirmation of his guilt. Just a conversation about the enigma of human nature.

"So, how are you treating Kevin when you see him?"

"Same as I did before," Elliot said. "If he's found guilty, they'll fire him, and he and I won't work together any more. If he's found innocent and he stays here at Beyond Adventure, then we'll work together again." He paused. "You might as well take the same approach."

"You mean pretend it never happened? This is the guy seeing my daughter."

"Did he hurt her? Physically, I mean?"

"No."

"Did you ever hear of a budding post-teen romance without a little emotional angst?"

"No."

Elliot nodded. "There you have it. Let the church investigation do its thing and let the chips fall where they fall."

Zahn nodded without enthusiasm. This wasn't why he'd come to talk to Elliot. On his earlier visits, he'd left feeling wiser than when he had arrived.

He'd worried about the time Daria spent at the camp and was curious about what Linzmeier had said about the odd happenings with the church visits downtown. Elliot's sage advice on the religious views of the Christian Scientists and his keen observations on human nature had eased Zahn's concerns.

He didn't feel better this time. Elliot had switched from philosophy to a treatise on the unknowable mysteries of human behavior.

Screw that. All Zahn cared about was whether the young man got his kicks pulling his junk out of his pants, or whether he was the victim of false accusations.

"Gabe, I sure appreciate you listening. This whole thing's got me wound up, and I needed to talk."

Elliot nodded. "Not sure if I helped, but come by anytime."

Zahn nodded. He agreed—Elliot wasn't much help.

He trudged back to his house in the waning light, paralleling the fence for a half-mile before wedging between two strands of wire, and he thought about Elliot's words and his own response.

Back home, he decided on two things.

Elliot might be right about the unknowable nature of the human soul.

But Zahn knew the best way to deal with evil was to root it out.

It was time for action.

CHAPTER 33

Click.

The deadbolt sounded like the pump of a shotgun.

Clunk.

Janae pictured Jefe lowering the handle and latching the outer door.

She couldn't hear Jefe on the ladder, but she imagined the sound of his boots climbing the rungs.

Janae turned and faced the bunks. Rachel lay prone, eyes open, ignoring Janae. Nicole stood next to her own bunk, staring at Janae with a questioning look.

"Well?" Nicole's voice was quiet.

"I don't think we have to whisper," Janae said. "He's still walking back to wherever he goes, right?"

"What if he records us?"

"You mean like he bugged this place?" Janae had read about bugs in *Spy Kids* before watching the movie on TV. She hadn't really thought about that. Maybe Jefe listened to their conversations. She moved closer to Nicole.

"Well?" Nicole repeated.

"I was so scared."

"Did he break the rules?"

"No. But it was really weird." Janae grabbed Nicole's arm. "I never want to do it again."

"You look different," Nicole said, eyeing Janae.

"He didn't touch me."

"What about your clothes?"

Janae looked down at herself. "I took them off. I put them on. Here they are."

Nicole's eyes widened. "Where's your jacket?"

"What?"

"When you left, you were wearing your windbreaker."

Janae spread her hands and looked at herself, surprised at Nicole's question. Where *was* her coat?

She remembered taking it off when she went into the man's trailer. He did something with it. When it was time to go, he hadn't brought it back. Instead, he had just walked her to Jefe's car.

Jefe hadn't asked about her coat either. It wasn't very cold, and neither of the men wore jackets. They had stood at the car while Janae sat in the back, the cameraman smiling a little toward her. Jefe didn't smile.

Jefe asked her questions on the return drive.

Did he follow the rules?

Did he touch you?

Did he like you?

Yes. No. I think so, Janae had answered,

But no *where's your coat* question.

Janae raised her eyes to Nicole. "I left it at his house, I think. Do you think Jefe will be angry?" Her heart pounded, and she breathed faster. What if Jefe made her go back?

Nicole furrowed her brow. "Maybe," she said. "Or maybe he won't notice. Maybe you can get it next time. Or maybe he'll bring it back."

"Should I tell Jefe?"

"No!" Rachel looked at Janae for the first time since she returned. "He'll punish you. Don't tell him. There's an extra coat there, by the door." She pointed toward the exit. "You can use that."

Janae nodded.

It was warm in their cells, under the stable. That's what she thought of the space as—cells. Like in a jail.

So, she didn't need her jacket.

Maybe Jefe wouldn't notice.

Her breathing slowed, but she still felt a pang of fear in her belly. Funny how this morning all she had worried about was the cameraman. Now she all she could think about was a lost pink windbreaker.

CHAPTER 34

In through the nose, out through the mouth. Zahn was already relaxing, and he hadn't even arrived at class yet. Ruth's calm voice and breathing techniques always cleared Zahn's head. He needed to think.

Perez and Williams had shared a big bunch of nothing yesterday over coffee regarding Janae's disappearance. No progress. The Linzmeier episode across the street had interrupted their conversation. Then he got the double whammy at home: the allegations against Kevin and Daria's announcing she was leaving. Gabe Elliot's philosophical musings had provided no help. Things were going to shit around here, and he was tired of just watching it happen.

Buena Vista was too small for this. The missing girl was the biggest event of the year. Until an hour later when they had found kidnapped Kendall. Then Janae's uncle's porn, the Linzmeier thing, and Kevin's exposure allegations? Adults. Kids. It didn't add up.

Zahn slowed, passing between the elementary school and the police station. The police weren't really involved anymore in the Janae Longmont case, with US Marshal Williams in town and the case originating in the sheriff's jurisdiction. Most likely, they were wrapped up in the Linzmeier affair. Perez had mentioned yesterday that Linzmeier was on an indefinite suspension until they cleared up the school incident. Accelerating from the slow zone, Zahn heard the shrieks of the kids tearing through the playgrounds behind the school.

The thrift shop's empty parking lot flashed on the left. Not open until ten. Zahn did a double-take. Not quite empty either. A tan Blazer sat at the far end of the lot next to the pickleball courts.

He recognized it from the last yoga session. Roger. Maddie's nephew. Must be dropping Maddie off again.

Zahn tapped on his brakes and pulled into the next parking lot between the courts and the softball fields. Both the pickleball courts and the parking lot were empty. Roger wasn't dropping off Maddie. It must not be a pickleball day. He looked at the city playground across the street. Empty.

Zahn winced as he shut the truck door. He was seeing perverts everywhere. He walked toward the community center then halted halfway across the parking lot. The voices from the school playground echoed at his back.

Got to check it out.

He returned to the pickleball courts and skirted the perimeter to the trail system heading north. These trails wove between a Frisbee golf course, paralleling the river on one side and the school, and residential properties on the other. Zahn had jogged here before, dodging dogs on leashes, as well as the land mines they left behind. A popular spot for moms to walk after dropping kids off for school.

Three minutes up the trail, Zahn spotted Roger. He was also walking north, at a much slower pace. Ambling along with his head turned toward the playground and the screaming children. Staring at the kids like Zahn had expected.

And doing absolutely nothing illegal.

Hell, he knew local moms made the same walk, staring the same way at the children, trying to spot their own. Was the kid fitting in? Did the other kids tease him or her? How did my kid behave when out from under mom's thumb?

Zahn stopped in his tracks, shaking his head. Wasted trip. Roger was weird. Zahn needed to stop making him more than that.

He walked back toward his truck and then veered around the right side of the pickleball courts to the thrift shop parking lot. Roger's Blazer still sat alone, the only vehicle in the lot. Passing the SUV, a flash of pink caught Zahn's eye from the back seat. He cupped his hands next to his eyes to block the sun and pressed them against the rear window. A jacket lay across the rear seat.

A pink jacket.

No yoga today. Pretty circumstantial, but his gut wouldn't let it go.

He pulled out his cell phone and called Randall Williams. Marshal Williams didn't care a whit about circumstantial.

"I'll be there in less than five."

Zahn knew Williams had been investigating a bunch of dead ends, resulting in a bunch of nothing to advance the case. He reached the courts in four minutes.

Williams pulled his black SUV next to the older Blazer and got out. Zahn walked over to join him, pointing through the rear window.

"See that?"

"Yup."

"I don't know—probably a good reason for it."

"Yup," Williams said. "But that's not for me to decide without talking to this guy first. What did you say his name was?"

"Roger. He's related to a lady I talk with before my yoga class." He nodded his head across the street to the building just east of the police station. "Roger's her nephew." Zahn paused. "He doesn't talk so well with adults."

Williams nodded and raised an eyebrow. "Yoga, huh? You missing your class just for me?"

Zahn smiled until he spotted Roger coming back from the trails.

"Here's your chance to meet Roger. He's coming back."

Williams turned and looked at the young man walking toward the Blazer. Roger's head pivoted from Williams to Zahn and back to Williams. Zahn figured Roger knew something was wrong. Two men at his car, one of them six-foot three and Black. Not an everyday sight in Buena Vista.

Roger's eyes darted to Williams's black SUV with *US Marshal* stenciled on the side. He looked confused. Zahn wondered if Roger knew what a US Marshal was.

"What're you guys doing to my car? What do you want?"

"Hey, Roger, remember me?" Zahn tried to meet the young man's eyes. "I met you over at the community center." He nodded his head over his shoulder. "I know your Aunt Maddie."

"Yeah, so? I didn't drive her this morning," Roger said. "You want her number?"

Williams stepped forward. "Actually, I wanted to have a word with you, Roger." He hooked his thumbs in his belt. "I'm US Marshal Randall Williams."

Roger looked at Williams. "Marshal? Like a sheriff or something?"

Williams nodded. "Something like that. I work at the federal level rather than the county level, though."

"I know the thrift shop isn't open, but sometimes I park here when I go on my walks," Roger said, glancing over at the CLOSED sign on the thrift shop door. "I don't think Ms. Holly, the owner, minds." He paused. "Am I in trouble for parking?"

Williams chuckled. "No, Roger, parking's not the issue." He pointed at Roger's Blazer. "It's what you've got in the back seat here." He pointed through the window.

Roger walked over and stood next to Williams.

"What?"

"That jacket, Roger. Looks a little small for you. Is that yours?"

Zahn watched Roger's eyes grow wide. He turned his head to Zahn, then back to Williams.

"No, that's not mine. That's not mine."

"Do you know whose jacket it might be?"

"No, that's not mine. That's not my jacket."

Zahn stared at the man. Looked like Roger was shutting down.

Williams nodded. "I heard you the first time, Roger. Whose is it?"

Roger stood as if frozen, his lips moving but no sound emerging. Zahn could practically see his brain struggling for a plausible response. And he thought he smelled fear.

"Someone must have put that jacket in my car," Roger said, nodding. "Yeah, see it's unlocked. Someone must have stuck it in there." He reached for the door handle.

Williams stuck his hand out and grabbed Roger's arm. "Hold your horses there, Roger."

Roger looked at Williams with a question in his eyes.

"You think someone got into your car? Left this jacket behind?"

Roger bobbed his head in the affirmative.

Zahn smiled to himself. Roger was sure he had gotten himself an out, and he was going to stick to it, hell or high water.

"Yeah, they got into my car. Planted it so you would think I took her."

Williams froze.

Zahn froze.

Roger looked at the two men.

"What?"

Williams stepped back and lowered his hands to his sides.

"Took who, Roger?"

"What do you mean?"

"You said 'took her,' right? How do you know someone was taken? How do you know it's a 'her?'"

Roger remained silent, his mouth hanging open.

Williams moved quickly and pulled Roger's hands individually behind his back, cuffing them.

"Roger, you're under arrest. You have the right to remain silent…"

CHAPTER 35

"So, what'd you think of our little valley?" Perez set his coffee in the console between the seats of his Jeep.

"I loved it," Daria said. "I hope no one is thinking I'm heading home because I didn't like Buena Vista. The people are great, there's a ton to do, and I couldn't have asked for better weather."

"Uh-huh."

The deputy didn't appear quite satisfied with her answer. Either that, or he just wasn't used to making conversation with a college student at 4:30 in the morning. Sure worked out good for Daria, though. Perez had a law enforcement conference in Manitou Springs this morning. It was only another twenty minutes to drop off Daria at her mother's house. When Perez had heard she was heading home, he'd offered to give her the ride, with the warning that she'd have to get up early.

Zahn had hemmed and hawed, arguing he could drive her, and muttering something about a father's role. But then he and Williams found the girl's jacket. Zahn didn't think that changed his responsibility to Daria, but Daria did.

"Come on, Dad. You guys are busting this thing wide open. You're involved, so finish it."

Perez wanted Zahn to stay too. The feds were in the lead, but it was mostly Williams running everything on behalf of the feds. Perez still had a peripheral role. But he was really looking forward to this conference and figured Zahn could be his eyes and ears back at Buena Vista.

Daria was okay with Perez taking her because it avoided Zahn having to meet up with his ex-wife. Not that she had any reason to think those two didn't get along. But they hadn't seen each other since she was a kid, so why tempt fate now?

She felt Perez ease off the accelerator as he crested Trout Creek Pass and coasted into South Park. At the bottom of the hill, after the turn to the east, she watched him set the cruise control and switch on his high beams.

"We got like thirty miles of straight road ahead of us before we hit Wilkerson Pass," Perez said. "Then it's mostly downhill all the way home."

Daria nodded. "You're probably wondering why I'm going home."

"Nope."

That was the answer she expected. Perez wouldn't push it. So why did she feel such a need to justify herself?

"It wasn't just one thing," she said. "It simply felt like it would make everything easier."

Perez said nothing.

"First off, Dad was driving me crazy with his adventure plan. Hiking, fishing, ropes, rafting—he had me on a two-activities-a-day schedule, just killing himself to make sure I had a great time. And I would have put up with it. But then he started prioritizing that over Search & Rescue. And even the missing child. You know, the Janae girl."

Perez nodded.

"I couldn't take that. My dad is useful in those situations. When you got to figure stuff out, he's the guy you want around."

"Don't I know that. Saved my butt last year."

"Well, with me gone, he can't justify staying out of the case," Daria said. "And then there was Kevin. You heard about Kevin, right?"

Perez dimmed his lights for an oncoming car and glanced at Daria. "Yes, I…"

A flash of brown crossed the shoulder of the road on Daria's side, and she leaned as Perez instinctively wrenched the wheel of his Jeep to the left to avoid the elk. The brown mass filled her windscreen as she heard the scream of Perez's tires skidding on the highway. Then the elk disappeared, and her face smashed forward into something. Everything stopped.

Her eyes opened to tapping on her window.

"Are you okay? Can you hear me?"

From her left came a muffled call. "Daria? Daria?"

"Rick! Are you okay?" She moved her good arm to touch the fabric pressed against her body. An airbag. She shoved it to the side and saw the pinhole light of a cellphone aimed at her through her window. She looked left and saw Perez staring at her.

"I'm okay," Perez said. "What about you? What about your arm?" He nodded toward the sling.

"I'm opening the door," came a voice from behind the cellphone light.

The door swung open, followed by a man's head. "How's everyone?"

"We're just figuring that out," Perez said. "How'd you get here so fast?"

"I was in the car coming the other direction. Nothing'll slow you down faster than watching an elk doing a half-gainer through the air toward your car."

"Oh, shit. Where is it?"

"Between my car and yours. I didn't check on it because I wanted to see how you all were doing first."

Perez unhooked his seatbelt and looked at Daria. "I'm going to call you an ambulance and go see about this elk. You hold tight, okay?"

"I don't need an ambulance." She lifted each leg and tried her good arm. She rotated her neck from side to side. "Everything's working."

"We'll see," Perez said. "Stay here." He pushed his way out his door and buckled when he stood.

"Rick, you're hurt!"

The deputy grabbed the door and stood upright. "Banged my knee. It'll be all right."

Perez hobbled around the car and nodded at the man who had stopped to help. Both men disappeared, leaving Daria to ponder how she and Perez had hit what appeared to be an 800-pound elk without injuring themselves. *Except for Rick's knee.* Like a miracle or something.

For us, she thought. Bet there's no miracle for the elk.

Suddenly, she had to know the fate of the animal they had struck. She lifted the airbag draped over her and stepped out her open door. Flares marked the road, arcing toward the other car. Between the cars she saw a small grouping of men. A strong coppery scent filled the air. She watched Perez lift his revolver and press it against the elk's head. A splintered antler drew Daria's eyes from the elk's blood-covered head, but only for a moment. The animal's eyes stared at Daria, as if asking for rescue.

And then Perez shot it.

The Park County sheriff took all the required information. Perez and the other man moved the carcass off the road, and Perez offered the meat to the tow-truck driver who arrived from Johnson Village, just south of Buena Vista. Her father would meet them at the towing company and drive Perez to the hospital to get his knee checked out. Gunbarrel Towing ran a salvage business on the side, and there wasn't a chance in hell Perez's Jeep would ever drive again.

The elk's eyes haunted Daria all the way back to Buena Vista.

She spotted her father waiting at the salvage gate as they pulled up. Daria considered the irony that she and Perez had been lauding Zahn's ability to help in a crisis seconds before the crash. So odd that after years together with her mother, she would be singing her dad's praises in what might have been her final moments. Was it fair to leave him over this incident with her boyfriend?

As Zahn folded his arms around her, carefully avoiding her sling, she looked past him wondering if Kevin might have come too. She hadn't really been fair to him either.

She thought back to the elk. The animal was just in the wrong place at the wrong time. Like Kevin.

Daria realized she had made his suffering about her, directing anger at him for not telling her first. And then she had poured fuel on the fire of his own misery by packing up and heading home.

She wasn't any better than Kevin when it came to doing the right thing.

"Did you call Mom?" Daria stepped back from her father's embrace.

"I did. I told her you were okay and that we'd call her when we had more info. When we'd decided about rescheduling your trip home."

"Can we talk about that? Not that I'm hurt, but I think I could use a couple more days here to get over what just happened. Is that okay?"

She saw her father's eyes glistening as he wrapped one arm back around her.

He said nothing, but his head nodded.

CHAPTER 36

Zahn didn't intend to follow Kevin. It just worked out that way.

He was downtown at the hardware store buying sand for his walkway project. One condition of Daria's return was for him to stop micromanaging her time. Might as well get some work done. He'd parked his truck on the store's side where the rocks and stones, cement forms, and bags of sand lay on wooden pallets.

As Zahn rounded the corner to the main entrance, he spotted Kevin exiting his truck and entering the store.

Buena Vista was a small town. Zahn couldn't help himself. He went back to his truck and pulled it to the front of the store, where he could watch Kevin exit.

Something about Kevin bothered Zahn. Even before the exposure accusations, Zahn hadn't been completely comfortable around his daughter's new friend. He had chalked the feeling up as normal since Kevin was the first guy he'd watched interact with his daughter.

Zahn had missed Daria's teenage years. Sheila, her mother, had done a great job caring for Daria while Zahn had spent the next five years contracting in southern Florida for the government during the day, and losing himself in alcohol-induced numbness at night.

The lost years.

Those years...darkened by the loss of Jacob, by the crash of his aircrew in Kuwait, and, by the subsequent disintegration of his family. The years where he raked in money from a contracting job he hated, most of it going to Sheila and Daria, some of it going to a meager sampling of weekly groceries, rent, and an ample supply of booze.

By the time he'd become self-aware enough to realize he was slowly killing himself and was wasting other people's oxygen, Sheila was engaged to an Air Force officer in Colorado Springs, and Daria was heading off to college.

Oops. Missed that.

So, Kevin and Daria. The blossoming of a relationship. This was unfamiliar territory for Zahn, and he figured his discomfort was just his protective father instincts kicking in.

Until they had suspended Kevin for indecent exposure. Accused by girls almost half his age. And all of this after finding Kendall, the young girl held against her will, and law enforcement still trying to catch a break on the Janae Longmont investigation.

No proof these incidents were related. But they certainly factored into Zahn's sudden paranoia about all the shit going down in his adopted town.

Kevin eventually emerged from the store, holding a brown paper bag in one hand and a small canister of propane in the other. He tossed the stuff he had bought in the truck's passenger seat, then climbed in to the driver's seat and drove away.

Next stop for Kevin was the Dollar Express. No way Zahn could follow him into the tiny store without being noticed. Wedged between the new grocery and the liquor store, the Dollar Express was the last resort for obscure items when you really needed something and didn't want to drive thirty-five minutes north to Leadville or thirty-five minutes south to Salida. Zahn parked at the liquor store and waited.

Kevin's venture in bargain shopping didn't last long. He exited the store with a single plastic sack, a set of jumbo red plastic cups jutting from the top. Something else in the bag's bottom, but Zahn couldn't identify it.

Zahn hunched his shoulders over his cell phone and hoped Kevin didn't head for the liquor store next. Then he remembered.

Christian Scientist.

Hitting the liquor store or drugstore probably wasn't high on Kevin's to-do list.

The library was next on Kevin's tour of the town. Not like Zahn was going to lose sight of him—a maroon truck driving 35 mph for less than a half mile. When Kevin walked through the library's double doors, Zahn gave up the charade. Covert surveillance in a two-stoplight town. Right.

It wouldn't be unusual for Kevin and Zahn to bump into each other at the library. Especially since Zahn volunteered there. He fiddled with his phone, using the library's parking lot Wi-Fi, while waiting to follow Kevin inside.

Zahn pulled up his search engine and typed in *"Roger Fullhart" Buena Vista*. Three pages of entries popped up, mostly about another Buena Vista in Florida. He went back to his original search and added *Colorado* to the parameters.

Did you mean Roger Fulhart? The search engine replied.

Zahn wasn't sure whether it was one L or two Ls in the last name. Randall Williams had arrested the young man, so he knew. Zahn clicked the search query question and scanned the results. The first four entries were all *people-finder* websites. White pages. Yellow pages. Facebook. Ancestry.com, etc. All stuff you had to pay for.

Zahn was simply trying to get a sense of where Roger stood in the community—not ascertaining his heritage or obtaining a listing of his last five addresses. He knew he was focusing on the right Roger Fulhart, though, because he could see a *Madison* in the text included with each search engine result. Relatives. Maddie.

Zahn scrolled down the results. One entry was definitely click-bait. *Your party has four arrests. Join ArrestRecord for only $9.95/mo and see details.* Zahn wasn't sure if he was ready for that yet.

Then he saw a result for the Chaffee County Tribune. A small county newspaper with a hefty subscription rate. Zahn didn't subscribe to it, but he'd read it a few times in the library during slow shifts.

Buena Vista Man Cited For Lewd Behavior.

When Zahn tried to click on the article, it demanded he sign up for a subscription. He finished half the form before remembering he had access to the paper in the library. He checked his watch. Ten minutes had passed since Kevin walked in the doors.

Zahn entered the double doors and turned toward the main lobby as Kevin walked out. The two men looked at each other. Zahn nodded and said, "Kevin."

Kevin pulled up short and looked Zahn directly in the eye. "Sir, I did not do that."

Zahn stopped. *We're having that conversation here? Now?* "I didn't say you did."

"I know you didn't. But I need you to know I respect your daughter and I'm embarrassed either of you are seeing my name associated with all this. It's not true, and I hope you'll give me the benefit of the doubt."

Zahn stared back at the young man. Not the shifty gaze or constant look of guilt someone like Roger wore. If Kevin was guilty of this charge, he certainly was a master of misdirection.

"Kevin, I'll be straight with you," Zahn said. "I don't know what to think. I've known you for less than two weeks. My daughter is all I've got, and so you can understand I might be a little cautious about who she spends time with."

Kevin nodded, and Zahn kept talking. "So thank you for explaining yourself, and I'm sorry about what's happening. I guess I'd prefer it if you and Daria took it easy on the whole relationship thing while it's all getting sorted out."

Kevin nodded again, a little more slowly, his brow creasing.

Zahn said, "Of course Daria's old enough to make those decisions on her own, and she'd probably kick my ass if she heard me telling you to back off. But there you have it. That's what I'm thinking."

"I can understand that. And I can respect that, sir." Kevin paused. "Just wait. You'll see." He pressed his lips together and walked out the double doors.

Zahn watched the young man leave. The conversation had done nothing to make him think Kevin was guilty.

Passing the front desk, Zahn stopped and talked with Judith. The matriarch. The woman looked like she might have been working behind the counter when Zahn was a boy checking out Hardy Boys mysteries at his own library.

"Tyler, good to see you." Judith smiled. "We've been missing you." She leaned closer. "All those new volunteers have been asking where you've been. New girlfriend?"

Zahn chuckled. "I wish. My daughter's in town and we've been spending some time together."

"Oh, I can't tell them that." Judith laughed. "Those gals hear that you're a good father *and* a local hero—they'll give you no rest."

Zahn smiled. "Best keep it secret, Judith." He paused and glanced over at the computer carousels. Four had users and two were unoccupied. "Anybody signed up for those free computers? I need to do some work."

Judith followed Zahn's gaze and shook her head. "They're free. That young man just left the one on the end." She leaned farther across the counter. "And he forgot to sign out, as well."

Zahn pulled a pen from his pocket. "I got it. I'll sign him out and sign myself in."

As he settled into the chair at the computer, Zahn glanced toward the reception desk. Judith had already disappeared into the back office. Instead of logging out, Zahn opened the internet browser. Then he went to *Settings* and looked for *Search History*.

Bingo.

Kevin had been to four or five different websites during his ten minutes. A quick history scan showed a list of all four lawyers in town, plus another in Salida. Zahn smiled at the *Phil White* website. Same guy who defended Galen Sullivan last year for the dam bombing. No win for Lawyer Phil on that case. Sullivan was in prison and despite White's best efforts, it didn't look like he'd be up for early release for at least another twenty years.

The last website Kevin used was an online Bible. Zahn clicked the link and brought up the page. The entire book of Revelations filled his screen. He squinted at the numbers in the URL.

2-10.

He scrolled down to the chapter and verse of Revelations.

Do not fear what you are about to suffer. Behold, the devil is about to throw some of you into prison, that you may be tested, and for ten days you will have tribulation. Be faithful unto death, and I will give you the crown of life.

Zahn looked up from the screen and stared out the library window. He'd just spent an hour following a young man around a town the size of a normal high school, and he was no closer to answers. Lawyers and a Bible verse could be obvious signs of an innocent man looking for both representation and encouragement.

But Revelations?

Could it be a warped mind using the Bible to justify his actions?

Was his daughter's boyfriend wrongly accused? Or was he a mental case?

• • •

Perez called Zahn at six thirty in the morning.

"Rise and shine, old man. How are you doing?"

Zahn smiled into the phone. Perez had the *old man* part right. Zahn had been up for an hour and a half already. Second cup of coffee. Reading the news on his computer.

"What's up? Didn't the doctor tell you to get some rest?"

"Nah, I'm good. Thought you might want to join Randall and me for a cup of joe down at the Elkhead in thirty. Can you make it?"

Zahn looked toward Daria's bedroom. No light under the door. She definitely needed the rest after the accident.

"Yeah, I can be there. Social invite, or we talking business?"

Perez made a coughing sound. "Since I'm not heading to the Springs and no longer have a car, Randall's letting me help out with the case. They got some info yesterday. Related to the girl."

"Janae? Did you find her?"

"No. But we might be close. Come on down."

Holy shit. There had been a week of nothing, except for Zahn finding the coat in the back of Roger's car. They didn't even know yet, if it was Janae's.

"Yeah, I'm on my way."

He scribbled a note—*Daria, coffee with the boys. Home by 9 or so. Love you. Dad*—and left it on the dining room table. He silently twisted the knob on Daria's door and ducked his head around the corner. She lay propped up against a pillow with her slung arm at her side. Didn't look comfortable. But she was sleeping.

Williams and Perez sat at the same table, Perez with another slice of quiche on his plate, crutches propped against the wall, and Williams cradling a cup of coffee with both hands.

"That was quick," Williams said.

"Hey." Zahn thought about asking the Marshal about Kristee, but then glanced at Perez and decided that would be a good question for when it was just Zahn and Williams. He suspected Perez might still be a little sore about Kristee and her relationship with Randall Williams.

"Go get yourself some coffee," Williams said, as Zahn pulled out a chair. "We promise not to say anything important until you get back."

Zahn nodded and headed to the counter.

"Let me guess, house black, no room for sugar or cream, right?" Maddie's granddaughter gave him a cheery smile, pausing before she turned back to the coffee dispenser.

Zahn smiled. "You got it." He still didn't know the girl's name, or exactly how she was related to Roger. *Wonder what she could tell me about him?* he thought, followed by *wrong time to ask.*

He collected his coffee and joined the two men back at the table.

"So, what's up?"

Williams tilted his chair and looked at Perez before answering. "Well, first thing is, nice job on the whole jacket thing."

"Was it Janae's?"

Perez jumped in. "It was. Our friend Roger will be staying behind bars for a while."

"But you said you didn't find her. Do you think he—? That he might have—?"

"Roger is singing like a canary, but he's just a pawn in this whole thing," Perez said. "And not a very smart one at that."

"Don't underestimate him. His aunt says he's pretty computer savvy," Zahn said. "Got some social issues, though. So, what is he saying?"

"Roger says he's a marketer," Williams said.

Zahn wrinkled his nose. "A what?"

"Yeah, so he goes on the web and hires himself out to shoot video. We think that's what he did with Janae."

"How do you know it's Janae?"

"The family identified the jacket," Perez said. "Roger described the girl. It's either Janae, or it's someone that looks like her—that's probably with her—using her jacket. Really, it doesn't matter if it's Janae or not, right? I mean someone local is leaving an underage girl with someone like Roger…"

"And not just one girl, right, Rick?" Williams glanced at the deputy. "Roger said there was a menu. He could have picked another job. With another girl."

"Holy shit," Zahn said, shaking his head. "So, some guy is running a pool of gals, underage gals, and farming them out?"

Perez nodded his head and Williams shook his.

"That's what it looks like," Perez said.

"Except, it seems like he's trying to get these guys to film them. To market them so they can be farmed out later," Williams added.

"Any leads on where the girls are being housed? Or who's behind it all? What about the drop-off guy?"

"Roger claimed he drove a truck and wore a mask. The girl was wearing a mask when she arrived, as well. No more details," Perez said.

"No idea where the girl, or girls, are," Williams said. "Roger says you have to order them and set up the drop-off at least two days ahead of time. Two days? Maybe they're coming from out-of-state?"

Zahn thought about that. "Maybe. But you said it's Janae's coat, right?"

"Right," Perez nodded. "Why?"

"Well, why would you kidnap a girl just outside of BV, take her to somewhere eight hours out-of-state or wherever, and then bring her back to the same town you got her from? That doesn't make sense, does it?"

Williams looked confused. "Sure, I can see that, but riddle me this. If you're keeping the girls around here, then wouldn't it be just as risky to kidnap a local girl and then keep her local for this 'hiring out' business? That doesn't seem very smart either."

Zahn nodded. Williams was right. Janae wasn't exactly a local, though. She was from Oklahoma. Which was just north of Texas. Which was where Kendall was from.

Kendall.

Zahn set his coffee in front of him and pressed his palms onto the table. "How about this for a theory, gentlemen?"

The two men looked back at Zahn.

"You remember Kendall, right? The girl we found instead of Janae? The one who escaped?"

Both men nodded.

"Not a stretch to think she might have been one of these girls we're talking about, right? One of the ones being rented out?"

"Not a stretch," Perez said, nodding.

"Right," Zahn said. "So what if they were looking for Kendall and took Janae instead?"

"Why would they do that?"

"I don't know," Zahn said. "Maybe they got mixed up, maybe they saw a target of opportunity, I don't know. But you agree that her disappearing at the same time we found Kendall is more than a coincidence, right?"

"Right," Williams said.

"So I think that makes the argument that they're being held locally—but could still be from out of state. The fact that Janae was captured locally is an outlier. An accident that happened related to Kendall's escape."

Perez smiled at Williams. "Told you it was worth a coffee." He nodded at Zahn, "He might be ugly, but he sure knows how to put a fresh angle on an investigation."

Williams laughed and looked at Zahn. "When are you going to start that Reserve Sheriff job? It's obvious they need you. Or at least Perez here does."

"Everything's on hold with that." Zahn smiled at the two men's banter, then turned serious. "So what's the next step in this thing? How are we going to find Janae?"

"Right," Williams said. "We were just talking about that." He looked at Perez.

Perez leaned forward. "So we're working with the BV police and local press to keep Roger Fulhart's arrest low-key. Out of the papers."

"So the guy with the girls won't think you're on to him? How does that change things?"

"No, Tyler," Williams said. "So we can have Roger put in for another session with Janae. On the Dark Web. We're going to use him as bait."

CHAPTER 37

"Rise and shine, Ms. Sunshine," Jefe called from the doorway, flipping on the light switch. "We got ourselves another shoot."

The three girls blinked at him. Rachel rubbed her eyes. He kept his stare focused on the top bunk.

Janae's bunk.

"That's right, you're the Ms. Sunshine they're looking for today, Janae. Repeat client. The Boss. Same guy as last time." Jefe smiled at the irony of labeling milquetoast Roger as *the Boss*.

He watched the other two girls respond to his announcement, Rachel's eyes widening and Nicole craning her neck to see Janae's reaction above her.

"What's the matter, ladies? You jealous? Janae getting outside and enjoying some fresh air?" Jefe's gaze shifted between Janae and the two girls. "Good things come to those who perform. Take notes." He nodded at Janae. "You got an hour, and I'll be back to get you."

"What—"

"You two help get her ready." Jefe ignored Janae, and addressed the others. "No walk this morning. Do some jumping jacks or something."

He stopped in the doorway and glanced at Nicole and Rachel. "I was serious about taking notes. You gals talk to Janae about playing team ball. Seems like she might have some pointers for you. Like, if you want to catch a fly, try using some honey. Shit like that." He focused his stare on Rachel. "Maybe she can help you get your crap together."

Jefe walked out the door. Climbing the ladder to the barn, he mentally reviewed the encrypted message he'd received in the chat room.

Roger wanted another session. Only three days after the last one. Said he lost most of the last shoot in a computer crash.

Normally, Jefe would make a marketer wait at least a week. For a couple of reasons. First, he didn't want to be predictable when delivering the girls. Patterns could spell trouble for the team. And second? He didn't want his videographers to think they were in charge. That they had control of the schedule. That was Jefe's job.

But Roger was a different breed.

Jefe didn't personally know all his marketers, but Roger was somewhat of a fixture around Buena Vista. One of those idiot savant types. Most of the town thought he was mentally handicapped. The way he always mumbled and avoided direct eye contact. Problems in high school. Hanging out with younger kids. And maybe he was. Certainly, he was socially handicapped. Couldn't maintain an adult conversation if his life depended on it. Not conversant in societal norms. Couldn't recognize that a community would be wary of a scraggly guy who spent his days parked on the outskirts of public playgrounds.

But for Jefe's purposes, Roger was both harmless and useful.

Roger followed the rules. He didn't touch the girls.

Roger got an allowance from his mother. So he always paid on time.

Roger was the one who had set him up on the Dark Web. Downloaded the software. Checked the encryption. All the stuff Jefe didn't want to learn. And he shot good film.

That was the savant part. The town folk recognized Roger as *special*. Worth keeping an eye on. Very few knew Roger's true talents.

Computer genius.

Master videographer.

Jefe had worked with Roger for a while and couldn't decide if the young man was aware his social disability served as the perfect cover for their illicit work, or if he was simply clueless. Jefe wasn't even sure if Roger identified anything about Jefe outside their Dark Web connection. Roger had the tech savvy to figure it out. He had seen Jefe's car. Had a physical description. Chaffee County wasn't that big. But Roger had given no sign he was even interested in Jefe's real identity.

Jefe decided to approve Roger's request. Janae had returned no worse for wear from the experience. She claimed Roger had followed the rules. Roger had said Janae was perfect.

An hour later and Jefe was driving downtown with Janae perched in the back seat of his truck. The tinted windows allowed him to keep a blindfold on the girl without drawing attention.

"You fired up, Janae?" Jefe called. "It's showtime."

Janae said nothing. Just kept her head pointed forward. Her mouth showed no expression.

Jefe turned up the road toward Roger's trailer court as a BV police sedan passed him going the other direction. His fingers lifted from the steering wheel. The patrolman waved back and gave Jefe a long stare. Or at least it felt long. Long as a stare can last between two passing cars.

Jitters. He still got them when he left the stable with one of the girls. When things weren't completely within his control. In the rear-view mirror, he watched as the police car turned north on the county road away from town.

Away from town? Did he get a call? Outside city limits?

Jefe reviewed the mission for the day.

Roger wanted another meet—only days after the last one. Non-standard.

There had been a police car near Roger's trailer. Maybe non-standard. He wasn't sure yet.

One and a half strikes.

Jefe steered his truck into the parking lot of the computer repair shop a half mile before Roger's trailer court. He pulled out his phone and dialed Roger. Roger picked up on the first ring.

Jefe pressed the phone against his ear. "You ready?"

"Yes."

"Anything I should know?"

"No."

Jefe could hear Roger breathing into the phone.

"I'm not coming," Jefe said.

"Okay." Jefe heard Roger release his breath and disconnect.

Jefe jammed the phone in his pocket and backed the truck out of his parking spot. He turned on the access road to the main highway and started heading home.

Something was off.

No way Roger would accept a last-minute cancellation without whining. He would have argued.

Jefe glanced in his rear-view mirror and saw another police car next to Roger's turnoff. He pulled on to the highway and watched a plain black SUV turn toward Roger's. African-American driver.

In BV? Not likely.

Roger was compromised.

Jefe should have stuck to his own rules.

"Janae, how are you doing back there?"

Janae said nothing.

"We're going to take a little ride, okay?" Jefe glanced in the rearview mirror.

Janae nodded.

Jefe drove west toward the mountains, then took a county road south, skirting Buena Vista, before returning to the highway. Toward Salida.

Salida was twice as big as Buena Vista. That wasn't saying much. Five thousand residents instead of twenty-five hundred. Simple place to figure out if you were being followed. Jefe did what every local valley resident did when they went to Salida. He headed to Wal-Mart. Parked the truck, left Janae in the back seat, and ducked into the store. From the inside, he watched the parking lot for ten minutes.

Nothing.

He and Janae drove a mile farther into town to Ace Hardware. Same drill. He waited. And thought.

They knew about Roger.

Did Roger know enough to lead them to Jefe? Roger knew the truck. Probably knew his name.

Was this the inevitable precipitating event? The one that triggered the bug-out plan?

CHAPTER 38

Janae figured enough was enough. Hermione wouldn't just sit in a prison if Voldemort captured her. Annabeth wouldn't just wait for Percy Jackson to save her if Kronos held her captive.

She remembered her dad's voice during one of her three-hour reading stints—*Janae, it's time to get off your butt and move.*

Then Jefe's voice when he parked the truck. "I'll be back in a minute. I'm watching you and this truck. Don't even think about leaving."

Janae followed her dad's advice. When she heard the door close, she pulled off her blindfold and peered out the rear passenger door's tinted window.

Wal-Mart.

In a different town than where Boss lived. Nothing looked familiar. Not that she could find her way around Boss's town, either, with the blindfold and all.

She scanned the parking area. Jefe's truck sat in the far end of the lot, close to the highway. Other customers walked to and from their cars, but she didn't see Jefe. What did Jefe tell the Boss? *I'm not coming.* What did Jefe tell Janae? *We're going for a little ride.*

Janae wasn't a hundred percent sure what happened back at Boss's, but Jefe was acting differently. Maybe he was nervous about getting caught with Janae?

She looked around the parking lot again. No police cars. Nothing out of the ordinary. Was Jefe just buying something he needed, or was he standing in the store watching the truck and seeing if anyone had noticed them?

Janae unlatched her seatbelt and scooted across the seat to the opposite side of the truck, closest to the highway. She tugged the door handle. Locked. Reaching over the front seat, she hit *unlock* on the driver's door. The locks on all four doors jumped to attention. And this time the door opened. She could get out of here.

The girl looked toward the store entrance. *Uh oh.* Jefe was striding toward the truck. Whipping her head toward the open door, she searched for options. A highway. Houses on the other side—then fields backed against mountains. She turned back toward Jefe. Not enough time.

Janae pulled the door shut and pushed the door lock with her finger. *Beep.* The lock jumped back up, joining the other three. Jefe must have hit the button on his keys. Janae scooted across the seat and put her seatbelt on as Jefe walked to his door. He wasn't looking at her. She clicked her seatbelt and grabbed the blindfold, pulling it over her eyes.

The door opened, and she heard Jefe climb into his seat. The door closed.

Silence.

Then she felt Jefe's warm breath on her face as he leaned over the seat.

"Why are you breathing so hard, Janae? You get scared out here by yourself?"

Janae said nothing.

Jefe pulled away, and Janae tried to picture the winding route through the parking lot she had glimpsed. Left on the main highway. Mountains to the right. So west? Or east? She sighed, hearing her dad's voice again: *How do you know where you're going, if you don't know where you're at?*

The truck slowed.

"One more stop," Jefe said. "Then we'll head home."

Jefe parked the truck and got out. She heard the locks engage. Then the *beep*. She counted to twenty real slow and then tugged off her blindfold.

Across the parking lot, she watched Jefe enter a store—Ace Hardware. Four other cars sat in the lot. Different parking set-up than the Wal-Mart. This time, Janae looked across the empty bench seat toward the store and her door faced the opposite direction. She looked out her door window. More parking lot. A road. And then a neighborhood. Out the front window was another highway against the mountains; maybe the same highway as the one she saw from Wal-Mart. Should she make a run for it? She couldn't exit Jefe's side because if he stood inside the hardware store foyer, he'd see her, for sure.

She took a deep breath, unhooked her seatbelt, and summoned her inner Annabeth. Her book hero got scared too. But not so scared she couldn't move. Annabeth would at least try.

Janae hit *unlock* again and opened her door. Lowering herself to the parking lot, she pushed the door closed. The truck blocked her view of the store. Which meant Jefe couldn't see her unless he was on his hands and knees inside the store looking at her from the level of the truck's tires. She ran away, looking over her shoulder and keeping the truck between her and the store doors. Janae pulled up short of the road leading to the neighborhood to wait for a passing car and caught sight of a woman's head ducking under the rear-view mirror and glancing her way. She bolted behind the car and stopped for another glance at Jefe's truck. Still no sign of her captor. And now she faced a choice. Highway or neighborhood?

She aimed for the houses.

Janae took the sidewalk at a run. A deserted school loomed to her right. Empty parking lot. Playground, like the one back home. *Scaredy cat, scaredy cat.*

Ha! If they could only see her now.

Janae turned away from the school, veering into the neighborhood. She snuck a glance behind her and spotted a car coming her direction.

A car. Not a truck. Either Jefe didn't know she'd escaped, or he wasn't looking this way yet.

A skinny alley cut to her right, but it paralleled the busy school road. She pressed ahead, across another intersection and toward another alley. Turning the corner, she looked over her shoulder.

A maroon truck turned her direction from the school road.

Jefe.

She bolted into the narrow alley, then abruptly stopped. Like all the Oklahoma alleys, this one ran straight as an arrow to the edge of town. Jefe would spot her. Where was an invisibility cloak when you needed one most?

Fences lined both sides of the gravel alley—some wire, some wooden. She spotted a garage, a row of garbage cans, a gate. Pushing through the gate, she cut through a backyard, skirting the house and aiming for the road she expected out front. Gravel crunched in the distance. Jefe's truck. Janae rounded the house and took the walkway toward a wrought-iron gate. Locked. She stuck her foot between the rungs and swung her other leg across the gate.

"Hey. You. What are you doing?"

Janae twisted and spied an elderly woman wearing a wide canvas hat, holding a gardening trowel in one gloved hand.

"He's coming," Janae said, and dropped to the other side.

Checking both ways, she dashed straight ahead to the house across the street. No gate. The walkway looked clear. Nobody gardening at this place. She headed around the house, glancing back over her shoulder. The woman was waving her trowel and calling from her gate. But no truck. No Jefe.

She rounded the house, aiming for the next alley. Janae's eyes shifted to the rear garage entrance at the walkway's end. She tried the door. It opened. Janae stepped through and caught her breath, trying to come up with a plan.

Jefe was out there. He didn't know exactly where she was. But he knew she was close. If he didn't find her in the alleys, would he keep driving the roads, or would he search the houses and garages?

The two-car garage was empty on her side. The other bay held a long car, top folded back and hood raised. Janae had seen cars like this in parades. People threw candy from them, and Janae and her friends would scramble around on the ground, grabbing at saltwater taffy and Tootsie Rolls while her parents watched to make sure she didn't get run over.

A tarp-covered object sat near the front bumper of the old car. Janae walked over and lifted an edge. A snowblower. They had those in Oklahoma too. As she lowered the tarp, a movement in the garage window caught her eye. The maroon truck was working its way through the alley. The truck paused at the house next door, and she watched Jefe jump out and stride to the neighboring garage, pressing his hands to the window.

That settled it.

Janae lifted the tarp on one end of the snowblower and climbed underneath. The smell of gas and oil reminded her of their garage back home.

The tires crunched closer as the truck pulled between her garage and the one across the alley. She heard the door slam, then silence. Lifting the tarp, Janae peered across the garage. The raised hood blocked the garage door windows, but the empty bay was all that separated her hideout from the side windows and the open backdoor.

The *open* door. *When is a door not a door?* her dad would say, *When it's a jar. Get it, Janae? Ajar?*

She didn't laugh then. Well, maybe on the inside. She certainly wasn't laughing now.

Rookie move. Hermione or Annabeth wouldn't have left the door open.

Jefe would definitely notice that.

And he did. She heard the gate clang. Jefe's head bobbed past the garage window and she sucked herself closer to the snowblower, draping the tarp over her head so she touched the floor with the hand holding the cover.

Invisibility cloak. Freeze. The heck with magic, she was just plain scared now.

Janae heard Jefe's footsteps across the floor of the garage and guessed he was checking the seats in the old car. Then the steps moved closer, and she heard a loud crinkle of the tarp and saw it press in against the snowblower as Jefe's foot tapped it.

"Shit, shit, shit." Jefe grunted.

Janae tried not to shake. Jefe was real mad.

The footsteps started again. And then the sound disappeared. Janae thought about peeking. That idea lasted less than half a second. She tasted bile in her throat.

What if he hadn't left? What if he was just waiting for her to come out? She hadn't heard the door close. Or the truck leave.

Janae waited. And waited. And waited.

CHAPTER 39

Goddammit.

Absolute wrong time for this shit.

Jefe strode to his truck, clenching his fists as he walked. Climbing back into his truck, he rolled forward twenty yards to the next garage.

Where was she?

He opened another gate, then froze at a voice from the house.

"Can I help you?"

An angular woman wearing a floppy hat, flip-phone in hand, waited for his answer.

He waved at her. "Just looking for my dog, ma'am. He bolted back at the store, and I can't find him."

"Does he have opposable thumbs?"

What the hell? "Uh, no ma'am. He's a mutt, black and white and—"

"That's a bunch of bull crap," the woman said. "I'm calling the cops. I saw you open that gate and walk into the Knapik's place next door. I saw you open my gate and walk into mine. So, either your dog has paws that can open gates, or you're a liar. Which one is it?"

Shit. Jefe raised his hand in a farewell gesture and headed for the alley. Driving away, he glanced back at the woman. She stared straight at him with the phone pressed to her ear.

Shit. Shit. Shit. He swung his head from side to side between the remaining garages, looking for Janae. Nothing. Time to pull the plug. He figured he had roughly five minutes before a cop showed up to investigate the woman's call.

Jefe smacked the steering wheel with his hand.

He drove out of town and picked up the highway back to Buena Vista, contemplating his next move. His sequence of events. Which would necessarily correlate with the cops and their sequence of events.

They were going to find Janae sometime between the next several minutes and the next several hours.

They'd figure out who she was right quick.

The good news? Maybe the search would focus on Salida rather than BV.

But that damn girl was smart. She knew he had driven somewhere else. She'd tell them that. It wouldn't be long before they were coming back in the BV direction.

Jefe doubted she could find Roger's place. She'd worn a blindfold, after all. But hell, the cops already had Roger.

Could she find the stable? They had blindfolded her every damn time, except for when they first found her.

Kendall's escape and Janae's arrival marked strike one. He'd heard scuttlebutt around town that Kendall wasn't talking. But still…

The incident at Roger's was strike two. Roger was compromised.

Janae's escape was strike three.

Three strikes and you're out. Three strikes was Jefe's self-imposed limit before he triggered his bug-out plan.

The second and third strikes happening together? That was a surprise. He had always assumed he would have some *shut down* time to review the escape plan.

Jefe figured the only outcome worse than letting his team of girls go was getting caught and having the cops take them. If the team was breaking up, he would damn well dictate the terms.

He set his cruise control on sixty the entire way home and rehearsed how it would go down.

• • •

"Okay, ladies. Ten-minute warning. We're headed out on a little trip."

Nicole looked surprised. "Both of us? Are we going for a walk?"

"Both of you," Jefe said, staring at the two girls. The girls had never left the stable together unless they were doing their morning walk. "We're going for a ride."

He watched Nicole glance at Rachel and then back at him.

"Where's Janae?"

"We're going to pick her up. Don't you worry about a thing. Just have a jacket ready, and I'll come grab you in ten. We'll be using the blindfolds."

He looked at the two girls. Nicole gave him a skeptical look, and Rachel nodded, her face a blank slate.

"Move it. Go clean up. Brush your hair and shit." He turned on his heel and left the girls staring after him.

Jefe locked the doors behind him, climbed the ladder, and stopped at the wide barn door.

Dammit. His bug-out plan included his horses, but he'd left his trailer at work. No time to go get it. He'd have to use the horses stabled at the place he'd left the trailer.

He rolled the sliding door open and backed his truck from the driveway into the barn, stopping just shy of the bunkroom hole. Leaving the truck running, Jefe jumped out and opened the stall doors, waving his horses out into the bay. The horses ignored his directions and trotted to the corral.

Shit. There goes five more minutes.

He followed the animals into the corral and opened the gate in the fence opposite the barn. Then he circled the horses and scooted them toward the open gate. Jefe gave them a *hee-ya* as he jogged past them toward the house.

Got to move. Got to move.

He dragged the hundred-gallon cooler he kept under the porch to the front steps and opened the lid. A gallon zip-lock bag contained two long lighters and rested upon four gallon jugs of gasoline. Jefe liked to call this his *leave no trace* box. Stuffed with everything he needed to make the house and the barn disappear.

He pulled out the jugs of gasoline and set them in a row on the steps. Two for the kitchen and garage side of the house. Two for the bedroom side. First-floor flames would devour the second floor.

He emptied the first two jugs, the pungent odor burning his nostrils. Returning to the front porch, he retrieved the remaining gas containers. Jefe paused in the doorway of his bedroom before emptying the first jug. He wouldn't miss this lonely room. A plain double bed and a reading lamp. The bare walk-in closet.

The next bedroom was a different story. Christina's room. This was all he had left of her, besides memories. This had started it all. He'd miss this one.

Striding toward the front door, he tossed the empty jugs toward the dining room.

Time to move.

Jefe left the door open. He'd light the house last. He jogged back to the barn, scanning the driveway as he ran. The horses hadn't run; they were loitering on the driveway-side of the fields eating the green grass they hadn't been able to reach from the corral.

Entering the barn, Jefe headed for the equipment locker and grabbed the two gas cans he used to refill the tractor and the baler. He doused the entire barn, spending extra time on the walls. The floor was concrete. But the wooden walls, the strewn hay, and the gasoline left plenty of fuel. This baby would explode sky-high.

Tossing the cans aside, Jefe glanced at the ladder leading to the girls and ran through the sequence: girls in the truck, truck to the driveway, light the barn, light the house. Light a fire under his ass and get away from this ranch. Then he needed to ditch the girls and get out of Dodge.

He was done here. Time to move on.

If he got caught, it was the slammer. For life.

He paused. So why the hell was he risking getting caught by taking the girls with him?

Suddenly endowed with a dose of morality? *Screw that.*

Jefe got in his truck, rolled forward to the barn doors and pulled out his lighter.

CHAPTER 40

As Daria zipped her jacket around her slung arm, her eyes caught a flicker of movement in the driveway. She smiled—on her way to meet Kevin, and here he appeared on her doorstep. God working in mysterious ways.

She stepped outside on the porch, the breeze carrying a hint of pine while teasing her raven hair.

Kevin stopped at the foot of the steps, staring at her with a sad smile on his face.

A storm of emotions hit Daria. The first was relief. She didn't know how Kevin knew she was back. But here he was, ready to give them a second chance.

Then came anger. What was his problem before? Why did he duck and run?

Forgiveness won out, the same emotion that had changed her mind about leaving Buena Vista flooded through her, and she greeted Kevin with a smile. Here he was.

Kevin looked at her and opened his mouth to speak, but the words seemed to choke in his throat like a half cough.

Daria put her hand on Kevin's shoulder. "Are you okay?"

"You came back."

"I did. How did you know?"

"Elliot has a scanner. They were talking about Perez getting hurt, and they mentioned you. Thank God you weren't hurt."

"I came back in part because I thought maybe we could start over. Give you a chance to tell me what happened. This time I might listen."

Kevin took a breath. "It's over, Dar," he said. "It's over."

Daria's mouth dropped, and she felt a sudden pang in her stomach, like she was cresting the top of a roller coaster, only to discover her compartment had no seat restraints. She hadn't even considered that Kevin was through with their relationship.

And then Kevin smiled. A weak smile. A relieved smile.

"What?" Daria couldn't read his face.

"I'm innocent."

"*What?* I mean, of course you are. You already told me you were. But what changed?"

"One of the girl's parents got into their daughter's phone account through the cloud. They were doing a challenge."

"A challenge? What do you mean?"

"I don't know the details. It's some sort of truth or dare thing connected to that social media site *YesSir*. The one all the teenagers are using. You get points for telling a bizarre truth. You get more points for doing a dare. And you get even more points for challenging others to do the same dare."

"What kind of sick game does that?" Daria couldn't believe what she was hearing.

"I have no idea. It's horrible. But, both girls earned points for the dare. Both would lose points if they told. So, they weren't planning on telling."

"But what if it had gone to trial? What would have happened?"

"I don't know." Kevin paused, looking into Daria's eyes. "To be honest with you, I'm having a hard time feeling angry at them. I'm just so relieved. You know, to get my name out of the spotlight. To keep my job."

"Will they rehire you? Let you work at the stables again? With the kids?"

"I started back today. Elliot had to run some errands, and they needed me."

Daria blinked at Kevin, her eyes turning moist. He deserved this happiness. This sense of relief. She knew it had been eating away at him.

She touched her heart. "I'm so happy for you. I knew you didn't do it. You deserve this."

Kevin stepped forward and reached for her hand. "So, about starting over…?"

CHAPTER 41

"We got her!" Williams's voice boomed over the phone.

Zahn's face broke into a wide grin. "Janae?" Who else? It had to be Janae.

"Yep," Williams said. "They found her down in Salida. Evidently, she escaped and hid in a garage. Owners stumbled upon her this afternoon."

"Are we positive it's Janae? Is she okay?"

"Yep. It's her, and she seems fine. She's talking. Not like Kendall."

"Anything we—I mean, you—can use?"

"Yeah, we're all over it. She gave us a description of the vehicle. Maroon truck. Twin cab. But that's not the biggest news."

"Okay, I'll bite. What's the biggest news? She knows who was holding her?"

"Not yet—but we'll get to that. She definitely knows what he looks like. No, here's the deal. Two other girls are out there."

"What?"

"Yep. Two girls doing the same stuff he had Janae doing."

"Ugh. He was farming them out?"

"Right. Tyler, we got to move on this thing."

Zahn nodded his head. No shit. If Janae busted out, then this guy holding the girls would be in panic mode. He'd know the game was up. What would he do with the other girls?

"You said she saw him?"

"Uh huh. You know how we've been looking at Linzmeier and that kid up at Beyond Adventure—what was his name?"

Zahn felt a sinking feeling in his gut. "Kevin," he said. "His name is Kevin." *Shit*, he thought. *Kevin with the maroon truck.*

"Yeah, well, it's not either of those two. This guy's a lot older. Gray in his hair, gray in his mustache. He's holding them somewhere up next to the mountains in a barn. With horses."

"Which side of the river?"

"West side. Janae said they walk in the morning. She saw the sunrise across the valley."

"Sounds like you all have enough info to figure this out, Randall. Thanks for the call. This thing's been eating me up."

"Yeah." Williams paused. "It's been getting to all of us. But I didn't call just to give you an update."

"What's up?"

"Need you to do that thinkin' thing you do, Tyler."

"To find the place? Can't you just have Janae draw out what she remembers? Use air assets to narrow down the possibilities? Doesn't sound that hard."

Zahn sensed Williams nodding in agreement on the other end. "Right. We're going to find it. But what then? Hostages and a standoff? Destruction of evidence, and we got nothing? Or will they be gone?" Williams paused. "We cracked last year's bomb thing when you put yourself in the bad guys' heads. Perez says you got mojo. We need some."

"Got pretty lucky…"

"Enough. No time for the humble shit." Williams's voice hardened. "Put some brainpower onto this, okay? I want to hear your thoughts on this guy's next move. Let me know today."

"Yeah. I can do that."

"Thanks. No pressure."

Zahn remained silent.

"Zahn?"

"Right. No pressure. Just the lives of two girls."

. . .

"Randall, it's Tyler." Zahn stared at the notepad he'd been scribbling on at the dining room table. *Kevin. YesSir. Linzmeier. Longmont?*

"What's up? How's that pondering going?"

"I got nothing for you there. Calling about something else."

"I'm listening."

"Have you heard about this online site, *YesSir*?"

Williams paused. "*YesSir*? That's the teeny-bopper site, right? Our Task Force monitors it because of predators using it to lure in kids."

"You ever hear about kids doing challenges on it?"

"Oh, yeah. It's a problem. They had one a couple weeks ago where the post challenged kids to punch a teacher. This social media shit is messed up." Williams paused again. "What do you got, Tyler? Why are you asking?"

"You know Kevin, up at Beyond Adventure?"

"Yep. The guy who doesn't match Janae's description. Daria's friend. The one who was accused of dropping his drawers, right?"

Zahn grimaced. Society's *guilty until proven innocent* attitude pissed him off...and he wasn't immune. Williams had just associated Daria's name with a guy accused of exposing himself, and Zahn's gut clenched. Even after Daria had updated him on the fact that Kevin didn't do it. The stain of the accused never comes clean.

"Yeah, well, not only is he not Janae's guy, he's also innocent of the exposure thing," Zahn said.

"No shit? How'd they figure that out?"

"One of the girl's parents came forward. They figured out she was doing this *YesSir* thing. It was a challenge."

"You mean the girls challenged each other to do this?"

"Yep."

"That's just not right."

"Nope."

"Well, I appreciate the update. Guess you're pretty relieved about that. So is Daria patching things up with the young man?"

Zahn grunted. "Not so sure about that. I didn't really call to share the family news. I thought you might want to look into this *YesSir* thing." He circled the name of the website he'd written on the notebook.

Williams sounded puzzled. "That camp case was kind of internal. We knew what was going on, but we weren't really involved."

"That's not what I'm talking about. What about Linzmeier?"

"He's using *YesSir*? No." Williams exhaled. "Shit. I'm not the sharpest tool, am I? You mean maybe the girl at school was doing the same thing? Right?"

"Could be. If so, you could get Perez off the Linzmeier investigation and more involved in Janae's. Linzmeier screwed up, being alone with the girl, but if, in fact, she was doing this game thing, wouldn't that sway a lot more people into believing Linzmeier's side of the story?"

Williams paused. "That's what I'm talking about, Tyler. You always come at things from a different angle. Not sure any of us would have thought to look at that—even if we *had* heard about *YesSir* up at Beyond Adventure."

"It might not pan out. Worth checking, though, I think."

Williams changed topics. "Janae gave us a name for her guy. He has the girls call him 'Jefe.'"

"Jefe? Like 'boss' in Spanish?"

"Yeah, probably not his real name."

"You think?"

Williams laughed. "The county's not that big, you know. Considering what we have on this guy."

"Give it to me," Zahn said.

"Twenty thousand people in Chaffee County, right? Give or take a couple hundred."

"Go on."

"Let's say just over fifty percent are male. Call it ten grand," Williams said. "Now we can get the exact numbers from the database, but would you wager half of the men in this county own a truck? The other half own something else?"

"That's fair," Zahn said. "Might even be a little short on your truck estimate."

"Down to five thousand on suspects. You go into the census and find that sixteen percent of the male population is over the age of fifty-five. So let's throw that percentage bracket into the vehicle stats. What's sixteen percent of forty-seven fifty?"

"Ten percent is five hundred. Twenty percent is twice that. Split the difference and call it seven fifty or so?" Zahn poised his pen over the notebook in case Williams had more math for him.

Williams laughed. "Nice. I got a calculator in front of me. It's eight hundred. You're doing good. Now, sixty-five percent live in your two big—and I use that term graciously—towns of Salida and Buena Vista. So throw the remaining percentage against our seven fifty."

"You're making some assumptions here. Maybe more old people live out of town than young people. Got those retirees, you know. Like me."

"I'm trying to make a point here. Roll with me. Call it forty percent out of town if you like."

"Okay. We're down to around three hundred."

"Right. Now if we go into the property records and determine how many of those three hundred live out of town, west of the river, within a mile of the Collegiates, and look for horses and a pickup truck? And, what the hell, let's go back to Janae's abduction. How many of those live within ten miles of Mike Longmont?"

Zahn remained silent. Williams was right. A handful of suspects if the assumptions held. Older. Truck. Horses. Location. This filthy thing was happening somewhere near his own house.

"So, you've been back there, Randall. Any ideas?"

"We got a couple to recheck now that we have this information. *You* got any ideas?"

"Nope. I don't know—wait a minute." Zahn knew someone with intimate knowledge of the area. Someone who had lived there for over thirty years.

Zahn bet Elliot knew almost every resident in those ten miles.

"Gabe Elliot," Zahn said.

Williams was silent, then spoke. "The horse guy from Beyond Adventure? You think Gabe did it?"

Zahn laughed. "No, Randall. I mean, Gabe might know who we could narrow it down to with your new parameters. You should give him the info you just shared with me and ask him."

Zahn could hear Williams thinking on the other end.

"Got a better idea."

"What's that?"

"You're the one who's bonded with the guy. Saturday afternoon spiritual clubs. You give him the info. You ask him. Then share it with me. How about that?"

Zahn nodded into the phone. "Got it. I'll do it right now."

He hung up and closed his notebook.

Time to go find a bad guy.

CHAPTER 42

Zahn ducked under the fence, heading toward the barn and a discussion with Elliot. His step carried a bounce. If Elliot suspected any of his neighbors of foul play, Zahn was sure he would have told him earlier. But now that one of the neighbors was quite likely the culprit, Zahn felt confident Elliot could help.

Elliot's tan truck sat alone, blocking the main door as Zahn rounded the barn from the rear. Kevin must not have returned to work yet. Zahn squeezed through the half-open door and inhaled the scent of fresh hay. A man crouched, silhouetted at the opposite end of the barn, a horse's hoof cradled in his hands.

Zahn walked closer and Kevin turned his head.

"Hey, Tyler." Kevin grinned. "How's it going?"

Zahn smiled with a bit of reservation. He would have smiled wider if Kevin had called him "Mr. Zahn." Why was that? Zahn didn't expect that old-fashioned sign of respect from his young SAR teammates. So why would he demand it from Kevin?

Because he's dating my daughter. Or was...

He needed to ease up. It was a tough week for Kevin, and the young man deserved the smile he wore.

"Hey, Kevin. Good to see you. Congratulations." Zahn paused. "I guess 'congratulations' is the wrong word, right? I guess...I mean, I'm happy for you."

Kevin nodded. "No, I know what you're saying. Honestly, I'm so relieved it's over that it *does* feel like congratulations are in order. Weird, though—congrats on being not guilty."

"Daria told me about it. Bizarre. Who would have guessed it was pre-teens and computers and online stuff? It's a crazy world. Daria's thrilled for you."

"Not so sure about that." Kevin's smile dimmed. "I should have told her from the start." He lowered his head. "I was so embarrassed. Like, even though I knew I was innocent, my name was out there as some kind of pervert. And everyone knew it. Including Daria. I felt like I couldn't face her."

Zahn nodded and said nothing. He knew that feeling, but didn't want to talk about it. He wanted to talk to Gabe Elliot.

"I deserted her and left her to deal with my problem alone. Do you know what I'm talking about?"

Zahn remained silent. Was Kevin even aware his question wasn't rhetorical? Hell, yes, he knew what Kevin was talking about. The young man had basically retold Zahn's own story with Daria and with his wife, Sheila, eight years ago, after their son had died. He had taken off and left them to grieve alone. Zahn didn't have the time now, nor the inclination, to rehash that period of his life. Two more girls were trapped out here somewhere. He needed to help find them.

He continued to stare at Kevin. Yes, Zahn understood what the young man was going through. And he knew one thing for sure. Kevin shouldn't just give up on Daria and walk away.

But he also knew this was Daria's business.

Not his.

"Yeah, Kevin," he said. "I do."

Kevin held Zahn's eyes for a second longer, then turned back to working on the horse.

"Where's Gabe at? I was looking to talk to him," Zahn said.

"Not in yet. He called and told me he had to take care of some stuff."

Zahn glanced toward the door and then back at Kevin. "Saw his truck out front. Thought he was here."

Kevin looked puzzled. He stood and walked over to the barn door, poking his head outside. He turned back to Zahn. "Just mine."

Zahn had spent an entire morning two days before following Kevin around in a maroon truck. Not a tan truck. "Huh. I saw you in town the other day driving a maroon truck. I assumed it was yours."

"Nope. The maroon Dodge is Gabe's. Tan Toyota is mine. But I used Gabe's truck all morning that day I saw you in the library. My Toyota was in the shop getting a new fuel pump. Gabe let me borrow his for some errands." Kevin laughed. "His Dodge is nice. But it ain't no Toyota. Mine's going to last ten years and two hundred thousand miles longer than his. Guarantee it."

Zahn stared at Kevin. When Perez had described the maroon truck, he had immediately thought of Kevin. Then, he'd dismissed the thought just as fast because Janae had said *older man*. And Kevin's accusers had confessed to making up the exposure story. Kevin was no longer anywhere close to being a suspect. Zahn felt a tingle at the top of his spine and his gut suddenly ached.

Maroon truck.

Older man.

Lives on west side of the valley.

Horses? Maybe.

No way.

Zahn's heart pounded. He'd never met a man as confident, introspective, and grounded as Gabe Elliot. Absolutely no way could he be involved. No way. *Could he?* His gut cramped as he thought about the afternoons Daria had spent in this stable. He bent over and leaned on his knees.

"Are you okay, Tyler?"

Zahn looked up. "Cramp," he said, and straightened. Kevin had concern in his eyes. Zahn thought about Perez and how the deputy had always warned him about not letting friendships blind you to facts, to be objective.

Zahn wasn't ready to share his suspicions with Kevin. "I was thinking I'd swing by Gabe's and see if I could catch him at home. Have you been to his place?"

"I have. Why don't you call him? He's probably not home. He said he had errands."

"Yeah, I don't want to interrupt that. It's close, right? If he's not there, I'll leave him a note."

Kevin's phone rang and he accepted the call. "Kevin here."

Pause.

"Yep. Give me five minutes."

He hung up and looked at Zahn. "They want me up at the lodge. You want directions, right?"

Zahn nodded.

Kevin said, "It's only like ten, fifteen minutes away. You know Deer Meadows off of Highway 24?

Zahn nodded again.

"Drive past the Deer Meadows entrance about two miles and take a right on the gravel driveway. It's not marked, but it's the only driveway with gravel."

"Thanks, Kevin," Zahn said, striding toward the door. He paused and looked back at Kevin. "Does Gabe have horses there?"

Kevin laughed. "Does a duck live near water? He's got two of them."

Zahn didn't laugh. Couldn't. He tasted bile in his mouth, but his face felt too numb to swallow.

Gabe Elliot?

Was it even possible?

CHAPTER 43

It took longer than fifteen minutes to get to Elliot's place and not because of Kevin's directions. The redeemed boyfriend had provided Zahn the correct route. It was the fire trucks. And Zahn's frantic calls to Perez.

"I think it's Elliot," he said, putting his phone on speaker.

"You talked to him?"

"No. I can't find him. But I think the girls might be at his place up by Frenchman's Creek. I'm headed there now."

"Don't approach that place without me. I'm on my way. Share your location on your phone." Zahn heard Perez click off.

As he turned north, he immediately spied a smoke plume billowing from the valley's edge. He had to pull over three times, allowing the screaming emergency response vehicles to pass him.

The smoke didn't register at first. A fire somewhere. But as he followed Kevin's directions and wound his way west up paved and then gravel roads, he pushed harder on the accelerator. No coincidence. Elliot's place was on fire.

Zahn ran through the facts.

Janae found.

Description matched Elliot.

Vehicle matched Elliot's.

Janae said he kept two more girls under the barn.

Elliot knew the game was up when he lost Janae. So this fire was definitely not an accident. Was he burning evidence of his crimes? And, more importantly, was the evidence human?

As he skidded around the corner of the gravel driveway, movement filled his windscreen, and he jammed on his brakes. The truck slid and slowed, just grazing the side of a horse. The animal bumped sideways, stumbled forward, then regained its feet, facing Zahn. He gripped the wheel and stared at the horse. The roan stared back, wild-eyed, its flanks heaving and nostrils flaring. Then the animal shook and bolted into the woods. Zahn let out his breath and hit the gas again.

A pumper truck straddled the turnaround facing the house, dowsing a fire leaping a hundred feet into the air. Several firefighters brandishing hoses augmented the pumper on both sides, and Zahn spotted an orange-haloed silhouette of another pumper truck furiously spraying the house. Beyond, another fire raged. The barn was also on fire.

He plowed his truck into the brush on the house side of the driveway. They would need more than the two fire trucks currently working the fires. The first pumper sat angled between the house and the second pumper, forming a vee to attack the flames. The firefighter teams concentrated on the house. No one noticed Zahn.

Zahn glanced from the burning house to the burning barn. The barn fire was even bigger, folding itself toward the house like a bear protecting its young. Emergency response must have assumed any trapped people would be in the house.

He ran to the back end of the pumper, where a man barked into a radio.

"Hey," Zahn rasped, the acrid smoke choking his voice. "What about the barn?"

The man looked up at Zahn with a quizzical glare.

"Who are you?" he yelled. "Get the hell back from here."

Zahn stopped, and the firefighter stepped forward.

"Is this your place? Are you Mr. Elliot?"

"No," Zahn said. "But I know him. I think he set the fire." Zahn stepped forward to meet the firefighter. "And I think there might be at least two girls under the barn."

"What the hell? The barn?"

Zahn nodded. "The barn."

A firefighter from the hose crew rounded the corner of the pumper. "What's the status on the other trucks?" He stopped when he saw Zahn. "Zahn? What're you doing here?"

Zahn recognized Craig Lucas, a SAR volunteer who also donated his time to the fire department. "I'm trying to—"

The radio operator interrupted. "He says there could be people under the barn. Kids."

Lucas turned back to Zahn, and Zahn nodded.

"I vouch for him. Move the teams, Benny."

The radio operator nodded and thumbed his mic. "Attention on scene. Attention on scene. Abort the house. I say again, abort the house. Move the main effort over to the barn. We have reports there might be people over there."

Zahn's gut ached. If the girls were in the house, then he had just blown any chance of saving them. He looked at the inferno that was the barn. Zahn didn't see any way they could survive that either. Damned if you do. Damned if you don't.

Another firefighter, closer to Zahn's age, strode around the pumper and walked up to the two men. "What's going on, Benny?" He turned to Zahn and Lucas. "What's happening here?"

Zahn opened his parched mouth, but Lucas interrupted. "Listen, Chief. This is Tyler Zahn from Search & Rescue. You know, from that Dillon reservoir thing last year? He says there may be kids under the barn. I trust him."

"In the barn?" The chief looked over the two men's shoulders at the tree-high flames. "Little late for that."

"No." Zahn jumped in. "Like in a bunker. Under the barn."

"A bunker? What the hell—"

"It's a criminal case, Chief." Zahn interrupted. "I mean, we're just going off eyewitness statements right now, but I can tell you we have a witness saying that at least two young girls are being held hostage in a barn, on the west side of the valley, by an older man with a maroon pickup."

The chief scanned the property. "Don't see a truck, except for that one." He pointed at Zahn's truck.

"That's mine."

The chief squinted at Zahn, then punched his radio. "This is the chief. You heard Benny right. Move the main effort to the barn. Now."

He looked at Zahn and said, "I don't know why I'm questioning you. It's obvious this thing was no accident. The barn and the house are independent fires. And we get like three calls a year out here, max. If you say there might be girls under the barn, then I'm sure the hell going to have my boys find out."

Zahn heard a yell, and Benny reached out for him. "Move back. We're going to turn the trucks around."

Zahn scrambled aside as the firefighters pivoted their effort toward the barn.

He glanced back at the house and prayed it was empty. Daria believed in prayer. It felt right.

A scorching wind pressed his shirt to his back and he turned to face the flames. The flames of hell.

Zahn prayed the barn was empty, as well.

CHAPTER 44

"Perez, what's your status?" Zahn watched the firefighters pivot their effort to the barn.

"I'm almost there—turning off 24 right now. Where are you waiting?"

Zahn said nothing.

"Shit. I told you to wait." Zahn knew Perez wasn't surprised at his failure to follow instructions. "What's the situation?"

Zahn described the fire and his theory about the girls.

"I'm three minutes out," Perez said. "Tell me again why you think it's Elliot."

"Because he's not here. The horses are loose. And his truck is gone." Zahn paused. "His maroon truck."

Silence.

"Maroon truck?"

"Maroon truck." Zahn paused a beat. "It all matches up. Yes, there could be more than one older guy out here with horses and a maroon truck. Those maroon Dodges are everywhere. But a deliberate fire when we're so close to breaking this thing open? I think it's him."

Perez said nothing for a few seconds, then broke the silence. "I'm coming up the driveway. Talk to you in a sec."

"Got it," Zahn said, and stabbed his phone's screen to hang up.

Shit. All those discussions with Elliot about a higher authority and trusting in it. Doing the right thing. The power of faith. Was Elliot playing him the whole time? Talking up the good Christians over at

Beyond Adventure while playing the devil himself? Or was Elliot just fricking crazy? Some sort of deranged evangelical? Zahn wasn't sure. Regardless of Elliot's mental state, the man had fooled everyone. He'd earned Zahn's complete trust in just weeks. The wise mentor. The man who'd also lost a child and dealt with it better than Zahn. Or maybe not.

Zahn pressed a button on his phone and called Daria. Five rings and the call went to voicemail. Which was odd. Ever since she'd injured the shoulder, she'd picked up his calls on the first two rings. Bathroom? Shower?

"Hey, Dar, it's Dad. I'm out with Rick Perez. Good news. They found Janae. Down in Salida. She's safe now. Uninjured."

Zahn paused. "But, listen. Some of the evidence is pointing at the church camp again. Not Kevin. We all know he's innocent. But listen, Dar? I need you to stay away from there until I say it's okay. You understand? Call me when you get this message."

Zahn hung up the phone. He wasn't sure why he didn't mention Elliot to Daria—just didn't seem right to tell her on an answering machine he suspected another friend of hers of a crime. Zahn stepped around his Toyota toward the fire trucks, which now aimed their twin beams of water at the barn.

The firefighters had changed from their vee set-up to a crossfire formation assault on the fire. The barn's rear had already collapsed, and the bulk of the conflagration roared at the front, closest to the house. Attacking the flames from the side, they tried to push the fire toward the smoldering remnants leading to the corral.

Zahn recalled Perez's debrief. *Janae said they walked between the stalls to a place where they climbed down. By a feeding trough.*

Nothing remained of the stalls. No feeding troughs. Charred beams and wood and ash blanketed the floor.

The chief approached Zahn and stood at his side. "No way anyone survived if they were above ground. You still figure something's underneath?"

Zahn nodded. "I think so."

The chief shook his head, staring at the barn. "Unless they've got some kind of fancy ventilation system drawing and expelling air from a distance…" He hesitated. "And unless the place is fire-proofed…well, I'm not very optimistic."

Zahn glanced at the man. "I know, Chief. I know."

Perez's vehicle sped up the driveway. The deputy parked behind Zahn's truck and opened the rear of his department Tahoe for his crutches. Zahn watched him swing forward two steps, then drop the crutches and hobble toward the two of them. Perez's eyes tracked the firefighters' efforts, then turned toward the house where the larger fire still raged.

The chief followed Perez's gaze. "Yeah, that thing's going to burn to the ground, Rick. We shifted over to the barn based on what Mr. Zahn here told us. You okay with that?"

Perez looked at Zahn. Zahn raised his eyebrows.

"Yeah, Chief. Good call. We believe our suspect kept two to three girls under a barn in this area of the valley. Don't have proof they're here, but we certainly have enough to assume they might be."

The chief nodded. Zahn heard a yell from their left, and the three men turned.

"Chief! Chief! Come check this out," shouted a firefighter manning a hose.

The chief moved toward the woman, then turned back to Zahn and Perez. "Come on, but stay behind me, okay?"

Zahn and Perez followed the chief. The woman on the hose cut off the stream and pointed toward the barn's center, where the fire had reduced the structure to ground level.

"See that defined area in the middle?" She looked back at the chief.

"You mean where the wood fell to the sides? Like a walkway or something, right?"

The woman nodded. "That's what I'm thinking. That's how my barn's set up."

"So, what? What are you trying to say, Chandra?"

"Okay, so track it down the center. There's a pile of wood. See that?"

"Got it."

"Watch this," Chandra levered open the nozzle on the hose, aiming the stream of water at the smoldering heap of wood. The powerful jet blasted at the beams, hardly moving them. Chandra angled the stream left two feet against a thin section of joined planks. This time, the pressure lifted a corner of the wooden slab. The stream caught the edge, and Chandra crouched lower for a better angle, lifting the planks several inches.

The slab covered a hole in the barn floor.

"I see it," Zahn said, as the trapdoor slipped from the water stream and slammed back down.

"What?" Perez turned at Zahn's voice.

"It's a hole. Like a tunnel thing, right?" Zahn looked at Chandra.

The young woman nodded.

Tunnel. Elliot. Fire. Zahn reached for his phone. He should have told Daria specifically to stay away from Elliot.

"Yep, I saw it, too," the chief called, striding away from the group. He pulled his radio out of his holster. Zahn could hear his words from where he stood. "All stations, all stations: listen up. Circle to the back of the barn. I say again, use your hoses from the rear. Focus on the center of the barn. We need to suppress and cool it, so we can send a team in."

As Zahn tried to get through to Daria, he watched the firefighters levering off their hoses and turning their faces toward the chief. Several of them traded skeptical glances. Another firefighter levered open his hose and re-attacked the wall of flames to his front.

The chief saw it as well. He reached for his radio again. "I may not have been clear. We've got potential victims *under* this barn. I need you to clear the entry. Move it. Now."

The reaction was immediate this time. The men shut down their hoses and moved with the trucks, repositioning near Zahn and Perez.

Zahn still couldn't reach Daria and left a more detailed message this time, including Elliot's name. His gut twisted. Go check on his daughter? Or wait and see if he was wrong about the girls under the stable?

Twenty minutes passed before the flames and embers and hot wood and metal were under control. Two firefighters in protective gear advanced on the trapdoor, picking their way through the smoldering debris obstructing the center of what remained of the barn. Zahn recognized Chandra, carrying an ax, her teammate in trail wielding a six-foot long pry bar.

Chandra hooked the ax on the trapdoor's edge, prying it open. A plume of smoke billowed from the hole. Both firefighters aimed their headlamps down the pit.

Chandra raised her radio. "We can see the bottom. Just concrete. Maybe another doorway down there. We'll need the ladder. I don't trust the rungs built into this thing."

The chief turned to a nearby firefighter and nodded. "Cooper's team is bringing it. What about the floor you're on? Stable?"

"Looks that way. It's a concrete slab until this hole. It looks like he built rooms under the concrete. You know what I mean?"

"Roger. So it looks structurally sound?"

"Best we can tell. We're comfortable going down. Maybe send someone to man the top of the hole while we're below."

The chief turned to Perez. "Do you think there's any chance the guy who took these girls is down there with them?"

Perez glanced at Zahn. "Well, his truck's not here. I don't see him lighting a fire and then crawling underneath it. Doesn't make sense." Zahn nodded in agreement.

The chief pulled the radio to his mouth. "Roger. I was asking the deputy about whether there might be a suspect down there. Have the guys bringing the ladder stay and monitor. You think they need masks where you're at?" He took a few steps closer to the barn.

"No. We'll keep them on below, but they don't need masks up here." Zahn heard a pause on the radio, then Chandra's voice again. "And, Chief? I don't think we need to worry about a suspect. There's a lot of smoke."

Cooper rejoined the group, and the two firefighters hauling a ladder vectored toward the crew at the hole.

The three men and Chandra lowered the ladder into the smoldering pit.

The chief nodded as the lead crew disappeared, then turned to Zahn and Perez, shaking his head.

"She doesn't think they're down there?" Perez's voice was quiet.

Zahn's head shook. "More likely, she doesn't think anyone's alive."

CHAPTER 45

Kevin's news left Daria's heart full. He couldn't stay—he had to get back to the stable because Elliot wasn't working. Another errand or something.

Daria felt such a sense of relief for her friend. He didn't deserve what had happened to him. No one did—except the guilty.

She heard her father let out his breath when she told him. Then suck it in when she revealed they were talking again. "Don't rush things, Dar," he had said. "I'm sure he's still processing everything that happened."

Daria hadn't replied to her father's advice. The silence between Kevin and Daria had made the whole situation worse. Kevin had stopped talking, and Daria had packed up and left. Not talking had turned out to be a poor solution.

You would have thought she had learned this lesson by now. She was no stranger to what silence did to a relationship. Her dad was living proof of that. Here she was, six years later, trying to rebuild the ties between them. Her dad was also trying hard—she could tell. Daria knew remorse over those lost years weighed heavily on Zahn. And he'd changed. No more long silences or refusals to talk. Heck, now they were even discussing religion with each other.

She wondered if she should have tried harder to engage him after her brother had died. Before her dad had left. She knew Zahn wished he would have tried harder with her. And her mom. No one blamed

Daria. She was just a kid when it happened. It all could have been different.

Daria stared out the window. Should she have a *sit down* with her dad, like she'd just had with Kevin? It couldn't make things worse.

She grabbed her journal and a pen. How would the conversation go?

Dad,

Thank you for understanding about Kevin. He's a good man. I like him.

When I told you we were talking again, I felt like you were almost jealous. Which is weird, right? Why would you be jealous of a boyfriend?

But, as I considered my feelings and guessed at yours, I realized I'm making an assumption that you already know my feelings. And that you're uncomfortable with Kevin.

Daria nibbled on the pen's clicker before continuing.

It's not about Kevin, though, is it? It's about you, right?

Dad, I love you. I don't judge you. I feel like you're trying to make my visit with you perfect to make up for our years apart.

But you have nothing to make up for. I forgave you the day you left. I know, I was just thirteen, and it was all crazy and so, so sad about Jacob's death. But I never blamed you. Not for Jacob. Not for leaving. I know you had a hole in your heart—I did too. So did Mom. That hole is still there for all of us.

So yes, it's been awkward getting reacquainted. Yes, you can be over-controlling. And yes, I'm going to keep seeing Kevin.

I just want to say sorry. I'm sorry for not sharing my feelings with you sooner. I thought you knew.

She reread her words. Her father needed to hear this. She'd tell him tonight.

Daria snapped a picture of the entry before tucking the journal into her backpack next to her bed. She'd share the pic with Kevin and see what he thought. Get his opinion. After all, she hadn't seen him in what? A whole two hours? She guessed he was finishing up at the stables.

She stood and walked to the mudroom where her coat hung. Stuck her arm through one sleeve and draped the other over her shoulder.

Daria locked the house and walked the thousand yards to the stable, awkwardly ducking under the fence at the edge of Elk Trace's property. She still wasn't putting weight on her shoulder, and the sling helped to keep it tight to her chest.

As she skirted the copse of trees next to the barn, Elliot's truck came into view, a trailer hitched to the back. It was the first time she had seen his truck pulling a trailer. Daria guessed he was moving some of the Beyond Adventure horses somewhere. The other barn on the north end? The vet? She hoped nothing was the matter with her horse, Gus.

Kevin's truck was nowhere to be seen. Maybe Elliot knew where he had gone.

As she rounded the trailer, she heard a muffled thump. From inside the trailer. Were the horses already loaded?

Daria raised the canvas flap hanging above the rear ramp and got a face full of Gus's rear end, loaded on the left side of the trailer. She wondered if he was sick.

Daria heard a hoarse cry from the other side.

"Help!" A loud *shhhhh* followed the plea.

Daria shifted to the right, poking her head around the partition bifurcating the trailer. She scanned the empty slot.

Which wasn't empty.

Two girls huddled atop a bale of hay at the trailer's front, staring at her.

CHAPTER 46

Elliot dropped the horse packs he'd pulled from the Beyond Adventure barn and stared at Zahn's daughter peering into the rear of the trailer.

Shit.

Nothing was going even close to right.

"Daria, how's it going?"

The woman whirled, and Elliot recognized confusion and, yes, fear in her eyes. And it wasn't from staring at a horse's ass.

"There're girls in here," Daria said. "We need to help them." She stepped from the trailer's rear bumper and moved toward the handles, which locked the ramp in the upright position.

"There sure are," Elliot agreed.

Daria looked back at Elliot. "But what—I don't understand…"

"No," Elliot said. "You probably wouldn't." He sighed. "Go ahead. Lower the ramp and we'll put you in the back with the girls? Okay? You can keep them company. Hell, you can join our team here."

Daria stepped from the trailer and backed away from Elliot, shaking her head. "I don't get it, Gabe. What's going on?"

Elliot stared at her with a thin smile.

"I'm calling my dad," she said.

Elliot nodded. "All right, Daria. You do that."

Daria kept edging backward.

"But as soon as you call, I'm going to shoot one of those girls in there. Do you understand that?"

Daria stopped moving. Her mouth dropped open. "Shoot?"

A voice called from the trailer. "Please come. Don't let Jefe kill us."

Elliot raised his voice. "Shut up, Nicole." He looked back at Daria. "Well, golly, Daria. I can't figure out if you're more surprised that I'm going to kill a girl, or that I'm only killing one of the two. Which one is it?"

Daria said nothing.

Elliot kept talking. "See, I have to keep one of them alive, in case a hostage is useful. But with you along, I can keep them both alive. Maybe I can even let you go later." He paused. "So what's it going to be, Daria? Should we make it a threesome? An 'alive and breathing' team? Or should I let you go, and just dump a body on my way out?"

Daria met Elliot's eyes, then looked at the pistol packed in his belt holster. A girl sobbed quietly in the background.

"Don't kill anyone, Gabe."

"Well, now, that's what I guessed you'd say. The Good Book says something like, 'no greater man than one who would lay down his life for a friend.' I know you're not a man. And you just met your new friends here. But I think your decision says a lot about your character, Daria. Well done."

Daria said nothing.

"So, go ahead and lower the trailer ramp, would you? Grab the handles up there at eye level on each side? Think you can do that with your one good arm?"

Daria raised the handle on the girls' side of the trailer. She glanced back at Elliot. He nodded toward the opposite handle. Daria walked over and lifted the handle, pushing her good shoulder against the ramp.

"Now lower it on down," Elliot said.

Daria moved her hand from the latch to the ramp and eased the pressure off her shoulder, lowering the ramp to the ground. A chain looped behind the horse. The girls huddled on the other side, staring at Daria.

"Climb on in, little lady," Elliot said.

Daria gave him a sharp look, then turned and walked up the ramp. She ducked under the canvas curtain and disappeared into the trailer.

"Stop," Elliot called.

Daria returned to the curtain and leaned out so she could see Elliot. "Your cell phone. Hand it to me."

Daria slid her phone from her back pocket and thrust it toward Elliot. He snatched it and stuffed it into his front pocket. Daria shuffled back to join the girls, and Elliot stooped and grabbed the saddle packs, hoisting them to his shoulder and climbing into the trailer. He dropped them inside, then raised the ramp and latched the handles before draping the canvas over his shoulders and folding his arms across the top of the gate. He gazed at Daria and the girls in the dim light.

"Those girls are too short to climb this ramp. You're too crippled to get over it. But I don't know." He scratched his chin. "Rachel. Get on over here. Daria, you come too."

Daria returned to her feet and waited as Rachel rose beside her. She grabbed her hand, and they approached Elliot.

He dug into his pocket and pulled out two zip ties, nodding at Daria's good hand. "Hold that out here. Rachel, you stick one of your hands up here too." Elliot watched a bead of sweat roll from Daria's brow, and he took a deep breath. The familiar scent of hay mingled with the pungent odor of fear.

Good.

Elliot used both the zip ties to link their wrists together, then nodded toward the front of the trailer. "Off you go now."

He ducked back outside from under the canvas and fastened it, dropping a padlock over the cinch holding the cover. He paused and scanned the barn and open fields leading toward the lodge. Still no one here. Kevin was probably done for the day. Elliot walked around the trailer and gave it a loud slap as he approached the truck's door.

Time to move out.

The good news? He had a Janae replacement. Older than his customers liked, but…fuck the customers. He was freelancing now.

The bad news? The bigger the team, the slower they moved.

He smiled. Just an hour ago, he'd considered letting Nicole and Rachel burn. Then he had changed his mind. He wasn't giving up on the team.

Elliot recalled his daughter's journal: *Christina never gave up on the team. The team failed her.* Sure, three girls might be a hindrance. Or maybe leverage. He'd just have to see. If they failed him, he'd get rid of them. Including the newest member.

CHAPTER 47

Think. Think. Think.

Elliot couldn't decide if adding Daria to the team had been a stroke of genius or a dumbass move. Of course, she wasn't a fit for normal operations. None of his customers liked college girls. Wasn't their thing. Their shtick.

But these were not normal times. Elliot had a sense they were approaching the end—and desperate times called for desperate measures.

Taking Daria meant extra time; she only had one good arm. And it also meant extra risk. Elliot wasn't sure what the law enforcement guys had figured out, whether they knew he had the other girls. But once they knew he had Daria, it was game on. They'd be after him in force with their pal Tyler Zahn leading the charge. Fire in his eyes and vengeance on his breath. Of that, there was no doubt.

When Elliot had met Zahn, he'd sensed a soul in need of guidance. He'd fed the younger man decent lines of philosophical shit, and made him feel better. But, at the same time, he had also clearly recognized Zahn's inner warrior. You mess with his family, and that boy was coming out swinging.

Daria could be a help, though. She wouldn't run so long as he was threatening the lives of the two girls. Maybe she could help keep the team moving. Take on that camp counselor role and inspire those young ones for what lay ahead.

Keeping the girls was always the long pole in the tent for the bug-out plan. That's why Elliot had seriously considered just letting them burn. The remainder of the steps were straightforward:

1. Burn the house and barn
2. Decoy the cops toward an I-70 escape
3. Ditch the truck and head west into the mountains on the horses
4. Hole up in his mining shack until the search stopped.
5. Figure it out from there.

Step one was complete. He doubted his ranch structures had taken more than a couple of hours to burn to the ground. There was no doubt he was a wanted man.

The next step was in motion. He pulled the truck and trailer into the broad shoulder of the gravel road leading to Aspen Lake, nodding at Janae's original captor—ATV man—who sat parked at the trailhead in a shiny blue Chevy Silverado truck.

Elliot grabbed the duffel bag from his passenger seat, stepped from the truck, and met the man by the tailgate.

"What do you need? Lose another girl?"

"Nope. Need logistical support."

"How soon? I got—"

Elliot unzipped the backpack, reached inside and pulled out a fistful of hundred-dollar bills.

"How about right now? I don't got time for your shit. I got ten grand in this bag. I want you to get someone to drive my truck as far down I-70, heading west as they can, and then ditch it. Can you do that?"

ATV man eyed the money. "That, my friend, is something I can do." He looked over Elliot's shoulder. "Trailer, too?"

Elliot followed his eyes. "Nope. Here's how that will work." The two men walked together toward Elliot's truck. "I'm going to unhook here, and I want you to take my truck and give me your keys. You leave. I'll hook the trailer to your truck. I'm going to drive it farther up toward the lake and leave the keys on the tire. When you get back, you take the trailer and ditch it wherever you want. But away from here. Got it?"

ATV man nodded slowly. "What's in it?"

Elliot cocked his head at the man. "Horses, dumbshit. It's a horse trailer."

"Right." ATV man said, staring at Elliot. "Got it." He grabbed the backpack of money from Elliot's outstretched hand.

Elliot cranked the trailer off his truck and pulled the Dodge over next to ATV man's Silverado. He handed the man the keys and watched him drive away.

It only took him five minutes to hook the Silverado up to the trailer. He plugged the electrical connection in—wouldn't want someone out here missing his turn signal—then walked around the back of the trailer and spun the lock on the cinch ties. He lifted the flap and shone his flashlight inside.

One little, two little, three little girls, he hummed. Well, two little ones and a biggie.

"Hey, hey, hey, team. Let's get this show on the road. You ready?"

Nicole and Rachel stared at the flashlight beam and said nothing. Like the dead fish they were.

Daria had her hand up to her brow, shielding her eyes from the light.

"Gabe?" she called.

"Right here, honey."

"Gabe, you can stop this right now. My dad knows all the law enforcement guys around here. I'm sure he can work something out."

Elliot laughed out loud. "Sweetheart, that's perfect. You are just as naïve as I guessed." He laughed again. "That train has already left the station. There's no turning back, no re-dos or do-overs." He paused. "You've got an important role in this, honey."

"What?"

"We're heading to the mountains. You girls on foot. Me on the horse." Elliot smiled. "It won't be easy. Harder than anything these young ones have ever done before. Don't know about you. You're in good shape, but you got that shoulder thing going on."

He moved the flashlight beam from Daria's face to her sling. "Anyway, you're going to be my team motivator. If things get too slow for me, I'll lighten the load. Get rid of a girl or two. Or you can use your life skills coaching abilities and keep us together. Think you can do that?"

Daria's good shoulder slumped. "Gabe, you wouldn't."

Elliot laughed. "Oh, Daria. You have no idea."

CHAPTER 48

"What's happening to us?" Daria turned her head toward the young girl's shaky whisper. The rumble of the trailer on the gravel road kept the volume at a constant roar, making conversation difficult.

"Hey, there. Nice hearing something from you guys," Daria said. She put her good arm around the girl. "What's your name?"

"I'm Nicole," the voice said. "And I want to know what's happening."

"She doesn't know," the other girl said. "She wasn't there. She doesn't know Jefe."

"And what's your name?" Daria shifted her eyes to the new speaker.

"That's Rachel," Nicole said. "We both know Jefe. When things go bad, he puts us in the hole."

Daria watched Rachel shake her head before speaking. "Nicole, have you ever even seen the hole?"

"No, but you know—"

"I know that Jefe keeps threatening us with the hole, but when things go wrong, girls disappear. They don't come back talking about the hole. They just don't come back."

"You mean, like Janae?"

Daria's head jerked. "You guys know Janae? Janae Longmont?"

Nicole nodded. "I don't know her last name, but we know a Janae. She's the newest girl. Jefe said he put her in the hole because she was bad."

"But we haven't seen her. And we probably won't see her again either. She's dead," Rachel said. The trailer hit a pot hole, launching the three girls airborne, then careening them back to the floor.

"You don't know that," Nicole said. "Maybe he let her go home. You're so negative."

Daria moved back to a sitting position. "Why do you think she's dead, Rachel? By the way, my name is Daria."

"We know. We heard Jefe talking to you," Rachel said. "I've just been thinking, is all. Jefe has us going to these video shoots and doing bad things..." Rachel paused and looked beyond Daria. Daria turned. Nicole was shaking her head.

"OK, *we're* not doing bad things. No touching. But it's not right. I mean, the marketers are taking movies of us in our swimsuits. Is that normal?"

"Oh, honey. No. That's not normal. I'd give you a hug, but I've got this dumb thing." Daria raised her bad arm.

"What happened?" Nicole eyed the sling.

"Fell off a horse."

"See, Nicole. Even Daria thinks it's bad," Rachel said. "So I figured, if anyone actually got to go home, they would have told people about it, and Jefe would get caught, and all of this would stop. But it hasn't stopped. So, that means the girls aren't going home. They aren't coming back from this 'so-called' hole, either, so I think they're dead."

Daria said nothing. Unfortunately, she thought Rachel might be right. But agreeing with her wouldn't help.

"Listen," Daria said. "Something is happening with this—what do you call him, Jefe?"

The girls nodded.

"Something is happening. Have you taken trips like this before? In a horse trailer?"

"No," Nicole said. "This is the first time."

"Right. I think he's afraid of getting caught, and he's moving you guys to somewhere new."

"What about you? Why are you here?"

Daria smiled. Rachel was starting to talk.

"I think I'm what you might call collateral damage," Daria said. "I found you guys, and I wasn't supposed to." She paused. "But that's a good thing. You know why?"

"Because you'll help us escape?" Nicole sounded hopeful.

"I don't know," Daria said. "I've got this bad arm, and there are two of you. I'm scared if we don't all escape together, he might hurt the person who gets left behind." She gave a thin smile. "No, the good thing is something else. It's my dad."

"Your dad?"

"My dad." Daria nodded. "My dad is a real bad ass—whoops, sorry. When he figures out I'm gone—and that I might be with you guys— he's going to come after us."

"Really?"

"Really. And you know who his friends are?"

"No. Who?"

"He's got friends in the sheriff's department and friends that are US Marshals. They're all going to come save us." Daria paused. "So that should be our plan."

"To get rescued?" Nicole frowned. "That doesn't sound like a plan."

"Yeah," Rachel said. "My dad is in the Army, and he always says, 'hope is not a plan.'"

"No. The plan isn't to just hope," Daria said. "We'll help. To make it easier for them to find us."

"How are we going to do that?" Rachel looked doubtful.

Daria smiled. "I've got an idea. It's called 'go slow and let them know.'"

"What does that mean?"

"It means we've got to slow Elliot down—"

"Who's Elliot?"

"He's the one you guys are calling Jefe. I know him as Elliot. He told me slow would be bad for us, so we need to be careful with this part of the plan. Try to get lots of rest breaks. Try to fall once in a while. But if he gets too angry, then we'll need to speed up."

"What about the 'let them know' part?"

"Did you girls ever hear about Hansel and Gretel?"

"Yes," both girls said in unison.

"How did they keep from getting lost?"

"Breadcrumbs!" said Nicole.

"Right. We need to figure out how to leave a trail. How to leave something behind for my dad and his guys to follow. You guys got any ideas?"

"I got something," Rachel said.

"What do you got, honey?"

"Kleenex. I've got two tissues in my back pocket. Can you reach them?"

"Maybe. But I'm not sure how long Kleenex will last." Daria turned to Nicole. "How about you?"

"I'm sitting on a towel. It's all dirty, though." Nicole pressed her back toward Daria. "If you use the end of that plastic tie thing on your hand, you could tear it up."

Daria looked over her useless arm at Nicole. "Not from this side I can't. Can you move over between Rachel and me?"

Nicole scooted forward and then backed between the two other girls. Daria and Rachel leaned forward and poked at the towel while she held it taut behind her. The hard plastic punctured the terry cloth.

"It's through," Rachel said.

"Right," Daria agreed. "But if he keeps our hands tied, she won't be able to reach it. Rachel, use your free hand with the plastic, and see if you can rip the towel around toward the front."

The girl pulled on the plastic while Nicole leaned forward and the towel gave away. Nicole reached back and pulled until she had a handful of cloth.

"Got it," she said.

The trailer slowed suddenly, and Nicole fell back into Daria and Rachel.

"Get back to where you were, Nicole. I think we're stopping," Daria said.

Nicole scrambled back to Daria's side.

Rachel twisted her wrist and clasped Daria's hand. "What's going to happen now?"

Daria squeezed the girl's small hand. "I don't know, sweetheart." She nudged Nicole with her bad shoulder. "Remember the plan?"

Nicole nodded, thumbing the torn material at the bottom of her shirt. "Go slow and let them know."

CHAPTER 49

There were no bodies under the barn. Which didn't prove the girls were alive, but at least lent a glimmer of hope.

Zahn wracked his brain as he drove back to his house. Where would Elliot go after torching his ranch? If he had taken the girls, Zahn guessed that he'd already departed the county. Elliot had to know he was a fugitive the second the barn had burst into flame.

He loosened his tight grip on the steering wheel. If Elliot *was* long gone, then Zahn didn't need to worry about Daria. Still—she deserved an update on the man she'd considered a friend. And Kevin needed to know, as well. The cops were going to want to talk to him about his boss—or former boss.

Zahn hit his phone's shortcut key again and listened to his daughter's voicemail message. This certainly wasn't the most convenient time for ignoring his calls. Zahn planned to stop by the house and shower, change out of his smoke-saturated clothes for something fresh, and meet Randall Williams to talk through this Elliot situation. But he'd feel better if he could just make contact with Daria first.

Zahn tapped the horn as he rolled into the driveway, but saw no movement in the window. Daria's car was parked out front in its usual spot. He punched the code into the locked front door.

"Daria!" Zahn called, closing the door and twisting the deadbolt. "Daria?"

His daughter had spent most of her recovery time on the big easy chair facing the living room TV. Not that she was watching the screen all day. Instead, she had plowed through a series of electronic books on her Kindle.

Which sat next to the empty chair.

Zahn walked through the house. No Daria.

He gave her another call.

Nothing.

The town was almost six miles away, but her car was out front. She wouldn't have ridden his bike there with her arm in a sling. Could Kevin have driven her?

Kevin.

She might have gone to the stables at Beyond Adventure to talk to Kevin. Zahn knew his daughter had forgiven the young man already. Not for the offense—Daria never believed he was guilty—but for keeping it to himself.

Over Daria's extended spring break, Zahn had discovered forgiveness was one of Daria's superpowers. She didn't judge, and when people made mistakes, she gave them the benefit of the doubt.

Unless it was her dad.

She had never said a judgmental word to his face. When he had asked Sheila about Daria's reaction to his abrupt exit from their lives eight years before, his former wife had said Daria didn't talk about it.

But Daria hadn't ever said anything to him about forgiveness either. It was a topic they just didn't broach.

The bad years. The lost years.

Zahn should have been the one to bring it up. After all, he was the adult. But he hadn't. So, he didn't know whether his only daughter had forgiven him.

Enough about me. She must be at the stables. Zahn headed out the door, jogging toward Beyond Adventure.

Approaching the corner of the barn, Zahn held his breath. He released it with a whoosh as he surveyed the empty parking area. He had hoped to find Kevin's tan Tacoma parked out front and had been nervous he would see Elliot's maroon truck instead.

Zahn ducked his head into the barn.

"Kevin? Anybody here?"

Silence.

"Daria?" he called out.

The barn was empty.

Maybe Kevin took her for a ride? He scanned the corral, counting the horses he'd grown accustomed to visiting. They were all accounted for except for Gus.

No way Kevin would take Daria riding on Gus with her broken collarbone. The boy was smarter than that.

He looked back to where Kevin usually parked. Did he take her to town in the truck?

He stood with the barn at his back, facing the mountains and the Beyond Adventure administration buildings and the dormitories. It was a ten-minute trip on foot, and his churning gut didn't want to waste the time. He pulled his phone from his pocket and checked the signal.

Three bars.

He typed the words *Beyond Adventure* into the phone and hit *Call* when the church camp popped up.

"Beyond Adventure, this is Shannon. How can I help you?"

"Hi, Shannon. This is Tyler Zahn. I'm a friend of Kevin's? Kevin Kilgore? He works there."

"Sure, I know Kevin. What's going on, Mr. Zahn?"

"I was wondering if I could get Kevin's number. I need to talk to him."

Shannon paused. Zahn realized he didn't sound like much of a friend if he was asking for Kevin's number.

"Or at least, can you tell me if he's up there? Do you have a way to contact him? I'm right down the road at your stables."

"Sure, I can tell him you're here. His truck is outside, so he's around. I'm seeing your number on caller ID. Is this the number you want him to call?"

"That'll work. Thanks."

Zahn punched off the phone and looked around the stables. Nothing here. He started walking up the road toward Beyond Adventure.

Was Daria up at the camp? She hadn't spent time up there with Kevin before, as far as he knew. They had always hung together at the stables and at Zahn's house. He doubted Beyond Adventure would allow one of their workers to bring a member of the opposite sex back to a dorm room, especially so soon after suspecting that same worker of inappropriate behavior with minors.

Zahn looked up from the road and saw Kevin's Tacoma trundling his direction from the main lodge. He stepped to the shoulder as the young man slowed and lowered his window.

"Hey, Tyler. How's it going?"

"Have you seen Daria? I can't find her." Zahn didn't have time for chitchat.

Kevin shook his head. "No. We talked a couple of hours ago at your house, but I haven't seen her since. You want me to call her?"

"Sure, but I've already been calling. She's not picking up." Zahn cocked his head at Kevin. "She wouldn't have taken a horse out by herself...do you think?"

"One of our horses? No way, not without asking. And not with her shoulder, right?"

"Right. You're right. It just seems weird that I can't reach her. I noticed Gus missing and thought—well, I'm not sure what I thought."

"Wait." Kevin gripped his truck's window frame. "Gus is gone? Are you sure about that?"

"He's not with the other horses. Maybe in another pasture?"

"No." Kevin shook his head. "He's supposed to be there. But I still don't believe Daria would have taken him out." He scrunched his nose. "She's not up at the lodge. I need to go check out this Gus thing. Hop in. We'll head back to the stables."

Zahn nodded, circling the truck and climbing into the passenger seat. It was time to tell Kevin about his boss too. Let him know law enforcement would want to talk to him.

"So, you've been tracking this Janae Longmont case, right? The lost girl?"

"Yeah, I've heard about it," Kevin voice sounded hesitant.

Shit. He thinks I'm still suspicious of him, Zahn thought.

"Kevin, relax. No one suspects you. They found the girl."

"That's great!" Kevin's eyebrows raised.

"We have a suspect. Not in custody yet. But we're pretty sure we've identified who's involved."

"Okay…"

"It's Gabe. Your boss, Gabe Elliot."

Kevin jammed his brakes fifty yards short of the stable and turned to Zahn.

"No, it's not. Not Gabe." Kevin's head swiveled back and forth. "No, it's not."

Zahn exited his side of the truck and circled over to where Kevin sat, opening his door for him. The young man remained frozen to his seat, still shaking his head.

"I can't believe it either," Zahn said. "But everything points that direction. You heard about the fire this afternoon, right?" He pointed north.

Kevin's dull eyes followed Zahn's gesture.

"That was Elliot's place," Zahn said.

Kevin climbed out of his truck. He approached the stable door, staggering like a sleepwalker, before pausing.

"Trailer's gone." He walked through the stable and stopped at the corral gate. "You're right. No Gus." Zahn heard no emotion in Kevin's voice. "Something's off. The trailer. Gus missing. I need to call Gabe."

"Look at me." Zahn watched as Kevin's eyes came into focus at his command. "That's what I'm trying to tell you. Everyone's looking for Elliot. He's in trouble."

Kevin pressed his phone to his ear, staring at Zahn. "No answer."

Zahn nodded his head. Both men were silent as the wind from the mountains rattled the barn door.

Kevin jerked as if he'd just awoken. "Okay. I need to go talk to Admin before I make a call to the police about Gus. I'll ask around at the lodge and see if anyone's seen Daria, but I'm not optimistic about that. Not sure she hung with anyone else up there but me."

"The police might be here before you make that call. They're going to need to talk to you about Elliot." Zahn paused. "I'm going back to the house. Maybe she was just on a walk." He cocked his head to the side. "I need to tell the Sheriff and my Marshal friend about your horse situation, though."

"Why's that?"

"What if it was Elliot? He knows the horse. He can pull the trailer. Who would question him if they saw him taking Gus?" Zahn eyed Kevin. "Right?"

"I mean, yeah, I guess so." The young man slowly nodded. "I don't know why he'd take the trailer and Gus, but it makes more sense than someone stealing those two things in broad daylight. But Elliot kidnapping girls? I just can't believe it." He froze.

Zahn noticed Kevin had switched to using Gabe Elliot's last name. Maybe he was coming to grips with Elliot's guilt.

Kevin looked at Zahn. "You don't think he's got Daria, do you?"

Zahn jerked and stared at the young man. "No, I don't. Actually, I didn't consider that. Why would he take her?"

"If he's on the run, why would he take a horse? None of the stuff you're saying about Elliot makes any sense."

"We're talking in circles and getting nowhere. You go to the lodge. If you hear anything about Daria, call me. I'll check the house again and give Deputy Perez a call. If I find her, I'll call you. Sound good?"

"Got it. You want a ride?" Kevin nodded toward Elk Trace and Zahn's house.

"Couple hundred yards. It's quicker for me to walk than for you to drive around."

Kevin backed out and turned toward the lodge as Zahn walked around the barn and picked up the trail to his house. He made it fifty feet before breaking into a slow jog, the taste of dust from Kevin's truck still lingering in his mouth.

His mind raced. What did Perez say last year during the bomb case? *We're trained not to believe in coincidence.*

Gabe Elliot, the man he trusted, was on the run with kidnapped adolescent girls, while Daria simultaneously goes missing?

Coincidence?

CHAPTER 50

"Daria?" Zahn burst into the living room, hoping his daughter had returned while he was at Beyond Adventure. "Daria?"

Nothing.

This time he noted every detail in the house. Walking through the mudroom, he tried to remember how many shoes and jackets his daughter had brought for her visit. Her windbreaker hung on the coat rack, trail runners parked underneath. She wasn't running.

Her hiking boots were missing, though, as was the green fleece she'd used for mail runs. He bounded up the stairs, knocked twice on her door, and entered.

Empty.

The bed was made, but Daria's clothes were strewn about the room.

Zahn let out his breath. No evidence that she'd changed her mind and decided to return home again. She was around somewhere.

He checked the closet, then the dresser, unsure what he was looking for. Daria's backpack lay next to her bed, zipper open, but Zahn had studiously avoided inspecting the bag. She always took it with her for long hikes or for downtown trips. The Colorado Rockies version of a handbag.

Zahn hesitated. Ten years ago, Sheila had spotted him dumping her purse out on the table, searching for the car keys. This was before Jacob's death, when all was normal, and arguments were as rare as snowstorms in July. The look in her eyes had never left him. Not angry so much as incredulous. It was as if she had walked in and caught him reading her email or something. *How could you do this?*

His first lesson in the privacy of the purse was his last. He hadn't touched his wife's or daughter's personal bag since. But he also hadn't run into this situation before: no contact with Daria, a boyfriend clueless as to her whereabouts, a suspected kidnapper on the loose, and at least two missing girls in the mix—condition unknown.

Zahn eyed the knapsack one more time, then snatched it and rifled through the contents. Wallet. Sunscreen. Lip balm. Journal. Water bottle.

All things she would take with her if she was going further than a short visit over to see Kevin.

He grabbed the journal. *Crossing the Rubicon.* It was one thing to open the bag. Reading his daughter's diary was the point of no return. But he needed to be sure.

He didn't have to read the whole notebook—just the last day or two. He flipped through the filled pages and opened the journal wide when the writing stopped. Thumbed back a page and read today's date.

Dad... Zahn's stomach dropped.

Thank you for understanding about Kevin... back to Kevin? He scanned forward as Daria switched to talking about her father. Him.

I forgave you the day you left. Someone was pounding on Zahn's heart with a mallet. He sank to his knees and reached up to touch his welling eyes. He did not deserve forgiveness, but here it was. Like Elliot had described the church. *Grace with no cost.*

The words he had desperately sought, but she never said. Until today. He returned his trembling finger to the beginning of the sentence, then stopped. What was he doing? Basking in redemption or finding his daughter? He continued to read, his hands shaking as they held the pages.

...I'm taking him a card today.

Zahn felt his blood rush to his face as he remembered Kevin's innocent expression when Zahn asked about Daria. How could—*Stop!*

Daria didn't write the word, but Zahn heard her voice ring in his head. *Think.*

He tucked the journal inside the backpack and sat on the bed.

Daria was the smartest young adult he knew. He trusted her judgment, even if it was tough to admit that to her. And his controlling issues didn't reflect that trust either. But she knew people.

Kevin wasn't acting confused about Daria. He *was* confused. A missing girlfriend, horse, and trailer all in the same day? Finding out his boss was on the run with two little girls and a ranch burning to the ground?

I'm taking him a card today.

Kevin hadn't seen Daria since he left Zahn's house. Daria had been taking him something, so she would have gone to the stables first. Then the lodge after not finding Kevin. But Kevin hadn't seen her there.

Zahn bolted down the stairs, digging in his pocket for his cellphone. He barreled out of the house and stopped next to his truck, thumbing Perez on speed dial.

"What's up?"

"Are you guys looking for Elliot's truck yet?"

"What? Are you kidding? We've got an Amber Alert covering four counties, and if we don't get a hit in the next hour, we're taking it statewide. Of course we're looking." He paused. "What's going on?"

"He's—he's…" Zahn choked, then swallowed, wincing at the sour taste in his mouth. "He's got my girl. He's got Daria."

"What are you talking about? We're not even sure if he still has the other girls. How would he get Daria?"

Zahn ran his theory through the deputy. Perez peppered him with questions.

"So you think Elliot's pulling a trailer? He's got a horse?"

"And possibly my daughter. And those other two girls, maybe."

"A horse? Why the hell would you delay for a horse? And a trailer? I mean, he has to drive over a mountain pass no matter which direction he goes. That stuff's just delaying his getaway. Especially if he has the girls. They'd slow him down too."

"Rick, I'm in on this. I need to help."

"Yeah, yeah. Of course. Get your ass down here to the police station. Meet me at the desk they gave Randall for his Marshal shit. I'll bring him up to speed on your info, and I'll update the alert to mention the trailer."

"I have to…"

"Zahn, get down here. Pull it together. You told me how you did it back in the desert, right? How you operated under family and combat stress. Compartmentalization, right? Do some of that right now."

Zahn nodded, forcing himself to take a long, deep breath, even though Perez couldn't see him. Compartmentalization. He was good at that. But the last time he did it, people died.

CHAPTER 51

A single tear trickled down Janae's cheek as she pressed the phone against her face. She sat in the Buena Vista Police Department listening to her parents sobbing on the other end of the line.

"I'm okay, Mom," she repeated. "I'm okay, really, truly." If she could escape from Jefe, then she was strong enough to keep from crying.

Janae was having a hard time understanding her parents between their choked voices and the lump she felt in her own throat. She couldn't believe it was over.

For her.

It wasn't over for Nicole and Rachel, and she knew she had to help them. And she would. Because the new Janae was brave. Well, not brave like she would ever run off alone again, but definitely courageous enough to act when bad things happened. Her hardware store parking lot escape had changed everything.

Make a move? She had swallowed her fear and moved.

Janae had hidden under the snowblower tarp for over an hour, her head throbbing from gas and oil fumes, before she heard them talking at the open garage door.

"He came through my gate and walked right into this garage. No knocking. No asking. Not anything. Like he owned the place."

"Right, ma'am. Did you see him carrying anything when you talked to him? Are you missing anything from in here?"

"Well, I'm not sure I remember. I think I would have noticed if he stole something of mine."

"Ma'am, you did right by calling the police. I don't know if we'll—"

As soon as Janae heard him say *police*, she ripped back the tarp, staring at the startled pair.

"I need help," she had said.

And that was that. Followed by a flurry of activity that had landed her back in Buena Vista several hours later on the phone with her parents, and with all kinds of police people lining up to ask questions.

She listened intently as her mother assured her they would arrive in Buena Vista in three hours. They were currently in Denver, pleading with the CBI to keep searching for Janae.

"Uncle Mike and Aunt Marcie are already on their way to come pick you up."

Janae felt a twinge of fear when her mother mentioned Uncle Mike. He made her uncomfortable, and she was done putting up with that.

"I'm not going home with them, Mom. I'll wait for you and Dad."

"But…"

"That's what I've decided."

Her mother didn't argue, and Janae guessed they would have a discussion about Uncle Mike later.

She handed the phone to Mr. Randall, the large African-American man from the US Marshals sitting across from her. She had learned about Marshals in social studies, but all she remembered was them wearing silver stars and chasing bad guys out of old Western towns. Mr. Randall didn't look like any of those guys.

"Yes…we do… probably another hour. Let me write that down."

It sounded like her mother was giving Mr. Randall instructions on how long he could ask Janae questions.

Janae smiled. It had never occurred to her that she would look forward to her mother controlling her life again.

•   •   •

Janae sat on the edge of a large roller chair halfway along a meeting table, nibbling on a sugar cookie. A mixture of uniformed and non-uniformed grown-ups surrounded her, all wearing big smiles. Which was weird. Like fake smiles or something. Janae studied their faces. Then it dawned on her. They all thought she was about to cry. They were using the *everything's going to be okay* smiles.

She smiled back at them, then spoke. "Don't worry. I'm okay. I'm ready for questions."

Janae literally heard a collective sigh of relief as the grown-ups traded glances, their expressions changing to genuine smiles. The woman next to her lay a hand on her arm and said, "You're a brave girl, Janae. I'm sure you've been through a lot. If you need a break or the questions get too hard, you let us know."

Janae nodded.

The next thirty minutes reminded her of an experiment they had done in one of her fourth-grade classes. Her teacher had given the kids sixty seconds to memorize everything they saw in the room, then they moved to a different room and wrote everything they remembered. That was what this was like. They wanted every detail on ATV man. *Red hair. Red sideburns.* Everything about Jefe. *Gray hair. White mustache.* They asked specific questions about the room under the stable.

"The door by the ladder led to the room," she said, reaching for the juice box next to her plate of sugar cookies.

"Actually, there were two doors. The ladder door and an inner door," a male voice interjected.

Janae whipped her head toward the man. "You found the room? Did you find Nicole and Rachel? Did you rescue them?"

The man, soot staining his face, looked to Mr. Randall like he needed permission to continue.

"Go ahead, Tyler," Mr. Randall said. He turned to Janae and the others. "Mr. Zahn helped us find the bunkroom after the fire."

"Fire? Were—" Janae stuttered.

Zahn interrupted. "Janae, it was empty. No one was there. I'm sorry we still haven't found your friends, but they weren't inside the bunkroom."

"Jefe must have taken them away. Were the horses still there?" She remembered morning exercise with Jefe and the girls. *We might have to leave in a hurry. Got to keep my horses in shape.*

Another man, wearing a star pinned on his uniform, looked at Janae.

"Horses? What's so important about the horses?"

CHAPTER 52

"All right ladies, time to move. Got to get out of there." Elliot slapped the side of the trailer, the clang of metal like a thunderclap.

Daria struggled to her feet, pulling Rachel up with her, and waited while Nicole stood.

"Let's go, guys. Be brave," Daria said.

She led the girls toward Elliot's silhouette, shielding her eyes as they approached the sunlight. The horse stood tethered to a tree, loaded with saddle bags and a rifle stuffed in a scabbard. Daria stepped off the ramp, and her eyes adjusted to the brightness. A glint of reflected sunlight made her squint again. Water. A large lake sat about a half mile below them in the valley. A familiar lake with mountains mirrored on the surface.

Daria knew this place. From the fishing trip with her dad. The trailer was perched above Aspen Lake, home to the elusive rainbow trout. Something told her they would not do any fishing today.

Daria turned to the mountains and frowned. There were no other cars, and she didn't recognize the truck pulling the trailer. She had heard the trailer's adjustments at the stop. Jefe must have switched tow vehicles. Gone was the maroon truck, replaced with a bright blue pickup. He was mixing things up. Definitely on the run.

"Take a good look around, Daria. Recognize anything?"

"No." She wasn't sure why she knew to lie.

"This campground is the last sign of civilization you're going to see." He pivoted and pointed up the valley. "Nobody goes where we're headed. Gets a little rugged."

What's he thinking? Daria couldn't see disappearing into the Rockies as a viable escape option. How would they survive?

Elliot dug into the tack box on the side of the trailer, retrieving a coil of rope with tied loops spaced along it.

"The exercise rope," Rachel muttered.

Elliot laughed. "The girls call it the exercise rope. We use it for our morning constitutional. Should work out well for our trip." He pulled a clear plastic bag labeled *Flex-Zip* out from the box and raised it. "Especially with these." He started with Nicole, draping the rope loop over her hands, then zip-tying her wrists to the loop. After severing the tie joining Daria and Rachel, Elliot used a fresh plastic strip on each of them, securing them to the rope.

He paused at Daria. "I can't decide where to put you. Up front, so the little ones have to keep up? Or back here to kick 'em in the butt if they slow down? Going to start with you in the rear, Daria."

Daria turned and stared into Elliot's eyes.

"What?" Elliot stared back, nodding. "Oh, I get it. You're a little worried about my 'in the rear' comment, aren't you? Like I'm talking about your rear? Your little butt?" He gave a short laugh. "Let's get something straight, Daria. Okay?"

Daria said nothing.

"I know you're disappointed in me. That I'm not the man you thought I was. But you need to understand what kind of man I am." He smiled. "I brought these girls together and made a team. A team of performers. Girls who film good. Making it on the big screen. Maybe not mainstream movies, but broadcast over hundreds of screens across the country." He paused. "I never touched them in that way. That way that you're thinking. I won't touch you that way either. That's not what I do."

Daria glared at Elliot. "Is that supposed to make me think you're not a bad person? That what you're doing with these girls is acceptable in any way?"

"Nope," Elliot said. "I just want you to know I'm not a pervert. I don't mess with the girls. Not expecting you to think I'm Mr. Morality. I'm not." He stared back at Daria. "I might not fool with the girls, or you, but make no mistake…if you all slow us down? Put this team in jeopardy? I will start making cuts." He laughed. "This is the final tour. If we get cornered, we're going out in a blaze of glory." He patted his holstered pistol at his side.

Daria kept her expression blank. *This man is crazy. He's going to kill us all.*

She couldn't escape alone. If she left these girls, she was leaving them to a certain death.

· · ·

An hour later, Elliot reined in Gus and pulled to a stop.

Rachel kneeled on the ground at Daria's feet, sobbing and gasping for air. Nicole remained standing, breathing heavily and averting her eyes as Elliot walked toward the weeping girl.

"Get up, Rachel," Daria said, in a quiet voice. She stepped forward and reached under Rachel's armpit with her zip-tied good arm, trying to raise her to her feet.

Rachel shook her arm away and hunched her shoulders, still whimpering.

Elliot stood next to the girl, staring at her.

"You heard Daria, Rachel. Get off the ground and walk. Now." He grabbed Rachel from under her armpits and stood her up. The girl dropped back to her knees.

"We're going to play it that way, Rachel? Really?" Elliot pulled his pistol from the holster.

Daria stepped forward. "Gabe, don't do it. Don't shoot her." She scrambled to find the words Elliot had used. "Don't hurt someone on your team."

Elliot turned to Daria. "Back up. NOW!"

Daria edged away from Rachel, shaking her head.

"You ready, Rachel?" he raised the pistol, and Rachel tracked it with her eyes.

Elliot stepped backward toward Nicole, who still stood, eyes forward. He pressed the gun against Nicole's head and then turned to Rachel. "Maybe you can't keep up because Nicole's in your way. Would you hike faster if she was the one who was gone?"

He turned back to Nicole and released the safety on the handgun.

CHAPTER 53

Zahn flinched at the rap on the meeting room door. The station duty officer strode past Zahn's chair and slapped a printout on the table in front of Perez.

"What do you got, Cecilia? Another maroon truck?" The phone lines had been barraged with multiple sightings matching the description. Only one was pulling a trailer, and that remained their most promising lead. It was spotted heading south only four miles from Beyond Adventure.

She gave a smile, pushing the sheet at Perez. "Got the truck, Rick. Your sheriff's dispatch just sent this over. They're on it, but asked you to phone in if you have questions." Cecilia walked toward the door, turning before leaving. "I'll be up front. Call if you need anything."

Perez scanned the paper while Zahn and Williams waited. His brow furrowed.

"Share it," Zahn said. "We got Elliot? Daria? The girls?"

"They pulled over the pickup in Eagle County on I-70 headed west," Perez said, handing the paper to Zahn. "It's Elliot's truck all right, but I think he set it up as a decoy. The man driving it, a Dennis Kamp, got paid to move it out of state. He claimed a guy handed him $1000 and told him to drive it to Utah and drop it in the Richfield Wal-Mart parking lot."

Zahn looked up from the paper. "How'd Kamp describe the guy who paid him? We think it was Elliot?"

"Read the bottom, Tyler. That last section has the description."

Zahn returned to the printout, following Perez's instructions. "Red hair? Clean-shaven? That's not Elliot."

"Maybe hair dye? A shave?" Williams suggested.

"Kamp described him as 30-40 years old," Zahn said. "Elliot's ten years older than me. Close to sixty."

Perez nodded and rose from his seat, his knee encased in a brace, but crutches nowhere in sight. "He's right. Doesn't look like Elliot. I'm calling the office to see who they're sending. Maybe throw some questions to ask this Kamp guy. You guys got anything we should ask?"

Williams nodded. "What about that horse trailer? The girl, Janae, thought Elliot would use his horses."

Zahn raised his hand. "And what happened to the red-headed guy after he offloaded the truck? Is he on foot? Another vehicle?"

"I'll ask," Perez said, and walked out of the room.

Zahn looked at Williams as Perez closed the door. "What're your thoughts? You think they're up north? Should we head up there?"

Williams stared at Zahn and squinted his eyes. "I'm not sure. I don't think we have enough info yet. And we're running out of daylight. But my gut says no. I figure it's a decoy like Perez said."

"Why?"

"Because our APB calls for a maroon truck pulling a horse trailer, and no one outside the county reported that combo. If it happened up I-70, heading out of state, then why no reports? They would have had to unhook it, and either leave it or transfer it, before they pushed the maroon truck off on the guy they paid."

"But they proved it's Elliot's truck. They ran the plates." Zahn paused. "And before you say, they could have swapped the plates, just think about it. Why would they switch to another maroon truck? That'd be a dumbass move."

"No. They didn't swap plates. They wouldn't have sent that printout to us if they hadn't cross-checked the VIN. It's Elliot's."

"So you think the trailer's between here and there somewhere? Or is the trailer a red herring?"

Williams shook his head. "I'm not sure. I just don't think it's up by Beaver—"

"Wait a minute." Zahn snapped. "Red hair, right?"

"That's what the report says."

Zahn nodded. "Janae described the guy who grabbed her in the woods. Not Elliot, the other guy. Remember, she said camo baseball cap? Orangish hair and sideburns."

"There's a lot of red-haired guys out there, Tyler."

"But if it's the same guy, it supports what you're saying. That maybe Elliot ditched the truck down here rather than up north. He swapped it to the red-haired guy for whatever the other guy was driving."

"Could be," Williams agreed.

"So let's walk that back. We got one sighting of a maroon truck with horse trailer, southbound on 361 this afternoon. Four miles south of the church camp. That was our best lead until we found the actual truck up in Eagle County."

Williams nodded. "361 is a back road. Probably trying to stay off 24 and avoid being seen. But southbound?"

"Maybe driving to the swap point. Maybe it's near red-hair guy's house or some other place."

"Or," Williams reflected. "he might not have even swapped. What if he gave red-hair guy the truck, ditched the trailer, and took the horse?"

"One horse, three girls, and heading down the valley? Not very stealthy."

"It's not. But how about this? Drive as far as you can, give up the truck, ditch the girls in the trailer, and Elliot takes the horse west into the mountains instead of south?"

Zahn rubbed his face. "Possible. Can we check that?"

"You're the local. How many trailer-friendly roads get up into those hills? And what are we going to find in the dark?"

"What are you saying, Randall? Just give up?"

Williams shook his head. "I know you're not going to do that. But you got to think smart. Do you want to look all night, in the dark, on half-assed leads and not be able to do anything tomorrow because you're exhausted? Or do you want to catch some hours of sleep and let these leads develop so we can be full speed tomorrow?"

Zahn stared at the floor. "I want my daughter back."

"Did you call Daria's mother yet?"

Zahn stared at his friend. "Oh, shit."

CHAPTER 54

Elliot tapped the pistol barrel against Nicole's head, instantly drawing blood.

Nicole dropped to her knees, and Rachel screamed. Daria stared at him, a look of total disbelief carved onto her face.

He should have just done her. Actually, now that he thought about it, he should have taken out Daria. She wasn't part of the team, anyway. That would have sent a message to the younger girls.

But damn if Daria wasn't proving useful. Pushing the girls. Encouraging them. They wouldn't have made it this far, this fast, without Zahn's daughter picking up the coaching duties from the rear. He was giving them all another shot. *No pun intended...*

He glanced forward at the trail. The bend marking his turnoff lay only yards ahead. Then it would be bushwhacking through the brush uphill to the miner's cabin.

"Get up, girl," Elliot said. He frowned at the smell of urine and the dampness showing on Nicole's pants. "That was a love tap I gave you. We're almost there. Get your butt off the ground and help your friend back there." He waved the pistol at Rachel.

Daria stepped toward Nicole, her zip-tied hand dragging the rope. "I got you, sweetheart," she said, glaring at Elliot.

She guided Nicole back to Rachel, who now stood on her own. Rachel raised her bound hands and wiped the trickle of blood running from Nicole's forehead to her cheek.

Elliot moved to the front of Gus and grabbed the reins. He clicked his tongue, and the party shuffled forward again, the girls jostling as they tried to line up to support one another on the trail. Elliot checked they were all moving, then continued down the path.

At the bend, he brought the horse to a stop.

"Sit down." He nodded at the girls and reached under Gus to loosen the saddlebags.

"You're going to like this one, Daria." He smiled. "Come on up here."

Daria rose and stepped forward as Elliot pulled the bags from Gus.

"Turn around and bend over."

"What…"

"I didn't say ask questions." Elliot pushed the saddlebags at Daria's chest, forcing her to back away. "I said to turn around."

Daria met Elliot's eyes, then whirled around.

"Bend forward a bit," Elliot said.

The young woman leaned over, and Elliot swung the saddlebags onto her back. Daria's knees buckled slightly, and she almost fell before shrugging the weight forward where she could still stand. Elliot dropped a strap from the bags over each shoulder.

"Grab it by the straps," Elliot said.

Daria reached behind with one hand, but the other strap dangled over her shoulder, swinging against the sling.

The sling. Her arm. She'd been doing so well at this hiking and coaching thing that Elliot had almost forgotten about her broken collarbone.

"Guess you'll just have to use one hand," he said. "Get back with the girls."

As Daria stumbled back to Rachel and Nicole, Elliot pressed his mouth against Gus's ear. "Good luck, boy." He took off his hat and slapped Gus on the flanks. "Now get out of here."

The horse jerked at the hat swat and moved forward a couple of feet. Elliot waved his hat again, and the horse trotted around the trail bend.

"All right, ladies. That's the end of our trail ride. Now for the final stretch. You ready?" Elliot grinned.

The girls stared back at him and said nothing.

"Oh, the team spirit here is killing me." Elliot pointed up the hill in the opposite direction of the trail. "Rachel, you lead the way. Straight up here. Nicole, you follow and help her on the steep shit. I'll bring up the rear behind Daria and make sure she doesn't drop our supplies." He stared at the motionless girls. "I said *move it,* ladies." He pulled his pistol and tapped it against his palm.

"Rachel, do what he says. Start climbing," Daria said, hunching under the weight of the pack. She took a step forward.

Rachel ducked under the branches bordering the trail and began the climb. Nicole followed, raising a limb for Daria behind her.

Elliot nodded. "That's what I like. A little teamwork." He surveyed the main trail before following Daria up the hill. Holstering his pistol, he reached forward to boost Daria's load with his other hand. The girls probably thought he brought up the rear so they couldn't escape.

Wrong. They weren't going anywhere while zip-tied to the rope.

He was riding caboose because he knew Daria couldn't haul those bags up the hill without his help. He'd considered rucking the bags himself, but hesitated at turning his back on the others while dismounted.

The group hadn't scrambled fifteen feet up the slope when a flash of white caught Elliot's eye.

"Hold up."

The party stopped while he retrieved the piece of fabric from the edge of the log at his feet. He dangled the torn material, cocking his head at the girls.

"Where'd this come from?"

"I don't know, Jefe." Nicole said.

Rachel shook her head.

"Hold up your hands."

Both girls raised their hands and showed Elliot their palms.

Nothing. Did he leave it behind on an earlier trip? He jammed the material in his pocket.

He'd promised the girls this was the last stretch. He hadn't been lying about that. But he didn't mention the duration—they had another hour of slogging. Elliot wouldn't badger them about their pace on this leg of the journey. He had already climbed this route three times, alternating his approach to the hideout while stockpiling cabin supplies, and he had struggled every trip. Forty pounds on your back while climbing a near vertical slope was no simple task.

His strategy? Fifty steps up the mountain, then two minutes of rest. Fifty more steps. Two minutes of rest. Every third rest, he'd pull the water bottle from Daria's load and hydrate the girls. They could take their time. Anyone on their tail would follow the horse tracks. And Gus was heading the opposite direction.

CHAPTER 55

Daria leaned against the log wall of the miner's shack, her two charges huddled in her arms, and tried to breathe. Dust, suspended in the fading sunlight from the cabin's sole window, coated her mouth and clogged her nose. Elliot was right. The uphill slog from the trail was the hardest thing she had ever done. The horse pack slung over her shoulder hadn't made it any easier, even with Elliot's help.

Through the log chinks, she spotted the man propped against a boulder. He looked spent too. Upon arrival, he'd shoved them into the cabin.

"Rest. We're spending the night."

Then he had slammed the door and locked it from the outside.

Daria's breathing had slowed as she suppressed her panic. *I've got this.*

She studied the two girls resting at her side. When she had first met the girls in the trailer, Nicole was the chatty one, describing how Elliot, who they both called *Jefe*, had captured them and what life was like in the stable. Rachel had remained mostly quiet.

But Elliot's threat to shoot Nicole in the head had stifled the girl's outgoing personality and silenced her. Nicole moved like a zombie on autopilot, numb to her environment. She hadn't complained once during the climb, just putting one foot in front of the other until they arrived.

Rachel, however, had emerged from her shell. Elliot's threat to kill Nicole seemed to have jolted Rachel from her malaise. She was talking and suddenly moving with purpose. She'd even snatched the strip of material from Nicole's shirt and taken over the trail marking duties. It was as if the two girls had swapped personalities.

Rachel turned to Daria. "Do you think we're staying here, or are we resting?"

Daria surveyed the shack. Large plastic containers formed a row underneath a single bunk on the opposite wall. Two gas canisters stood sentinel in the corner next to the window. She spotted a stove and a pile of sleeping bags.

"Looks to me like we're staying. Look at all these supplies."

Rachel nodded and turned to Nicole. The silent girl's head remained between her knees.

"How did Jefe get this stuff here?" Rachel pointed at the containers. "If the horse couldn't climb it, how could he move those?"

"He didn't go up," Daria said. "He hauled them in. Like on an ATV or something. Did you see the trail up behind the cabin?"

Rachel shook her head as Daria continued.

"Probably the first miners came from the other side of the mountain. Our route was too steep, so they built a road from the top down."

She paused, thinking. *Could they get out that way?* If they could escape from Elliot, could they make it over the peak?

Daria wasn't even sure if she could stay ahead of Elliot on her own, with her injured collarbone. Herding these girls up the slope? Not an option.

But what about sending one girl? She sized up the exhausted captives, evaluating which of the two had the best shot at escape. Nicole was in better shape, but she was practically catatonic. Rachel's recent adrenaline charge might help, but how long would that last?

"Rachel, what do you think about trying to get away?"

Nicole looked up and tugged on Daria's arm.

"No. He'll kill us."

Daria didn't share her thoughts. *I think he might kill us, anyway.*

"He hasn't done it yet. Maybe he's just scaring us from trying to escape." Daria paused. "I mean, think about it, you guys. Why is he keeping us? If his only thought is getting away, he could move three times faster on his own."

"Hostages?" Rachel said. "Maybe he's keeping us as hostages, so the police will let him go free when they catch him."

Daria nodded slowly. "Could be. But I don't think so. Without us, he could have driven out of the state by now. Or he could have ridden the horse alone over the pass. No need for hostages because he'd be long gone."

She looked at the girls. "It's because he wants to keep you. After everything that has happened, he doesn't want to leave you two behind. Do you understand that?"

Nicole monotoned, "It's because we're his team. He's always talking about keeping the team together. Doing things for the team."

Rachel turned to Daria. "What about you? Why did he take you? You're not like us."

"Right, I interrupted his plan. If he let me go, I'd run to the police, and they might have caught him," Daria said. "Plus, maybe he hasn't killed anyone yet. Maybe he doesn't want to kill."

"So why keep you when we left the trailer?" Rachel shook her head.

"Maybe he used me to help you guys?"

Rachel nodded. "You did help. Thanks for that."

"So here's what I'm thinking," Daria said. Both girls turned their heads to listen. "If I try to escape, then he's not going to come after me."

"So you should do it," Rachel said.

"Don't leave us," Nicole whimpered.

Daria looked at each girl. "Here's the problem with that. He'll still have you two together. What did you call it, Nicole? The 'team?' He won't have any reason to stay here. By the time I get help, he'll have moved you guys, and we won't know where to find you." She raised her good hand and squeezed Rachel's arm.

"I've got a different idea. We'll do like Jefe said. We'll rest…spend the night. Then tomorrow?"

Rachel looked up at Daria. "What?"

"Tomorrow, you're going to escape."

CHAPTER 56

"We found the trailer," Perez's voice barked over the phone.

Zahn flipped on the lamp next to his bed and sat straight up, the phone to his ear. The clock on his nightstand read 5:52. He'd been on the phone with Sheila until past 1:00. That hadn't gone well, and he expected her in town later this morning. Gray light filtered into the room through the half-drawn curtains.

"It's empty," Perez said. "Up above Aspen Lake in one of the campground sites. No vehicle pulling it; the tongue's just sitting on a block of wood."

"What're you seeing? Any sign of the girls? Elliot?"

"I'm not an expert tracker, but there are definitely horse tracks."

"People?"

"Yeah, I can't tell. I mean, there's something. And the horse didn't unload itself, so you'd expect that, right?"

"Can you figure where the horse went? Was it this morning or yesterday?"

"I'm pretty positive we've got tracks heading north, although I'm not sure why because I don't think you can get a horse over the tops of those mountains." Perez paused. "I can't tell how long ago it was. My guess is that it was probably yesterday."

Zahn pictured the lake and surrounding mountains. "If it's Elliot, he's got to be moving west. You're right about the mountains, though. He probably angled north to intercept the trail farther up the valley. He wouldn't park at the valley's end because it would telegraph his route."

He could practically hear Perez's gears turning.

"Yeah, that makes sense. I'm going to follow what tracks I can," Perez said.

"Oh, that's smart. You hobbling alone on that knee brace to face Elliot? I'm on my way. I'll have my 24-hour pack with me. You hold tight, and I'll meet the guys you called for back-up, and then hike with them."

"Uh, that's a problem, Tyler."

"Why's that?"

"The sheriff's department is on an active call. Guy holed up with his girlfriend. Some hostage thing. I can't even get a helicopter to respond to us. They want me to sit tight until they get someone out here."

"No one is coming?"

"Just you and Randall. At least initially. The Marshal's due in ten minutes. Already called him."

"Well then, sit your ass in your Tahoe and wait for us. Okay?"

"But Elliot's making time. I can…"

"No, you can't, Rick. That knee will give you a mile, at best. Let me and Randall hike after them, and you run the radios out of your vehicle."

"I can't let you go. I mean, I can send Randall—hell, he doesn't need my permission—but you're not, you know, law enforcement."

"Screw that. Elliot could have Daria with him. I'm going no matter what. See you in twenty." Zahn hung up.

He grabbed his pack and jumped into his truck. He punched out a text to Sheila while keeping one eye on the road.

I'm out looking for Daria. Go to the police station when you get here.

Then he gave Cecilia a call at the station and let her know about his ex-wife.

"We'll take care of her, Tyler," she assured him.

As Zahn cut south toward the mountain pass, he reviewed his plan. Or at least the plan he'd have by the time he arrived. Perez was in no condition to hike. Williams didn't know the area, but he was in shape. Zahn was the one familiar with the terrain.

He ran through Elliot's conceivable courses of action. Zahn had to assume the girls were alive. He couldn't think straight if that assumption proved false. If Elliot were solo, they'd never catch him on foot.

But it made little sense for Elliot to take off into the mountains on a horse. Much easier to just bolt out of the state in a car. He'd already proven he had the resources to switch vehicles. He could have made it…if he were alone.

Hiding in public with three girls was a different story. Practically impossible.

Zahn smacked the steering wheel with his palm. Elliot was here. He had the girls. Zahn and Williams had a shot at finding them. The two men would be slow, deciphering the trail, but Elliot would most likely be slower, trying to drag the girls along at his pace. Best Zahn could tell, Elliot only had the one horse, Gus. The same animal that had thrown Daria just weeks before at Beyond Adventure.

Zahn reached to his glove box and popped it open. His Glock 26 sat holstered inside, right where Daria had discovered it when this whole thing started.

Zahn didn't need to check the load. The only time it wasn't full was when he cleaned it or used it on the range. He was still a good shot, even if he'd only used the local range twice. Twenty-four years of annual M-9 training in the Air Force had left him comfortable with handguns. Not comfortable, like he wanted to always carry one. But confident in his proficiency.

He turned off the main pass onto the gravel road, which ran three miles to the lake. The mountains reflected off the water's surface like a National Geographic cover. Zahn spied three early-morning anglers on the near shore. He considered stopping, asking if any of them had seen the trailer come through, perhaps girls in the back seat of whatever pulled the trailer. But he couldn't take the time. Every minute wasted was an opportunity for Elliot to move further into these mountains. Possibly with his daughter.

The sign for the campground flashed on his right, and Zahn spun up the road, hitting the loop counterclockwise and scanning for Perez's Tahoe. Three football lengths later, he saw the flash of white through the trees, then two flashes. The deputy's Tahoe and the trailer. He pulled into the site and skidded to a stop parallel with the deputy sheriff's vehicle.

CHAPTER 57

Zahn and Perez studied the hoof prints leading north as Williams pulled his black SUV into the campsite. The Marshal jumped out of the vehicle and strode toward Zahn.

Zahn stepped forward. "You ready to go?"

"Yeah, I'm ready. Can't believe this shit." Williams turned to Perez. "How is it we're on the tail of a suspected kidnapper, and all you got is a single US Marshal and a civilian?" He looked at Zahn. "No offense."

"None taken. But let's get our ass in gear and worry about manning later. I'm getting my pack."

"They'll be here," Perez muttered. "It's not like we're manned for simultaneous felonies in this podunk county."

Zahn snatched his gear and watched Williams organizing his pack in the rear of his SUV. The Marshal's semi-automatic rifle reminded him of his Glock in the glove box, and he returned to his truck and holstered it under his arm. The Glock was easier to carry. Williams's M4A1 carbine was more practical. Either choice made Zahn nervous. With every passing minute, he was more convinced that Elliot had his daughter.

The two men met Perez at his Tahoe.

The deputy glared at Zahn. "I'm saying this one more time. I think you guys should wait until we've got more bodies."

"Ain't happening. We're going. Even without Williams here, I'd be going." Zahn gave Williams a grim smile. "Every minute we waste makes it harder to find him. And if he's taken the girls…"

"I'm good." Williams looked at Perez. "Not the optimal situation, but I agree with Zahn on this. We got to move if we're going to stay on this guy."

Perez nodded. "Figured as much." He tapped the center console. "Here's the comm plan. Williams, I've got you on a digital and VHF. We'll use TAC 5 for the digital frequency. You need to take it off SCAN if you want to stay quiet. Otherwise, you'll be listening to that mess the whole time." He pointed at the Tahoe's blaring speaker where the hostage situation up the valley played out live for every citizen with a police scanner.

Williams keyed a button on the digital radio.

"We'll be on MRA-1 for VHF," Perez said.

Williams pulled a smaller radio from his vest and confirmed the frequency.

Zahn disagreed. "If you call us and we're close, he'll hear us. We need radio silence to take him by surprise."

Perez shook his head. "There's no way I'm letting you guys go out there without radios. I'm already putting my ass on the line by not waiting for everyone else to get here." He stared at Zahn. "I won't talk to you, but you figure out a way to talk to me. And this 'take him by surprise' bullshit is just that. You two are going up there to fix his position—not take him. You pinpoint where he's at and then fall back and radio in for reinforcements. Understand?"

Zahn stared back and said nothing.

Williams nodded. "Got it." He tugged on Zahn's arm. "Let's get moving."

"Wait," Perez said, squinting at Zahn's chest. "That a GPS on your pack? Satellite texting?"

"Yep," Zahn said, palming the device and raising it so Perez could see better.

"What's your address? I can text you on that with my GPS, and it won't make any noise. Or at least it shouldn't if you fix it in your settings."

Zahn nodded. "Z-man@roam.gps.com," he said, fiddling with the buttons on his device. "Set. You can text away. Send a text after we start, and I'll reply to test it out."

Perez tilted his head. "Z-man? That's what Kristee calls you, right? Thought you didn't like that."

Williams looked at Perez upon hearing Kristee's name.

Zahn nodded. "That's what all the SAR guys call me, so I picked an address they would remember." He turned to Williams. "Ready?"

"Let's go."

Perez pulled himself from the car and looked from Zahn's holster to Williams's rifle. "Self-defense only, men. Self-defense only."

Zahn said nothing. He nodded at Perez and pivoted to follow the tracks at the edge of the campsite.

Williams followed.

• • •

"Check this out," Williams said, holding up a piece of cloth. "I found one outside the campsite, as well."

Zahn moved closer to Williams and inspected the piece of material in his hand. Dirty. White. Nothing about it stood out.

"I don't know…"

"Yeah, that's what I thought at the campsite. I mean bottle caps, plastic, and stuff; all of it probably left over from campers. But now this, the same color and all, and we're what…? A quarter mile from the camp? Might be something. Keep your eyes out."

The two men continued north until they took the *T* onto an established trail.

"I'm checking left. You want to check the other way?" Zahn pointed east.

"Right, like he's going to head that direction." Williams shook his head. "I'll check."

Zahn scanned the ground as he moved west on the trail. Same prints he'd seen leaving the campsite before the path had blurred into the undergrowth. Here on the packed dirt, the tracks were easier to spot. And there was something else.

"Got something," he called.

The Marshal rejoined Zahn at the trail's side, so as not to disturb any evidence.

"You see the hoof marks here, and here?" Zahn pointed at the ground.

"Yeah, I see them. I see those other marks too. Someone on the ground, right?"

"Right. I'm thinking he either dismounted, or we got people on foot with him. We wouldn't have seen the footprints back in the brush. Now they're visible."

"You said Elliot was a cowboy, didn't you?"

Zahn nodded.

"Ever notice him in tennis shoes or running shoes?" Williams ran his finger next to a soft indent on the trail.

"Nope. Cowboy boots every time," Zahn said. "Those aren't boot tracks, are they?"

"No. Boots would have defined edges. These are from a softer shoe. And see the way we have these soft marks next to each other?" Williams pointed to another mark. "Either the person is circling the horse...or there's more than one."

Zahn nodded and started walking up the trail. He looked over his shoulder at Williams. "He's got them—he's got the girls."

Zahn found the next cloth strip, lying on the side of the path. Smudged with dirt, same as the ones Williams had spotted. He held it up in front of Williams and raised his eyebrows.

"Not a coincidence," Williams said. "They're leaving a trail." He looked at Zahn with a thin smile. "That's your girl, isn't it? You don't think those young ones would think of that, do you?"

Zahn didn't know the other girls. Hell, he was just getting to know his daughter. But this felt like the way his daughter's brain worked. "I'm thinking it's Daria. Her idea, at least."

The two men pointed west, following the route as it wound along the base of the mountains forming the northern valley boundary. Zahn felt his GPS vibrate and raised his hand for Williams to stop.

Status? Perez checking in for an update.

Zahn manipulated the clumsy keyboard, thumbing the cursor through the entire alphabet to punch out a reply.

Still tracking. We've got more tracks. Think he's got the girls. We're 3.8 miles west of you on the trail.

Zahn pushed send and re-hooked the GPS to his pack. With satellite connectivity, he knew it would be another five minutes before Perez responded. If he did.

Another hour of hiking. The morning sun warmed their backs, shortening the shadows in the direction they hiked, and drying the trail, making the tracks harder to identify. Fortunately, the terrain didn't offer many alternatives beyond the trail they followed. Zahn couldn't imagine Elliot taking the girls up the north mountains, and he doubted the horse could bushwhack to the river to the south.

Williams gave a low whistle and raised his hand, bending to retrieve another strip of cloth. Zahn nodded, but said nothing. Each marker meant the two young girls were still alive—but also that his daughter was probably with them.

Zahn looked ahead where the trail abruptly jagged left, south toward the river. He stopped at the turn, scanning for side trails. Nothing. A bed of dry pine needles covered the path here, instead of the soft dirt they had been following. He and Williams rounded the corner and stopped.

Williams pointed at the indentations in the needles at their feet. "Looks like they're still on the trail. These look like they're from the horse," he said, in a low voice.

Zahn nodded and continued south, the river's dull roar increasing as they moved away from the valley slope. They hiked another quarter mile before hitting the banks of the Aspen River, where the path veered back to the west and paralleled the stream. A layer of thin mud, deposited during the spring runoff, replaced the pine needles.

Williams raised his voice to be heard over the river's flow. "Here's where I'd try to throw us off."

Zahn nodded. "Use the river. No tracks. No scent."

"Yep. It's only thirty feet to the other bank. They could wade it if they were hanging on to something."

Zahn turned up the path as it paralleled the surging stream. He still followed horse tracks. He turned back to Williams, moving close so the Marshal could hear him. "I don't think so. Still got hoofprints here."

"Right. But where're the people tracks? Those tennis shoe tracks we saw before."

Shit. He's right. The trail's mud veneer highlighted perfect tracks, but they were all in the shape of a horseshoe. The soft indents they had tracked at the base of the mountains had vanished.

He frowned, wrapping his head around Williams's logic. Yes, the river could confuse trackers, but how would Elliot use it? If he had the girls, would he trust them to cross the stream on their own while he managed the horse? Or did he put a girl on the horse and have her ride it? Or…what if Elliot had someone helping him? That might make sense. But he hadn't seen any large footprints.

"Okay, let's check out the other side," Zahn said, nodding across the river. "You're right. No people tracks here."

"No need both of us getting wet. I'll check it out." Williams handed Zahn his rifle and shrugged out of his pack, setting it against a tree at the river's bank.

Zahn leaned the rifle against the same tree and opened the screen on the GPS, checking for updates from Perez. Nothing. He glanced up to check on Williams.

The US Marshal was nowhere in sight.

Zahn had only focused on the GPS for five seconds at most. *Where did Williams go?* He shoved the GPS in the pack's side pocket and dropped the bag to the ground.

Stepping forward, Zahn scanned the far bank of the river. The rocks where he expected Williams to exit were bone dry.

Zahn weaved through the trees lining the banks downstream. There was no trail to the east along the river, and he thrust twined cottonwood branches out of his way, while carefully placing his feet on the slick rocks forming the river's bank. He scanned the stream for his friend between steps.

A large deadfall loomed in front of him, damming up two-thirds of the river, and funneling the water to the south side in a chute that would excite his river rat friend Kristee. The branches thrusting from the water like fingers were just the strainer hazards she taught her students to avoid.

Zahn squinted. The closest branch looked different.

It was a hand.

He glanced upstream toward his 24-hour pack, mentally inventorying the contents. Bivy sack, rain gear, first aid kit. But no rope.

He whipped his head back to the hand and watched it slide underwater.

No time.

The cottonwood forming the deadfall had fallen from the river bank, roots splayed halfway ashore and halfway in the water. Zahn dropped off the crumbling edge of the bank and splashed through brackish water pooled against the shore, grabbing a fist-sized root. He wove through the gnarled roots to the trunk and pulled himself atop the fallen tree, pressing his feet on a root behind him while tugging on the remains of a branch to pull himself up.

The downed tree was too narrow to stand upon. Or maybe not, but Zahn wasn't confident he could perform a balance beam routine the length of the tree without doing a sloppy dismount and joining Randall in the water. Instead, he remained on his belly and began scooting himself toward the river's center, reaching forward with his hands and sliding his torso along the tree, then digging his heels into the trunk and scooting more. Ignoring the pain in his forearms where the smooth bark was rubbing his skin raw, he propelled himself forward, pausing only long enough to twist through branches jutting into the air from the fallen tree. In seconds, he lay above the deluge of water where he'd last seen Williams's hand.

Peering over the edge, he scanned the roiling water. This was where the bulk of the stream runoff smashed into the tree, then swirled sideways, seeking the path of least resistance. If Williams's hand had disappeared, then he'd most likely already washed downstream. Zahn's eyes traced toward the swift channel sweeping around the tree's crown.

Then he saw it. The dark outline meshed against a lighter, almost white color, just below the surface. He could see the pinks of Williams's palms struggling against the underwater branches. The entire weight of the mountain stream was crushing Williams against a snarl of cottonwood limbs.

Zahn stared at Williams's scrabbling arms. If the Marshal extricated himself from the tangle, his body was going one of two ways. Sideways, down the water chute at the tree's end, or straight under the tree on which Zahn straddled, and into whatever protruded from the tree or the riverbed. Snagged by branches or crushed by rocks.

A branch the width of Zahn's arm thrust at an angle over the top of Williams, and Zahn grabbed it like he was in a desperate a tug-of-war. Unlike his brush with death the year before, where memories of Jacob had flooded his mind as he considered his impending demise, this time his thoughts were blank. He swung the rest of his body off the tree trunk and splashed his boots into the raging river below him, barely registering the icy water already at his knees.

Zahn's foot contacted something hard, and he dropped his eyes from the branch to the water. He was kicking Williams's head.

Not good.

Wait.

It was good.

Williams's flailing hands immediately pulled away from the tangle of branches and clawed at Zahn's boots. Zahn's body assumed Williams's weight as the man below him wrapped his ankles in a bear hug. His own hands slipped, and Zahn jerked his head toward the branch above him, seeking a better purchase. He found it a foot higher on the same branch where a broken limb formed a Y. Struggling against his newly increased bodyweight, he walked his hands the twelve inches and secured his grip just as Williams's face broke the surface.

A raspy, high-pitched sound escaped from the man's throat as he gasped for the air he'd lacked for the last two minutes. Zahn struggled to keep his grip as Williams's panicked arms squeezed hard and tried to scale his torso. He saw the khaki-clad legs below him drifting toward the channel as Williams's weight released from the side of the tree and transferred to Zahn.

Williams vomited water as Zahn pondered their options. He felt Williams's grip around his legs loosen and he watched as his friend slid several inches lower.

"Zahn!" Williams gasped for air.

"Hang on."

"Fuck!"

"I know. Are you functional, or am I going to pull your ass out by myself?" Zahn yelled.

"No, man, hang on." Williams puked another stream of water into the river, scanning the tree in front of him. He pulled one of his legs forward and thrust it against the same bundle of underwater branches trapping him only seconds before. With his right foot secure, he pulled his other foot forward and jammed it next to the first boot.

Zahn felt the load on his own legs lighten as Williams's weight transferred toward the tree trunk.

"Don't let go of me," Williams gasped. "I have nothing to grab with my hands."

"You're the one doing the holding, man. If I let go, we're both going in."

"Can you get me closer to the tree? I'll use my legs to take the weight off," Williams yelled.

"Right." Zahn felt the load lighten further as Williams arched his body toward him. Zahn moved one hand forward on the branch, toward the trunk, then the other, inching Williams's torso toward the log. He felt his hands slipping on the smooth, wet bark, and he began moving his hands faster.

"Slipping!" Zahn yelled.

Williams reached forward with one hand and grabbed at a limb pointing skyward. Swinging himself onto the tree, he transferred his other hand from Zahn's pants and reached toward his friend.

"Shit." Zahn grunted as his other hand slipped. He swung it over, hanging on to Williams's dangling arm with both hands.

Williams swung the arm to the shore side of the tree, and Zahn wrapped his arms around another branch, resting his feet on a wide limb just below the surface.

The two men stared at each other. Williams shook his head.

"Should we f-f-find a different way across?"

CHAPTER 58

The GPS dangling from Zahn's shoulder strap lit up as he yanked his down bag from the bottom of the pack. Williams stood next to him on the trail, visibly trembling, struggling to bounce on his toes to warm his frozen limbs.

Zahn seized the locator, tilting the screen to read the message. Had to be from Perez.

Status?

Shit. His last reply reported status unchanged. They hadn't found Elliot. Now, they were worse than *unchanged*. They were off track. Zahn needed to warm Williams up, or they weren't going anywhere.

Ignoring the text, he focused on Williams.

"Take your clothes off, Randall, and crawl inside." Zahn held up the bag.

"Let's g-g-go." Williams shivered. "If-f-f I keep moving, I'll be okay."

"No, you won't. You're hypothermic, and if we run into Elliot, you're going to be slow, at best—ineffective at worst."

Williams shook his head.

"Are you willing to put my daughter at that kind of risk? Life or death, and you can't hold a rifle steady?"

Williams cast his eyes at the ground. "R-R-right." He fumbled at the buttons on his shirt, unsuccessfully attempting to disrobe.

Zahn took over, undressing his trembling friend, and zipping him into the bag.

"Try to warm up. I'll make you some hot water or tea or bouillon if I can find it in my bag."

"I'll focus on the w-w-warming part. I'm scared if I close my eyes, you'll s-s-strip and crawl in the bag with me. T-t-that's what they do in the movies."

Zahn gave Williams a thin smile. "That's my plan after you finish your tea…if you don't thaw out. You motivated now?"

Williams's eyes widened. "I'll be warm. I promise. Keep your clothes on and m-m-make me that drink."

Zahn pulled his backpacking stove from his bag and screwed on the fuel canister. Filling his aluminum pot from his water bottle, he lit the burner. He rummaged through his first aid kit. No tea. He found a plastic sleeve of electrolytes in the pack's side pocket and dangled it in front of Williams.

"This will be like hot Kool-Aid. You remember that, from Boy Scouts, right?"

"Dammit, Zahn. D-D-Do I look like a graduated Boy Scout? I'm from the city. They had Boy Scouts in the suburbs, but I lived d-d-downtown. No fording rivers. No making fires."

"You missed out."

"Uh, not really. L-L-Look at me now. I went on my f-f-first hike in Marshal training. I climbed my first m-m-mountain with you guys last year. Now I-I-I'm hypothermic in the middle of the R-R-Rockies. Why don't you go skin me a r-r-rabbit or something?"

Zahn removed the bubbling pot of water from the stove and stirred in the drink powder. Then he transferred the steaming concoction to his camp cup and handed it to Williams.

"Drink up. How're you feeling?"

"Better. Warming up."

Zahn noticed the color coming back into Williams's cheeks and his use of full words rather than the stuttering mess he'd been using since the rescue. Maybe ten more minutes and they could see about moving again. He unclasped his GPS from his pack and sent a message to Perez, omitting the river mishap.

Taking a break. Should be moving again in ten.

No sense riling up Perez over something they couldn't control.

"I'm checking across the river. Like you were going to do," Zahn said, taking another quick glance at Williams to make sure he was warming.

"Yeah, I'm not sure that makes sense. Maybe Elliot could have crossed, but not the girls. Not in that current."

"Maybe upstream. I'm thinking your log wasn't the best choice." Zahn smiled at Williams, then glanced above his shoulder. "I'm checking for a crossing up that direction."

Williams nodded. "I'm not going anywhere. Leave your pack."

Zahn leaned his backpack against the tree beside Williams and moved up the trail paralleling the stream to the junction where they'd first arrived at the river. He followed the hoofprints west, scanning the ground again for other signs of traffic. Same as before. The same prints from the horse, now mixed in with Zahn and Williams's scuff marks.

Except for that one. And that one.

Zahn stared at the ground, then dropped to one knee. He ran his finger around the rim of a fresh track embedded in the mud on the river side of the trail.

Not just a scuff. A full shoe print. Sneaker-style, and not Elliot's size unless Zahn had failed to notice that Elliot had ballerina-sized feet.

Zahn snapped his head up. No way had they missed this track the first time. Someone had walked this trail while he and Williams were playing water rescue games a hundred yards downstream.

He started up the trail, ignoring the urge to call out. It had to be one of the girls. Not Daria. He knew her feet were bigger than that. One of the younger girls.

But what if Elliot was with her?

Didn't make sense. None of this made sense.

As Zahn scanned the shoreline for a longer log than what Williams had tried to use, he spotted movement between the trees lining the bank. Not just movement, because the whole river was moving, but movement out-of-synch with nature. Colors moving in a different direction than the river.

Zahn stared through the trees and watched a young girl leap from a rock to a stump wedged in the river bottom. She stumbled, then stood again, searching for the next rock. Glancing over her shoulder, she met Zahn's eyes.

Her eyes widened, and she whirled back to the rock she had spotted and jumped.

CHAPTER 59

Elliot rarely lost his temper. No matter how his associates fucked up a photo shoot, regardless of the close calls with the authorities, and despite his recalcitrant team members, he never blew up. Sure, he'd dressed down people for incompetence. And there was that marketer he outed for kiddie porn when he broke the rules—before Elliot had switched from direct sales to marketing. But violence and revenge were different, more calculated responses than blowing your stack.

He hadn't been gone long. Woke early, the girls still asleep, and headed for the outhouse for his standard constitutional. When he'd crossed the shack's threshold on his return and counted two girls instead of three, plastic zip-tie remnants hanging from the rope loop next to the open window, he lost it. Almost as bad as when his daughter, Christina, announced she was off for the bright lights and big city so many years ago.

Elliot stared at Daria. "You. Stupid. Girl." He stepped toward her and Nicole. "Both of you, really. But you, Daria. You should have known better."

He drew back his boot and kicked Daria's shoulder where the sling held it to her side.

Daria screamed and shrank against the log wall. Nicole jerked the opposite direction.

He flinched his foot toward the tiny girl, shaking his head as Daria tried to move between them. Then, he whirled around, bolted outside, raced around the cabin, and scanned the access road switchbacking up the mountain. No sign of Rachel.

How long had he left them alone in the cabin? Absolutely no more than ten minutes. She had to be close. But if Rachel had escaped, then so could the others. He had to prevent that from happening before pursuing Rachel.

Elliot circled the shack before rejoining the huddled girls. He stared as Daria draped her good arm around Nicole, squeezing the two together.

That was the problem, he thought. They're working together. He snorted at the irony. He'd been encouraging teamwork all along, with little success. Rachel giving the videographers the silent treatment. Kendall running away.

Now, just as the entire scheme was disintegrating, they start to gel? Elliot suspected Daria's influence played a role. He could fix that. Shut Zahn's daughter up, and she won't be able to plan. Immobilize her, and she won't be able to help. Easy-peasy.

Elliot pulled his knife from his pocket and flipped open the short blade. He reached down and grabbed Daria by her good shoulder, yanking her to her feet.

"Need to do a little rearranging, sweetheart."

Tears streamed from Daria's eyes to her chin. Were the tears a response to Elliot's well-placed kick, or a result of fear? He wasn't sure which. She winced as he slid the knife between the rope and the zip-ties, slicing through the plastic.

He pointed to the metal bunk in the back corner of the shack next to Rachel's escape window.

"Lay down." He nodded as the young woman obeyed. He might need to incorporate more corporal motivation.

Elliot then grabbed Daria's hand from the sling and yanked it above her head. The young woman shrieked and twisted on the bunk as he grabbed her other arm. He zip-tied her wrists together above her head with a fresh plastic strip, then ran another through the vertical metal rods making up the headboard. He looped more ties over both ankles and pulled them tight, leaving Daria's legs slightly opened and secured to the base of the bed. He stepped back and surveyed his work.

Probably the first time she'd been in this position.

He suspected those Dark Web guys would pay money for some of this action.

Maybe. Maybe not.

His marketers told him their targeted customer base liked them closer to Nicole's age than Daria's. And the whole *tied to the bed* thing might be too conventional.

Elliot turned to Nicole, who sat bug-eyed, pressing herself into the wall, a look of terror on her face from his handiwork with Daria.

"Okay, Nicole. Got the big girl taken care of. What to do about you?"

He searched the room for somewhere to secure Nicole. Nothing. Elliot jerked her to her feet and cut her tie from the rope.

"Think we'll keep you outside."

"Nicole, be strong!" Daria whimpered from the bed.

He froze for several beats before continuing. That team-building thing again. He needed to shut her up. Stepping from the porch, he tugged Nicole toward the outhouse. The privy, as some liked to call them. Flinging open the door, he scanned the cramped space for a tie-down solution.

The roof spanned only two feet, so no rafters, but the two-by-four frame looked promising.

"You climb up next to the hole, Nicole," he said, tugging her hand and pulling her up onto the platform where she straddled the oval cut-out. "Hey, you see what I did there, honey? A rhyme. Hole. Nicole. You like it?"

Elliot was pretty sure she didn't. She had been shaking since they left the cabin. Now she was eyeing the outhouse hole between her legs and probably trying to guess what Elliot had in store for her. Not in the mood for poetry.

He yanked her wrists above her head and zipped them together. Elliot bought these zip-ties in bulk for a reason, and today he was pleased with his foresight. He eyed the targeted two-by-four and ran a tie in that direction. Just enough length so he could close it with the girl perched on her toes. But too short, unless torture was his only goal. He pulled out another tie, using loops in a chain to secure her in place. Like those construction paper chains he and his mother had strung around the Christmas tree.

Elliot heard a voice from the shack.

"Nicole?"

Too fucking loud.

He strode to the horse packs leaning against the cabin and dug through the front pocket. His hand found the familiar round shape, and he pulled out a roll of duct tape. Barging through the door, he walked toward Daria while pulling the tape from the roll. He used his teeth to rip off six inches and plastered it across the young woman's mouth.

"Oh, so much better," he said. "Don't you think?"

Daria glared at him.

Elliot returned to Nicole and repeated the process with the tape. No one was comfortable here, but he wouldn't be gone long.

He grabbed his rifle and moved around the outside of the shack to the window, scouring the mountainside for signs of Rachel. The trail turned to road as it wound up the mountain, the surface composed of rock instead of soil. No tracks. He looked closer at a slash of dark gravel where a rock had overturned. Another disturbed rock lay ten feet up the road. Elliot scanned the downhill side of the ATV track and saw nothing. Rachel was heading up and not down.

CHAPTER 60

Shit. Two water rescues in one day?

Zahn bolted for the bank, aiming just downstream from where the girl had jumped. Maybe he could catch her before she swept into the same mess as Williams.

As he scanned the river, he caught movement where he'd last seen the girl. And another. The girl was still rock-hopping her way across the stream. She hadn't fallen.

"Hey!" Zahn called. "Wait up."

The girl paused on the far shore, her head twisted toward him, eyes wide with fear. Then she spun and started scrambling up the bank.

"Daria?" Zahn yelled. "Have you seen Daria?"

The young girl froze, her hands locked on a root, her feet no longer churning. She turned around, eyeing him with a look of suspicion.

"Does he have her? My daughter?" Zahn called. He stepped to the first rock, scanning a route across the river.

The girl inched backwards, her lips moving.

Zahn heard her voice, but couldn't understand her over the current. He cupped his hand to his ear.

"I asked you if Daria is really your daughter?" she yelled louder.

"She is. Is she okay?"

"Prove it. Prove she's your daughter."

Zahn thought, then tapped his shoulder. "She's got a broken arm. Collarbone technically, but she should be in a sling still."

The girl nodded and yelled. "How did she hurt it?"

"She fell off a horse." Zahn paused. "Actually, if I'm guessing right, she fell off the same horse Elliot took. Was its name Gus?" He watched the girl's shoulders sag in relief. Something he had said made the girl believe him.

"He let Gus go," she said.

"Are you Rachel or Nicole?" Zahn called.

"Rachel. He's still got Nicole." She paused. "And Daria."

"Where? Where are they at?"

Rachel pointed straight at him, then pointed her finger to the mountain behind him. "They're all up there. In a building. Or a shack, or something." She sobbed. "Daria told me to run away up the hill, but I got too tired. And I heard him yelling. So I went down instead."

Zahn raised his eyebrows. *Elliot was on this girl's trail?* "Cross back over. Do you want me to help?"

Rachel widened her eyes. "No. He's on that side."

Zahn nodded. "But so am I. And so is my police friend." He pointed first toward Rachel and then upriver. "That way is the wrong direction. There's nobody for a hundred miles, and it's all uphill. Cross over, and let's get you home."

Rachel's eyes snapped to his when he uttered the word *home*. Not in surprise. Not in shock. Almost in disbelief. Like he was spinning a fairy tale.

"You'll take me home?"

Zahn felt an ache in his gut imagining what these girls had endured. He nodded and stepped out across the first two stones of the steam crossing.

"Let's go, Rachel."

The girl popped to her feet and worked her way to the river's edge, eyeing the reverse course to join Zahn. She proved just as nimble on the return. He tried to grab her hand as she neared the rock on which he stood, but she motioned for him to back away. *She still doesn't trust me.*

He stepped farther up the bank as Rachel leaped from the last rock and stood on the shore.

"Can I see your badge?"

"I don't have one." He watched the girl's eyes widen again. "I'm here because of Daria. I have to find her. She's my daughter." He paused. "Rachel, if your parents knew where you were, don't you think they would come get you, too?"

Rachel looked at her feet. "I'm not sure I remember what they look like."

The dull ache in Zahn's belly turned to a burn, and he felt his anger at Elliot return. "We're going to take you back to them. I promise you, they will remember. And you will remember too."

He stepped onto the trail and pointed east. "Let's go. My partner's just downstream, warming up from falling in the river." Zahn skipped a beat. "And guess what he has?"

"Food?"

Zahn laughed. "Sure, we got food. But he's also the one with a badge. He'll show it to you. He's a US Marshal."

Rachel gave a thin smile and followed Zahn.

Rounding the corner, Zahn saw Williams, still in his bag, reaching for his carbine against the tree. He dropped his hand when he recognized Zahn, but his eyes widened as he looked past him to the young girl following him.

"Is that…?"

"Randall, I want you to meet Rachel."

"*The* Rachel? As in…?"

Zahn nodded. "The Rachel we've been looking for." He pointed up the mountain behind him. "The other girl, Nicole, is up there. With Daria." He moved closer to Williams and said in a low voice. "And Elliot's probably close, searching for Rachel." He reached into his pack and pulled out two granola bars and a Pop-Tart. He handed them to Rachel. "Your choice."

She thanked him and lowered her back against the same tree as Williams.

The marshal moved the rifle away from the girl. "I'm warmed up. Going to get dressed, and we can move out."

"Yeah, that's a problem." Zahn scratched his chin. "We can't go after Elliot with Rachel here. But we can't take her back yet either. We're cutting off his western and southern escape route right here. Perez is blocking the east. Elliot's only option is north, over the mountain."

"We need to give Perez an update," Williams said.

"Got it." Zahn unclasped the GPS unit from his pack and started working the keypad.

"Mr. Randall?" Rachel turned to the Marshal, her mouth stuffed with Pop-Tart. "Can I see your badge?"

CHAPTER 61

Elliot didn't find it difficult to track signs of Rachel's hurried departure up the old mining road. Until they disappeared. He was striding up the path, alternating between following the dislodged rocks and scanning the sparsely forested mountain above him for signs of the girl, when suddenly the scuff marks vanished. He backtracked, moving to the road's uphill side, where he assumed she veered off, short-cutting her way to the mountain's top where the path cut down to the neighboring pass.

Nothing.

He moved to the road's downhill side, scoping the loose embankment and tree line below.

There.

About six feet down the dirt slope, Elliot spotted two divots in the loose scree pointed in the direction of the treeline. He scrambled lower and followed the tracks.

Stepping forward into the trees, Elliot kept his head on a swivel. The dry needles revealed fewer tracks than the road above, but the broken underbrush told the story. Rachel had changed her mind. She was heading downhill.

Their trip up this same slope, five hundred yards to the east, had taken over an hour. With gravity on his side and Rachel's obvious pell-mell escape leaving a clear path through the brush, Elliot reached the bottom in twenty minutes. He recognized the river's dull roar as he paused to confirm Rachel's direction of travel. Turning left would take her back to Aspen Lake and the campground. Toward civilization. He'd need to catch her before she made it that far. A right turn pointed her farther up the valley. Away from people. But into a line of cliffs as the river bent against the mountain.

A broken branch straight ahead brought a smile to his face. Her route vectored to the river and the same trail where he'd released Gus. Ten minutes later, he paused, peering left and right for signs of the girl. Or anyone else, for that matter. The trail was a mess. He could see Gus's hoofprints, as well as a slew of footprints. When he'd tugged the girls on this same trail, a mile to the east, it was clean. No longer. People were out here. They might have already found Gus.

Elliot scanned the riverbank on the trail's far side and spotted the large stones positioned for a stream crossing. Did the girl take the trail or cross the stream? Hopefully the latter.

As he approached the water, he froze. Then raised his rifle.

A voice. Downstream. On his side of the river.

He stepped back into the woods and crouched, thinking about his next move. He'd just heard the one voice, high-pitched. Like a girl. Now he could hear lower tones but couldn't distinguish them over the sound of the river. Couldn't ignore them, though.

He recrossed the trail and picked his way through the forest, pausing every twenty feet. The third time he stopped, he saw it. A flash of blue in the distance. Elliot dropped to a crouch and parted the branches of the shrub he used as cover. He was close enough to see faces.

Close enough to recognize trouble.

The patch of blue morphed into a sleeping bag, a dark face poking from the top. Rachel sat under the same tree, munching away on something. Elliot couldn't tell what. Pacing in front, head bent and fingers moving, was Tyler Zahn.

Shit.

Zahn had Elliot's girl. Kind of ironic since he had Zahn's girl. And if Zahn was here, then sleeping bag man was that friend of his...Marshal Williams. Elliot was positive about that. Chaffee County was lucky to have ten African Americans within its boundaries on a tourist weekend, let alone on a daily basis. Of course it was Williams.

Elliot retreated, ducking behind a large tree.

The game had just changed.

Keeping the girls, keeping Daria—these were all efforts to preserve his dream, to hang onto the team as long as he could. Maybe use Zahn's daughter as leverage.

Honestly, he had thought the mining shack could remain undetected for months, as it wasn't easily visible from the air. Not accessible from the valley floor. Well, accessible if you bushwhacked like him and his girls.

Instead, the game was up after only a single night in the hideout.

Rachel knew where to find them. Disoriented or not, all she had to do was point up the fucking mountain. *They're in a cabin up there*, he imagined her telling Zahn. Probably already had told him.

Which meant these two men had to be eliminated right here. Right now. The search parties would find the bodies and continue up the valley, following the horse tracks. He could snag Rachel and return to the shack.

He craned his head around the tree, searching for Zahn. Daria's father still poked at whatever was in his hand. Cell phone? No coverage out here. GPS? Could be. Marking his position for others to find.

Elliot rolled from the tree and evaluated the terrain. Eyeing a dead log ten feet away, he low-crawled forward, his right hand wedged in the rifle sling, and silently positioned himself behind the deadfall.

He rehearsed his plan. Zahn first. Then the Marshal. Wasn't like Williams was moving anywhere fast in that sleeping bag. Then take the girl before she ran again. Three-step process.

Elliot propped his rifle on the log and put Zahn in his sights. *Squeeze, don't pull.*

CHAPTER 62

Pain exploded between Zahn's neck and shoulder a fraction of a second before he recognized the sound of a rifle crack. The bullet pinwheeled him to the ground as the GPS slipped from his hands. His face slammed into the dirt and another shot rang out. And another.

He opened his eyes, searching for Williams and the girl. The sleeping bag Williams used to warm himself was moving, and Zahn watched him roll it from the inside, skirting around the tree. Rachel was nowhere in sight.

Zahn thrust his hand sideways and seized Williams's M4, wincing at the pain in his left shoulder. He rolled a backpack in front of him, then slung the long barrel toward the shots and squeezed off three rounds.

Suppressing fire, he hoped. Maybe. He was a fricking pilot, an ex-pilot to be precise, and he wasn't a hundred percent sure if that was what you would call his errant bullet spray. But he didn't get an answering shot. Maybe it was working. Raising his eyes from the rifle's scope, he peered over the log.

Nothing.

He turned his head toward Williams. "Randall, you all right? Randall?"

A groan emerged from behind the tree, and Zahn's eyes caught the contrasting blue of the sleeping bag next to a large root.

"Randall. Where's the girl? Where's Rachel?"

Another groan. "Got her. She's back here."

"You okay?"

"Hit. In the back," Williams said. "I'm checking on Rachel."

Shit. Zahn heard Williams and Rachel talking in soft tones as he scanned the forest for movement. There it was. He spied a camouflaged jacket flashing between trees, moving to the north. Zahn sighted the rifle just forward of the position and shot.

Silence. No movement.

"Randall, can you move? Scoot around the tree toward the river." Zahn thought for a moment. "The south side. He's moving north and I can't tell if he's running away or circling around for a better shot."

"Got it." Williams's breath sounded ragged. "Rachel's not hit."

Zahn heard the swish of the bag as Williams pulled himself out of it and moved himself and the girl.

"What about you?" Williams croaked. "I saw you go down. How bad?"

Zahn removed his hand from the rifle trigger and patted his left trapezoid. It stung even more when he touched it. And it was wet. He wiped his hand on his pants and returned his finger to the trigger.

"He grazed me. Right across my trap. I'm still functional." He glanced at the tree and saw Williams's face visible, peering at him. "I'm coming over to check you all out."

Zahn lowered the weapon and crouched behind the pack. Spearing the rifle strap with his thumb, he low-crawled to Williams, rolling back toward the shooter's last location and raising the gun.

No shots.

He trained the rifle north and looked at Williams and the girl huddled next to him.

"Rachel? You all right?"

The girl nodded her head quickly, still shaking.

Zahn heard another crack, and Williams flinched. Not a rifle this time. Sounded like a branch. He saw movement up the slope of the mountain, several hundred yards away.

He lowered his weapon. "He's leaving." Zahn met Williams's eyes. "Rachel says he's got Daria and the other girl up there. I think he's going back."

Williams nodded and said nothing. His hands pressed against his upper chest and Zahn watched him push his toes into the earth to keep his back against the tree.

Zahn moved to his knees, closer to Williams. "Talk to me. What do we got?" He looked at the blood seeping between the man's fingers and moved toward his pack. "I'm going to get you something to staunch the bleeding. Looks like he nailed you right in the chest?"

Williams shook his head. "Exit wound." He leaned forward, and Zahn saw a splash of blood against the tree. "I saw you go down and heard the gunshot," he said. "So I covered Rachel, and the bastard shot me in the back."

Zahn heard a bubbling rasp in Williams's voice and smelled the coppery scent of blood. Might have nicked his lung. He looked at Rachel sitting next to Williams. She stared back at him, still shaking.

He lifted Williams's fingers and pressed an extra shirt against the wound. "Hold this," he said, and returned to his pack. He yanked out his first aid kit and rummaged through his supplies. He hadn't built the kit expecting a gunshot wound. But there, next to the Ace wrap, he saw the green plastic package he'd hoped he still had. Expired, but functional. He ripped the package open and pulled out the bandage.

"Lean forward again."

Williams complied and Zahn spread the unfolded gauze against the wound. "Now press against the tree."

His friend leaned backward and looked at the girl next to him. "It's going to be okay, sweetheart. Dr. Zahn is patching me all up." He looked from her eyes to her feet. "You sure you're all right?"

Rachel nodded and pointed at Zahn's shoulder. "What about him?"

"I'm okay," Zahn said, and turned back to his first aid kit, grabbing another elastic wrap. "But we can wrap me up too. With this." He held up the bandage. "You guys want to do that for me?"

The Marshal nodded and leaned forward.

Zahn pressed him back. "No way. You've got to stay against the tree. That's what's holding you together."

"I can do it," Rachel said, as she reached for the wrap.

Zahn was torn between trying to keep the girl from dealing with the blood and encouraging her to stay busy, so she didn't go into shock.

"Okay. Let's have you do it." He handed the supplies to the girl.

Zahn considered their position as he guided Rachel through the bandaging process. He hadn't contacted Perez—he was in the middle of that when Elliot had fired on them. Now the message he had drafted was irrelevant. They needed support, and they needed it now.

Zahn tried to put himself in Elliot's shoes—and found it difficult. He couldn't fathom the kidnappings, let alone this attempt to kill them. Everything had escalated with those gunshots. And Elliot must realize that, as well.

Did he come down the mountain to kill Zahn and Williams, or was he trying to recover Rachel? Zahn guessed the latter. He and Williams were simply obstacles. After Zahn's return fire, Elliot knew at least one of them had survived.

What was Elliot's next move? Everything the man had planned was unraveling, and he had to be desperate. Zahn guessed he'd either try to escape or make a last stand. If he ran, the girls would hinder his escape. Would he leave them or kill them? If he fought, he'd keep the girls. They gave him a bargaining position. Hostages.

Shit. Two scenarios where the girls' lives were in danger. Only one where they might survive.

Zahn couldn't wait for backup. He had to move now to save his daughter's life. And the other girl. Nicole.

Rachel finished patching him up and sat back. Zahn inspected her work. Not bad.

"Perfect job," he said. "You should be a doctor."

Rachel responded with a slight nod and an almost imperceptible smile.

Zahn scanned the trees for movement and saw nothing. He crouched and scooted over to where he had dropped the GPS. Scooping it up, he returned to the tree.

"Randall, you still with us?" He poked Williams with the orange GPS and watched the man's eyes flicker open. "I need you."

"Yeah. Yeah. Just resting," Williams rasped. "How long until backup gets here?"

"That's where I need your help. I was trying to send a message when Elliot started shooting. Need you to finish it."

Williams shook his head. "Don't you think—"

"I'm going after him. No time for me to send the message."

Rachel gazed over Williams's shoulder at Zahn's unfinished message on the screen, then met Zahn's eyes. "Why don't you just hit SOS? My dad has one, and he says if you're in trouble, you just hit that button on the side."

Zahn stared back at Rachel, then smiled. "Because I'm not as smart as you. I guess our situation counts as being in trouble, right?" He lifted the tab on the GPS and mashed the SOS button. Then he handed the locator to Rachel. "Hang on to this until help arrives."

"Hold on there. You ain't going anywhere." Williams's gaze settled on Zahn. "How can you possibly think that's a good idea? I'm incapacitated, you're shot, and you're going to leave the victim with me?"

Zahn nodded. *As if I have a choice.* "Think it through. When Elliot fired those shots, everything changed. He went from kidnapping to attempted murder. It's over for him when he's captured, and he's desperate. The question now is not if he gets caught, but when it will happen. He's thinking about his last stand. Letting the girls go would admit defeat. Killing them would mean he went out in a blaze of glory."

Williams stared at him, and Zahn saw recognition dawning in his eyes.

"Shit." He moved his eyes to Rachel. "Sorry." He paused a beat. "And the third option would be him holing up for a standoff with the girls as negotiating tools."

Now he gets it, Zahn thought.

Williams shook his head, talking to himself. "I'm going to get fired over this one. Chasing a fugitive with an uncredentialed civilian. Get my ass—well, my back—shot, and I send the civilian out alone after the bad guy while a child gets left behind to take care of me." He sighed, then groaned in pain. "Nice, Williams. Just nice."

"I'm not a child. I'm in middle school," Rachel interjected.

Williams gave a thin smile and nodded. "Okay, Tyler. Get a move on. You're taking the rifle, right?"

"Can't do that. You guys need it here in case he comes back down without me seeing him. He'd pick you all off easy from a distance if I just left you with your pistol. You can shoot the rifle if you have to, right?"

"Hand it here."

Zahn passed the weapon to the injured man, who hefted it in his hands.

"Yeah, I got it." He squinted his eyes. "I'm going to turn on the radio and try that. Screw radio silence if you're going to be chasing Elliot up that mountain." Williams stared at Zahn. "You're going to have to get close with your Glock, you know?"

Zahn nodded. "I know. But I'm only using it if it's a life-or-death scenario with the girls. If he leaves the girls behind, I'm done. I'll bring them back and let the rest of Perez's team chase him down." His voice choked. "We just don't know what he's going to do with them."

Randall reached forward and grabbed Zahn's arm, grimacing as his back peeled away from the tree.

"Go."

CHAPTER 63

Elliot's ragged breath echoed through the forest as he scrambled up the mountainside toward the shack.

That didn't go as planned.

The decision to kill Zahn and the marshal had been a serious one, a decision that would ultimately mean his own death or imprisonment. Not taken lightly. What he hadn't counted on was failure.

Elliot had dropped Zahn instantly. He was relatively certain he'd killed the man in the sleeping bag—Williams. Rachel had disappeared in the flurry of movement after he had started shooting.

But the gunfire coming from Zahn's position proved Elliot's first shot was off. Maybe he hadn't missed, but he definitely hadn't incapacitated his target. That first round of return fire had struck the tree trunk only twelve inches from his head.

Once Elliot had realized he was also now a target, he had moved clockwise around the party, seeking a better angle to finish Zahn off. After Zahn's second shot, he had changed his mind. Time to cut his losses and return to the team.

He paused halfway up the slope, leaning on the uphill side of a tree, catching his breath. After his heartbeat slowed, he raised his rifle and peered downhill around the tree. Tracking the barrel from left to right, he scanned for movement.

Nothing.

Elliot pulled the rifle back and tilted his head skyward, eyeing the branches shadowing his resting site and considering his next move.

This standoff with Zahn and his lawman friend forced a change in strategy. His original plan was to hole up in the cabin, positioned to defend it if searchers stumbled upon it. But now the searchers knew where to look. They'd be prepared.

Time to move the girls again.

He gazed through the thinning trees at the narrow ATV track. Winding past the cabin, the track led up and over the ridge, the same route Rachel had started to take when she bolted. Elliot had spent time in the adjoining valley, directing trail rides for Beyond Adventure, so he knew that—just after the path hit the tree line on the other side—it bisected a Forest Service road leading east to Buena Vista. If he could throw off his pursuers at the intersection, he and the girls might buy enough time to find a safer place to hole up.

Elliot slung the rifle over his shoulder and hoofed the last hundred yards to the shack. He glanced in the window on his way to the outhouse. Daria lay strapped to the bed, just as he'd left her. Yanking open the latrine door, he found Nicole in tears, eyes squeezed shut in exhaustion. Her eyes flew open at his entrance, and she let out a moan.

"You ready to get a move on, Nicole?"

The girl simply stared at him, her eyes dead.

"No sound now. I'm going to pull that tape and untie you okay?" He yanked the adhesive strip from her mouth, and she gave an audible gasp before sucking in the fetid air. Elliot wrinkled his nose at the girl's stale breath. Leaning his rifle against the outhouse wall, he pulled his knife and cut Nicole from the zip-ties, catching her as the girl sagged toward the gaping hole between her feet.

"Keep it together, girl. Don't have time for this shit." Elliot helped her from the bench, grabbed his rifle, and herded her out the door toward the cabin.

Inside, he cut Daria loose, as well. Although she immediately clutched her bad shoulder, she appeared to have weathered the whole bondage experience much better than Nicole.

Elliot pointed at the saddlebags with his muzzle, then turned to Daria. "Time to do your pack mule thing again."

The young woman gave him a blank stare.

Elliot thrust the rifle barrel forward and used the tip to guide Daria to the wall. "Move it. Move it. We're out of here."

Daria reached down and loaded the bags over her shoulders, then turned back to Elliot. "Where's Rachel? I heard shots."

He pondered the usefulness of telling Daria the truth. *She's okay. But I shot your dad and his friend, and now your dad is chasing us.* Elliot shook his head.

Not useful at all.

"Rachel is no longer a part of the team," he said. "She broke the rules. She escaped and paid the price."

"You killed her?" Daria's eyes widened. Nicole sucked in her breath, visibly sagged, and stared hopelessly at Elliot.

"A man's got to do what a man's got to do." Elliot smiled. "But I don't have to do it again. That's up to you." He pointed toward the exit with the rifle. "No more chitchat. Go."

He herded the girls out the door and along the road leading up the mountain. Leaving the trees, he scanned the slopes below, searching for any sign of Zahn on their trail. Nothing. He caught Daria staring at him with a questioning look.

She knows. She knows we're being followed.

"Drop the bag. It's rope time."

Daria lowered the pack, and Elliot rummaged through it.

"Shit." He'd left the rope and the zip-ties in the shack. Elliot surveyed their progress. Only a couple hundred yards back. He looked farther down the slope and caught a hint of movement. Maybe. He squinted. Couldn't be sure.

Elliot lifted the pack and thrust it at Daria. "Put it back on." She shouldered the bag while he grabbed Nicole's shoulders, positioning her on the road's downhill side. When Daria had the gear loaded, he moved her to the same position and motioned toward the cabin below them. "Listen up. I want you both to always be walking between me and the cabin, okay?" He pointed up the hill at the switchbacks. "We only got a quarter mile to the top. Maybe twenty minutes. Then it'll be downhill."

Daria turned to him. "You want us to be your shields? Is that it?"

Elliot looked from the girl back to where he'd last seen the movement below them. He nodded. "That's it, Christina. You got a problem with that? Or are you interested in the alternative?" He rubbed the barrel of the rifle on Daria's cheek.

Christina? Daria lowered her head and said nothing.

CHAPTER 64

Daria touched the side of her face where Elliot had scraped the rifle, her hand shaking.

He's lost it. Who was Christina?

She already knew the man was unbalanced. Leading a double life: avuncular Gabe Elliot, the horse manager at Beyond Adventure you could turn to with your personal problems, and the warped Jefe who kidnapped girls and let others film them.

Now add murder to the list. She'd heard gunshots, and Elliot pretty much told them Rachel was dead. Panic surged in her chest. She had sent the young girl to her death.

She fought to calm herself. Eventually, Jefe was going to get caught, and Daria doubted he intended to surrender peacefully. Or planned to give up her and Nicole. Nope. It would be like The Alamo. No survivors.

Escape? Look what had happened to Rachel. Daria had encouraged her to run away, and it had cost the girl her life. How could she ask Nicole to do the same?

Because the alternative is certain death, she reminded herself. Her breathing slowed as she forced away her fear.

A new variable was in play. Elliot had them on the run because someone had found them. Not a theoretical search in the future. She'd seen his body stiffen as he surveyed the mountainside, and now he was glancing behind them every twenty steps. Someone was following them. Someone was coming to help.

As they approached the final switchback, Daria scanned the jagged ridge only a hundred feet above. It ran the length of the mountain like the edge of a razor blade, interrupted only by the track they climbed. The loose shale at the start of the road had given way to massive boulders as they neared the mountain crest.

Elliot switched positions as they turned the corner, looking through Daria and down the slope. She followed his gaze and glimpsed movement at the cabin. Someone was exiting the door. She squinted and watched the man striding toward the road, face upturned.

Daria sucked in her breath and abruptly lowered her eyes, not wanting Elliot to see what she had spotted. She'd recognize that gait anywhere, especially after their daily walks around Elk Trace. That man was her father.

"Hold up." Elliot raised his hand, and the girls stopped. He peered over the edge of the track toward where Daria had seen her father, then glanced back at Daria and Nicole. "I want you guys right there." He pointed to the uphill side of the path and the series of boulders that formed the barrier, keeping rockslides from covering the road. "Don't you dare move," Elliot said, raising the rifle.

Daria grabbed Nicole's hand and tugged her to the side of the mountain as Elliot dropped to a prone position, laying his rifle beside him as he retrieved his binoculars. She could smell her own sweat—as well as Nicole's—from the climb. It smelled like terror.

Daria cupped her hand to Nicole's ear. "We've got to get away, Nicole. We've got to do it quick."

The girl shuddered, eyes wide as she mouthed the words Daria expected. "He'll kill us. Just like he did to Rachel."

"He's going to kill us, anyway. There's someone coming up the trail trying to save us. If we go soon, we have a chance." Daria nodded at Elliot. "If we wait until he finds a spot to hole up, then he'll just shoot us together."

"But how? How will we do it?"

Daria's eyes widened as she saw Elliot reach for the rifle. She motioned up the road toward the point where it crested the ridge.

"When we hit the top, I'm going to run for it. Down the other side. When he chases me, you go down this side. Where help is coming." She pointed down the slope. "Use the big rocks as cover and be careful. You don't have to be fast. If Elliot…er, Jefe, is chasing me, you can just crawl down. If he's chasing you, he has to keep from getting shot by the rescuers."

As Nicole nodded, Daria heard Elliot talking in a low voice and tracking the rifle.

"Uh huh, uh huh, right like that."

Daria reached for a fist-sized rock at her feet, stood, and heaved the stone over the edge to the right of Elliot. She would have aimed for his head if she thought she had any chance of hitting him. He whipped his rifle toward the sound, searching for its source. Daria sat back next to Nicole. Elliot turned to Daria. "Did you do that? Did you just throw a rock?"

Both girls shook their heads. Elliot stared at them.

He scowled, turned, and aimed his rifle below their position. A minute passed. Daria heard him swear before he swung the rifle around and rose to his feet. He crossed the narrow road and stood over the girls, the downhill edge of the road providing cover from whoever pursued them.

Elliot narrowed his eyes at Daria. *He knows I threw the rock.*

"We got company," he said. "He's holed up now, but he'll be coming. We need to move out." He nodded toward the notch a hundred yards away. "Let's go."

Daria squeezed Nicole's hand and helped her to her feet, hoping the girl was on board with the plan. Elliot had just pointed toward their split-up point for the escape.

Elliot fell in behind the girls, driving them at a brisk pace with taps from his rifle barrel. Daria kept her hand wrapped around Nicole's, alternating between tugging her in response to Elliot's rifle taps, and squeezing her hand, hoping Nicole knew Daria was getting ready to make a break for it.

CHAPTER 65

Zahn stepped out the cabin door and scanned the mountain above him. The snipped zip-ties and half-empty water bottles inside the shack convinced him Elliot and the girls had been there. Zahn must have just missed them. He caught a flash of movement on the switch-backed road above him, several hundred yards away, but it quickly disappeared.

The road made sense. He doubted Elliot would return to the river where Zahn had almost shot him. The logical choice led over the ridge.

Zahn jogged back to the cabin and grabbed a handful of zip-tie remnants. Kneeling outside the door, he fashioned an arrow out of the plastic pieces pointing toward the road.

As Zahn started up the path, he hugged the mountainside, using the boulders on the slope above him as intermittent cover. He weighed climbing straight up to the ridge, but decided the angle gave Elliot too much of a tactical edge. Zahn could narrow the distance on the road by hiking faster.

Five minutes from the cabin, he eyed the first switchback only a hundred yards ahead and then scoped the bare slopes above. The hairpin turn left him exposed. He started to jog—couldn't really run at this angle—and made it about ten steps before a fist-sized rock rattled off the mountainside in front of him.

Zahn dove to the uphill shoulder, pressing his back against the dirt and gasped for air. *What was that?* Did Elliot or one of the girls just lose their footing, or were they trying to lob rocks at him? That didn't make sense, because he knew Elliot had a rifle. Hell, the man had already tried to kill him. Zahn pressed his fingers against Rachel's first aid handiwork and winced. *Just a flesh wound*, he repeated to himself.

He evaluated the remaining distance before looking over his shoulder up the slope. Zahn was unsure about the source of the rock, but he wasn't taking chances. Reversing course, he moved fifty yards back, then turned uphill, using the large boulders as a screen until he intercepted the road switchbacking above him. It was harder going, but he needed the cover to close the gap between him and Elliot.

Zahn struggled to understand Elliot's motives. How do you climb inside a crazy man's head? Particularly one who had seemed so rational initially, and then so methodical, diabolical, and cunning.

Based on the brief glimpse of movement and the rock that had almost nailed him, Zahn was confident Elliot had the girls somewhere above him. They were going over the mountain.

Where would they go next? West into no-man's-land, east to the valley, or north over the next mountain? Where could Zahn close on Elliot to make a move? Or should he just keep his distance and leave a trail for the backup guys to follow? Lots of questions. No clear answers.

Zahn crossed the road above him and continued his vertical climb, moving from rock to rock and scanning the ridgeline. Still no one in sight.

A shout echoed above Zahn.

"Fuck!"

The roar sounded as if someone had smashed their finger with a hammer. Rocks trickled a football's throw away as he scrambled around the boulder to put eyes on the situation. The road above looked clear from what little of it he could see. He thrust his head farther around the rock and caught a flash of clothing moving down his side of the mountain. Blue jacket. The figure was slight and careening its way frantically down the rocks.

A girl.

Zahn squinted, trying to recognize his daughter. Daria didn't have a blue jacket that he remembered.

The girl paused behind a boulder and looked up the ridge.

Holy shit! It's the other girl. Zahn tried to remember Rachel's description of her fellow captive.

Nicole. That was her name.

He looked from the girl to the ridge crest, trying to spot Elliot. Did he release her, or did she escape? Based on the way she kept looking back, Zahn assumed it was the latter. Standing upright, behind the boulder he was using for cover, Zahn waved his arms at the girl, trying to attract her attention.

The girl was singularly focused on whatever was behind her and gave no sign she saw Zahn.

He glanced up the slope, looking for Elliot. No movement. Zahn began picking his way across the boulder-strewn mountainside toward the girl, who continued lunging downhill.

She stopped again, turning to scan the ridgeline. This time, Zahn watched her freeze when she spotted his waving arms. The girl edged around the boulder and peered back at him. Zahn looked up at his hands. *I might be a little less threatening if I wasn't waving a pistol.* He waved one hand and pointed it toward the top of the mountain. Then he aimed the handgun in the same direction. Maybe Nicole would understand he was a good guy if he pointed the weapon toward the bad guy.

He turned and saw the girl staring at him. Zahn raised his finger to his lips and pointed up the hill. He thought he saw the girl nod. He pointed at himself, then at Nicole. *I want to come to you.* The girl continued staring. Zahn made the signal again. Nicole nodded.

He skirted his way across the slope toward the girl, periodically checking the high ground for Elliot. When he got within ten feet of Nicole, he paused, watching the girl shrink back into the rocks as he approached.

"Are you Nicole?"

Nicole nodded again.

"Do you know Daria?"

"She's up there," Nicole mouthed, pointing up the mountain.

Zahn looked up the slope. Nothing. He returned to Nicole. "I'm her dad. Tyler Zahn. I'm here to help you guys."

The girl visibly sagged, as if relieved. She stepped from the rocks and said, "He killed Rachel. He'll kill us all if he catches us. Can you get us out of here?"

Zahn moved into the rocks and motioned Nicole to join him. "He didn't kill Rachel. She's fine."

"We heard the shots. Me and Daria. We heard them."

"He missed. He didn't hit Rachel. He got me here." Zahn patted his bloody shoulder. "And he shot my friend. But Rachel is okay." He pointed at the river valley. "She's right down there with Marshal Williams."

"Will you take me home?"

"That's the plan, Nicole. But I have to do something first, okay? That's my daughter up there, and I need to bring her home. You understand that, right?"

Nicole nodded slightly. "I don't want Jefe to catch me again."

"You aren't going back to him. And I can't take you with me to get Daria." He reached out to reassure the girl, but she shrank at his approach. He withdrew his hand. "This is the part where I'll need you to keep being brave. I want you to stay here. Just until we come back to get you."

"By myself?" Nicole's eyes widened. "What if you don't come back?"

"By yourself," Zahn said. "Look, Nicole, Daria and I are coming back. But there's also a posse of police heading this direction. They might even get here first."

"How will they find me?"

"That won't be a problem. I left a GPS with Rachel and the Marshal, and they activated the emergency beacon. The police are probably already on their way to them. And they know you guys were being held in the cabin down there." Zahn pointed down the hill. "So, when you see a crowd of people surrounding the cabin, that's when you know you are rescued. Jump up and down, and let them know where you're at."

Nicole nodded.

Zahn glanced up the hill before turning back to the girl. "Can you do that, Nicole? Because I need to go save Daria."

Nicole bobbed her head and shrank between the rocks. "I'll wait for the police." She paused for a beat. "Don't let him kill Daria."

Zahn watched as Nicole disappeared into the rock cavity, and then he turned up the mountain. Everything he'd told the girl was true. The police would rescue Nicole, and he would rescue Daria. But in order for that to happen, he needed to find Elliot.

Find Elliot, and bring Daria home.

CHAPTER 66

"Fuck!"

Elliot was as mad at himself as he was at the two escaping girls. His expletive was involuntary—a reaction to Daria bolting over the ridge while he had his back turned checking on the man tailing him—and had probably just given their position away. Nicole was sliding among the rocks only twenty steps in front of him. He raised his weapon and aimed at the girl's back. Easy shot. Put her down, then go after Zahn's daughter.

He sighted in and began the trigger squeeze. Slowed his breathing. Then he lowered the barrel. He knew he should take her out. Just like he'd tried to do with Rachel. But he couldn't resist imagining alternative scenarios. There were only two guys at the river. And he'd shot at least one of them. Rachel was still alive.

Hmmmm…new plan. Daria had lost her usefulness. In fact, she seemed to encourage rebellion among the team members. Time to take Daria out, and then return for Nicole. If his pursuer rescued Nicole first, then Elliot would eliminate him and recover his girl. Then he and Nicole would make another attempt at getting Rachel back.

He laughed. The Gabe Elliot-side of his brain told him his plan didn't have a snowball's chance in hell of success.

The Jefe-side answered. *Who the fuck cares about odds? Two potential outcomes: the team's back together, or we all die.*

Nicole was so damn slow. He watched as she carefully planted each step and paused behind rocks. He smiled, turned away from Nicole, and jogged around the road bend at the ridge.

Rounding the corner, Elliot paused and surveyed the mountain's northern slope. It looked a lot like the southern slope—a zigzagging path carved into loose shale. He squinted at movement a hundred yards below. Daria was lunging from boulder to boulder, short-cutting the road and barreling straight down the mountain. He saw her head swivel uphill as she tried to stay behind the large rocks checkering her descent, but he couldn't tell if she'd spotted him yet.

It wasn't clear to Elliot whether Daria had a destination in mind or was just trying to outrun him. Didn't matter, though. She was trying to get away. That meant his job would be straightforward. Track her down and take her out.

Elliot mentally marked Daria's location, then shuffled back to the mountain's south side, checking his pursuer's progress. Approaching the edge of the ridge, Elliot dropped to his belly and peered over the edge, scanning the winding road for movement. It didn't take long to spot the figure directly below him. He was picking his way laterally across the boulder field, aiming toward something at Elliot's ten o'clock. Elliot trained his eyes on the rocks and saw a flash of Nicole's jacket in contrast with the gray of the mountainside. The man had spotted the girl.

Elliot backed away from the ridge, regaining his feet and returning the way he came. He smiled. Yes, whoever was chasing him was going to get Nicole. He'd have to deal with that. But now he could take care of Daria without checking over his shoulder. His pursuer couldn't overtake him with the girl in tow, and Elliot thought it unlikely he'd leave her behind. He'd either hike her to the main roads or return with her to the camp spot where they had Rachel. He hoped it was the latter. After Elliot eliminated Daria, he could stroll back and recover the girls on his own terms.

One thing confused him, though. At least one man at the river had a rifle. The man behind him didn't. Why not?

Elliot worked his way down the north side, pausing every minute to relocate Daria. He spotted her again, a hundred yards lower on the mountain. Easy pickings. He looked in front of Daria's path and sighted in on a cluster of pines at the tree line, in case he lost sight of her.

He stopped again and watched Daria working her way around a mine tailing, the tan earth and rock piles in sharp contrast to the gray boulders on either side. Elliot focused on the tree line and continued skidding down the slope. Five minutes later, he rounded the mine tailing, eyeing the rotted remnants of a cabin on the ledge and the drop-off behind it leading to the trees. He stepped to the edge and scanned the terrain. No movement. The large boulder field tapered into slides of small rocks and gravel. The girl should be easy to spot.

Elliot dropped to a knee, catching his breath and patiently scanning the slope. Still nothing.

He whipped his head around, suddenly aware Daria might have stopped. No one was behind him. *Rookie move, not checking my six.* He rose to his feet and walked the old cabin's perimeter.

Elliot stared at the mine tailing Daria had skirted, his head cocked to the side. Dark earth lay exposed in even increments where movement had shifted the shale. Someone had climbed the small hill. The tailing flattened at the peak.

"Daria," he called, in a low voice. "You up there, sweetheart?" He picked his way around the tailing and up the rock slope's side, for a view of the mine shaft's remains.

"Not a good move, you running away like that." His boots slipped on the steep pile and he adjusted his footing. "Thanks to you, I had to—how do you want to say it?—immobilize Nicole. Kind of your fault, you know."

Elliot unslung his rifle. He stepped on a flat rock and lowered himself so he could peer around the boulder at Daria's possible hiding spot. Raising the rifle's barrel, he thrust himself forward and pointed the gun into the mine hollow.

Nothing. No one was there.

His breath left in a whoosh. A small black hole yawned at the rear of the depression. The remains of the mineshaft. Daria wasn't hiding in the concave entrance. She was down inside the mine.

Elliot smiled.

How could she make it any easier?

Pull her out into the light.

Shoot her.

Stuff her back in the hole.

One. Two. Three.

Love it when a plan comes together.

CHAPTER 67

Daria never looked back after she dropped Nicole's hand and ran. She prayed her hunch was correct—that Elliot would focus on her, not Nicole, giving the traumatized girl a chance to escape.

As she crested the ridge, her eyes traced the descending switchbacks wrapping the mountain's south side like a string of Christmas lights. If she kept to the road, Elliot would spot her. And if he cut directly down the mountain while she clung to the path, he would certainly catch her.

Daria ignored the road. Straight down, using the large boulders as cover, she barreled forward, not daring to turn around. Between the sounds of loose rocks, she listened for the crack of Elliot's rifle. A muted crack meant a shot at Nicole. A sharp crack meant he was aiming for her.

She didn't hear gun reports. But as she stepped around the boulder in her path, slowing to keep from falling, she heard the sounds of sliding shale behind her. Her heart pounded. Elliot had chased her instead of Nicole, just as she'd planned. Hopefully her dad would find the young girl.

Daria spotted the tree line, a football field away. She was exhausted, and her shoulder ached, but she knew she could move faster if she could reach the trees. A mound of fine rock and dirt loomed ahead of her, and she skirted around the side, using it as cover. Finally, she risked a glance over her shoulder and noted the pile of dirt completely obscured her from Elliot's view. She stepped backward, and her foot caught between two rocks. Daria fell, her weight shifting as she landed on her back while her wedged ankle remained stationary. Pain shot from her foot to her knee. Her momentum forced the base of her head into the gravel as her foot popped from the rocks, and she momentarily lay motionless, staring at the blue expanse above her. *Not now,* she thought. She scrambled to her feet, turning toward the slope.

One step, and the pain brought her to her knees, gasping. Not just a twisted ankle. She'd done something to it. Tears sprang from her eyes as she glanced at the tree line in the distance. She turned to the mountain, but there was no sign of Elliot because the pile of earth still sheltered her. The sound of sliding rocks in the distance startled her into motion. She looked back at the trees. *Not going to make it.*

She scrambled up the loose earth to the top of the berm. It made little sense to backtrack, but she refused to just sit and wait for Elliot. Maybe she could cover herself in the dirt. Or find a bigger rock. A thought struck her as she climbed. *Where did this pile of dirt come from?*

Daria crested the berm and rolled into the depression on the other side. She stuck her good arm out to halt her roll. It didn't work. Her hand disappeared into a two-foot gap at the bottom of the sinkhole, and her shoulder and head followed. Sliding to a stop, she stared ahead into the black void.

Daria guessed she had found the remnants of an old mine. She couldn't see a thing. She had no clue if the hole traveled vertical or horizontal—whether climbing inside meant a fall to her death, or if it was a dead end and Elliot would pull her out by her feet.

All she knew was she didn't have a choice. She used her good arm to drag her body farther into the hole, digging her toes into the rocks behind her to help push forward into the dank darkness.

Reaching forward again, she searched for a way ahead. No wall yet. Daria rolled on her back and raised her hand. The roof she had squeezed under at the entrance had suddenly gotten higher. She couldn't feel any rock above her. Daria worked her way up to her knees and began crawling forward. Ten more feet and she bumped her head into a wall. She shook it, trying to ignore the pain. Smooth rock blocked her path to the front. She groped to the right. Same smooth rock. She tried the left. Loose rocks plugged the route from the floor to the ceiling.

Dead end.

Breathing heavily, she turned toward the halo of light formed by the entrance of the mine. She leaned against the rock and tried to control her breathing. The tunnel's confines amplified her fear, and Daria was certain anybody on the outside could hear the pounding of her heart and her ragged breath.

Daria needed Elliot to keep searching down the mountain. Into the trees. Away from her. She could hole up here for hours and wait for help. If it came.

She squeezed her eyes shut. Of course, he would come. She'd seen her father in hot pursuit. He wasn't that far away.

Except that if Elliot was chasing her, then he wasn't going after Nicole. And if her dad found Nicole, he was going to have to take the girl back to the police. Daria might sit here for a while before Zahn returned to the business of rescuing his daughter.

How long would she have to wait?

She heard a rock shift from the entrance of the mine. She held her breath.

"Daaaaria? Oh, Daaaaria?" Elliot's sing-song voice drew out the first syllable of her name, mocking her efforts to hide from the man.

Sounded like she wouldn't be waiting long at all.

CHAPTER 68

Zahn crested the pass in a crouch, using the carved walls of the road as concealment while scanning the hillside below for Elliot and Daria. Movement immediately caught his eye a quarter mile down the slope—Elliot scurrying his way down the mountain. No sign of Daria. He scouted the zigzagging road cutting through the boulder field, but his best option was to vector straight toward Elliot, using the rocks as cover.

Descending the slope with an eye on Elliot, Zahn thought through the potential scenarios. Best case, he could catch Elliot and incapacitate him before the man caught Daria. Zahn stepped between two large rocks. *Incapacitate?* How would that work? Zahn waving his pistol at a rifleman, shouting, *'Drop your weapon and come with me?'* Not likely. Armed with only a handgun, he'd require the element of surprise and close quarters. And he'd need to take Elliot down.

Zahn didn't ponder the ethics. The man had stolen the lives of multiple children, kidnapped his daughter, attempted murder, and shot his friend. Justice would be served if Elliot died.

No, the real problem was the damn pistol. Zahn wasn't sure he could hit Elliot, let alone kill him. He needed to sneak toward him undetected, and not miss, for this plan to work.

The other scenario was Elliot recapturing Daria before Zahn caught up with him. That was by far the worst-case outcome. If Zahn worried about hitting Elliot as a single target, how could he possibly nail him if the man had his daughter? He'd need Daria to break free while he took out the madman.

Complicated. Communication required. Daria in even greater danger.

He picked up his pace. *I need to catch him before he gets Daria.*

A loose rock spun off his foot and tumbled fifty feet down the slope before coming to rest. Zahn froze. He'd closed the distance to Elliot by about a hundred yards.

He watched as Elliot skirted around a mine tailing, heading for the tree line. Once Elliot entered the forest, Zahn would have trouble keeping him in sight. But Elliot would also have to slow his pace to track Daria among the trees.

As Zahn neared the tailing, he scanned the openings in the trees where he expected Elliot to appear. Had he missed him? He paused. If Elliot had stopped on the tailing's far side, Zahn would walk straight into him. The slope curved slightly uphill above the tailing, and Zahn elected to scout the other side from the high ground rather than follow Elliot. He crept up the small rise and peered over the top.

Nothing. The slope tapered into an abrupt cliff with several large boulders about twenty feet below him. The remnants of an abandoned mining shack lay in front of him. No sign of Elliot. Zahn guessed the man had somehow made it into the woods. He stood, then dropped again at the sound of a voice.

"Daaaaria? Oh, Daaaaria?"

Elliot was below him among the rocks. Was Daria there, too?

Zahn inspected the ledge and carefully crawled west to get a different angle on the voice. That's when he saw Elliot's profile—denim jeans, and cowboy hat, rifle in front of him, pointed at the hillside.

"Come on out, Daria. Game's up." Zahn heard Elliot's commanding tone and cocked his head. *Come on out of where?* Behind a rock? Down a hole?

He looked to his left. Just enough room to cut across and get close to the man. But the closer he crept, the more he moved into Elliot's line of vision.

"Here's how it's going down, Daria. I'm counting to three. If I don't hear you coming out of this mine, then I'm going to shoot."

She's in a mine?

Elliot continued. "I don't know how far back you are. Maybe my shot will miss. Don't know. Don't care. You ready?" Elliot moved closer to the mountainside, his torso moving out of Zahn's view.

Silence.

Zahn moved farther to his left. If Elliot moved back, he'd be square in front of Zahn, maybe only ten feet. No way Elliot could miss seeing him. Not likely Zahn would miss shooting him. He raised his pistol, propping his elbows on the ledge.

"One…"

"I'm coming out." A voice echoed from inside the mountain.

Zahn tasted bile in his throat at the sound of his daughter's voice. He'd hoped Elliot was wrong. That Daria wasn't in the mine. That Zahn could shoot him alone, then go find his girl.

"Well, now, that's a smart girl, Daria. If I shot you back there, I might have to get all dirty."

Rocks shifted from inside the mine, the sound amplifying from the exit of the narrow opening. Elliot stepped back, his rifle still pointed forward, and his figure silhouetted in the sun.

That's when Zahn shot him.

From this distance, it seemed impossible to miss. Zahn was aiming for center of mass, the middle of Elliot's chest. Instead, he nailed the man in his left hip.

Elliot staggered at the shot and stepped backward, swinging his rifle toward Zahn. Zahn fired again. This time, the bullet hit Elliot square in the chest, knocking the man backward a step. Elliot's rifle clattered at his feet as he raised a hand to his heart. He looked at Zahn and scowled.

"It's over, Gabe," Zahn said.

Elliot stumbled, and his legs struck a boulder. He crumpled to the ground.

"Daria? It's Dad. Can you hear me?" Zahn called, climbing to his feet while keeping his weapon trained on Elliot.

"I hear you! Are you okay?" his daughter's voice echoed out of the shaft. "I'm coming out."

Zahn walked down the side of the tailing, his eyes locked with Elliot's. "Stay, Daria. Don't come out until I tell you." He kneeled in front of Elliot and grabbed the rifle, then stepped back and leaned it against a boulder out of the man's reach.

Blood trickled out of Elliot's mouth, and his lips moved.

"I'm going to patch you up. The sheriff's department is on their way."

Elliot shook his head, his mouth still moving. Zahn moved closer.

"Don't let her go," Elliot said.

"What?"

"I let my daughter go." Elliot sucked in a breath. "And Christina never came back." Elliot coughed and moved his eyes toward the tunnel. "Keep a tight rein on her." His eyes closed.

Zahn shook his head. "Why don't you save your bullshit advice—" He paused as Elliot's chest stopped moving.

Zahn released his breath and turned toward the mine. He stopped, then turned back to Elliot, kneeling to check the man's pulse.

Nothing.

He turned and scrambled toward the portal.

"Daria, come on out. It's safe now."

He grasped Daria by the shoulders to pull her through the entrance.

"Careful with that one, Dad," Daria tilted her head toward her injured shoulder. "Might have to get a new sling." She stared at Zahn's blood-stained shirt. "What about you?"

Zahn bent his head to where she stared. "It's just a graze. Looks worse than it is."

As Daria rose to her feet, she grabbed her father with her good arm and drew him in close. "He killed them, Dad. He killed those girls, and I couldn't stop him." Her voice trembled.

Zahn stepped back and gripped Daria's good arm. "No, honey. He didn't."

"But Rachel…we heard the shots. And he said…Nicole."

"Rachel's with Williams. Unless Perez and his guys already got her." He smiled. "I left Nicole by the pass." Zahn pointed over Daria's head. "How about we go get her? Are you okay to walk?"

"I twisted my foot…or my ankle, or something. I don't know if I can walk."

"Not a problem, sweetheart," Zahn said. "This place is going to be crawling with help in less than an hour. We'll get you out of here."

She looked over Zahn's shoulder at Elliot. "What about him?" Her eyes filled with tears. "He's a bad man."

"He *was* a bad man, Daria. Not anymore."

CHAPTER 69

Zahn smiled as Perez hobbled through the revolving door at the Salida hospital. The deputy had given up on the crutches, but it was obvious he wouldn't be running trail races any time soon.

Perez spread his hands to his side. "Why don't they have you in a bed? What're you doing in the lobby?"

"Waiting for you. The helicopter flew us in hours ago. What took you so long?" Zahn nudged the deputy's shoulder. After an overnight in the antiseptic hospital, his nose picked up on Perez's odor of sweat, coffee, and dirt.

Perez moved to return Zahn's shove, then hesitated, his eyes moving toward Zahn's sling. "Can't wrap up a crime and tend to the wounded all at once. How's Daria?"

"She's going to be fine. Minor fracture in her foot. She reinjured her collarbone, so she'll keep the sling awhile longer, but her spirits are high." Zahn cocked his head. "Her mom says she was tough as a kid. Guess that hasn't changed."

He grabbed Perez's arm and led him toward the elevator. "Daria's mother, Sheila—you know, my ex—is upstairs with her now."

"Are you guys okay being in the same room? What about Williams? How's he?"

"First, yes, Sheila and I are good. She's not convinced I didn't somehow put Daria in harm's way, but she's lightened up a lot since the doctors gave Daria the positive prognosis." Zahn smiled. "And you won't meet her yet, because we're going to see Randall right now. I haven't seen him since they pulled him out."

Zahn mashed the third-floor elevator button with his good hand and turned to Perez. "Randall got hit hard. Through the back and it tore him up pretty bad. The good news is they can take care of it all here. He doesn't need to go to Denver. The bad news is that he's going to be in here awhile and probably in a wheelchair for some weeks after that."

"Did someone call Kristee?"

"You'll see her in a minute. She's in his room right now."

Zahn led Perez down the hall and into Williams's room, rapping on the doorframe as they entered. "Knock, knock. The A-team is in town."

Kristee rose from the side of Williams's bed and strode to Perez. The deputy raised his eyebrows at Williams over her shoulder before returning her hug.

"I'm so glad everyone is here. And that everyone is okay," she said.

"Everyone's not going to be okay if that cop doesn't disentangle from my girlfriend," said a weak voice from the bed.

Zahn laughed at Williams. "Guess those pain meds are working? How come you're not on your stomach if you got shot in the back?"

Williams gave him a thin smile. "Because the slug came out the front." He pointed to his lower abdomen. "So six of one, half-a-dozen of the other, as far as sleeping positions go."

Kristee and Perez stood at Williams's feet, watching the two men.

"Where's Elliot?" Williams tilted his head at Zahn.

"He's here," Zahn said. "In the morgue."

Williams said nothing, but nodded.

"We got his accomplice, as well. The red-headed guy who took Janae on the ATV? He was the same one who helped Elliot switch trucks," Perez said. "Local guy named Mark Behring."

Zahn turned to Perez. "No shit? Where did you end up finding him?"

The deputy smiled. "Just good policing work on my part. Guess I'm a natural."

Kristee snorted. "That sounds like a story."

"I was sitting in my Tahoe at the trailhead where you guys left me, about a hundred yards from Elliot's trailer, and I see this truck pull up through the trees," Perez said. "At first I thought it was our guys from that other hostage thing—which all got resolved, by the way. No injuries." The deputy paused. "But then I saw it was a civilian vehicle. Moving in front of the trailer…"

Williams groaned. "You mean the dumb shit came back and tried to take the trailer away?"

Perez looked up and raised his eyebrows. "Like I said—just good old-fashioned police work."

"What about that other guy?" Zahn asked. "The one Behring paid to drive Elliot's truck out of state."

"He's still in custody. Not sure how that one's going to play out, but unless they find any connection to him and Elliot or Behring, I think he's just going to get a slap on the wrist." Perez wrinkled his brow. "It's unusual to take a grand in cash to leave a car in a parking lot. But not really illegal."

"Roger?" Williams croaked from the bed. "What about him?"

Perez nodded. "Well, the dust has got to settle on all this, but I think it's safe to say Roger is going to prison for a long time. They might cut him some slack for pointing us toward Elliot, but he's still not getting out any time soon."

Zahn watched Williams nod again and then close his eyes. The man needed some rest. Zahn turned to Perez. "What the hell was Elliot thinking? I mean, he was obviously mentally ill, but he was so damn functional most of the time. What would cause him to go off the rails like that and keep these girls?"

"I don't have a lot of answers today, do I?" Perez said. "That one's going to take some time, as well. But we might have some leads from Kevin."

Zahn met Perez's eyes. "Kevin? Daria's Kevin?" He coughed. *Not what I meant.* "Kevin from Beyond Adventure?"

Perez nodded. "He came down to the BV Police Station after you left to tell them everything he knew about Elliot. He suspected nothing unusual about his boss, but he had some interesting tidbits about his past. Like the fact that his daughter was killed."

Zahn's head bobbed. "Yeah, Elliot told me he'd lost a daughter. Christina. Didn't tell me how."

"Evidently she was an up-and-coming talent agent out in Los Angeles. Had a team of models she ran for the fashion industry. Something happened, and one of her clients murdered her," Perez said.

"How does that relate to what Elliot was doing?"

"We're not sure it does. But Kevin said he didn't think Elliot had completely recovered from the murder. Mentally, that is."

Kristee spoke. "And you said Elliot was using these girls in films, right? Sort of a talent agent—just like his daughter."

Williams's eyes opened, and he looked at Perez. Then he turned to Zahn.

"That's some kind of crazy."

CHAPTER 70

"Where are you, Janae? It looks like you're in trees." Nicole's voice sounded tinny through Janae's tablet computer. Janae turned her screen around so the others could see what she saw from her perch above the lake. She sat in a grove of cottonwoods outside Stillwater, Oklahoma, on a narrow bluff overlooking the picnic grounds where her mom and dad, Uncle Mike and Aunt Marcie, and two of Janae's friends were munching watermelon. The scent of roasted corn on the cob still hung among the trees.

Uncle Mike held Dobby in his lap with one hand, hiding his watermelon wedge from the small dog with his other. Turned out her uncle wasn't much of a dog guy before he met Dobby. He'd spent those nights in Colorado loitering near Janae's door, listening to see if Dobby needed to go outside to pee. Didn't want the dog messing up their house. Now they were fast friends.

Good thing Uncle Mike had Dobby to hang around with. Janae had overheard her mom tell her dad that Aunt Marcie was real mad at him about something.

Her dad waved at her and held up his cellphone. Then he gave her alternating thumbs up and thumbs down signals. Janae returned a thumbs up. They hadn't been certain whether her dad would have enough signal to provide a hotspot for Janae's scheduled video conference call. But it was working great.

Her mom just stared at her with a plastered smile. Janae figured her mother would probably keep staring at her with that smile until she graduated from high school. Or maybe forever.

Janae flipped the tablet and smiled at the three faces. Dr. Susan was there from Denver. She was the first adult Janae had talked with after the police found her in Salida. When Mr. Zahn had rescued Rachel and Nicole the week before, Dr. Susan had talked to them, too, and promised to call every week to check on them. That's what this meeting was—a check-in call. Rachel and Nicole were on the screen, smiling from somewhere in Texas. Kendall had never met Dr. Susan because her parents had come so quickly to whisk her away. The group had invited her to the check-ins, but she had yet to attend.

"Hi, guys! How's everybody?" Daria's face popped on the screen. Janae hadn't met Daria until it was all over. Rachel and Nicole had told her about how Jefe had captured Daria and put her in the horse trailer with them. And how Daria was the one who made them believe they could escape. Nicole said Daria tricked Jefe so Nicole could get away. Daria was really brave.

"Hi, Daria!" the girls said.

"It looks like you're still in Buena Vista," Rachel said.

"I am." Daria smiled. "Good thing my college is still shut down—it's giving me time to heal. We're having a barbecue this afternoon with all the people who helped rescue you guys. The police, the sheriff's department, Search & Rescue. And my friend, Kevin. Too bad you guys can't come back."

"Uh, no thanks," said Nicole. "I don't care if I never see Colorado again."

"Thanks for joining us, Daria," Dr. Susan said. "The girls love having you in our sessions."

"Wouldn't miss it. Thanks. And I have to be honest, you guys. Talking with you all is helping me too." Daria paused. "I thought I'd just put this behind me and move on. But it's not that easy. Sometimes I'm still nervous about things."

"Me, too," said Nicole.

"Good," said Dr. Susan. "Not 'good' that you get nervous…I mean 'good' that the talking is helping."

The girls all nodded.

"Daria, do you want to start? Tell us what's new with you and anything you've learned about yourself."

Janae smiled. Dr. Susan always started with Daria. Janae guessed it was because Daria was practically a grown-up and wouldn't be shy about going first.

Daria talked about her relationship with her dad. How they talked all the time now. When she had visited her dad this spring, that was their first time together in years. Now they were really close.

Nicole raised her hand next. She told how her family took her and her friends to the county fair, and they had deep-fried Twinkies.

"Gross!" Janae said. "That sounds disgusting."

Nicole smiled. "Delicious."

Rachel explained her family's reluctance to let her out of their sight. Just last night, they finally let her have a sleepover. The friend came to Rachel's house because her parents couldn't handle Rachel leaving. But Rachel said it was a blast. They made popcorn and watched a movie. Her father burst into the room halfway through because Rachel was laughing so hard he thought she was crying.

"I almost peed my pajamas," Rachel said. "I hadn't laughed in such a long time."

Janae told everyone about the picnic she was having and how she was making new friends.

The fun stuff was easy to talk about. It got a little tougher when they started talking about what they learned from Colorado.

"I learned not to be afraid to talk about how I feel," Daria said. "My dad was acting all crazy because he thought I was still mad at him from something in our past. And the whole reason Elliot caught me was because I wasn't talking to Kevin for a long time about my feelings. Keeping your feelings inside doesn't make things better—it makes them worse."

"Everything is easier with friends," Nicole said. "Rachel and I kept each other going after Kendall got away, but it was a lot better when Janae showed up. Friends make you stronger."

"I learned not to shut down," Rachel said. "When I was under the stable, I thought if I ignored everything and everyone, then I could just shut out the bad things. Daria convinced me I had to try. And it worked."

Dr. Susan nodded. "What about you, Janae? Last week you said books got you through it. Is that still the case? What are you reading today?"

Janae searched her backpack for the title before remembering she had left her book at home next to her bed. That was a first. She glanced away from the screen at her two Oklahoma friends splashing in the lake. Her mom still sat at the table, alternating glances between the girls in the water and Janae on the bluff. She was just as nervous about her as Rachel's parents were about Rachel.

"No book today." She smiled. "I learned books can help, and books can hurt." Her smile faded. "Before Colorado, I didn't have a real life. It was all imaginary. All contained in the pages of my books." She paused. "And that was a good thing and a bad thing. If I hadn't read those books, I wouldn't have found the courage to run from Jefe. I know I wouldn't have. That was the good part."

The other girls nodded, and so did Dr. Susan.

"But, before Colorado, I was living my life inside the books. Scared to meet friends. Scared to try new things. I didn't have to *be* brave because I could just read about it." She rolled her eyes. "Sorry, guys, this is a long answer."

"That's okay, Janae," Dr. Susan said. "Go on."

Janae nodded. "I'll keep reading." She laughed. "I don't think I can stop that. But I learned living is more important than reading. I'm going to take everything I learn from my books and use it to make friends, try new things, and face up to the things that scare me the most. That's what I've decided over the past week."

Daria's head moved side to side on the screen.

"What, Daria?" Janae stared at the square with Daria's face in it.

Daria smiled. "I'm just surprised you claim this is a new decision."

"Why?"

"Because you made that decision the moment you escaped that evil man. Your bravery made him run and put my dad and the police on our trail. You're a heroine, Janae."

Janae felt her heart swell. She was a heroine.

CHAPTER 71

"Jesus, Daria, this place looks like a hospital ward. I should have asked about visiting hours before I came over," Kristee said, shaking her head. The two women sat in lawn chairs facing the grill where Zahn wielded a set of barbecue tongs. Daria's shoulder sling matched the walking boot encasing her ankle.

Zahn shrugged his injured shoulder and wondered if Kristee was counting him among the walking wounded. He still wore a heavy bandage across the spot where the bullet had creased his shoulder, but he didn't think it was visible under his shirt.

A group of officers from the police and sheriff's department and friends from Search and Rescue circled the horseshoe pits in Zahn's backyard. Rick Perez had put one of the deputies in charge of making Kevin feel at home among the lawmakers, and it looked like it was working. Even though he refused the beers the men pushed his direction, his horseshoe tossing prowess was drawing cheers.

Zahn shifted his eyes to Officer Linzmeier while listening for Daria's response to Kristee. The man sat alone, apart from his fellow police officers, staring at the ground. Although found innocent of any wrongdoing with Alyssa Peterson, he had been reprimanded for his poor judgment in placing himself alone with the young girl. It didn't look like the rest of his unit was in a big hurry to make him feel like part of the team.

Randall Williams sat wedged in a wheelchair next to Zahn, providing unsolicited advice on his grilling skills. Perez still hobbled in his knee brace, passing out cans of light beer. The man had zero taste when it came to the nectar of the gods.

Zahn looked over the open lid at his daughter and smiled. Zucchini, bell peppers, onions, and asparagus rainbowed one side of the grill. The meat-eaters owned the ribs on the opposite side. It smelled like the 4th of July—and felt like family.

"It's not as bad as you'd think," Daria said, responding to Kristee's remark about the array of injuries. "Keeps my dad from scheduling the rest of my vacation."

"Right. No ropes course for you!" Kristee laughed. "So what did you do all day?"

"Very casual. We slept in a bit. I had a video conference with the girls Elliot kept captive. Dad took a walk to check the mail. We talked a lot. Tested out the beer before you all showed up." She smiled and looked across the yard at Kevin. "My favorite kind of day. The only thing scheduled was the video call and the barbecue with you guys."

Her favorite kind of day? If only Zahn had known that tidbit when his daughter first arrived. If only he had asked.

While they sampled the beers before the guests arrived, she had started the conversation.

"It took me a while to figure out you were saying 'sorry,'" Daria said.

Zahn nodded. "Me too. That I was doing that without ever saying it."

"I don't remember much about when you left. After Jacob. You always came home after your missions in the desert. And then you didn't."

Zahn had said nothing, waiting for Daria to continue.

"So, I wasn't mad then. And then I visited a couple of times. That seemed okay. But then the visits stopped."

"I'm not good at talking about it, either, Daria. I'm sorry. For everything."

"That's the thing, Dad. You don't need to be. Mom said you were broken after Jacob died, and you never got fixed. That made me sad. I was never mad at you. I just hoped you would get better." She shook her head. "I should have told you I wasn't mad sooner. I just didn't know that's what you were thinking."

"I don't feel broken anymore, Dar. It still hurts to think about your brother. I have a hard time with that. But things are getting better out here. Especially with you coming to visit. And with you forgiving me."

Daria smiled. "That's where we both screwed up."

"What do you mean?"

"If there was anything to forgive, I did it a long time ago. I just never told you."

"And I screwed up by not asking." Zahn stared at his feet.

"That was just part of your problem."

Zahn met Daria's eyes. "What else?"

"You never forgave yourself. I know I don't have a degree in this stuff...yet. But that's what it looks like to me."

"You're probably right."

"Well, now that's fixed."

Zahn cocked his head. "How so?"

"You saved my life, you dolt." Daria laughed. "Let's assume that little pilot brain was right about making up for lost time, and forgiveness, and all that crap. Don't you think that taking out a madman who kidnapped your daughter wipes the slate clean?"

Zahn smiled as he recalled that morning's conversation. He flipped the ribs, then swapped to a different set of tongs and did the same to the veggies. Closing the grill lid, he surveyed his back porch. Daria and Kristee deep in conversation. Linzmeier sitting alone, absolved of all crimes, except for being an asshole. Williams crammed in his wheelchair, talking to Perez, both men angled with a view of Kristee.

That whole 'two men, one woman' thing's still not worked out. Zahn guessed Perez still carried a torch for Kristee.

Zahn had put this barbecue in his day planner this morning with an empty box next to it. He turned from the grill toward the sliding glass doors. He could go inside right now and mark it off as complete. The barbecue was a success.

Or he could relax and ignore his to-do list.

He turned back to the grill and caught Daria smiling at him. Zahn shook his head and grinned at his daughter. Then he leaned forward and gave the ribs another flip.

ABOUT THE AUTHOR

Over a 30-year Air Force career, author Cam Torrens delivered combat supplies and personnel across Europe, the Middle East, and Africa. He piloted the first mobility aircraft into Iraq during the Iraq War, served as the United States Air Attaché at the US Embassy in Beijing, China, and spent four years as the Professor of Aerospace Studies at Virginia Tech.

A father of six, Cam and his spouse live in Buena Vista, Colorado where he serves as the Vice President of the Chaffee County Writer's Exchange and volunteers with the Chaffee County Search & Rescue team.

Stable is his debut novel. The next book in the Tyler Zahn series, *False Summit*, will be released in November, 2023.

NOTE FROM THE AUTHOR

Word-of-mouth is crucial for any author to succeed. If you enjoyed *Stable*, please leave a review online—anywhere you are able. Even if it's just a sentence or two. It would make all the difference and would be very much appreciated.

Thanks!
Cam Torrens

We hope you enjoyed reading this title from:

Subscribe to our mailing list – *The Rosevine* – and receive **FREE** books, daily deals, and stay current with news about upcoming releases and our hottest authors.
Scan the QR code below to sign up.

Already a subscriber? Please accept a sincere thank you for being a fan of Black Rose Writing authors.

View other Black Rose Writing titles at www.blackrosewriting.com/books and use promo code **PRINT** to receive a **20% discount** when purchasing.